THE FAMILY LAWYER

THRILLERS

JAMES PATTERSON

WITH ROBERT ROTSTEIN, CHRISTOPHER CHARLES, AND RACHEL HOWZELL HALL

GRAND CENTRAL
PUBLISHING

NEW YORK   BOSTON

Copyright © 2017 by James Patterson

Hachette Book Group supports the right to free expression and the value of copyright. The purpose of copyright is to encourage writers and artists to produce the creative works that enrich our culture.

The scanning, uploading, and distribution of this book without permission is a theft of the author's intellectual property. If you would like permission to use material from the book (other than for review purposes), please contact permissions@hbgusa.com. Thank you for your support of the author's rights.

Grand Central Publishing
Hachette Book Group
1290 Avenue of the Americas, New York, NY 10104
grandcentralpublishing.com
twitter.com/grandcentralpub

Originally published in trade paperback and ebook in September 2017
First oversize mass market edition: August 2020

Grand Central Publishing is a division of Hachette Book Group, Inc. The Grand Central Publishing name and logo is a trademark of Hachette Book Group, Inc.

The publisher is not responsible for websites (or their content) that are not owned by the publisher.

The Hachette Speakers Bureau provides a wide range of authors for speaking events. To find out more, go to hachettespeakersbureau.com or call (866) 376-6591.

ISBNs: 978-1-5387-5158-9 (oversize mass market), 978-1-5387-1134-7 (ebook)

Printed in the United States of America

OPM

10 9 8 7 6 5 4 3 2 1

CONTENTS

THE FAMILY LAWYER

JAMES PATTERSON

WITH ROBERT ROTSTEIN

Children are of the blood of their parents, but parents are not the blood of their children.

—Bouvier's Maxims of Law (1856)

CHAPTER 1

JUST AS DEBRA IS about to get to the punch line, my cell phone rings.

"Shut that damn thing off, Matt," she says. "If I were the judge, I'd fine you five hundred dollars for disrupting court."

"And I'd appeal your fascist ruling to the highest court in the land."

She smiles in spite of herself. She's rehearsing for a hearing tomorrow, and I'm playing judge. Our client, an amateur photographer, claims that the cops rousted him for filming on-street arrests, so we sued the police department for violating his civil rights. That's what we do.

I should ignore the call, but the ID screen reads *Westside Jail,* so I answer. It's probably someone looking for representation, and the law firm of Grant & Hovanes needs all the clients it can get. There's little money in public interest law, and Debra and I are soft touches. Her case for the photographer happens to be pro bono.

On the other end of the line, a female is weeping. She sounds so distraught that I suspect she's a psych case. No matter—I represent a lot of psych cases.

Then I hear, "Dad?"

I stand up in shock and sit down again when my knees buckle. "Hailey? What…? My God, are you okay?"

"No."

"Are you hurt?"

"No, I…"

"What's wrong?"

"They arrested me!" I can hear deep breathing, a heaving sound. She's trying to compose herself. This isn't like her, not even under these circumstances. She's the eight-year-old who wouldn't cry after she cut her chin on the playground slide; the kid who wouldn't cry even when she got six stitches. A fourth-grade teacher once called her "The Ice Princess." She has titanium nerves. Which is why she's a highly recruited soccer player who should earn a college scholarship and ease our family's financial burden. I can't pay for college, and I don't want her to start adult life a hundred thousand dollars in debt.

"Settle down and tell me what happened." Easy for me to say. How am *I* going to settle down?

Fraught silence. The uncertainty is agonizing.

Finally: "I was going to soccer practice after school, and these police walk up and ask if I'm Hailey Hovanes. When I say *yes,* they arrest me in front of all my friends and the team and the coach and some teachers and parents and…They handcuffed me and hurt my wrists, Dad!"

On hearing this, I want to punch the cops who did that. But I have better ways to get back at them—through the legal system. "Have you said anything to the police?"

"Just that I didn't do it."

"Don't say another word to them."

"Okay. Just come and—"

There's an adult male's voice in the background, his words inaudible.

"They're making me hang up, Dad."

"Don't hang up yet. Tell me why they arrested you."

The line goes dead.

"Hailey's been arrested," I tell Debra as I spring out of my chair. "She was so upset she couldn't even tell me what they busted her for. She was crying."

"Hailey? No way," Debra says as she follows me out of the room.

I'm not sure if she's incredulous about Hailey being arrested or about the crying.

"I'll come with you," she says. "She'll need a lawyer."

"I'm a lawyer, in case you've forgotten."

"Right now, you're only a parent."

She's right. And, even if I wasn't, I can always use her help. We make a good team. Six years ago, a judge separately appointed us to handle a habeas corpus appeal for a death-row inmate. We won, and ever since, we've shared an office suite, assisted on each other's cases, and divided our meager profits fifty-fifty.

"Thanks, I'll handle it," I say. "You need to prepare for tomorrow's hearing." That's not the real reason I decline her offer. My wife, Janet, doesn't want outsiders involved in our personal business. She considers Debra an outsider, though heaven knows I don't.

I grab my briefcase and laptop from my office and hurry to my car. In the concrete plaza that separates the parking garage from our building, the homeless are gathering to crash, as they do every night. When Debra and I opened up our law practice, we made sure to lease office space in a poor section of town. When you represent the downtrodden, you have to come to them—they're too intimidated and resentful to come to a lavish chrome-and-glass high-rise in the Golden Triangle.

As I race to my car, the homeless man known as Downtown Dennis shouts, "Attorney Hovanes!" Imposing at six foot eight, he played college ball, might even have made the NBA if he hadn't flunked out sophomore year of college for various infractions caused by his incipient schizophrenia.

"It's Mike and Byron time!" he says.

It's a ritual that we've shared ever since I represented him pro bono on a trumped-up assault charge—we replay in pantomime Michael Jordan's game-winning shot over Utah's Byron Russell in the sixth game of the 1998 NBA finals. It started when he found out that I played in high school. Dennis always gets to play Jordan.

"Dennis, I can't—"

I've never refused him before, and despite the silliness of our trivial game, his eyes fill with a combination of confusion and disappointment. I respond to the disappointment part, because I rely on the trust of people like him. I assume my defensive stance, he pushes off though the offensive foul isn't called, and he sinks the imaginary shot. And all the while, I'm thinking *Why am I letting my daughter languish in that jail even an extra thirty seconds?* Yet, I simply can't let these people down, can't let Dennis down. I'll just have to drive faster.

We slap hands, and I sprint to my car, then drive to the jail through a fog of disbelief, fear, and anger. I've had practice doing this, unfortunately. Three times over the past nineteen months, I've posted bail for my seventeen-year-old, Daniel. Trespassing on school property, shoplifting, vandalism—petty crimes, but escalating. Somehow, the rides to the station to pick up my son seemed easier than this drive. Maybe it's because he's had behavioral problems since preschool, so the outcome seemed inevitable. Hailey has never been in trouble. Not like this.

I don't call Janet. She'll learn about this soon enough.

By the time I reach the station, I'm primed for battle. The cops won't get away with this. My next lawsuit against the department will be filed on behalf of Hailey Nicole Hovanes.

Walking through the entrance, I'm assaulted by bleak fluorescent lighting, a fusty odor of unbathed derelicts and underfunded budgets, and voices of the cynical and the desperate. This is no place for my daughter. I approach the watch commander, a brawny, clean-cut man in his thirties, and identify myself as Hailey's father and lawyer.

"I'm here to arrange for her immediate release," I say.

"You're Hovanes," he says, his tone accusatory. The police don't like lawyers who sue them. Worse, I was once a prosecutor, so they consider me a turncoat.

"I'm glad my reputation precedes me, officer. I'm sure it'll make things go a lot faster."

The cop makes a grand show of checking his computer and says, "She's still being processed. Take a seat in the lobby."

I lean over the counter. "Hailey is sixteen years old, and you're not going to keep her here any longer than it takes to unlock her cell."

"How are you, Matt?" someone behind me says.

I turn to find Detective Ernesto Velasquez. We worked together when I was at the district attorney's office. He's an honest cop. We were friends until I left the DA's office and began suing the department. I haven't seen him in a while, and he's aged. Wrinkles from excessive stress and too much sun score his face. His formerly jet-black hair has gone mostly gray.

"What's this about, Ernie?" I ask.

He leads me to an interior conference room and asks me to sit down.

"I don't want to sit down. I want to take my daughter home."

"It's not that simple. She's been charged with violating the cyber-stalking law. Using the internet to harass a classmate with the intent to cause severe emotional distress."

I shake my head, as much to clear it as to disclaim his statement. "You know how teenage kids are, especially girls. Hailey isn't a bully. She'd never intentionally harm anyone."

"The victim was Farah Medhipour."

I shudder. Farah was the fourteen-year-old at Hailey's school who committed suicide six weeks ago. Hailey mentored the younger girl at the start of the semester, and they were soccer teammates, but that doesn't mean they were close. The school held the obligatory grieving assembly and offered the obligatory student counseling, the local media reported the tragedy, and then everything went back to normal in the space of a week.

"We have compelling evidence that your daughter orchestrated a vicious harassment campaign against Farah with knowledge that the girl was suicidal," Velasquez continues. "Farah left a video as her suicide note. She said she couldn't stand the torture any longer, and she identified Hailey as her tormentor." He takes another deep breath. "The victim hanged herself on video. The DA is all over this one. He wants to try your daughter as an adult."

"That's absurd. She just turned sixteen."

"Her mature demeanor works against her."

I raise my hands in defiance. My daughter is being charged with a crime that could bring her a life sentence. The cops are calling her a cold-blooded killer.

CHAPTER 2

HAILEY IS NO MURDERER," I say. "The other girl took her own life."

"The charge isn't murder. Under the penal code—"

"I know the law as well as anyone, but I'm not talking about that right now, damn it. You're saying my daughter intentionally tried to hurt another human being. Hailey would never do that. And, if you want to talk about the law, there's never been a successful prosecution against a cyber stalker where the alleged victim committed suicide." I raise an index finger and point it at him as if I, not he, am the accuser. "Hailey's a juvenile with a spotless record. More importantly, she's innocent. Now, release her. I'm not leaving this place without her."

"We need to bring her in front of a judicial officer who'll set bail, and it's late. There's no time to do that today."

"If she's not released now, I'll ring up every superior court judge and crime reporter I know and tell them that the department and the DA want to put a child in an adult jail with a bunch of dangerous adult criminals. For a crime she didn't commit."

"Don't threaten me, Matt. I'm the lead investigator

on this, and we have more than enough evidence against your daughter."

"Who's the assistant DA on the case?"

"Lundy."

"Now I get it. That son of a bitch is putting my daughter through hell because he has a vendetta against me." Back in my days with the DA's office, Joshua Lundy and I were work buddies. We played basketball in the city leagues together, he the point guard and I the power forward, though that was thirty pounds ago. Then I discovered that he was withholding exculpatory evidence from defense counsel in a kidnapping case. He lied and claimed it was an oversight. When I blew the whistle, our superior backed him, so I quit and went into private practice. Lundy has held a grudge ever since. So have I.

"That's not what's going on here," Velasquez says. "You've spent your entire career involved in the criminal justice system. You know that the parents are always the last to accept the truth."

In that moment, I transform from combative lawyer to desperate, frightened parent. "I know my child. She's innocent. She's certainly not a flight risk or a danger to herself or others. She should be released on her own recognizance. Please, Ernie." I pause. "How's Maggie doing?"

Eight years ago, his youngest sister, Margaret, was charged with possession of crack cocaine with intent to sell. He hired me to defend her, and not only did I get the charges reduced to simple possession, but his sister avoided jail time and got into a diversion program.

"She's doing real good." He thinks for a long moment, then sighs. "I'll see what I can do."

I nod in gratitude, return to the main room, and sit

down on an uncomfortable wooden bench. I pass the time speaking with a mother who's there to post bond for her son, another kid who's never been in trouble with the law. He had too many vodka and tonics at a frat party and then got stopped at a random highway-patrol checkpoint. I know she's hurting, but I envy her. This arrest will turn out to be a cheap but important lesson for her son. I don't know that I can say the same for my daughter. Just before her son is released, I give the woman the name of a friend of mine, the best driving-under-the-influence attorney in town.

Forty minutes later, Velasquez emerges from the back, escorting Hailey. She's a willowy brunette like her mother, tall like me. Statuesque like neither of us. Now, she's walking down the corridor poised and serene as an English duchess mingling with the commoners. The Hailey I know. All at once, I find this more distressing than her panicked phone call, because it isn't natural for a sixteen-year-old kid to behave this way. Not here and now. I blame those beauty pageants that Janet was obsessed with. Yes, my wife entered Hailey in kid beauty contests, JonBenét Ramsey's murder be damned. The pageants taught Hailey to pose and preen and behave like an adult when she was just a toddler. At the moment, *adult* is the last thing she should seem.

CHAPTER 3

WHEN I MAKE A right turn out of the station parking lot, Hailey asks, "Where are you going, Dad?"

"Home. Where do you think—?"

"My car's at school."

That's what she cares about? I thought she'd want nothing more than to explain what happened.

"I'll take you to school tomorrow."

"Dad, I don't want—"

"Consider me your own personal Uber driver who's desperate to earn five stars—we'll get the car tomorrow. Tonight, why don't you tell me why the police think you had something to do with Farah's death."

"I have no idea."

"What was your relationship with the girl?"

"I was her mentor when she started ninth grade. She was on the soccer team, so they assigned me to her. She became obsessed with me, started stalking me. I told her to stop. That's it."

"Stalking you how?"

"Didn't Mom tell you about this?"

"This is the first I've heard about it. How did she stalk you?"

"Like sending creepy text messages. Acting like we were best friends when I wasn't her friend at all. We didn't want her in our group. That upset her, I guess. Then she hit on Aaron." Aaron is Hailey's boyfriend.

"Why would she accuse you of bullying her?"

"She's trying to stalk me from the grave, I guess."

"That sounds insensitive, Hailey. Under the circumstances, it's important that you don't—"

"Please don't lecture me. I'm having a bad day."

"Hailey, the cops don't just arrest people for no reason."

"You *always* say they do! I can't believe you're accusing me!"

"I'm not accusing you. I'm just trying to—"

She folds her arms tightly across her chest and retreats into that teenager's impenetrable shell of silence. When my daughter goes into that place, she's unreachable.

I process her reaction. The lawyer in me suspects she's hiding something. The father in me wants nothing more than to believe in her innocence. I *must* believe in her innocence.

Night has fallen. When I finally turn onto our street, I squint at the glare of flashing red and blue lights. A police patrol car is parked in front of our house. Our family's nightmare is just beginning.

CHAPTER 4

JANET, ARMS CROSSED, IS waiting on the porch, along with two uniformed officers.

"Why are they here?" she says as soon as I climb the steps.

I inhale deeply. "It's a mistake. Hailey was arrested for—"

"I know that, and of course it's a mistake," Janet says. "Why are they still here? I assumed you'd clear up this mess by now."

I shrug helplessly.

Almost looking amused, the older of the two officers—his nametag reads OFFICER CRANE—holds up a document and says, "Mr. Hovanes, we have a warrant directing us to seize all computers, smartphones, and tablets belonging to your family or otherwise located on the premises. We'll need you to gather the electronics and give them to us, and then we'll search the residence for any other device. We waited until you arrived to enter the residence, counselor. As a courtesy." From this guy's smirk, I can tell they waited so they could enjoy turning our house upside down while I was present.

"How very, very kind of you, Officer Crane," I say. "I

wish the others in the department were so considerate of the people whose privacy they invade without probable cause." I take the warrant and read it carefully, searching for any irregularity that would allow me to quash it. Unfortunately, everything is in order.

An impassive Hailey hands her cell phone to the younger cop, an Officer Verlander.

I glance at Janet, who frowns but walks inside. The police follow, and Verlander begins in the living room, opening a drawer in the buffet in the dining area. I suspect the cops are going to use this warrant to tear the house apart.

"Please be careful," Janet says. "The china belonged to my mother."

"Yes, ma'am," Verlander says, and he seems to mean it, because he opens drawers in the buffet gingerly and doesn't throw anything on the floor. Crane begins rummaging through a media console, and he's much rougher.

My son appears from the hallway and moves within two feet of Verlander. Too close.

"Please step back," the cop says.

Daniel holds his ground. "This is an illegal search and seizure in violation of the Fourth Amendment to the United States Constitution. I know all about you fascist paramilitary types. I've been the victim of police brutality."

Daniel insists that after he was arrested the second time, the cops abused him in the patrol car. The cops told me he was lucky they didn't charge him with resisting. Since then, he's been obsessed with real or imagined police misconduct—not with the cases that I try, but with the dangerous drivel spouted by radical fringe groups that lurk in the dark recesses of the internet and call for violent resistance against the police and the US government. As hard as I've tried to explain that it's better to work within the system to effect change, he won't stop looking at that junk.

"Daniel, give the officer room so he can do his job," I say in my calmest voice.

To my relief, he steps back. But he says, "Why aren't you jerks out catching murderers and rapists instead of rousting an innocent family and harassing a sixteen-year-old girl? You guys have no balls. But I guess this is better than committing genocide against innocent black and Hispanic people."

Hailey goes into her bedroom and returns with her computer and smart tablet. "It's okay if you search my room," she says. "Just please don't make a mess."

"Show us *your* room," Officer Crane says to Daniel.

Daniel chortles, and then dashes into his bedroom and slams the door. The behavior is irrational for a seventeen-year-old, but Daniel is very immature. He's also something of a savant at using a computer and a whiz at video games. They're the only things that seem to interest him—that and his internet crusade against police misconduct. Now, these officers are about to deprive him of his most precious possessions.

The officers follow, and Crane orders Daniel to open the door.

"Fuck off, pigs!"

That's *not* what you say to a cop. Crane places a hand on his holster, and I take a step forward but stop when he drops his arm. Reason has overcome reflex for both of us—this time. What the cops don't realize is that Daniel is still a kid although he's a grown man physically—six foot one with a deep baritone. Grown men use profanity with cops at their own risk. I've represented quite a few clients who swore at cops and ended up hurt.

"Open the door, or we're coming in," Crane says.

When Daniel doesn't respond, Crane tries the handle. Daniel has locked the door.

"Last chance," Crane says in a tone that confirms he'd love to break in.

Janet looks on in distress, while Hailey observes this with a clinical frown, as if her brother were a lab rat in the midst of an experiment.

"Let me talk to my son," I say.

Crane doesn't react, but Verlander taps his partner on the arm, and Crane stands aside.

I knock and say firmly, "That's enough, Daniel. Open up and let them have your computer."

He opens the door a crack. "It's an illegal search and seizure. Stop them. You're a lawyer."

"That's exactly why we're going to follow the law. That's what lawyers do. These officers have a valid search warrant, and they're just doing their jobs."

Daniel glares at me, considering. It's that fragile moment when events could go either way. To my relief, he opens the door, fetches his computer, and shoves it into my hands. Then he tosses his cell phone and tablet at Crane's feet.

The officers spend the next half hour searching for other electronic devices, finding nothing. They do make a mess, but it could be worse, though I'm sure Janet doesn't see it that way. When they finish, they finally make the demand I've been dreading.

"You'll need to give us your computer and electronic devices, Mr. Hovanes," Crane says.

"I'm afraid that's not going to happen," I say. "It's my work computer and work phone. They both contain information protected by the attorney–client privilege. Including information about lawsuits that I have against your department. As far as my personal use goes, I borrow my wife's computer, which you already have."

"As you told your son, counselor, we have a valid search warrant and are just doing our jobs," Crane says. "Please surrender your phone and tell us where the computer is."

I pull out my cell phone, but instead of handing it over, I call Debra and inform her of the situation.

"I'm on it," she says and hangs up. She and I often read each other's thoughts.

Meanwhile, I stall for time. I argue the law, which doesn't impress the cops one whit. I call Ernesto Velasquez and ask him to tell his guys to back off, but he says he can't do anything without the approval of the district attorney. So I phone the DA's office and ask to speak with Joshua Lundy, but Lundy has left for the evening—or so the secretary claims.

"Hand over your electronic devices or we'll have to place you under arrest, sir." It's Verlander who makes this threat. So much for the good cop.

"Don't do it, Dad," Daniel says. "It'll bullshit."

"Stop it, Daniel," Janet says. "Matt, I don't understand what you're doing. Haven't—?"

And then my phone beeps, and the e-mail from Debra comes in. I open the attachment, and there it is—a signed order from a superior court judge prohibiting the police from seizing my computer, phone, or any device that has privileged information on it. Not only is Debra a top-notch lawyer, but she's surprisingly well connected.

I show the police my screen and say, "I think we're

done for the evening, officers. The judge's order has already been forwarded to your superiors and to the DA's office."

Crane makes a call, confers with his partner, and the two of them grudgingly leave.

"So you get to keep your stuff, but we don't?" Daniel says. "That's bullshit. Maybe *we* should've hired Debra."

I don't bask in my small victory. I fear the police will find something incriminating—on Daniel's, not Hailey's, computer.

CHAPTER 5

I SUMMON EVERYONE INTO the living room, and unlike most occasions when I call a family meeting, everyone complies. We sit in our usual spots—I on the threadbare occasional chair, Janet and Hailey on the overstuffed sofa, and Daniel off to the side on the wicker chair. As usual, rather than looking at us, he stares down at the floor.

"Tell me what you know about Farah's death, Hailey," I say.

"We already talked about this, Dad. I don't know anything about it."

"Of course she doesn't know anything," Janet says.

"Why didn't I know that this girl was stalking you?" I ask.

"Because you're never here," Janet says. "The law firm of Grant & Hovanes is your family."

"Lest you forget, the law firm of Grant & Hovanes puts your gluten-free pasta and free-range chicken dinners on the table."

"You work to save the world. If you wanted to pay the bills, you'd join a big law firm and do white-collar crime work."

It's an old argument that I don't want to repeat. "I'm speaking to Hailey," I say. "I want to understand. Was there a confrontation with Farah? Did you call her names or post bad things on the internet?"

"I told you no," Hailey says.

"Did Aaron know the girl?" I ask.

"What's that supposed to mean?" Hailey says. "You're always dumping on my boyfriends. That's fucked up."

"Don't use that language. Why would this Farah girl blame you on that recording, just before she—?"

"Because she was a crazy nutcase?" Hailey replies, her tone a verbal eye roll to accompany the real one.

"I think you should have a little more sympathy for her given what she did to herself," I say.

"Whatever."

"Why are you cross-examining her?" Janet asks. "You should support your daughter, not interrogate her. She already told you, she doesn't know anything about this."

"Bullshit," Daniel says, still looking down.

"You're horrible, Daniel," Janet says. "Maybe your father should be asking what relationship *you* had with that disturbed girl. Hailey says she saw you talking to that weirdo. Two peas in a pod."

Daniel stands so violently that he almost knocks over a lamp, then storms out of the room with his arm raised and his middle finger pointing upward.

"That was unnecessary," I say.

"That's all you can say when he's disrespectful and vulgar toward me?" Janet says.

"Did Daniel know Farah?" I ask.

Hailey shrugs. "I saw Danny talking to her a couple of times." Only his sister can call him Danny. "I don't know what they were talking about."

"Were he and Farah friends?" I ask.

Hailey and Janet glance at each other.

"Danny doesn't exactly have friends," Hailey says. "I mean a couple of the guys from grammar school still, but… The girls don't like to talk to him. It's sad. I wouldn't call Farah his friend. More likely she was trying to use him to get to me."

Intellectually, I know that Daniel is a loner, an oddball. But when it comes to their own children, parents are the ultimate self-propagandists. No matter how severe the problem, you overlook, minimize, spin until you can't anymore. Then you hope.

"The boy has problems, and you ignore them," Janet says. "You've always ignored them."

"He's a good kid," I say. "He's a teenager. He just needs to grow up."

"That's how you explain his horrible behavior?" Janet says. "If you were making that argument in court, the judge would laugh in your face. People are afraid of him."

"He's never hurt anyone."

"Not yet. But it's only a matter of time. That's my biggest fear in life. Maybe he would've turned out better if you'd acted like his father, not his lawyer."

And soon, Janet and I are yelling at each other, at which point Hailey gets up and removes herself, as if we were the children and she the grownup. The same scenario has played itself out countless times over the years: Janet clashes with Daniel, he blows up, I come to his defense, and soon we're quarreling.

"Maybe he needs an advocate because his own mother is always judging him harshly," I say.

She gets up and leaves the room.

Daniel was born when Janet was thirty, according

to plan. Janet conceived Hailey four months later, after a night of alcohol and carelessness. Suddenly, we were caring for two infants thirteen months apart. Daniel's problems started in preschool—biting, tantrums, defiance—and haven't gone away. Hailey was always easy.

In Janet's view, Daniel is our tarnished misstep and Hailey is our golden surprise. If that's true, why is Hailey the one who's been charged with homicide?

CHAPTER 6

DEBRA AND I SIT in the conference room, staring at the blank screen on the wall monitor. Ten seconds ago, I inserted a flash drive containing the video of Farah Medhipour's last moments on earth. I can't bring myself to click Play. I've tried many violent-crime cases, both as a prosecutor and a defense attorney, including brutal rape and murder cases. I've never been squeamish. Looking at gruesome photos, visiting the morgue is part of the job. Watching a fourteen-year-old kill herself doesn't feel like it's part of the job.

Finally, Debra reaches over and launches the video. I will myself to watch the screen. The seventeen minutes and forty seconds that follow are the most harrowing of my life. During the entire video, my heart hammers against my chest. Once it ends, there are tears in my eyes, and I want to run from the room and vomit. I force the bile down and stay where I am. If I'm going to defend Hailey, I have to stay where I am. None of this means anything, I tell myself. The girl was disturbed, delusional. So, why do I feel a simmering anger toward my daughter?

Debra stands and turns on the lights. There are no

tears, no signs of revulsion, just the impassive look of a defense lawyer objectively analyzing a piece of evidence.

"Hard to watch," she says. "Awful. But I'm encouraged. That video is going to form the centerpiece of the prosecution's case, and it's vulnerable."

"I want you to handle the lead on Hailey's case," I blurt out, surprising myself because we haven't decided which lawyer will defend Hailey.

She gives me a hard, businesslike stare. "You should go with Davies or Grutman, or maybe Thau."

She's named three of the top defense lawyers in the state, maybe in the country. But Debra Grant is the brightest, most tenacious lawyer I've ever met.

"I want you, Debra. I trust you with my life. No, more importantly, I trust you with Hailey's life."

CHAPTER 7

I SIT IN THE living room across from Janet and Hailey. I've just announced that Debra will act as lead defense counsel and that I'll sit second chair.

"I don't want that," Janet says. "She's not good enough. This is our daughter's life."

"She's a terrific lawyer," I say. "She knows Hailey, and she'll fight for her."

Janet scoffs. "So you say, but she's riding your coattails. You're the trial lawyer, not her. She's an elitist, a spoiled rich girl, and it shows. I can't believe jurors really like her." Debra's father was a successful real-estate developer, and Debra went to Princeton undergrad then Yale law school. Janet had a rough childhood. She was raised by a single mother who worked in a school cafeteria. Admirably, Janet graduated from state college with a degree in library science. But she's sensitive about her upbringing, suspicious of the privileged. Which didn't stop her from insisting that we send our kids to an exclusive private school.

I expect her to suggest that we hire one of the celebrity lawyers, but she says, "You should defend Hailey. She's *your* daughter."

"That's exactly why I *shouldn't* be lead counsel," I say.

"Mom's right, Dad," Hailey says. "Everyone knows you're the best trial lawyer around. You win all those impossible cases against the police, and they write about you in the news. Please."

"Hailey, it's a bad idea. You wouldn't expect a surgeon to operate on his own daughter."

"Of course I would, Daddy, if he was the best like you." She rarely calls me *daddy*.

Then something even more unusual happens—Janet comes over, put her arms around my neck, and kisses me. "We have faith in you, Matthew Hovanes," she whispers. "We love you. You're the only one who can protect us."

Manipulative, sure, but I've missed the affection, craved the harmony. So the kiss is meaningful no matter what the motivation.

"I love you, too," I say. And as impulsively as I asked Debra to take the lead, I now agree to do it.

There's also an objective reason for changing my mind. Debra might have a more incisive legal mind than I do, but I'm more effective in the courtroom. In fact, I feel that I'm as good as Davies, Grutman, and Thau—better, because I'm not a celebrity and so have to rely on skill, not press clippings, to persuade a jury. And Janet's right—no other lawyer will fight as hard for Hailey. The legal profession attracts egotists. You have to have an ego to believe that you're fighting for justice. I'm no exception.

"I have a suggestion," Janet says. "Why don't you hire Roy Davies to assist you?"

"Davies won't sit second chair for anybody even if he were to agree to sit second chair," I reply. "Neither would any of the superstars. Besides, if I'm going to do this, I'll need Debra. No one has a better legal mind."

Janet is about to protest, but Hailey says, "Yeah. I absolutely want Debra. She and Dad are awesome together."

First thing the next morning, I tell Debra about the change of plans.

"It's a mistake," she says. "You must know that deep down. I saw how you reacted to that horrible video of Farah—like a father, not a lawyer."

"If you want out, I understand. But I hope you'll stay involved. I need your help."

"I'll be beside you every step of the way, Matt. You know that."

Her intelligent green eyes are wide with sincerity. And then something unsettling happens. Throughout the years of our partnership, Debra has been my business colleague and my pal. But at rare moments, I'll notice how she brushes a strand of auburn hair away from her cheek or how she's applied a bit too much perfume, and I suddenly feel as if she's more than just a partner and friend. This is such a moment, and as always, I struggle to suppress the feeling.

"I appreciate your support," I say, trying to sound businesslike. "Good to have you on board."

"I have to go on record, Matt. You're making a huge mistake."

CHAPTER 8

IN THE FOLLOWING WEEKS, Debra and I prepare for *People v. Hailey Nicole Hovanes,* but we also have other clients to represent. On this morning, I stand at the lectern in a stuffy, run-down courtroom and try to convince a politically conservative judge that my homeless client has a constitutional right to sleep in public parks. I lose—of course I do—but I'll appeal.

"Where do I sleep, Mr. Hovanes?" Cecilia, my client, asks. She's thirty-seven but looks a hardscrabble fifty. "I like the parks. I can hide in the trees. The streets are too dangerous."

Because she's paranoid, I can't suggest a shelter. She believes they're under the control of a secret cabal run by Donald Trump.

"Come back to my office building," I say. "I'll speak with Downtown Dennis. He'll make sure you're not hassled anymore. If it's cold, I'll slip the night janitor some money and you can sleep in my lobby until we think of something better. Meanwhile, we'll pursue your appeal."

She nods in gratitude and walks off, and I can only think, what's wrong with this world that this troubled woman has to be grateful for an offer to sleep in a law-firm lobby?

Most attorneys, even those who love trying cases, find courtroom appearances physically exhausting and emotionally draining. I'm one of the lucky few who finds them energizing, and now I feel invigorated despite the loss and Cecilia's travails. Then I exit the courtroom and check my cell phone, and all my new-found energy dissipates like a drop of water on a hot skillet.

There's a text message from Daniel, sent twenty minutes ago: *DAD GET DOWN TO THE SCHOOL NOW! URGENT!* There's also a voice mail from the assistant head of the Star Point School, who in a somber tone requests my presence and informs me that she already spoke with Janet, who said I'd handle it.

I drive into the school parking lot. My Chevy is a jalopy compared to the foreign luxury cars and late model SUVs, most of which belong to the students at this tony private school. Even Hailey's used Toyota, a present on her sixteenth birthday that we couldn't afford, is nicer than my car. But Janet wants the best for our kids. I do, too. Daniel refuses to get his driver's license, so at least we didn't have to make two purchases.

As always when I'm on this campus, I feel like a hypocrite. I've built my career on fighting for equality, on breaking down distinctions between rich and poor. I wanted to send my children to public school. Janet wouldn't hear of it. "Not safe," she insisted. "Inferior education." I lost that battle and tens of thousands of dollars in tuition.

As I make my way to the administrative offices, I see Hailey talking with a group of her friends. She looks like a royal holding court. I don't know how she came by her charisma. As a kid, I was neither here nor there in the social hierarchy. Sure, I was a decent athlete, good-looking enough, I suppose, but too academic, too politically combative, too interested in skateboarding and Dungeons & Dragons to hang with the in-crowd. Janet doesn't talk much about her childhood, but she wasn't popular, either. More of an outcast like Daniel, I suspect. Maybe that's why they clash so often.

The good news is that the criminal charges against Hailey apparently haven't harmed her social standing. If her friends know she's innocent, so will a jury.

When she sees me, she waves but doesn't come over. Does she know what's going on with her brother?

I arrive at the assistant head's office to find a sullen Daniel sitting on the sofa. The assistant head—Miss Kirby—has her hands folded on the desk, looking more like a prison matron than a high-school administrator. Only then do I see the ugly scratch on Daniel's left cheek, oozing blood.

"Why isn't someone tending to that cut?" I ask.

"He refuses to see the school nurse," Kirby says. "There was a fight."

"Why were you fighting?" I ask.

He doesn't respond, won't make eye contact.

"What happened?" I ask Kirby.

"The other boy has been taken to the ER with a possible broken nose. He says that Daniel hit him without provocation."

"I can't believe that," I say.

Kirby gapes at me. Based on Daniel's history, she believes it.

"Why were you fighting, Daniel?" I repeat.

Again, no response.

"He won't tell us anything," Kirby says.

"Witnesses?"

"Two students say they saw Daniel punch the other boy in the face. That's all they saw. But let me get to the point. I'm afraid Daniel may no longer attend Star Point."

Without looking up, Daniel lets out a half-snort, half-guffaw.

"Excuse me?" I say.

"I'm being expelled," Daniel says. "Fine with me. I hate this fucking place."

"Wait for me outside, son. Better yet, go see the nurse and get that taken care of."

"No, I'm good." He stands and walks out, looking down at his shoes, hands in pockets. The posture gives him an odd, hulking quality.

Once he's out the door, I say, "You don't have all the facts, so why judge and pass sentence?"

"We do have all the facts. Your son injured another child without provocation. That's grounds for expulsion. And it's not the first time he's gotten physical."

"The other incident involved some minor shoving."

"Still physical, Mr. Hovanes."

I plead my son's case, ask for leniency, negotiate for a suspension. It's like speaking to granite.

"What happened to innocent until proven guilty?"

"This is a private school, not a court of law, sir. Read your contract."

"I'll do that. Remember what I do for a living. I'm good at finding loopholes. And I won't have to pay legal fees like the school will."

She inhales wearily. "May I speak off the record?"

"Sure, why not?"

"I'm sure you know that the school has received a

lot of negative publicity because of Farah Medhipour's suicide and the criminal charges that have been filed against your daughter. Your children aren't the most popular students among the administration or the trustees. There's a concern—a belief among some— that your kids did bully Farah."

The words anger me, but I'll only make things worse if I show it. "What evidence do you have against Hailey? And, what do you mean *kids*?"

"I've said too much. Just know that the school isn't afraid of a lawsuit from you. They're far more concerned about a lawsuit from Farah's family. Your son is no longer a student here. We'll e-mail you and your wife some alternatives for his education if you decide against public school."

I walk out of the room without a word, because my words wouldn't be nice. Daniel is waiting in the corridor, leaning against the wall, one leg bent at the knee with the sole of his foot on the wall. It's an attitude many of the homeless men loitering outside my building often take, and I shudder at the comparison.

We drive in silence. When we're halfway home, I ask, "What do you know about Farah's death?"

"That's Hailey's problem, not mine."

"What about the fight?"

"Oh, this jerky kid Adam came up to me and said Hailey is a murderer. I tried to walk away like you tell me to do, but he grabbed my sleeve, so I shoved him away. He took a swing and cut my face with his ring, so I hit him back."

"Why didn't you tell this to Miss Kirby?"

"She wouldn't have believed me. Besides, the asshole deserved it. I wish I'd broken his neck."

CHAPTER 9

IN CIVIL CASES, A lawyer can compel witnesses to appear for depositions, but in criminal cases, discovery is rare. So, Debra and I try to set up meetings with people who might know something about Farah and Hailey. We reach out to Adam, the boy who Daniel fought with, but it turns out he was just spouting off and knows nothing. His admission that he taunted Daniel doesn't cause the school to rescind its expulsion decision.

It seems that Farah truly didn't have any friends. Sad, but selfishly, good for Hailey's case, because there are fewer potential witnesses who might accuse Hailey of bullying conduct. We start with those close to Hailey, kids who'll testify that she had nothing to do with Farah's death. Or so we hope.

We first interview Aaron Crawford, Hailey's boyfriend. He's handsome, articulate, and confident, and like Hailey, a star athlete, the captain of the lacrosse team. He's also rich. Or at least his parents are—his father owns several sports arenas. I don't like the kid.

Then again, as Janet points out, I didn't like Hailey's prior two boyfriends, either. But there's something different about this kid. He's a senior, two classes ahead of Hailey, too old for her in my opinion. He's also a future frat boy, materialistic and snarky with his peers, unctuous with adults. And when he comes to our house to visit, he ignores Daniel.

Aaron and I sit in the conference room and talk baseball, waiting for Debra. When she arrives, he says without prompting, "I want you both to know that these charges against Hailey are bogus and that I'll do everything to help her. You know how I feel about her, Matt. She's awesome."

Debra asks him what he knows.

"At the start of the school year, Hailey was assigned as Farah's mentor because they were both soccer players. She was nice to Farah. She's nice to everybody. At first, Farah seemed cool, but then she got weird."

"Weird how?" Debra asks.

"That's the ironic thing. Farah was the stalker, not Hailey. She'd text Hailey constantly, claiming that they were BFFs—she really used that term, *BFF,* which is lame, because no one says that anymore. Then Farah wrote a text where she said she was in love with Hailey. It was creepy. Hailey told her to back off. I know because Hailey showed me the text before she sent it, because she didn't want it to sound harsh. But Farah kept on annoying everyone. Then, Farah started sexting me, saying she wanted to hook up. Totally creepy."

"Did you tell this to Hailey?" Debra asks.

"Absolutely. I showed her the texts. Obviously Hailey was pissed. What girlfriend wouldn't be?"

"Did you tell your parents?" I ask. "Or the school administration?"

"I didn't, Matt. Most kids don't share stuff like this with their adults. I think Hailey told her mom, though."

I wonder why Janet didn't tell me.

"What did Hailey do when she learned Farah had sexted you?" Debra asks.

"She and I met up with Farah at school and told her to stop. Hailey told Farah she didn't want to be her friend and that Farah should leave her alone. Farah started to cry, I mean really cry, like hysterically. So we just walked away. It was very disturbing."

"Did the sexting stop?" Debra asks.

"I didn't get any other texts from Farah. Hailey told me that Farah kept trying to communicate, but Hailey just deleted the texts. I do know one thing. There was no stalking and no bullying. No way. Hailey just ignored Farah. That's what a person should do in that situation, right?"

Debra asks some follow-up questions but doesn't get any more information.

"Is that it?" Aaron says. "Anything else you want to know?"

"Who else should we should speak with?" I ask. "Other kids that might have something to say about Hailey and Farah."

"You might talk to Brianna Welch. She's known Hailey forever. As you know, of course, Matt. Brianna is on the soccer team, and I saw her and Farah hanging out a few times. Other than that, I don't know. Hailey didn't do anything wrong, and it's hard to prove a negative."

We end the meeting, and Aaron stands and shakes our hands. "Like I said, I'll do anything for Hailey. If you need anything else, just text or call me. See you at the house, Matt."

Though tempted to say sarcastically, *I'll be counting the hours,* I nod.

"So what do you think of the boyfriend?" I ask after Aaron leaves.

"He said all the right things," Debra says. "And, he's very poised and confident. Good-looking, articulate. I think he'll make a very good witness."

"I don't like him."

"I'll bet Janet does."

"How did you know?"

"Because he's likeable. You don't see it, because you're a dad, and he's dating your daughter. Trust me, a jury will love him. Especially the female jurors." Her assessment should hearten me, but it doesn't. There's something I don't trust about that kid. And my daughter's future—her life—is partly in his hands.

CHAPTER 10

ALTHOUGH I'VE KNOWN BRIANNA Welch's parents since our girls started middle school together and became soccer teammates, they won't let me speak with her unless they're present. I don't want to do it that way—the father, also a lawyer, is overbearing, and the mother is overprotective. I'd be interviewing them, not their daughter.

So, I drive out to the Klatch, a coffee house in the strip mall across the street from the school. According to Hailey, Brianna is addicted to caramel mochas. Fifteen minutes after school lets out, Brianna walks in with Ethan Gold, a boy I've known since he was a preschooler. I hope Brianna will speak with me. Hailey asked her to do so a few days ago, and the girls are good friends.

Brianna and Ethan order their drinks and find a corner table. In contrast to Hailey, who carries herself like an adult, Brianna could pass for a twelve-year-old. I approach them and say hello.

She flinches. "Oh, hi, Mr. Hovanes," she says in a quivering voice. I can't blame her for being skittish. I've blindsided her.

"Hey, Matt," Ethan says. He's losing the gawky teenager look. He's apparently traded his glasses for contact lenses. His complexion has cleared up. He looks as if he's been working out excessively. Or, maybe he's had help building those muscles.

"Looking good, Ethan," I say. "Pumping iron?"

"Five times a week."

"Stay away from the steroids," I say. "They'll shrink and shrivel your…" I point downward in the general direction of a portion of his anatomy below his belt.

"Absolutely, sir. I'm totally clean."

"Good to hear," I say, hoping it's true. Facing Brianna, I say, "I was hoping we could talk about Hailey and Farah."

"I can't without my parents."

"It's important for me to speak with you alone. That's how lawyers do it."

"My dad's a lawyer, and he thinks—"

"He's a civil lawyer. It's different. I promise it won't take long." Without an invitation, I take a seat across from her.

She glances at Ethan and says in a barely audible voice, "Okay, I guess."

I'm strong-arming the girl, but this is how an effective defense lawyer operates.

Ethan stands and says, "I'll be at the counter."

"So, tell me what you know about Farah and Hailey," I say.

"Nothing, really. Farah was on the soccer team. She was really good. A center midfielder like Hailey. They were kind of competitive, but…"

"You're not saying that the competition resulted in bullying?" My tone is more abrupt than I intended.

"No."

"So, what *are* you saying, Bree?"

She shrugs.

"You can understand how, as a parent, I'm so upset at these charges. Please tell me what you know."

"I guess Hailey mentored Farah and Farah got, like, inappropriate? Not just with Hailey, with all of us. She tried to force herself into our group, which was weird not only because she didn't fit in, but because she was a freshman and we're all sophomores. A couple of times, she showed up uninvited at group events—at a party once and a movie one time. We didn't know how she even heard about them. She'd do favors for us, which was nice, because we didn't ask for them, but then she'd expect us to do bigger favors for her in return. Hailey finally got sick of it and told Farah to leave us alone, that she should find friends in her grade."

"Did Farah listen?"

"Not really. Then there was a collision between Hailey and Farah on the soccer field, and Farah got hurt."

Hailey hasn't told me about this. "I assume the collision was accidental?"

"Yeah, I guess so."

"You guess so?"

"Yeah. It was an accident. Of course it was."

"Anything else I should know?"

She thinks for a moment and shakes her head.

"Thanks for the time, Brianna. You've been very helpful. I'm sorry I surprised you. Apologize to your parents for me, too. I hope they'll understand. You understand, don't you?"

She nods.

Before I can get up to leave, Ethan comes over and says, "Matt, could I talk to you?"

I sit back down. Ethan and Brianna trade places, and

the girl walks away as if she'd just been released from the penitentiary.

"What's up, Ethan?"

He folds his hands on the table and pauses for a moment. "So, this is awkward, because Hailey is my friend. But I think it's only fair to tell you. A couple of weeks before Farah died, I got some texts from Hailey telling me Farah was air. Invisible, you know? And I'm not the only person who got the messages. After that, Farah got frozen out, not just by our group, but by most people in the school. Word travels fast. People didn't want to be seen with her because it would hurt their reputations."

I have trouble processing this. "Brianna didn't say anything about text messages like that."

"She's a girl in the group. Hailey didn't have to text her."

"When did this happen, again?"

"A few weeks before Farah…before she killed herself."

"Do you have copies of these texts, Ethan?"

"No, sir. Hailey asked me to erase them a couple of days after Farah died." He hesitates. "And you should know something else. I've spoken with the DA's office—Mr. Lundy? I told him about the texts. My parents said it was my obligation. I feel really bad about it because I don't want to hurt Hailey."

"Are you seriously implying Hailey was trying to cover something up?"

He shrugs.

"I'm sorry, Ethan, but I find this hard to believe. This doesn't sound like Hailey."

"Really? You're her father. I assumed you knew."

"Knew what?"

"Hailey has a dark side. She has ever since we were little kids. She'll cut you dead if you cross her—or sometimes even if you don't. People listen to her even when it's the wrong thing to do."

"Why do people listen to her?"

"Because she's Hailey Hovanes," he says as if there's nothing more obvious in the world.

CHAPTER 11

WHEN I GET BACK to the office, Debra shares some more bad news—the DA's office just sent over a stack of e-mails gleaned from Farah's computer that came from an anonymous, so far untraceable address. They seem to have been written by Hailey: *leave Aaron alone bitch or you're dead*; *stay away from me and my friends or you'll be sorry*; *quit the team we all hate you*; *find a school for special needs morons before it's too late.* And on and on, a barrage against the girl—sometimes a dozen messages sent in a single day. We can argue lack of authentication under the Evidence Code all we want, but the DA will scorch the earth to get these documents before a jury.

I tell Debra about my conversation with Ethan. She doesn't respond, but I know what she's thinking: I've been too trusting of Hailey, have been behaving like a parent, not a lawyer. I call my daughter and demand that she come to the office immediately. She pleads schoolwork, says we can speak later at home, but I won't hear of it. The conversation will take place between attorney and client, and it has to happen in my domain. It has to happen without Janet.

Hailey walks in a half hour later.

"What do you know about these?" I say, showing her the e-mails.

She sits down and reads through some of them. "Oh, my God, they're horrible. I didn't send these. I swear on my life."

"Then who did?" Debra asks.

"No idea," Hailey says. "Maybe Farah sent them to herself to set me up? Look at the lies she made up about me on her suicide note." Hailey hasn't seen the actual video but has only read a transcript. I've decided to spare her the actual video as long as possible.

Debra flashes me a concerned look.

"I met with Ethan Gold," I say. "He says you sent texts to him and some others telling them to exclude Farah—to treat her as if she was invisible."

"She hit on my boyfriend and stalked me and was totally annoying. We didn't want her around. It's a free country, right?"

"Your attitude stinks," I say. "And you hid this from us. That was stupid."

Debra holds up a hand to me. In a soft but firm tone, she says, "Your behavior can be viewed as bullying, Hailey. That's how the district attorney is going to spin your texts. He's going to say that you harassed Farah and convinced other kids to do it. He's going to argue that you wanted the texts deleted to cover up your actions because you knew you were guilty."

"Oh, my God, it was the other way around. I just wanted her to stop harassing *me*. I can't believe *you're* against me, Debra. My dad told me about a case for a photographer where you're fighting for free speech. Don't I have the same rights?"

"I'm not against you," Debra says. "It's quite the

opposite. I'm trying to protect you. The only way your father and I can do that is to be completely honest with you and for you to be honest with us."

"Anyway, Ethan is exaggerating. Actually, he's probably doing this because he's jealous of Aaron. Do you know that the day before spring break started, he said he has a crush on me? Why did he tell me that and ruin our friendship? What did he expect? He's like a brother to me. I guess I hurt his feelings, so maybe this is his way of getting back at me."

"How did Ethan exaggerate about your texts?" Debra asks.

"I just know he did. They weren't that big a deal. People text things about other kids all the time, and no one takes it seriously. Ethan is a huge gossip himself. I mean, come on, it's just texting."

"Hailey, look at me," I say, and she looks me straight in the eyes. "You're going to stop defending those texts. You're going to say that it was a mean thing to do in hindsight, but Farah was making you uncomfortable, and you didn't know what else to do. You're going to say that you asked people to delete them because you were embarrassed and that you're very sorry, but things never went any further. You're going to say those things because it's the truth."

Debra glances at me, clearly surprised at my forcefulness. I usually take a soft approach with clients. But Hailey isn't just any client.

"Of course, Dad," Hailey says. "If that's what I need to say, absolutely."

"You need to tell the truth," Debra says.

"It is the truth," Hailey replies.

I reach across the table and take Hailey's hands. "Is there anything else you're not telling us?"

"No, Dad. Absolutely not. I swear."

"Okay. Good. Because we need to know everything, even if you don't think it's important."

"Got it."

I ask Hailey to wait outside. After she leaves the room, I say, "Do you think she's hiding something?"

"I honestly don't know what to think, Matt."

"Then there's a major problem."

"Is it just my problem?"

All at once I'm overcome with that overwhelming current, that wellspring that refuses to let us hide our emotions, and my eyes brim with tears of disappointment, confusion, and most of all, dread. "What if she did this, Debra? What if my daughter really is some monster who…? I thought I knew who she is. I don't know who she is. I…" Struggling not to break down entirely, I bury my face in my hands.

Debra walks behind me and gently touches my shoulder. "We're going to do what we always do, Matt. We're going to represent her to the best of our abilities and fight to get her out of this. We're going to see that justice is done."

Through the tears, I wonder if justice is what I really want.

CHAPTER 12

THE BAILIFF CRIES OUT, "All rise!"

We're in court for Hailey's preliminary hearing, a proceeding in which the prosecution must show that it has probable cause to bind her over for a full-blown trial. The security door to the judge's chambers clicks open, and the Honorable Brady Sears takes the bench. The bad news is he was once the district attorney, so he leans prosecution. The good news is he hired both me and my nemesis, Joshua Lundy, and he's a fair person. When I discovered Lundy concealing evidence, Sears had already left to become a judge. I like to think that if Sears had still been in office, he would've done the right thing—unlike his successor, the political hack who'll do anything for a conviction.

I glance back at Janet, who's in the gallery. She gives a nod of encouragement. We've had our issues, but she's always made me feel like a great lawyer.

The judge instructs the defendant to rise—I still find it unimaginable that my daughter is a defendant—and asks her to enter a plea.

"Not guilty, Your Honor," Hailey says, her tone steady and confident.

"We'll conduct the preliminary hearing now," the judge says.

I stand and say, "The defense has a motion, Your Honor."

"Proceed, Mr. Hovanes."

"Your Honor, there's no dispute in this case that the tragic suicide of Farah Medhipour was just that—a suicide. We vehemently deny that Hailey Hovanes harassed or bullied Farah, and a trial would prove that. But we shouldn't have a trial. Under the law, a person can't be held responsible for another's suicide. We can never know what causes a person to take her own life, can never get inside a troubled mind. There's also no dispute that Farah was depressed, on medication. There's no dispute that she had emotional problems for years. There simply isn't legal causation. The charges against my client should be dismissed." The key to good courtroom advocacy is leaving the listener with the impression that you're sincere. Flash, oratory, and presence are great, sure, but they're not as important as sincerity. I believe in what I'm saying.

"There's another reason why this case should be dismissed," I continue. "The cyber-stalking laws impinge upon free speech. Even hateful speech is entitled to protection under the First Amendment. Sad as it may be, it's human nature to gossip, to needle, to ridicule. Allowing even vulgar and offensive speech is essential to a democratic society." I go on to discuss some helpful legal opinions that Debra found. Then I sit down and hope.

To my surprise, Hailey takes my hand. Usually, she's not physically demonstrative.

Lundy stands, and rather than using the lectern, he

remains at counsel table—his way of conveying that my argument is so feeble that he needs only a brief moment to refute it. He's still a lanky man, athletic, with angular features. Good-looking except for residual scars from childhood acne. And the eyes and ethics of a serpent.

"The cyber-bullying laws are constitutional because harassment, bullying, and torture are actions, not words," he says dismissively. "As for defense counsel's argument that a bully can never be responsible for the consequences of her conduct, that's absurd. Under the statute, whoever with the intent to kill, harass, or intimidate another person that causes severe emotional distress has committed the crime of cyber bullying. The People will present evidence that Hailey Hovanes caused Farah Medhipour severe emotional distress and drove her to suicide." With that, he sits down.

I stand to reply, but the judge says, "Defendant's motion is denied."

Hailey releases my hand and slumps in her chair. I don't have to turn to look at Janet, because I can feel her dismay. Winning the motion was a long shot with a law-and-order judge like Sears, but that doesn't lessen the disappointment.

"The People will present evidence," the judge says.

"The People call Detective Ernesto Velasquez," Lundy says.

Velasquez takes the stand and testifies about the anonymous threatening e-mails, about Farah's video accusation against Hailey, about the texts she sent Ethan Gold. All hearsay, but hearsay is admissible in a preliminary proceeding, and unlike in an actual trial, the prosecution's burden of proof is very low. So far, no surprises.

Then Lundy asks, "Detective Velasquez, did you take a statement from one Nicholas Volokh?"

"I did."

"Who's Nicholas Volokh?"

"The upper-school soccer coach at the Star Point School."

"What did Mr. Volokh tell you?"

"Objection," I say. "The defense hasn't been provided with a copy of Volokh's statement."

"It was just signed this morning, Your Honor," Lundy says. "I thought my office sent over a copy to Grant & Hovanes."

I glance at Debra, who shakes her head.

"My bad," Lundy says. "I apologize." He reaches over and hands us a copy of Volokh's sworn statement. In it, the coach claims that during a practice, Hailey intentionally tried to injure Farah, shoving the girl from behind.

"The document is signed under penalty of perjury?" Lundy asks Velasquez.

"Yes, sir. The witness was very concerned about its accuracy."

"No further questions," Lundy says.

"Cross-examination?" the judge asks.

I want to interrogate Velasquez, to batter him into conceding that Lundy intentionally withheld Coach Volokh's statement. Cops are tough witnesses to crack, but I've made a living accomplishing it. As I rise, Debra touches my arm.

"Save it for trial," she says, chilling, because I now fully realize there will be a trial.

"No questions," I say. "But there's one other issue we need to discuss. My daughter…*my client* is a juvenile. The defense would request that the court—"

"Stop right there, counselor," the judge says. "Bullying with intent to inflict severe emotional distress or death is horrific, and that makes it an adult crime. The defendant will be tried as an adult."

Suddenly, the prospect that my child will serve the rest of her life in prison is all too real.

CHAPTER 13

DEDICATED CRIMINAL DEFENSE attorneys can represent society's vermin—terrorists, murderers, even pedophiles—and still sleep at night. That's because we never ask if the client is guilty, don't give a rat's ass if the client is guilty. Under the American justice system, even a guilty person is entitled to a defense.

Such willful blindness might be a blessing for a defense attorney, but it's a parent's curse. So, I almost drag Hailey into the attorney conference room after her disastrous preliminary hearing and say, "Did you harass and stalk that girl? Did you try to hurt her like Coach Nick says? I want the truth."

"I can't believe you're talking to me this way."

"Answer me, Hailey!"

"Keep your voices down," Debra says in a harsh rasp I've heard her use with opposing counsel and recalcitrant witnesses but never with me. "You and Hailey discuss this alone." Before waiting for a response, she walks out. She doesn't want to know whether our client is guilty.

"I didn't do what they say, and I didn't try to hurt her on the soccer field," Hailey says. "We were scrimmaging, and it was a fifty-fifty ball. You asked Brianna Welch, and she said it was a clean hit. She was there."

"Then why would Volokh say—?"

"Coach Nick is a jerk. He's been against me ever since I quit the Dynamo. Farah was his little pet because she joined his club team. I did not do what they say, Dad."

My genuine sense of relief is tempered by a lingering skepticism.

"I can't really go to jail, right, Dad?"

"Hailey, the charges against you are very serious, and you made it worse by not telling us everything. You're in trouble, and you have to tell us everything." I reach over to take her hands, but she pulls them away.

"No. I didn't do anything wrong. I'm going to play soccer in college and have a modeling career. Mom and I have been looking for talent agents."

Suddenly, I'm acutely aware of something that people forget about my daughter, even me. She's still a clueless child.

Or, is that explanation too facile, a father's rationalization? Are her words a symptom of something far darker and more disturbing than mere childish naïveté?

CHAPTER 14

WHEN I GET BACK to the office, Debra is typing on her computer. I report my conversation with Hailey.

Debra slams her laptop cover shut and says, "This is bad."

"It's not really—"

"Oh, it really is. The prosecution hasn't divulged even a fraction of the evidence they have against her. Lundy always hides the ball—as you know better than anyone. Worse, Hailey hasn't been forthcoming. When she gets found out, she comes up with these ridiculous explanations: her close friend Ethan is a vindictive rejected suitor; the coach doesn't like her because she quit a youth soccer team; Farah created bogus e-mails and committed suicide just to get back at Poor Little Hailey. Well, she's not the victim. Farah Medhipour is."

"You've known Hailey since she was ten years old. Do you honestly think she's guilty?"

"It doesn't matter what I think. What matters is that the wrong jury could convict her. She's not appealing."

"She's beautiful and poised. At least all those beauty contests helped with that."

Debra shakes her head. "People hate the popular

girl. And I don't mean to offend you, but she's cold. What's the word? Imperious." She takes a deep breath. "I have something to tell you. You won't like it. I called Josh Lundy a little while ago and floated the idea of a plea bargain."

"You did what? How dare you do that without consulting me? Do you want to ruin Hailey's life? All you've done is make Lundy think we have no confidence in our case."

"He says he'll agree to a maximum of five years as an adult, but I think he'll go for eighteen months in juvy if we make a deal now."

"No fucking way."

"If she weren't your daughter, you'd consider it."

I walk out of Debra's office, collect my things, and go to my car. As I drive, my viscera begin to twist in indecision, because I do know that Debra is right. A plea bargain is something to consider.

When I arrive home, I ask Hailey and Janet to join me in the living room. When Daniel starts to follow, Janet says, "This is a private conversation."

"I want Danny to stay," Hailey says.

Once everyone is seated, I broach the subject of a plea bargain, explain the risks of going to trial.

"This is Debra's doing," Janet says.

"It's part of any discussion when you represent a defendant," I say. "Most cases plead out."

"No. This is Debra. She's gotten you to doubt your own daughter."

"That's not true."

"I want that woman off the case," Janet says. "I want her out of our lives. End the partnership. She's been holding you back for years, anyway."

"I'm not going to fire Debra. She's my partner."

"And what the hell am I?"

All the while, Hailey has, as usual, sat silently and watched us argue, her demeanor reminiscent of a tennis referee. Daniel is more like a ball boy, hunched over, subservient, and unobtrusive.

Finally, Hailey says, "Stop fighting, you guys. Dad, I'm not going to make a deal. I'm innocent. Mom, I want Debra on the case. Dad needs her. I need her."

Janet frowns.

"You have to consider this, Hailey," I say. "A plea bargain could mean that you'd avoid a possible sentence in an adult prison, that you'd be out in a year and a half and start your life. Sometimes guilt and innocence don't matter. Freedom always matters."

To my surprise, Hailey asks Daniel's opinion.

He thinks for a moment. "Aren't guilt or innocence the only things that matter, Dad? Aren't you always telling us that the law is all about justice? If Hailey's innocent, wouldn't it be unjust if she spends a second behind bars?"

And that ends the discussion. Only later do I realize that Daniel said *if* Hailey is innocent rather than because she *is* innocent.

CHAPTER 15

BEFORE THE FINANCIAL CRISIS in 2008, O'Mahoney's Irish Pub in mid-city was a popular sports bar where stockbrokers, bond traders, and big law attorneys went to drink and dine after the markets and their offices closed. These days, it's mostly a hangout for middle-aged soccer fanatics, Irish expats, and broken-down former athletes. At five o'clock in the afternoon, a few days after Hailey's preliminary hearing, I walk into the bar to find Nicholas Volokh, coach of Hailey's high school and former club teams, sitting alone at a back table. Although O'Mahoney's touts its array of ales on tap, Volokh is a whiskey drinker. He's been known to show up at soccer practice with an obvious hangover. But he's a good teacher of the game, and more importantly, a winner, and even in youth soccer, everyone loves a winner.

He's a tough guy—he played a bit of pro soccer in the UK—but I'm a larger man. When he sees me, he starts and makes a move to get up.

"Sit back down, Nick," I say, moving to within six inches of him.

"Why should I?"

"You wouldn't want the school to know that its soccer coach and recovering alcoholic smells like he's been guzzling Tennessee moonshine during school hours, would you?"

He complies, and I sit across from him.

"The DA told me I didn't have to talk to you, Hovanes."

"I just want to know why you threw Hailey under the bus when you know it's all lies. My God, you've coached her since she was twelve. You could've at least given me a heads up. You didn't even have the loyalty to do that."

"You're not one to talk about loyalty after moving her to the Southern City United." Although Volokh coaches the high school team, the true competitive soccer is played in the club leagues. The colleges, and sometimes even the pros, recruit from the club leagues.

"We've been over this. She needs that college scholarship, and you don't get scholarships playing below premier. Is that really what this is about? Your star player leaves your team, so you accuse her of a crime?"

He chugs the rest of his drink and signals to the server to bring him another. I order a glass of water.

"Hailey intentionally set out to hurt Farah," he says. "She was jealous because Farah was about to take her position, and I think your daughter saw that scholarship flying out the window. So she tried to injure the girl. One of the dirtiest tackles I've seen in girls' competition; hell, in boys' competition. Farah's down, writhing in pain, and Hailey taunts her and yells, 'I warned you, bitch. Next time I won't be so nice.'"

Interesting. This fact wasn't in Volokh's declaration.

"And the attack wasn't only physical," he continues. "Hailey got the other girls to freeze Farah out, in practice and in games. They wouldn't pass to her even when she was wide open, wouldn't come to the ball when she was double teamed. It was disgusting. Cost the team a victory, maybe two."

"Hailey isn't that kind of player."

"How would you know?"

He's right. I saw only one high school game this season, and Hailey received a yellow card for an overly aggressive play. I'd never seen that before. But the girls have gotten older and stronger, and the competition has gotten more intense, so you'd expect more physical play. Hell, one of Volokh's techniques is to have them scrimmage against boys' teams to make them tougher.

"It's tragic," he says. "If Farah had continued to develop, she would've been a special player."

"According to Hailey, Farah was stalking her."

His tippler's laugh is derisive. "What I saw was that she looked up to Hailey—admiration, not stalking. She was nerdy, and your ever-so-cool daughter doesn't like nerds." The server brings Volokh another shot, which he chugs down. "I have nothing against you. The fact is that Hailey didn't behave well. At least your daughter is alive. Farah's mother is a broken woman. Do you know she came to see me afterward? I was afraid she was going to shame me for not protecting her daughter. She thanked me for making Farah's life a little happier. I spoke with the district attorney because I want to see justice done for that girl. Now, this interview is over."

"I'm not finished talking to you, Volokh."

"Oh, I think you are." He glances over my shoulder, and I follow his eyes. Two roughnecks are standing over me. I recognize one as Vlad, who spent a month as Volokh's assistant coach until the parents found out he'd been arrested two years earlier for assault and battery. More accurately, I did a records search and found out. Vlad doesn't like me. I don't recognize the second man, whose most prominent characteristic is a massive chest.

"Well, if it isn't the lawyer," Vlad says, smirking. "The lawyer bothering you, Nick?"

"Mr. Hovanes was just leaving," Volokh says.

I know a credible threat when I see it, so I get up. "More soon, Coach." And there will be more soon. I'm going to destroy this guy because of what he's trying to do to my daughter. I know just how to do it.

CHAPTER 16

ALL ATTORNEYS SEEM TO have the ability to convince themselves of their own righteousness. It's an occupational hazard. Which is why I'm able to persuade myself that it's a good idea to visit Farah's mother unannounced even though she's steadfastly refused to meet with Debra.

On a Saturday morning, I drive to Shirin Medhipour's Tudor-style house in the Hillcrest district, a neighborhood far more upscale than mine. The home seems too spacious for only the girl and her mother. How empty it must feel now.

I park my car, climb the stonemasonry steps, and reach out to ring the doorbell. My hand begins to tremble. What am I thinking, invading this grieving mother's privacy? If I were only Hailey's lawyer, this might be all right, but I'm not only Hailey's lawyer.

Impulsively, I press the button anyway.

There are footsteps, and the door opens. Shirin is an attractive woman in her mid-to-late thirties—black hair, full lips, a Greek nose. She's dressed casually, in yoga pants and a long T-shirt. What did I expect, mourning garb? Her doleful brown eyes indict me for having the temerity to show up on her doorstep—indict me for being Hailey Hovanes's father.

"I'm sorry for your loss," I say, and flush hot with embarrassment at the trite words.

"Thank you. I mean that sincerely. But you must leave now." Surprisingly, there's no venom in her tone. She has a slight Persian accent, but she's obviously spoken English most of her life. I've already seen enough to know that she'll make an appealing trial witness. She starts to shut the door.

All the stratagems for easing my way into this "interview" elude me, and all I can think to say is, "Wait! I just want you to know that my daughter is a good kid. She didn't do what they say. It's all a misunderstanding. Teenagers sometimes—"

"What do you want, Mr. Hovanes?"

"I just want to talk so we can get to the truth."

"I know the truth. Your daughter is a bully, and my daughter is dead because of it. If you're looking for forgiveness for yourself, you don't need it, because I don't blame you. If you're looking for forgiveness for your daughter, it's too soon, because there can be no forgiveness until justice is done. And if you're here as her attorney to get me to say something that will help in your daughter's defense, well, sir, that would be unforgivable."

From inside the house, a man shouts something in Farsi.

"It's nobody, Kamron," she replies in English. To me, she whispers, "Go now. Before my brother—"

Too late. The brother comes to the door. He looks at least ten years older than Shirin.

"What are you doing here?" he says, his accent much thicker than hers.

"He came to give his condolences," Shirin says. "He's leaving now."

"Leaving? That is bullshit. You are running because a real man came to the door. It is very easy to harass a woman. You are a coward and a bully, just like your daughter!"

I turn and take two steps toward my car. He runs out the door and shoves me. I almost tumble down the stairs but somehow regain my balance and only go down to one knee. The brother is glowering at me in hatred. Although I have at least six inches and forty pounds on him, he charges and takes a wild round-house punch, which I deflect with a forearm.

"Kamron, don't!" Shirin screams.

He swings again, and all I can do is tackle him. Like absurd characters in an antiquated Saturday-morning cartoon, we grapple and grab and tug, rolling down the lawn. I finally subdue him and pin him to the ground, but he continues to struggle, so full of rage that foamy spittle leaks from the corner of his mouth. I understand his feelings completely. So, why do I have an almost ir-resistible urge to punch him in the face?

Shirin runs down the lawn. "It's enough! Both of you, it's enough." When her brother struggles again, she says something to him in Farsi and then begins to cry.

Still glaring at me, he relaxes under my grip. Though his anger hasn't diminished one whit, the fight is over. I rise, and fortunately, he stays down.

"I'm sorry I intruded," I mumble. I hurry to my car and speed away, dazed and mortified. Somehow, I manage to get back to the office without crashing into anyone. I don't even remember the drive.

"Oh, my God, what happened to you?" Debra asks when she sees me at her office door.

I take inventory. There are grass stains on the elbows of my coat. My pants are ripped at the right knee, and the fabric is soaked with blood. I didn't notice any of it until now.

I explain what happened, and instead of giving me the expected—and well-deserved—dressing down, she says, "We'll get through this. Now, go wash that cut off and put a Band-Aid on it."

I clean up in the men's room, raid the first-aid kit for an alcohol swab and a bandage, and go back to my office, trying to work on some other case files but getting nothing done. Unwittingly, I just tortured a woman whose daughter died in torment.

Thirty minutes later, my office phone rings. "Matthew Hovanes. It's Detective Ernesto Velasquez. I'm here with Joshua Lundy."

I wait.

"I'm going to say this once, Hovanes," Lundy says. "If you ever bother the Medhipour family again, I'll have *you* arrested for stalking." The line goes dead.

CHAPTER 17

JUDGE SEARS SCHEDULED THE trial to begin in early July so school would be out for Hailey and the student witnesses. Not the way any of us planned to spend our summer vacation. It's hot and humid, and even in my summer-weight suit I'm drenched in sweat by the time I walk the half-block from the parking lot to the courthouse steps.

Debra, Hailey, and I make our way to the courtroom and take our seats at the defense table, and now I'm shivering because the air conditioning has been turned up so high. Or maybe I'm shivering because Farah's mother and uncle are in the gallery, sitting in the first row behind the prosecution.

Hailey has tried to dress "young." But because of her poise and good looks—and what after all these years I finally recognize as a kind of haughtiness—she could pass for a twenty-two-year-old. The good thing is that she doesn't appear anxious. Or maybe that's not such a good thing, either. Maybe the jurors will see her as cold and uncaring. I fear that my dual status as lawyer-parent is already affecting my judgment.

The judge takes the bench, and during the morning

session, we pick a jury. In the end, a decent draw. Six of them have children, and five are young and might understand that kids use the internet to say things to each other that seem vile but that are actually benign in the world of a teenager.

Judge Sears says, "The attorneys will give their opening statements. We'll hear from the People first. Remember that what the lawyers say isn't evidence."

Openings might not be evidence, but usually they're the most important part of a trial. Studies show that 80 percent of jurors have made up their minds immediately after opening statements. I've got to win this phase, or at least stay even.

Lundy takes the lectern and faces the jury. He was a plodder back in the day. I hope that's still true.

"In every homicide, there's a weapon," he says. "Usually, it's a gun or a knife or a blunt instrument. In this case the weapon was a computer keyboard, but just as lethal. And that weapon was wielded by Hailey Hovanes, who harassed, bullied, and, yes, tortured Farah Medhipour, knowing that Farah was suicidal, knowing that words and deeds could kill Farah. That's what Hailey's words and deeds did—drive Farah to her death." The best trial lawyers don't use notes, and in the old days, Lundy relied on them extensively. Now, he's speaking extemporaneously. He summarizes the evidence, succinctly, powerfully. He describes Farah's video and warns them what they're going to see is disturbing, horrific—but also Farah's way of bringing her tormentor to justice. He tells the jurors that they'll hear from people who were close to Farah—her friends, her longtime coach—who'll testify she was harassed by Hailey.

Then, as he holds on to the lapels of his coat like

some down-home country lawyer, he says, "Ladies and gentlemen of the jury, when all the evidence is in, you will conclude beyond a reasonable doubt that Hailey Hovanes bullied Farah to death knowing of the girl's fragile emotional state. At the end of this trial, the People will ask you to return a verdict of guilty."

Experienced trial lawyers never look at the jury during opposing counsel's opening so as not to give credence to what the opponent is saying. I don't need to see the jurors to know that they're riveted. Joshua Lundy is a plodder no more.

"Counsel for the defendant, do you have an opening?" the judge says.

When Lundy began speaking, my heart was pounding, but now there are no nerves, only the burning desire to refute what he's said. My adrenaline level is so high I have to force myself to slow down.

Instead of walking to the lectern, I stand behind Hailey and put my hands on her shoulders. I didn't tell her that I was going to do this, and she starts slightly in surprise. Good. I don't want the jury to think this is rehearsed. I'm a lawyer humanizing my client; a father showing I love and trust my daughter.

"Members of the jury, Hailey Hovanes is a sixteen-year-old rising high school junior who's had an exemplary record. She's a star athlete, a mentor to younger kids, and a good student. She's never before been in trouble, never before been accused of bullying anyone. She didn't bully Farah Medhipour. Farah's death is a tragedy, but not every tragedy is a crime. There's not a shred of evidence that Hailey caused Farah's death, much less evidence beyond a reasonable doubt. No, sadly, Farah died by her own hand."

I move to the lectern and make eye contact with each juror. "Farah was one of those younger students who Hailey mentored. There's no dispute that Hailey was kind to Farah, helpful. That, members of the jury, isn't the profile of a bully but rather the opposite of bullying. You'll hear evidence that Farah Medhipour had profound psychological issues long before she entered high school, that she had a history of conflict with other children, that she was being treated for severe depression. And because of those issues, she took Hailey's acts of kindness the wrong way, expressed romantic love for Hailey, and eventually stalked Hailey. What the prosecution calls bullying was just Hailey's way of protecting herself."

I point out that the threatening e-mails are anonymous and could've come from anyone; that a schoolyard confrontation doesn't amount to bullying; that you can't criminalize every harsh word or insensitive act, especially where teenagers are involved. I note that other important forces—parents, other kids, teachers, therapists—all influenced Farah's state of mind.

Then I confront the most damning piece of evidence. "Yes, you'll see a horrible video that no parent, no person should have to see. But that video will show one thing beyond any doubt: Farah Medhipour died by her own hand." Two of the jurors are nodding, and that's a good thing, especially so early in the case.

As I'm about to finish, I momentarily turn away from the jury so I can stand near Hailey when I ask the jury to acquit her. My eyes fall on Daniel, who's sitting slouched in a chair in the third row of the gallery. His long legs are in the aisle, crossed at the ankles. He looks as if he's lounging. He has a disrespectful—no, disbelieving—smirk on his face. I struggle to remain composed: if even one of the jurors notices Daniel's demeanor, this opening statement, no matter how effective, could be worthless. How could Hailey be innocent if her own brother thinks she's guilty?

CHAPTER 18

THE JUDGE CALLS FOR a fifteen-minute recess. As soon as the jury exits and the judge leaves the bench, I tell Hailey to stay with Debra, half-sprint toward Daniel and Janet, and usher them into the attorney conference room.

"What the hell, Daniel?" I say.

"I tried to nudge him, but I didn't want to make a scene," Janet says.

He seems genuinely confused. "What did I do now?"

"Slouching like that, with your legs in the aisle," I say.

"Those chairs are hard, and it's cramped. This courtroom sucks. Anyway, so what?"

"You were smirking, like you were ridiculing what I was saying."

"Jesus, Dad, that's the way I always look. I wasn't doing anything."

For all his issues, Daniel isn't stupid. How could he be unaware of his behavior? Of course, I don't want to believe he's trying to sabotage his sister's case, but I can't take the risk.

When he takes out his cell phone and starts playing

some game, I lose it. "You're not going to set foot in this courtroom again while this trial is going on! Take an Uber back home now and don't come back."

He recoils as if I've slapped him in the face. I expect him to hurl invectives at me, but he just pockets his phone and shuffles out.

Janet nods, as if this is a triumph rather than yet another crack in our family's foundation.

I worry that I've been too harsh. Maybe his behavior wasn't intentional. Daniel has difficulty reading social cues. It doesn't matter. He can't come back.

"Do you think the jury noticed?" I ask.

Janet shakes her head. "They were all focused only on you. You were terrific. Riveting."

I've always craved her praise, and her words lift me out of the gloom that this incident with Daniel has caused. We share a sweet awkwardness we haven't experienced in a long time.

"You'd better get back," she says.

CHAPTER 19

THE PEOPLE CALL DETECTIVE Ernesto Velasquez."

Dressed in a tailored charcoal-blue suit—Velasquez is a flashy dresser, especially for a cop—he lumbers to the stand. He's testified hundreds of times before and has a good courtroom demeanor. The perfect first witness.

Velasquez recounts his investigation, which began with Farah's video suicide note and continued when police forensics found the anonymous threatening e-mails on the girl's computer. Lundy offers into evidence the message that reads *leave Aaron alone bitch or you're dead*.

"Objection," I say. "No foundation as to authenticity." What I mean is that because the e-mails are anonymous, they can't be traced to Hailey and are irrelevant.

"Overruled," the judge says. "I'm going to admit them for the limited purpose of showing that the victim was harassed. The jury is instructed that unless authenticated, these e-mails can't be used as evidence that the defendant sent them."

Honest jurors try to follow limiting instructions, but

it's like telling someone not to think of giraffes for ten seconds. Our jury can't help but conclude that Hailey sent these disgusting messages.

"In your investigation, did you discover a video in which Farah Medhipour discussed committing suicide?" Lundy asks.

"We did." Velasquez spends the next ten minutes testifying about the investigation and forensic analysis surrounding the video.

"At this time, we'd like to play that video for the jury," Lundy says.

"Objection," I say. "Hearsay."

"It comes in under the dying declaration exception," Lundy says. "The victim had a belief in her impending death."

"But she hadn't suffered her injuries yet, and the case law holds that injury is required before the statement is made."

"Not unprecedented at all," Lundy says. "West Virginia and the federal courts in Illinois hold that a suicide note is admissible as a dying declaration."

"Those cases involved written notes," I say. "And California and Louisiana don't even let notes in."

"The medium doesn't matter, it's still a dying declaration, Your Honor. The California and Louisiana cases that Mr. Hovanes mentions are outdated and ill-reasoned. And besides, Farah Medhipour *had* suffered injury when she made the video—the taunts and harassment and bullying and psychological wounds inflicted by Hailey Hovanes."

"Objection!" I shout.

"Lower your voice, Mr. Hovanes," Judge Sears says. "And don't do anything like that again, Mr. Lundy. The jury will disregard Mr. Lundy's statement about the defendant inflicting wounds. That's for you to decide after all the evidence is in."

"Very well, Your Honor," Lundy says with false contrition.

"As for the hearsay objection, it's overruled," the judge says. "The video will come in as a dying declaration. I know this is a case of first impression, but I agree with Mr. Lundy—the medium doesn't matter. And it's highly relevant to this case, whatever the prejudice."

Debra exhales audibly. This is a major defeat and a mistake on my part. I should've asked to approach the bench so we could argue out of the jury's presence. We have grounds to appeal, but that assumes a conviction—a nightmare scenario.

"What we'll do now is clear the courtroom of everyone but the media, law enforcement, and family members of the defendant and the victim who choose to stay," the judge says.

Farah's mother and uncle leave. Janet stays. I warned her about the video but also advised her that remaining in the courtroom would signify a strong show of support for our daughter. I admire her willingness to sit through this.

And then, to my shock, I see Daniel sitting in the back row. Why is he here after I demanded he stay away? His mother doesn't seem to notice him.

Hailey has never seen the video, and it will be hard on her. More than that, her reaction will influence how the jury views her.

Lundy's assistant taps on her keyboard, and the five courtroom monitors power up. The video starts like any other kid's selfie, with Farah looking down as she adjusts the camera. Because she made the recording on a cell phone, the video quality is slightly fuzzy on the large high-definition screens. She's a kid, a pretty girl with raven hair and olive skin, at fourteen still a child in a way that Hailey wasn't at that age. She looks into the camera, her dark-brown eyes clear and sad—but no tears. She's wearing her school soccer uniform.

"Maamaan, if you're watching this, I'm already dead and at peace," she says, and what's chilling is that she sounds at peace. "Please don't blame yourself. You were a great mom, did everything for me. I love you." She adjusts the camera to zoom in. "I'm ending my life, yes, to stop my own pain, because I've been hurting so bad for as long as I can remember. But that's not the only reason. I want to help other kids who are in pain so they don't have to do what I'm doing. I just can't stand the torture anymore—the horrible, mean words, the texts, the shoving, the loneliness. Maybe that's the worst, the isolation. The torture has gone on for so, so long." She takes a deep breath. "Why, Hailey? I just wanted to be your friend. You were supposed to be my mentor, my teammate. So what if I liked you more than you liked me? So what if I'm not as cool or pretty as you and your friends? So what if I said I loved you? You didn't have to be mean, you didn't have to torture me, to get the other kids to torture me. Don't you have any feelings at all? Why did you hurt me like that, with those ugly e-mails, and the…? I warned you, Hailey. I told you that you were making me want to die. I hope you see this video someday soon. It's for you, too, to help you and other bullies. So you won't do to other kids what you did to me. We're all just teenagers, in the same boat, right?" She pauses, showing no signs of fear. "I guess that's it. I love you, Maamaan." She repeats the words in Farsi, her last.

She maneuvers her cell phone upward so the camera

is focused on the second-floor balustrade. A heavy-duty orange extension cord—industrial grade—dangles from the top railing. You can hear her climbing the stairs. Then interminable silence, as if she's reconsidering, but, of course, she doesn't reconsider. The extension cord is pulled upward. There's another long pause as she forms the noose and wraps it around her neck—we don't see this, but we know. Then she maneuvers her youthful, athletic legs over the railing, and she seems to be sitting for a moment, and the decisive drop, and a short high-pitched shriek, and the gurgling and the convulsions—legs and arms and torso flailing helplessly against death despite what her brain and soul may desire, and her face a bloated, hideous death mask before actual death, and the spasms subside and become tremors. Then even that paltry indicator of life ceases. Only just before the screens go blank does it become clear that Farah soiled herself.

Three jurors are in tears, and several glare at Hailey, who, as the video played, showed no emotion at all. It would've been better if she'd become hysterical.

I scan the gallery. Janet stares at the ceiling, jaw clenched, hands clasped tightly on her lap. Daniel is nowhere to be seen.

CHAPTER 20

I JUMP OUT OF my chair and go to the lectern, a message to the jury that I can't wait to have at Velasquez, that nothing about his testimony or the video bothers me. I hope I'm a good actor.

"The e-mails that you found on Farah Medhipour's computer were sent anonymously, weren't they, Detective Velasquez."

"Yes, sir."

"In fact, the sender uses the name *Farahs_Nightmare*."

"That is correct."

"And no one in law enforcement knows who sent them."

"Correct."

"The police department examined Hailey Hovanes's computer and smartphone?"

"Yes."

"And after a thorough forensic analysis, you found no evidence that Hailey Hovanes sent those e-mails from her computer or phone."

"No. Not from those devices."

"Well, detective, have you found evidence that Hailey sent the e-mails from any other devices?"

"No, sir."

"Let's talk about the video we just saw." I show him a transcription of Farah's words. "Farah said, 'I've been hurting so bad for as long as I can remember.' That would seem to mean that she was in pain since she was a small child."

"I've seen reports that she suffered from depression for a number of years."

"And that depression was a reason she gave for committing suicide?"

"You could interpret it like that."

"That's how you interpret it, isn't it, Detective?"

He shrugs.

"And Farah only met Hailey at the beginning of the school year?"

"Correct."

"So, the pain Farah was suffering that led to her suicide predated her meeting Hailey?"

"It's hard to know what the victim was thinking," he says. He tugs at his tie, a tell that he knows he's made a mistake.

"If we can't know what Farah was thinking, we can't know what caused Farah to commit suicide, can we, Detective?"

Then another unfathomable error from an experienced witness—he glances at Lundy.

"Do you need Mr. Lundy's help to answer that question?" It's a low blow, but effective.

"No, counselor. The video speaks for itself. Farah mentioned Hailey by name."

"Farah also said, 'The torture has gone on for so, so long.' But according to your investigation, the alleged dispute between Farah and Hailey only went on for a matter of weeks."

"That's what the investigation turned up. But in those weeks, the harassment was unrelenting."

"Farah had been bullied in middle school, correct?"

"I don't know that to be true."

"Did you investigate whether she'd been bullied in middle school?"

"Based on the e-mails and videos, there was no reason to do that."

"So, you just saw the video and read the e-mails and assumed that Hailey Hovanes was guilty without pursuing any other suspect, without investigating who else might've bullied Farah?"

"There were no other suspects."

"Did you come to that conclusion because the police department didn't want to find any other suspects? Because Hailey Hovanes's father is in the business of holding the police accountable for their civil rights violations and acts of brutality?"

"Objection, argumentative," Lundy says.

"Sustained," the judge says.

It doesn't matter. I've made my point. "In the video, Farah says, 'I warned you, Hailey.'"

Velasquez nods.

"Isn't that an odd word for Farah to have used—*warned*?"

"I wouldn't say so."

"Doesn't the word *warned* indicate that Farah made some sort of threat?"

"It might or might not."

"As you pointed out, we don't know what was in Farah's mind."

No answer.

"So, detective, Farah might have taken action to carry out some sort of threat she'd made against Hailey?"

"Anything's possible, counselor. But—"

"You've answered, sir. No further questions."

I've chipped away at the testimony and evidence. But nothing I did on cross could possibly blot out the image of that poor child in her death throes. The jury will want to blame someone for Farah's demise, and the easy target is Hailey Hovanes.

CHAPTER 21

THE PROSECUTION CALLS COACH

Nicholas Volokh, who describes Hailey's abusive behavior toward Farah—the threatening words, the freeze-out during games, the dirty play. Worse, for one of the rare times in his adult life, the son of a bitch isn't drunk or hungover.

On cross-examination, I ask, "Hailey Hovanes played on your club team for several years?"

"She did."

"Good player?"

"Hailey's okay."

"She was your captain, your leading goal scorer, and your assist leader for three years running, wasn't she?"

"I don't pay that much attention to statistics. I coach kids." Except that when Hailey played on his club team, Volokh knew every statistic for every child on his team and on the opposition.

"Your club team, the Dynamo, played at the gold level?"

"Yes."

"One level down from the premier level?"

"Yes."

"And Hailey left to play for a premier-league team?"

"I thought it was a mistake. She wasn't ready."

"And yet, she's been a star on her new team at the higher level?"

He shrugs. "I haven't followed her career. It's youth soccer. Anyway, it depends on your definition of *star*."

I establish that his teams won when Hailey was on the team and lost after she left, that he can't survive on his high-school coach's salary alone, that even youth club soccer coaches eventually lose their jobs if they don't win. I try to shake his testimony that Hailey's tackle of Farah during practice was a dirty play, but he holds firm. Which makes me decide to engage in a dirty tactic of my own—a tactic that Debra vehemently objects to.

"Now, you were fired from your previous job as a girls' high-school soccer coach, were you not?"

Lundy is on his feet, objecting on relevance grounds.

"This goes to Coach Volokh's motivation for testifying the way he has," I say.

"Overruled," the judge says. "You may answer."

"I resigned," Volokh says.

"Resigned because if you didn't the school was going to fire you."

"I guess you could say that."

"Let's explore the circumstances of your termination. You have an alcohol problem, do you not?"

"I did."

"You were terminated after you came to a practice drunk?"

"That's what they claimed. I was not intoxicated at practice. As I just said, I did have a drinking problem. I went into a step program afterward. That's why I was able to get hired at my present position."

I'm tempted to bring up our encounter at the pub but let it go.

"At the time you were fired, you coached a girl named Ellie Jones?"

The coach doesn't answer, only regards me with hatred. He shakes his head in disgust.

"You're shaking your head, sir, but you did coach Ellie Jones."

He silently appeals to Lundy for help.

"Objection," Lundy says, confused about the facts but obviously aware that one of his star witnesses is in trouble.

"Overruled," Judge Sears says, clearly curious about where I'm going.

"I coached Ellie," Volokh says. He clenches and un-clenches his jaw. If we weren't in a court of law, he'd attack me. He might anyway.

The other reason he resigned was that the player, Ellie Jones, complained to her parents that he'd groped her breast. In fact, he was showing her a move called the dodge, and the girl turned in such a way that the touching was inadvertent. Fortunately for Volokh, the high-school newspaper was recording practice, and the video confirmed his story, though that didn't come out until three days later. But his tenure with that team was over. His problem now: Ellie Jones resembled Farah Med-hipour and was also of Persian descent.

He actually brought the claim up in the job inter-view and asked that someone verify the facts. I was the person the school appointed to make the inquiry, be-cause I'm a lawyer and was an involved parent then. Though the allegation wasn't true, it was made, which means that I can use it to discredit this loser and make it look like he was attracted to Farah and engaged in behavior that contributed to her suicide. Let Lundy bring the truth out on redirect if he dares. Volokh's credibility will come into question either way.

Just as I'm about to go in for the kill, I glimpse the gallery. There are quite a few reporters and bloggers in the courtroom. I'm about to propagate a vicious lie, and a falsehood that finds its way into cyberspace always takes on a peculiar truth. If I pursue this line, use the video, Volokh will be ruined no matter what the reality. I look at Debra, who's gazing down at a legal pad. Almost involuntarily, I say, "No further questions."

Confused, Hailey whispers, "Why didn't you finish, Dad?"

"We'll talk about it later."

I glance back at Janet, who's glowering at me. She knows why I cut the cross-examination short—my precious ethics and my need for Debra Grant's approval. If Hailey is convicted, Janet will never forgive me for passing this witness. I'll never forgive myself.

CHAPTER 22

AFTER COURT, I USUALLY go to the office to prepare for the next day's testimony, but tonight I go directly home for a rare family dinner. Since I banished Daniel from the courthouse, he's said little to me. He enters the kitchen, but instead of sitting down, he shovels a pile of lasagna on his plate and leaves.

"Daniel, come to the table," I shout, but he ignores me.

"Let him go," Janet says. "It's more pleasant without him."

In the past, I'd have to reprimand Hailey for texting her friends while we eat, but lately she hasn't had anyone to text.

"I guess they don't want to be associated with a criminal," she explains. "Their loss." She claims Aaron is still in the picture, but I haven't seen him around in a while. Though she speaks in a matter-of-fact, almost defiant tone, there's a sheen in her eyes. She uses an index finger to swipe several times at the corner of her right eye, pretending to scratch an itch rather than brush away a tear. On the rare occasions when Hailey cries, the tears start in that right eye. And still, she doesn't yield to emotion.

"So, we're winning, right, Dad?"

"We're holding our own," I say, a euphemism for *I don't think we're winning at all*. "It's the prosecution's turn, so the jury only hears their evidence."

"We'd be winning if you hadn't let up on Volokh," Janet says.

"It was wrong, Janet. Fiction."

"The great defense lawyers do whatever they must to protect their client," Janet says. "Even when they're only in it for the money and not representing their own child in a life-and-death homicide case."

"I don't get it," Hailey says. "Did you decide not to do something that would help me? Why would you do that?"

Suddenly I have no appetite. "I think I'll eat later. I'm going to get ready for tomorrow."

On the way to my study—well, I call it that, but it's really a cramped bonus room tacked onto the rear of the house—I pass Daniel's bedroom. I knock and without thinking walk in before he responds. He's sitting in front of his computer, and when he notices me he jumps and immediately slams down the cover of his laptop, just as most teenage boys do when their father catches them looking at porn.

But Daniel wasn't looking at porn. Oh, how I wish he were. He was viewing a still image of Farah Medhipour's lifeless body dangling from the second floor railing immediately after she hanged herself.

CHAPTER 23

BRADY SEARS HAS ALWAYS had a temper, and now he's so furious that his cheeks have flushed crimson, and purple veins bulge from his bald pate. "That video was filed under seal," he bellows. "Whoever took that photograph violated the law. When I find out who did this, I'll hold them in contempt and make sure they spend a long, long time in jail, First Amendment be damned. The police will be speaking with all of you."

Because he cleared the courtroom before the video was played, the judge blames the media for surreptitiously snapping a photo and posting it. There's another possibility that gnaws at my gut. Daniel was in court the day Farah's video was played. Could he somehow have captured that image using his cell phone without anyone noticing? Of course he could. He's more tech savvy than anyone I know.

When I confronted him about it, he denied knowing how the photo got onto the web. Of course he did.

The posting of that image could severely damage our case. Public opinion has never favored Hailey, but now it will turn overwhelmingly against her. The jurors have been instructed not to watch TV, read the newspapers, or surf the internet, aren't supposed to know about events like this. But juries always find out, as if by osmosis.

CHAPTER 24

DR. NATHALIE TYLER, MD, received her medical degree from Johns Hopkins and did her residency in psychiatry at the University of San Francisco. A tall, elegant woman in her fifties, she specializes in adolescent behavioral issues and has been in private practice for about twenty years. She was Farah's treating therapist at the time of the suicide.

Under questioning from Lundy, Tyler recounts the history of Farah's psychiatric issues. She testifies that Farah suffered from depression starting at age ten. Farah also suffered from dyssemia—the inability to pick up on nonverbal cues and body language, typical of a child who doesn't fit in socially. A dyssemic child can wish someone *happy birthday* and unknowingly sound sarcastic and insincere, Tyler says. Despite these issues, Farah didn't become suicidal until the bullying started.

"During the last therapy session before Farah died, did she mention Hailey Hovanes?" Lundy asks.

"She did."

"What did she say?"

"Objection, hearsay," I say.

"Under Rule 803 it's a statement made for and

reasonably pertinent to medical treatment, and describes the cause," Lundy says.

"Don't argue against the objection unless I ask you to, Mr. Lundy," the judge says. "I know the law. The objection is overruled."

"Unbelievable," Debra says under her breath.

"Did you say something, Miss Grant?" Judge Sears says. He either has astounding hearing or he reads lips.

Many lawyers would quail at the judge's tone, but Debra half stands and says, "I was just telling Mr. Hovanes that I'd like the opportunity to argue the validity of your ruling on the hearsay issue. It's clearly erroneous. May I be heard, Your Honor?" My partner is certainly no wimp.

"You may not," Sears snaps. "If you don't like my ruling, you have your remedy. That's why the legislature invented appellate courts. Proceed, Mr. Lundy."

"Dr. Tyler, what did Farah tell you about Hailey Hovanes?"

"That Hailey Hovanes was bullying her. Freezing her out of social events. Intimidating students who wanted to befriend her. Sending threatening, offensive e-mails. Tried to injure her on the soccer field. Assaulted her in the locker room. She said she confronted Hailey and told her she'd started cutting herself again, felt like dying, and would kill herself if the abuse continued. Farah told me that she pleaded with Hailey to stop."

"What did you do in response?"

She knits her brow. "May I check my file? It's been a while, and I want to be accurate."

Lundy hands the file folder to the witness, who peers through the reading area of her bifocals and nods.

"Farah and I spoke about her pain, and as always, I tried to impress upon her that these horrible events were situational. I confirmed that she was still taking her SSRIs—selective serotonin reuptake inhibitors, brand names Prozac and Zoloft, among others. She promised she was. I urged her to report Hailey Hovanes's behavior to school authorities, which she steadfastly refused to do. Farah said she still had feelings for Hailey, and besides, if she reported the bullying, the kids would hate her all the more. I found that troubling, because that's how bullies control their victims. I told her to call me any time if she had thoughts of harming herself, if she was bullied again, and she promised to do that, too. Then, three days later"—Tyler shrugs helplessly, and her eyes mist over—"Farah ended her life."

Lundy ends his examination, and I slowly move to the lectern. "Dr. Tyler, did Farah Medhipour ever express romantic feelings for Hailey Hovanes?"

"She did."

"Sexual feelings."

The witness folds her hands in her lap, clearly uncomfortable. "Yes."

"Did Farah, to your knowledge, engage in stalking behavior toward Hailey?"

"There was an obsessive-compulsive element going on with Farah. So, yes, Farah told me that she did pursue Hailey. It increased the depression, because Farah knew it wasn't productive behavior."

Now, I ask a question on instinct, and though I don't know the answer, it can't hurt me. "Did Farah come from a religious family?"

"It's my understanding that her uncle is quite religious and that her mother is observant as well."

"Was Farah conflicted about her feelings toward another female because of her religious upbringing?"

"She was."

"That contributed to her depression as well?"

"It did."

"Now, Dr. Tyler, you said in response to Mr. Lundy's questioning that Farah was taking SSRIs for depression. Hasn't the Food and Drug Administration issued what's called a *black box warning* that the drug could increase the risk of suicide in teenagers?"

"The studies only show a small increase in suicidal ideation—suicidal thoughts—among adolescents, and none of the participants in the study actually committed suicide."

"The FDA study reported that the incidents of suicidal thoughts doubled, correct?"

"At a very low percentage. From two to four percent."

"Exactly. Double the risk. And despite the black box warning, despite Farah's suicidal ideation, you encouraged her to keep taking the drug rather than insisting that she stop."

"In my professional opinion, the FDA warning does more harm than good." She sounds defensive and condescending. Perfect.

I hammer home other aspects of her treatment protocol that might've been lacking: she didn't recommend that Farah participate in group or recreational therapy. She failed to suggest a term at a residential treatment center. She didn't refer Farah to an expert in remediation of dyssemia.

"*I'm* an expert in dealing with adolescents," she says pompously.

"I also note from your file that Farah didn't have family therapy," I say.

"That I *did* recommend. She refused, didn't want

to impose on her mother and uncle, with whom she resided. She was the patient, so I had to abide by her wishes."

"So, you couldn't convince Farah to take the actions that you thought were necessary to help her, could you, Dr. Tyler?"

"Alas, no, Mr. Hovanes."

"That was a failure on your part?"

"One I regret every second of every day."

"And maybe if you hadn't failed, Farah Medhipour would be alive today?"

"Perhaps."

"Do you think you should be on trial for causing Farah's death, Dr. Tyler?"

This question causes many in the gallery to gasp, and before Lundy can even object, Judge Sears shouts, "That is an inappropriate, argumentative question, and Dr. Tyler will not answer it." It's not often that a judge sustains his own objection. But I've made my point.

During my last few questions, Debra has been riffling through the psychiatric file, and because I'm about to end my cross-examination, I briefly consult with her. She points to a medical record that we've both read several times. It takes me a moment, but then I see it—this piece of paper might set Hailey free.

I pick up the document and start to ask Dr. Tyler about it but stop myself. "No further questions," I say.

When I sit down, Debra whispers, "What the fuck, Matt?" This time she covers her mouth with a legal pad so Judge Sears can't read her lips.

"It's under control," I reply.

I just hope the bombshell I intend to lob later doesn't blow up in my face.

CHAPTER 25

WE'RE FORTY-FIVE MINUTES short of the morning recess, so I can't question Hailey about whether Farah really confronted her and threatened suicide if the bullying didn't stop. I'm tempted to request an early recess, but doing so would make us seem worried about the shrink's testimony. My concern about this issue becomes less paramount when Lundy says, "The People call Brianna Welch."

Debra and I exchange a quick look. The girl is supposed to be *our* witness, helpful to *our* case. Why is the prosecution calling her?

Hailey's discreet wave to Brianna goes unreciprocated. Brianna doesn't even look over at the defense table.

To my shock, after testifying that she's known Hailey well for years, Brianna recounts a long history of perceived maltreatment at my daughter's hands. I've always thought of Brianna as sort of Hailey's devoted sidekick, but the girl now characterizes herself as Hailey's toady. Throughout the direct examination, Brianna seems timid, which makes her sound more credible.

After eliciting testimony that Hailey commanded all her friends to ostracize Farah, Lundy asks, "Did you ever witness a violent confrontation between Hailey Hovanes and Farah Medhipour?"

"Yeah…yes."

"Tell us about it."

"There were two. During a practice, Hailey did a slide tackle from behind, and Farah twisted her ankle. The bad thing was that the whistle had blown and the play was over, so Farah wasn't expecting it."

"Did Hailey say anything to Farah after the play was over?"

"I was across the field, so I didn't hear it. But I saw her say something. She looked mad."

"And was there a second confrontation?"

"So, like, I walked into the girls' locker room after soccer practice. This was two days after the tackle. I forgot my backpack in my locker. It was pretty late, so I assumed everyone was gone. Then I hear shouting, and I peek around the corner, and I see Hailey shove Farah hard against the locker, and then Hailey shouts, 'If you don't stop, I'm really going to fuck you up bad.'"

"What did you do?"

"Like I…I'm embarrassed to say it, but I got out of there before Hailey saw me."

This kid didn't say anything about this when I interviewed her. Hailey has never mentioned it, either. We've been blindsided from two directions.

Fortunately, we had decided—when *we* were going to call Brianna as our witness—that Debra would examine her, so we were prepared.

Debra chips away at Brianna's credibility—over the years, she pursued the friendship with Hailey, hung out with her at school, and roomed with her when the soccer team traveled. She told others that Hailey was her best friend. She froze Farah out of the group and team. She doesn't know whether Farah leveled the first blow in the locker room.

"Farah was physically strong, wasn't she?" Debra asks.

"Yeah, she was real strong."

"Did you know she received more yellow cards in actual games than Hailey did?"

She shrugs. "Maybe. Yeah."

"Farah got into a couple of fights during games this past season?"

"Yeah, but they weren't her fault."

"How many fights did Hailey get into?"

"None in games. Just what I saw in the locker room and at practice."

Finally, Debra asks, "You had a meeting about this case several months ago with Mr. Hovanes, didn't you, Brianna?"

"Yes."

"And you didn't tell him about a fight between Hailey and Farah, did you?"

"No."

"And you didn't tell him you thought Hailey's tackle during practice was a dirty play."

"I didn't."

"In fact, you said you didn't really know anything about a dispute between Hailey and Farah."

"Yes, ma'am."

Debra sits down. That's all she can do. On cross-examination, you don't ask "why" if you don't know the answer already.

But Lundy has another shot on redirect, and he *can* ask the why question. "Brianna, why didn't you say anything to Mr. Hovanes about the fight?"

"Because I was afraid."

"Afraid of who?"

"Hailey Hovanes. And her brother, Daniel."

"Physically?"

"Not physically of Hailey, really. I am afraid of Daniel physically. He's really big, and everyone knows he's kind of crazy. I really believe...I think one or both of them drove Farah to kill herself. I saw Daniel talking to Farah a couple of times. Real intense discussions, you know? Sometimes...well, Hailey can use the threat of her brother to get what she wants. Everyone knew Farah was messed up. She just wanted to have friends. Who doesn't? Hailey wouldn't allow that."

The answer is objectionable speculation, but Debra doesn't dare object. It will only make things worse.

"Have you finished your answer?" Lundy asks.

"No sir. I"—she glances at me for the first time—"I was also afraid of Mr. Hovanes. My parents told him that he couldn't talk to me if they weren't there, and he didn't listen. He ambushed me at the coffee place and sat down at a table in the corner where I couldn't get out. He kept asking me these questions, telling me what to say. I thought if I told him about the fight he'd get mad at me, and then what would Hailey and Daniel do to me if they found out?"

CHAPTER 26

MERCIFULLY, JUDGE SEARS CALLS the morning recess, and we retreat to our dank, stuffy attorneys' conference room, while Lundy, the son of a bitch, takes the elevator up six floors to his air-conditioned office. I'm sure he's gloating, holding court with those sycophants he calls his assistants.

Hailey sits at the head of the table. Debra and I flank her.

I say, "Hailey, I can't believe—"

"I'll handle this," Debra says, her tone so peremptory that I shut up and Hailey's eyes widen to oversized bottle caps. "Did Farah Medhipour come up to you and ask you to stop bullying her, Hailey?"

"Sort of."

"Why didn't you tell us this before?"

"I didn't think it was important."

"You didn't think it was important?" Debra stands. "I have better things to do than listen to this." She storms out of the room. I can't blame her.

"You attacked Farah in the locker room," I say. "Did you think that was unimportant, too?"

She looks down at the table. "I knew it was important. That's why I pretended it never happened. Sometimes I do that. Like when you and Mom fight, or Daniel—"

"Don't hand me that bullshit. This has nothing to do with how much your parents argue or how your brother behaves. You threatened that girl with physical harm."

"I didn't mean it. Kids at school were beginning to talk, saying shit like Farah and me had something going on sexually. It was embarrassing."

"Did you send those e-mails to her?"

"How many times do I have to tell you I didn't do it? I wouldn't know how to send anonymous e-mails anyway."

"You could've had help. Daniel or Aaron."

"I didn't have help because I didn't do it."

"You threatened Farah knowing she was fragile. You're strong, Hailey. The strong should never attack the weak."

"Maybe I'm not so strong, Dad."

Debra walks back in and shakes her head. "Lundy smells blood."

"I figured as much."

"What?" Hailey asks.

"Debra approached the prosecutor about the plea deal we talked about before." I know this because that's what I'd do if the roles were reversed.

"I thought we agreed no deal," Hailey says.

"That was before Brianna made you look like a serial bully," Debra says.

Hailey regards me with a look of genuine fear, and suddenly my sixteen-year-old daughter seems old. Not like a precocious child who's poised and sophisticated beyond her years, but old like an elderly, world-weary person. Her bearing jolts me back into reality. She's a kid, and no matter what she's done, she deserves a chance at redemption. That's how we treat our children in a civilized society. This trial isn't over.

"We'd better get back," I say. "We're already late."

CHAPTER 27

WE ENTER THE COURTROOM just four minutes late, but Judge Sears has already seated the jury in the box. Usually, judges wait until all counsel are present before calling in the jury. Lundy is at the lectern, and the witness is on the stand. Sears is a control freak, and this is his way of punishing us for our tardiness. My son would call it a dick move. He'd be right, especially because the witness is Farah's mother, Shirin Medhipour.

I'm sure the judge expects me to apologize, but it's not going to happen. This is no time to appear obsequious.

"Proceed, Mr. Lundy," the judge says, glowering down at me.

Shirin testifies that her daughter was a smart, talented girl who loved soccer and who just wanted to have friends. She was too sensitive for her own good, socially awkward, but a sweet child. Shirin's husband walked out when Farah was only four years old, so Farah was her best friend—her life. Still, growing up without a father was hard for the girl.

"Did your daughter tell you she was being bullied at school?" Lundy asks.

Shirin takes a deep breath. "No. I learned about it after from the therapist. Farah was afraid I'd complain to the school and make it worse. Victims of bullies don't always speak to their parents. I wish she had told me. Farah and I were so close, and yet, she couldn't talk to me, her own mother." There are tears in her eyes. "I'm sorry. I promised myself I wouldn't cry."

"It's understandable that you'd cry," Lundy says.

It's an objectionable statement, but I don't dare object.

Lundy elicits testimony about the horror of finding Farah dead, a horror compounded by watching that video.

"Farah was always saying such nice things about Hailey Hovanes," Shirin volunteers. "I truly believed them to be close friends. Farah didn't have many friends, and I was happy that she had an older girl as a mentor. A soccer player, too. I had no idea what was really going on."

Several jurors appear on the verge of tears. Others glare at Hailey. The jury clearly sympathizes with Shirin. *I* sympathize with Shirin.

"No further questions," Lundy says solemnly.

"Cross-examination?" the judge asks.

I'm sure he and Lundy expect me to pass the witness because she's unimpeachable. They're wrong.

As I'm about to stand, Debra grabs my sleeve. "Let me do this. Better coming from a woman."

"If I'm not up there, the jury will think I'm running."

She nods.

"Did you physically abuse your daughter, Miss

Medhipour?" I ask. This is the bombshell that I could've asked the psychiatrist but saved for Shirin.

The courtroom is abuzz with reproach. There's no doubt that the jury thinks I'm an ogre, a man whose daughter became a bully because he's a bully himself.

Lundy shouts, "Objection!" though he gives no grounds. He has no grounds, because my question is relevant.

Judge Sears gives me a hard stare, and I look back at him just as hard. He nods his head slightly. "Overruled. The witness will answer."

"Never," Shirin says, her eyes agape. "I did not touch Farah. I would never."

"Did you argue with Farah?"

"All teenagers argue. But no, we did not argue much."

"How long was Farah in therapy?"

"We tried a child psychologist for the first time when she was seven. The kids were teasing her, and Farah became sad—depressed. We tried several psychologists, but they did no good. The middle school counselor recommended Dr. Tyler, a psychiatrist, who could prescribe medication. Dr. Tyler helped a lot. Or so I believed."

"Why was Farah seeing Dr. Tyler?"

"Same reason. Farah was still having trouble with other children, was depressed."

"Bullied by other children?"

"Teased. Middle school was more difficult for her. Children that age...I just wanted to help my daughter to be well and happy. And Farah was improving, especially when she started ninth grade, until...until your daughter—"

I hold up my hand like a traffic cop, and she doesn't

finish her thought. "Now, Greenbriar Insurance Company provided your health insurance?"

"Yes."

Debra projects a document on the courtroom monitors as I hand a physical copy to the court clerk. "I'd like to have marked as next in order a billing statement from Greenbriar Insurance Company showing a claim for reimbursement for Farah Medhipour. This form comes from the psychiatric file, already admitted into evidence. Please tell me if you recognize this document, Miss Medhipour."

"I have never seen this," she says.

"I'm not surprised. This is a form that doctors use. But I want to refer you to the box for DSM coding. Do you know that *DSM* stands for the Diagnostic and Statistical Manual of Mental Disorders, published by the American Psychiatric Association? A catalogue of mental disorders?"

"I know this because of Farah's problems, yes."

"And the box for DSM is coded 'roman numeral V15.41 & 15.42 – non-reimbursable.'"

"I have no idea what that is."

"Well, I'll tell you, Miss Medhipour. I'll represent to the Court, and we'll recall Dr. Tyler if necessary, that these entries mean that there's no insurance coverage for physical abuse in childhood and psychological abuse in childhood. Which means that Farah's psychiatrist believes that abuse was a contributing factor to her condition."

The courtroom falls silent. Then there are murmurs of surprise and comprehension, which grow louder as the import of this document sinks in.

"Farah had problems," Shirin says. "Sometimes she would exaggerate…I did not abuse Farah, ever."

"How about her uncle?"

"Never."

"Sometimes Farah would say bad things about people even if they weren't true?"

"Sometimes, yes. That must be why Dr. Tyler…" She catches herself, too late.

"So, it would be just like Farah to make up this entire story about my daughter bullying her?"

"No, she…" She stops talking because there's no way out for her.

CHAPTER 28

ETHAN GOLD CALMLY TESTIFIES to what he told me—that Hailey sent texts telling other kids to ostracize Farah. And like Brianna, he reveals something he hid from me.

"At anytime in the two weeks before Farah Medhipour died, were you shown a photograph of Hailey Hovanes and Farah Medhipour together?" Lundy asks.

"Yes, sir." These pampered kids have no regard for the truth, apparently. And that goes for my daughter.

"Please describe it."

Debra is handling Ethan's cross-examination, so she stands and objects. "The defense wasn't provided with any such photograph. The testimony is improper under the best evidence rule."

"The defense doesn't have it because the People don't have a copy ourselves," Lundy says. "Which means that the witness can testify to the contents of the photo under the best evidence rule."

"The objection is overruled," Judge Sears says.

Ethan glances at Hailey. "It's kind of embarrassing. There was a group of the senior guys gathered around the weight room, laughing and stuff. They called me over, which was weird, because I was only a tenth grader. They were passing around this phone that had…it had this image of Hailey and Farah together, and"—he inhales deeply—"both girls were naked. It was, what do they call it, really suggestive?"

Hailey gasps audibly.

"How was the photo suggestive?"

"I'd rather not—"

"You have to answer, Ethan."

"Like maybe the girls were going to have sex. Or already had?"

"Who did the cell phone belong to?"

"Aaron Crawford. Hailey Hovanes's boyfriend."

"I have no further questions," Lundy says.

I glance at Hailey, who's flushed with anger and mortification. She huddles with Debra and me and says, "Farah took a photo of me while I was showering after a game. Then she photoshopped it to mash it up with a picture of her. I only wanted her to delete it, that's all. I didn't know Aaron…oh, my God."

"Cross-examination, Miss Grant?" the judge asks.

Debra rises and goes to the podium at a deliberate speed. Which means she intends to cut Ethan to shreds. "You say you got texts from Hailey Hovanes asking you to shun Farah Medhipour?"

"Yes, ma'am."

"And you in fact shunned Farah after getting that text, didn't you?"

"Not really. I never hung out with her in the first place, so…"

"Did you think what Hailey was doing to Farah was nice? Fair?"

"No, ma'am."

"What did you do to help Farah?"

"Nothing. Hailey wouldn't have liked that."

"Has Hailey ever physically threatened you?"

"No, she's a girl. I don't mean that in a sexist way, but…"

"So Haley couldn't beat you up. Could she affect where you're going to go to college?"

"How could she…? No."

"Make the teachers give you bad grades?"

"No."

"Get you kicked off the lacrosse team?"

"No, ma'am."

"Make you mother and father upset at you?"

He shakes his head.

"You grew up with Daniel Hovanes. Did you always get along with him?"

"Yeah. We're not friends anymore, but I've never had a problem with Daniel."

"He never threatened you?"

"No. He's fought with other kids, but never me."

"Do you have a crush on Hailey Hovanes?"

Now he's flustered. "Not really."

"Not *really?* Didn't you tell Hailey the day before spring break that you wanted to be more than just friends?"

He shrugs, and his cheeks become splotchy.

"You wouldn't fall in love with a girl you thought was a bad person, a girl who bullied people, would you, Ethan?" It's a risky question, because the boy could answer it in so many damaging ways. But now, we have to take risks.

"Objection," Lundy says. "Irrelevant."

"Overruled," the judge says. "Answer the question, young man."

"I guess not," Ethan says.

And then a line of questioning that sets up the cross-examination of the witness we know Lundy will call next.

"Let's talk about the photograph of Hailey and Farah that Aaron Crawford showed you. Did it look photoshopped?"

"I only saw it for a second. But Aaron said it was real, so..."

"Did Aaron tell you why he would show you a nude photograph of his girlfriend with another girl?" This is also a *why* question, but the answer can't hurt us.

"He was bragging about how it proved he had the hottest girlfriend in the whole school. That's how Aaron is, I guess. Always bragging about the girls he sleeps with. Or claims to."

"How do you know?"

"I heard him do it. Even though I was only a sophomore, we both played on the lacrosse team. He even said some sexual stuff about Hailey once."

"Did you respond to him on that occasion?"

"No, I...no. But I didn't believe him."

"Because you thought Hailey was a nice girl?"

"Yeah."

"Did Aaron say anything else about why he was showing other boys a sexy photograph of his own girlfriend?"

"He said he was looking forward to having a three-way with these hot athletic girls."

"No further questions," Debra says.

It was effective cross, but there's no doubt that Lundy will use that photo to show that Hailey had a motive to want Farah dead.

CHAPTER 29

THE PEOPLE CALL AARON Crawford."

The parade of adolescent liars continues.

I force myself to look confident, even combative in front of the jury. Inside, I'm in turmoil. Debra was right when she warned me that I'd make mistakes if I took the lead. An objective, dispassionate, hired-gun defense attorney would've seen through Hailey's bullshit, would've pushed her for the truth. He would've exposed Aaron as a creep long before trial.

While Aaron walks to the witness stand, Hailey sits with hands folded, her face like granite, her eyes virulent. Just the impression she shouldn't convey in front of this jury. Why the hell can't she play the weepy school girl for once?

Lundy announces that the district attorney's office has entered into an immunity agreement with Aaron. In exchange for his testimony, he won't be prosecuted for displaying a prurient picture of nude underage girls.

"How did you come to be in possession of the photo of Farah and Hailey?" Lundy's voice sounds taut, irritated. Even a jerk like Joshua Lundy can't disguise his contempt for Aaron.

"Farah texted it to me. It was a group text to me and Hailey."

"Did Farah write anything in the text?"

"She wrote, 'I'd love to fuck you both.'"

"Did you talk to Hailey about the message?"

"Of course. She's my girlfriend."

When he uses the present tense, I have the urge to charge the witness stand and pummel him. When Debra and I interviewed him, he mentioned a text from Farah but said nothing about the photo. Was he protecting Hailey or himself?

"How did Hailey react?" Lundy asks.

"She went ballistic, screaming and shouting. She said Farah must've taken the picture of her in the girls' locker room and photoshopped it. She said she was going to kill that Persian bitch." He doesn't even have the guts to look at Hailey.

"He's a fucking liar," Hailey says, her harsh whisper much too loud.

"What happened next?" Lundy asks.

"Hailey and I confronted Farah at school. I didn't want to do it, but Hailey insisted. She told Farah she hated her, to stay away or she'd kill her."

"I never said that," Hailey whispers. "I told her to stop bothering me."

I believe her for once, because that's precisely what Aaron told us during his interview at the office. But to get immunity, he needed to give Lundy something better than *Hailey told Farah to leave her alone*.

"Was Ethan Gold telling the truth when he said you showed the picture of Hailey and Farah to other students?"

"Unfortunately, yeah. It was a horrible mistake. Sometimes teenagers do stupid things. I want to apologize to Hailey and to Farah's mother for that."

Debra glances back, then whispers to me, "Not even Farah's mother bought that bullshit."

"But the jury is buying his testimony about Hailey," I reply.

"Do you have a copy of the photo?" Lundy asks.

"No, sir. I realized what I did was wrong. So I deleted it."

"Your witness," Lundy says to me.

I stand. Aaron looks at me with no fear, as if he's waiting for Hailey in our living room on date night.

"Did you ever tell Hailey Hovanes that you loved her, Aaron?" I ask.

"Sure, lots of times, Matt—Mr. Hovanes."

"Do you think a boy who loves a girl would show a nude, sexual picture of her to random boys?"

"I was just—"

"Answer my question. Is that an act of love?"

"No, sir, but—"

"When you told Hailey you loved her, you were lying?"

"No."

"So, you're just a sleazeball?"

Lundy half-stands to object, but he sits down again—Aaron *is* a sleazeball.

"Do you think a boy would do anything for the girl he loves?" I ask.

He puffs out his chest and preens, a chance for redemption, or so he thinks. "I know I would."

"So maybe if you thought Farah was bothering Hailey, you'd send some obscene and threatening e-mails to get her to stop?"

He looks at me in confusion. I always told Janet the kid is a dim bulb. Finally, the light flickers on. "I didn't do anything like that."

"You told Hailey that you'd delete the photo of Farah and her, didn't you?"

"I did delete it."

"But not right away."

"No, sir."

"Does that make you a liar?"

He shrugs. "I guess you could say I didn't tell Hailey the whole truth. I don't know if that makes me a liar."

"Well, if you didn't tell the girl you love the whole truth, how do we know you're telling the whole truth now?"

"Because I'm under oath."

"Except you wouldn't testify until you got immunity from prosecution. You're testifying so you can avoid a prison sentence."

"But I'm telling the truth."

"Now, Ethan Gold said you talked about a threesome with Hailey and Farah?"

"It was just guy talk."

"Right. 'Teenagers.' You knew that Farah Medhipour was fourteen years old and Hailey was sixteen?"

"Yeah."

"And how old are you now?"

"Eighteen."

"A grown man. Do you think a grown man should be making sexual comments about a fourteen-year-old child? Showing nude pictures of her?"

He hesitates, fidgets in his chair, and then blurts out, "I was seventeen at the time."

Someone—a spectator or a media member—guffaws so loudly that the entire gallery breaks up in the kind of laughter that's uncontrollable because it's so morbid. Judge Sears admonishes the room that further outbursts won't be tolerated.

"I'm done with this...witness," I spit.

No one in the room likes Aaron, including the prosecutor, judge, and jury. It doesn't matter. I haven't overcome the damage that he's done. I can see it in the jurors' faces.

CHAPTER 30

ANOTHER RECESS, ANOTHER LITANY

of excuses from Hailey. She was embarrassed to tell me about the nude photo. What girl would want her father to know something like that? After the arrest, she thought the photo would make her look bad, and no one was supposed to find out about it. She trusted Aaron. Besides, she told her mother, even showed her the photo, and Janet told her to keep it secret—even from me.

"Why ever would your mother do that?" I ask.

"Because she thinks you would've complained to Aaron's parents or the school, and I didn't want that. It would've been humiliating. You're a crusader, Dad. I didn't want to be your—what does Mom say—your Holy Grail. So, I handled it my own way."

That last is very close to an admission that she harassed Farah. I don't think I've ever been intentionally cruel to my children, but now I'm cruel to Hailey. "How did it feel to have Aaron betray you like that? To show your naked body off to other boys?"

She gawps at me for a moment, and then for once her emotions overcome her, and she starts crying.

"Feels terrible to be the object of public ridicule,

doesn't it?" I say, unrelenting, surprised at the insensitivity in my voice. "Well, now you know how Farah Medhipour felt. Remember that feeling, Hailey. Remember it every day for the rest of your life. Otherwise, you won't truly be human."

I RESIGNED FROM THE district attorney's office because Joshua Lundy was an unethical shyster willing to do anything for a conviction. When he calls a surprise witness, Special Agent Grace Mogren, an FBI computer forensics expert, it becomes clear that Lundy hasn't changed a bit.

I ask the judge to exclude the witness because we didn't have notice that she'd be testifying and so haven't had a chance to prepare a cross-examination. Lundy claims that the information just came to his attention a day earlier. It's a lie, exactly the kind of sharp practice he engaged in when we worked together.

"I can't say I'm comfortable with this, Mr. Lundy," the judge says. "But I'm going to let the testimony in. If I find out that you knew about this witness's testimony before yesterday, I won't be happy."

Lundy starts with Mogren's credentials: a bachelor's degree in engineering, a master's degree in computer science, twelve years with the FBI's forensics unit, an expert in hacking, spoofing, and other cybercrimes. The Bureau lent her out to help on the Farah Medhipour investigation. There's no way to attack her qualifications.

"Did you run a forensic analysis on Farah Medhipour's laptop computer?" Lundy asks.

"I did. The police department had already located a number of threatening e-mails, and you asked our office to examine the Medhipour girl's computer for additional evidence. The FBI has jurisdiction because internet use involves interstate commerce." This woman is slick, prepared, and experienced. Talkative, but not so much that I can object that she's giving a narrative answer. A dangerous witness, in other words.

"Did you attempt to identify the source of the harassing e-mails that Farah received?"

"We did. No luck. It appears that the sender used a Tor browser and a secret e-mail client—Hushmail, Guerilla Mail, and, believe it or not, Hide My Ass are examples. That software enabled the perpetrator to keep his or her identity confidential."

"Is it difficult to use this software?"

"It takes some work, but anyone with moderate computer knowledge can learn how to do it by searching the web, unfortunately. We call this the Dark Web. There's some bad stuff that goes on there."

"Did you find anything else of interest on Farah's computer?"

"We examined Farah's internet browsing history, web cache, and what's called an *ntuser.dat* file—a registry file that contains browsing history. Based on that examination, we located a link to a social media page set up by someone called *Farahs_Nightmare*. We tried to open that page, but it had been deleted."

"What happened next?"

"Your office subpoenaed the social network provider for information as to what was on the website and who might have posted the information."

"And what did you learn?"

"The social media site had archived the webpage. It had purportedly been set up by a group of students at the Star Point School." On cue, the courtroom monitors light up. Mogren clicks through a series of increasingly harassing messages and images directed at Farah—criticizing her physical appearance, her heritage, and her intelligence, and suggesting that she shouldn't be alive. The posts seem to come from many different people, as if the whole school is against her.

"At this point, because of the sensitive nature of this next image, I'd ask that the courtroom be cleared," Lundy says.

I don't object, not only because it would be the wrong thing to do, but because I'm numb. I glance over at Debra, who seems to be as shocked as I am. Hailey stares straight ahead, a defiant expression on her face. Is she silently proclaiming her innocence or justifying her guilt?

"Everyone but law enforcement and family members will leave the courtroom," the judge says.

When a reporter protests, Judge Sears says, "Get one of your overpaid First Amendment lawyers down here if you don't like my order. Right now, you're either outside in the corridor or sitting in jail. Your choice."

The reporter exits along with everyone else.

"Please tell us what else you found, Special Agent Mogren," Lundy says.

"This image." She points to the screen, which displays a capture of a social media page depicting a nude, sexually suggestive photo of Farah with the caption, "Drink Drano and die, you skanky Persian ho!!!"

Farah's mother and uncle bolt out of their seats and hurry out of the courtroom. Why didn't Lundy warn them about what was coming? The answer is obvious. Their reaction makes for better drama in front of the jury. No matter that he's torturing them.

"Have you determined when this image was posted?" Lundy asks.

"Our forensic analysis indicates that it was posted the day before Farah Medhipour died."

The screens go dark, and Judge Sears instructs the bailiff to allow the media and the spectators back inside.

"Agent Mogren, were you able to identify who posted these statements and images on the internet?"

She nods solemnly. "You know, it's interesting about people who commit cybercrimes without a lot of hacking experience. No matter how careful they are, there's always a slip. The person who posted this filth was fairly careful. But there was a mistake. One of the images of Farah on the soccer field is accompanied by a demeaning ethnic slur. This image wasn't sent anonymously, according to the social media service's logs. The Tor browser works through a standard web browser, but it's slower. The perpetrator apparently got confused or impatient and used the standard browser on this one occasion, which allowed us to obtain information about the poster's identity."

"Please explain how that worked."

"The social media service logged the user's internet protocol, or IP, address. To locate the user, we had to issue another subpoena to the internet service provider. Only yesterday, the company responded."

"Did you identify a user?"

"We've narrowed it down. The person who posted on that website did so from a computer that had an IP address assigned to the internet account of Matthew Hovanes."

CHAPTER 32

ALL IS NOT LOST. We still have the defense case to put on, and the law favors us, as it does every criminal defendant. We don't have to prove Hailey's innocence; we only need to raise reasonable doubt. Farah took her own life, so Hailey can't be criminally responsible. All is not lost.

This is my mantra. I don't believe it for a second.

Debra and I go back to the office and spend the next hours phoning and e-mailing forensic computer experts who might jump into the case at the last minute and try to poke holes in Mogren's testimony. The response is bleak—too busy, too much regard for Mogren, animosity toward Hailey. At nine thirty, Debra says she's leaving for the night and advises me to do the same. I'm not going anywhere.

I knock off at midnight, lock up, and head to my car. Just as I reach the parking lot, a hulking figure emerges from the darkness, as if lying in wait. I stop when the guy blocks my way. It takes me a moment to identify him—Downtown Dennis, my pantomime basketball buddy and former client. Only now, he wears an expression I've seen only once, when he was angry at a cop—menacing and foreboding.

"Hello, Dennis," I say. "I'm just heading home." I start past him but he holds up a hand, and it's clear that I'm not going anywhere.

He looks back, and with a wave of his arm beckons someone from the dark parking structure. The person shuffles over almost casually. Only when the floodlight hits his face do I recognize my own son.

"Daniel, what—?"

"He's been hanging out on the streets the last few nights, Attorney Hovanes," Dennis says. "Almost got into a fight tonight until I showed up and recognized him as your boy. He should stay off the streets, Attorney Hovanes. It's dangerous." Before I can reply, he turns and, with long, athletic strides, disappears back into the night.

"Thank you, Dennis," I call after him, but he doesn't respond. I wish I could've hugged the man, though he wouldn't have liked that.

With eyes lowered, Daniel says, "She had a gun, you know." He sounds as if he's in a trance.

My knees buckle at the words. "Who had a gun, Daniel?"

"Yeah, Farah. She was going to use a gun and blow her brains out." As chilling as the words are, his tone is affectless. Has he been doing drugs again?

"Let's get in the car. We'll talk on the way home."

"No! In your office."

I nod. As we pass the contingent of homeless in the plaza, a few of them greet him by name. As a child, he spent a lot of time at my office. I even dreamt that he'd follow in my footsteps and become a lawyer someday. How naïve that dream was.

We sit on the faux-leather sofa in the lobby.

"What's this about Farah and a gun?"

"I told you. She was going to shoot herself. She stole her uncle's gun."

"When did she tell you that, Daniel?"

"Three weeks before she killed herself. I told her a gun was too messy and sometimes it doesn't work, and, boom, you're a vegetable. Poison isn't dramatic enough and even less effective than a gun. But hanging yourself like Robin Williams—that makes a statement."

I shudder, not only because he has knowledge of Farah's death but also because he must've researched suicide methods himself.

"I liked Farah—you know, outcasts bonding, shit like that—but she didn't really want to be seen with me." He laughs sardonically. "She thought I'd hurt her reputation. One day, she came up to me at school and asked to talk. She told me Hailey was harassing her and that if it didn't stop she'd shoot herself. She showed me the e-mails that the DA is using in court. Anyway, that's when we talked about ways to kill yourself. I thought it was a funny conversation. I didn't think she'd really do it." He shakes his head in childlike wonderment, though kid stuff is the last thing this is.

"Did you send those e-mails, Daniel? Set up the phony social media account?"

"If I was going to go after some kid, it wouldn't be Farah. Anyway, I went to Hailey, told her what Farah said, and she laughed. She said that Farah was crazy."

"I can't believe—"

"She said she was sick of Farah bugging her. She wanted me to do my enforcer act."

"Hailey really would ask you to intimidate other kids? And you'd do it?"

He shrugs. "She's my sister. Besides, most of the guys

I strong-armed are assholes. I wouldn't do it to a girl, especially not to a sweet girl like Farah. I told Hailey that."

"You really think Hailey did what they say?"

"Who else would it be, Dad?" He picks at his fingernails, a habit Janet despises. "I guess Farah wasn't angry enough."

"What do you mean?"

"That's the only reason I don't kill myself like she did. I'm too fucking pissed off. If Farah had more hatred like I do, she'd be alive today."

"Daniel, I'm…I don't know what to say. I'm so sorry I didn't realize you felt this way. But…why are you telling me this now?"

"Because I want Hailey to tell the truth. I don't want her to go to prison, but I can't stand her lies anymore. She could've left Farah alone. I should've stopped Hailey."

"Come home with me, Daniel." I place my hand on his shoulder as gently as possible, but he recoils.

"You're going to defend Hailey anyway."

"That's my job. She's entitled to a defense."

"I'm not going to the DA. But if he does call me, I'll tell the truth."

"That's exactly what I'd expect. Now, let's go home."

He thinks for a moment and then nods. On the ride home, he hunches over and plays a game on his phone.

"What are you playing?" I ask. I need to connect with my son, and there's no time like the present.

There's an insolent frown on his face. "Postal."

"I thought we talked about…" When he was younger, we forbade him to play that game, which is about an average person who goes "postal" and embarks on a serial-killing spree. The object of the game is to kill every living thing in sight.

THE MOMENT I OPEN the front door, Daniel hurries into his room. Hailey is already asleep.

Janet is in our bedroom watching some reality TV show. On the screen, a voluptuous redhead confides in a friend that her husband had an affair and has been fired from the show.

"Why was Daniel with you?" Janet asks.

I recount what he told me.

She shakes her head, a mocking glare in her eyes. "Do you believe him?"

"I don't know what to believe."

There are sobs and hugs on the reality show. Janet picks up the remote and aggressively hits the power button, as if she's firing a weapon. She tosses the device aside with such force that it hits the floor.

"You've fallen for his bull ever since he was a child. Don't you get it? The cops traced that webpage to our house, and all of a sudden he shows up at your office and blames Hailey. Damn it, Matt, he's the expert in computers, not her. She's lucky to be able to turn on her cell phone. Tor browsers? HushMail? The authorities are hot on his trail; they just don't know it yet. He's try-ing to cover his own ass. He did this."

"I can't believe—"

"Believe it for once in your life. He hacked Hailey's computer and found that horrible nude photo of the girls. Maybe he heard about it at school. It probably aroused him, and he started stalking Farah. He's stalked other girls, you know. The girls think he's creepy. That's why the other parents avoid us like the plague. Because he's a weirdo, and he's dangerous. He did this and wants Hailey to take the fall. He's always been jealous of her." She sits up, reaches over, and grabs my arm with both hands, and now she's not hostile but beseeching. "The trial is a disaster, and she's innocent. Let me take the stand tomorrow and tell what I know about Daniel."

"You'd seriously testify against your own son?"

"To save my innocent daughter, in a heartbeat. The boy is so troubled. Maybe it's for the best. Hailey didn't do this. He did."

Janet could be right. Daniel has a history of breaking the rules. He's a computer whiz who could cover his tracks. Especially for a kid her age, Hailey isn't all that good with computers—she can e-mail and text and use social media, but Tor and the Dark Web? Doubtful. Unless, as I suggested to her, she had help.

"I'll talk it over with Debra."

That's not what she wants to hear. "I'll be ready to testify. I expect you to be ready to protect your innocent daughter."

I feel like the mother in *Sophie's Choice,* forced to sacrifice one child to save the other. There's a different way to look at it, though—the lawyer's way. Maybe if Janet names Daniel as the stalker, the jury will find reasonable doubt, and both my kids will go free. They'll never be exonerated, of course, but maybe they'll both avoid prison.

I leave the room. Daniel is entitled to know what we're thinking. As a civil rights attorney, I have an obsession for due process.

I knock on his door, and he tells me to come in. When I explain what Janet and I discussed, he doesn't deny involvement as he did earlier, just lets out an eerie, chilling laugh and tells me to get the fuck out of his room.

An hour later, just as I'm finally on the verge of sleep, the front door slams. I roll out of bed and run outside to see Daniel sprinting away like a felon fleeing the scene of the crime. Worse, under his arm, he's carrying my laptop computer—the one computer that the police didn't seize and didn't search.

"Wait, son!" I shout.

He doesn't wait, only runs at full speed and disappears into the night.

CHAPTER 34

BEFORE TRIAL RESUMES THE next morning, I hurriedly explain to Debra why we're going to call Janet as our first witness, and that we've been up all night mapping my examination strategy and going over prep. I expect her to argue, at least to question, but she just nods in agreement. We don't tell Hailey—she's protective of Daniel and might try to stop us.

Lundy stands and says, "The People rest." Why wouldn't he? Special Agent Mogren was the perfect denouement for the prosecution's case.

"Does the defense have a witness?" Judge Sears asks.

I stand, but Debra beats me to the lectern and says, "The defense calls Janet Hovanes."

Bewildered, I say, "May we take a moment to confer, Your Honor?"

"Make it quick, counsel," the judge says.

"We don't need to confer," Debra says. "I'm ready to proceed with my examination of Mrs. Hovanes." She turns and beckons Janet, who walks to the witness stand. My wife is clearly not happy that Debra is handling this. Neither am I. But we can't let the jury think we're disunited, so I yield.

"Why is she calling Mom?" Hailey whispers.

I don't respond. How can I tell Hailey that her mother is going to try to save her by implicating her brother?

After posing some background questions about Janet's education and work experience, Debra approaches the bench. Lundy joins her, but when I try to follow, she shakes her head. I sit back down. Again, we can't make a scene in front of the jury. What the hell is going on?

The sidebar conference lasts for a full ten minutes. Finally, the judge says, "We're going to clear the courtroom again. Meanwhile, Detective Ernesto Velasquez, will you go out in the hall and bring Daniel Hovanes in?"

Janet looks at me in confusion. I shrug, as shocked as she is. More. What does Debra have in mind? Why is Daniel here? Did the police arrest him?

Velasquez returns with Daniel at his side. They sit in the third row. Daniel is dressed well, at least for him—jeans and athletic shoes, but also a collared shirt and sports jacket. I can't remember the last time I've seen him in a sports jacket. He's carrying what appears to be my laptop under his arm.

When the courtroom is clear, Debra says, "Mrs. Hovanes."

"Miss Grant." The edge in both their voices is palpable.

"Do you remember that the police seized your family's computers in connection with the arrest of your daughter?"

"I'll never forget that intrusion. We were violated."

"And all the computers and devices came back clean?"

"They did."

"But there was one computer that the police didn't take."

"Yes. My husband's computer. Attorney–client privilege. You managed to stop the police from seizing it, Debra." There's a patronizing tone in Janet's voice, as if Debra had intruded, too.

"By the way, did your husband, Matthew Hovanes, post the nude picture of Farah Medhipour?"

Janet flinches. "Of course not. It kills me to say this, but it turns out that my—"

"You've answered my question," Debra says in a tone so harsh that Janet reacts as if she's been slapped in the face.

"Did I post the nude photo of Farah?" Debra asks.

"You, Debra Grant? No, I…Is this some kind of joke?"

Without making eye contact with me, Debra turns and nods to Daniel, who walks to the bar and hands her my computer. She spends a couple of minutes hooking it up to the court's audiovisual system and logs in. Then she presses some keys, and the disturbing, sexually suggestive nude photo of Farah appears—but this one shows only Farah. "Only three people have passwords to this computer, don't they, Miss Hovanes? Your husband, as well as you and me in case of emergencies. Is that right?"

"That's right."

"And we've already established that neither your husband nor I posted those horrible things about Farah Medhipour. Which leaves you, doesn't it?"

The gallery breaks out in restrained buzzing. Janet shakes her head in disbelief.

"As a library science major and a librarian, you know a good deal about computers, don't you?" Debra asks.

"It was part of the college curriculum and the job. I'm certainly no expert. And what you're implying is absurd."

I almost believe her—want more than anything in the world to believe her. I shut my eyes, praying that I've made a mistake, that I've misunderstood.

"You know more about computers than your daughter, don't you?" Debra asks.

"I do. But not nearly as much as my son, Daniel. Not even close. He's a known stalker of girls, and he would have no trouble hacking Matt's password. That's what he does. As a mother, it rips me apart, but he did this. Not Hailey and certainly not me, if that's what you're implying."

"As a mother, it rips you apart, huh? How poignant. Except that Daniel couldn't have hacked into this computer."

"Of course he could. He's a computer genius." Strangely, as she tries to destroy our son, there's a tinge of pride in her voice.

I'm about to become physically ill from the humiliation, the anger, the despair. My stomach settles only when Hailey grasps my hand.

"But to access Mr. Hovanes's laptop you don't just need a password," Debra says. "You also need a separate device called a secure token." Debra reaches into her pocket, retrieves her key chain, and shows the token first to the judge and the jury and then to Janet. "These were issued by the law firm of Grant & Hovanes. There are only three in existence. Matt and I each have one. And you have the third on your own key chain, don't you, Janet? A key chain that you guard zealously because you don't trust your son with your keys." Debra approaches the witness—lawyers aren't supposed to do that without the judge's permission despite what you see on TV—and dangles the keychain in Janet's face.

Lundy appears too shocked to object, and Judge

Sears seems too interested to put a stop to Debra's tactic.

Janet squeezes her eyes shut for a moment and says, "Daniel could've hacked into—"

"Oh, come on, Janet. This thing has eight numbers that change every minute. It's manufactured by one of the top security companies in the world. There's no way Daniel could've hacked that."

Janet straightens in her chair like the prim librarian she's never been. "I didn't have anything to do with this, Debra. Neither did Hailey. Or Matt." She looks at me, as if pleading. Does she really expect my support? I glare at her with growing fury. Only when she lowers her eyes do I look away and bury my face in my hands.

"You know what, Janet?" Debra says. "Daniel came to me last night with Matt's computer, and I used Matt's password and my secure token to get access. And you're right, your son is a computer genius. Once Daniel had access, he verified that someone tried to delete this photo of Farah. But because Matt's computer automatically connects with my law firm's server, the image was saved in a backup cache." Without waiting for a response from the judge or an objection, Debra pushes another button on the computer keyboard. This time, it's the photograph of Farah and Hailey apparently posing nude together. Debra points a finger at Janet. "This was the photograph that Farah Medhipour sent your daughter, isn't it? Hailey showed it to you, and you copied it from her phone. And then you edited it back to eliminate Hailey from the image, after which you posted Farah's photo on that phony website that you set up. And you sent the harassing messages."

"That's absurd."

"Please, Janet. Don't make me call your son to convict his own mother. You've already sunk so low."

"That girl killed herself," Janet says. "You can't convict another person for someone else's suicide." She looks at Judge Sears. "I don't care what you think. It's not the law. Hailey should never have been arrested."

"Mrs. Hovanes, stop talking!" the judge says. And like a cop on the beat arresting a perpetrator, he advises Janet of her rights, tells her that she's entitled to an attorney.

"I know my rights," Janet says, then looks at me with what I can only interpret as hatred. "I've been married to a man who's obsessed with civil rights. So you don't need to tell me what I can and can't say, Judge Sears."

"I made it stop, Mother," Hailey says, trying to keep her composure, though I don't know why. "Farah got the message in the locker room that day. It was all over."

"It would never have been over for as long as she lived," Janet says. "The girl was miserable, *wanted* to kill herself. It was inevitable." Then she points to our son. "Daniel did her a favor."

"Oh, my God, Mother," Hailey says in horror and then gets up and runs out of the courtroom. I wish I could follow her, but I'm paralyzed.

Buying none of Janet's words, Judge Sears discharges the jury, dismisses the charges against Hailey, and calls Joshua Lundy to the bench. Lundy confers with Detective Ernesto Velasquez, who arrests Janet.

Defiant, Janet says, "There's no way you can convict another person for someone else's suicide. This trial was a farce."

"Oh, we're not only arresting you on charges of cyberbullying," Lundy says. "You're also under arrest for distribution of child pornography. You posted that picture of Farah on the internet. The girl was fourteen years old. That will be a no-brainer to prove."

As Velasquez escorts Janet out of the courtroom, Lundy catches my eye. He hoped to destroy my family by convicting Hailey. Well, he might not have convicted Hailey, but he's destroyed my family nonetheless. From that smirk on his face, I know that's good enough for him.

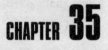

CHAPTER 35

IN THE FOUR MONTHS since Janet's arrest, the kids have returned to school. Not the chichi Star Point private school—they wouldn't have taken Daniel back anyway—but John Greenleaf Whittier, the local public high school. I'm worried about Hailey. She's decided not to play soccer anymore, she's given up aspirations for a modeling career, and she's had trouble making new friends—or hasn't tried.

"It's okay," she says when I express my concern. "It helps me remember."

Janet is in prison after a plea bargain. At her sentencing, rather than showing remorse she tried to justify her conduct, insisting that Farah was crazy, obsessed. Janet firmly believes that Farah would've used the photo to ruin Hailey's future. "You can never delete what's on the internet," she told the court. "I had to protect us." She blames Daniel for making our family outcasts, believed Hailey would redeem us with her popularity, would make us normal again. In Janet's warped mind, Farah threatened to steal it all.

Hailey won't visit her mother. I don't want to see Janet, either. I've filed for divorce. But I do see Janet, because Daniel asks me each week to take him to see his mother. Once inside the visitors' room, I stand in the back and watch them. Daniel does most of the talking, while Janet looks at him with a vacant stare. When I ask him why he keeps going, he says that Janet needs someone.

Meanwhile, at Debra's urging, we hired Daniel part-time to handle our IT issues. Recently Debra has been working on a law journal article about cybercrimes—particularly *spear phishing,* where a hacker sends a text or e-mail that appears to come from a colleague but that contains malware or a Trojan horse. Daniel is helping her understand the technology.

On this afternoon, I'm preparing for an upcoming suppression hearing. Suddenly, Debra runs into my office and asks me to come into the conference room. When I demur because of workload, she says, "Come on, Matt. This is important."

I grudgingly follow her down the hall. Daniel is sitting at the conference table. The television is on, tuned to the local news.

"Ernie Velasquez called and gave us the heads up," Debra says.

"What are you talking about?"

"Just watch. Daniel, turn up the volume, please."

After a commercial, a photo of Joshua Lundy appears on the screen. In the wake of Janet's arrest, he announced that he was running for district attorney against his boss—an act of betrayal typical of Lundy. The early polls have him leading. Hailey's trial was highly publicized, and Lundy benefitted from it.

The beauty-pageant gorgeous anchorwoman says, "Assistant District Attorney Joshua Lundy announced his withdrawal from the race for district attorney this afternoon after it was revealed that he's under investigation for posting on the internet the horrific image of fourteen-year-old Farah Medhipour immediately after the girl committed suicide. Investigators say that they began looking into Lundy's involvement after receiving a tip from an anonymous source who claimed to have hacked into the district attorney's office computer network and traced publication of the image in question to Lundy's top assistant. The assistant, who's cooperating with law enforcement, has reportedly stated under oath that he posted the image at Lundy's behest. Lundy allegedly hoped that release of the gruesome photo would sway public opinion and ultimately influence the jury to return a guilty verdict in the cyberbullying trial of Hailey Hovanes. Lundy has been placed on leave by the district attorney's office, which is considering filing criminal charges against him. Lundy and his attorney couldn't be reached for comment."

Daniel still rarely smiles, and he isn't smiling now. But Debra is.

"You wouldn't happen to be the anonymous hacker, would you, Daniel?" I ask. "It's a crime to hack into a government computer, you know."

"I instruct my client not to answer that question," Debra says. "The Fifth Amendment applies in this office, too."

"This was the so-called law journal article you two were working on?"

Debra gives a noncommittal shrug.

"I've gone straight, Dad," Daniel says. "Maybe I'll work for Special Agent Mogren at the FBI someday."

"I have a feeling she'll be working for you," I say. "Or trying to arrest you."

"She'll never catch me."

Debra takes my arm. "Come on. Why don't we all get some coffee? It's really not nice to celebrate a man's downfall, but when it comes to Joshua Lundy, I'll make an exception."

"I have homework," Daniel says. "This public school crap is tougher than I thought it would be."

Debra looks at me and tilts her head, and though I enjoy Daniel's company, I relish any opportunity to spend time alone with Debra outside of work. As we start for the front door, my cell phone rings. I show her the screen: *The Downtown Jail*.

"Take it," she says. "We need the work. Fee receipts are down this month."

I press the Answer button and say, "Grant and Hovanes."

NIGHT SNIPER

JAMES PATTERSON
WITH CHRISTOPHER CHARLES

CHAPTER 1

I'M ALMOST STARTING TO like it here. It isn't as stuffy and stale as the phrase "in-patient residential facility" suggests. It's not a gymnasium full of bunk beds made up with thin, scratchy blankets. I've just got the one roommate, and mostly she sleeps.

There are activities, too. Pottery and beadwork and storytelling. Tuesday mornings we go for a guided walk along the beach. There's even a garden with a fountain in the courtyard, where we're allowed to sit or walk after lunch. And the food is good. Students at the local culinary school try their recipes out on us. Every meal is like a *prix fixe* at a fancy restaurant. But without the wine.

I'm in a "program" for women looking to start over. They call it I.S.H.T.A.R. (Independence, Sobriety, Hope, Total Acceptance, and Recovery). Despite the pretentious name, it's working. I almost never think about the incident anymore, and I'm starting to believe I could be something besides a cop. A teacher, maybe. Or a youth counselor. Someone who reaches people before the damage is done.

* * *

I'm sitting on a bench by the fountain, sipping a cup of green tea (not a beverage you'd find in most squad rooms), when a baby-faced nurse who never stops smiling tells me I have a visitor. I've never had a visitor before. No one knows I'm here.

"Someone wants to see me?" I ask.

She gives a painfully slow shrug.

"He has a badge," she says. "I think he's a detective. I can bring him out here, if you like."

"Can't you tell him I'm not home?" I ask.

She looks at me like I cursed in church.

Randy Hall, my ex-partner, sits on the bench beside me. Randy was a fat kid from Ozone Park who grew into a lean cop with ironclad instincts and a knack for talking to whoever you put in front of him. He has a wife and an ex-wife and three kids between the marriages. Even the ex-wife loves him.

"Hello, Detective Mabern," he says. "You don't look half bad. I was afraid you'd be wearing a hospital gown and drooling into a paper cup."

I flash my most biting grin.

"Don't be so nonchalant," I say. "You must have jumped through hoops to find me. You ought to be proud."

"I've been worried about you."

Randy's just kind enough for that to be true.

"Worried?" I ask.

"Turning in your badge and gun is one thing," he says. "I didn't expect you to disappear from the face of the earth."

He's right: he deserved better. We worked Homicide

together for seven years. Randy always had my back. Still, I sense a lurking motive.

We're quiet for a while. Randy watches a sparrow splash around in the fountain.

"Why now?" I ask. "You're a good cop. You could have found me months ago."

He leans forward, plants his elbows on his knees. In the interrogation room, that always meant he was closing in on the real question.

"You get any news in here?" he asks.

"If I do, I tune it out. News is bad for my recovery."

He shakes his head: cops don't believe in recovery.

Then he tells me.

Chief Branford has dubbed this one the Night Sniper. A marksman who kills his victims from great distances with a single bullet through the heart. No connection between the vics. No geographical pattern. Always in the early morning hours.

"The mayor's putting the city on lockdown as of midnight," Randy says.

He waits for me to start talking. All I come up with is:

"That's horrific. But what's it got to do with me?"

His look says: *Are you really going to make me ask?* I gesture to the sign over the back entrance that reads: LIFELINE: A HAVEN FOR WOMEN.

"Maybe you haven't noticed," I tell him, "but I'm not a detective anymore."

He stands, stares down at me.

"Fine," he says. "I'll put out a citywide bulletin asking the killer to take a three-month vacation."

"What's wrong with the other hundred Homicide detectives on the city's payroll?" I ask.

"You caught Bryzinski when no one else could."

"That was dumb luck."

He doesn't bother to contradict me. He starts to walk away. He gets as far as the door before I call him back.

"The curfew is a mistake," I say. "You'd be inviting the killer to escalate."

CHAPTER 2

THE VICTIM IS A lunatic strung out on PCP, hemorrhaging from a stab wound to his abdomen. He's thrashing, screaming in tongues. A team of orderlies strap him to the table and hold his head still. He bites wildly at the oxygen mask. Dr. Amy Winston, anesthesiologist extraordinaire, doesn't hesitate: she slaps the man's face with all of her force, then clamps the mask in place before he can recover.

Dr. Miles Caffee watches his patient's skeletal frame go slack.

"You're a marvel, Amy," he says.

"You're the one who keeps them alive," she says. "I just keep them quiet."

Miles catches a hint of her country-girl smile beneath the paper face mask.

At three in the morning, paramedics carry in an elderly bag lady who broke her hip running from a gang of juvenile thugs. She's whimpering, crying out for the Lord to take her. Amy brings the mask down like a caress.

Night after night, Miles watches her calm the weary and drug addled, give the gift of sleep to victims of the most violent crimes and horrific accidents. She brings people peace in their worst hour.

And then Miles patches them up, sends them back out into the world.

At 3:30, Dr. Miles Caffee operates on a sixteen-year-old boy who shot himself in the leg with his father's hunting rifle. The hole appears surprisingly small until he cuts away the pants leg, finds the major artery obliterated. Judging by the boy's lettered jersey, this marks the end of a varsity career.

"The cops asked me to sedate the mother," Amy says.

"Hysterical?" Miles asks.

"More like hell-bent on killing the father."

Miles removes dead skin and tissue from the wound. Extracting the bullet is the easy part; if he can't restore blood flow, he will have to amputate to prevent gangrene.

Amy hovers in the back, watching Miles and a small team of nurses transplant a blood vessel from the boy's good leg.

"Stellar work," Miles tells the head nurse.

He uses cadaver skin to fashion a temporary graft, then turns the boy over to the orthopedic surgeon on call.

Later, back in the break room, Amy says:

"That was amazing. I thought for sure he'd lose the leg. I've never seen anything like it."

Miles enjoys the adoration but finds it misplaced. In the ER, he is a mere technician. He can do nothing more than react to whatever trauma materializes on his table.

* * *

At 4:00 a.m. their shift is over. As always, Amy's be-trothed is waiting just outside the hospital doors. Ron's an ambitious young prosecutor, six months into an al-ready promising career with the DA's office. According to Amy, he sleeps just three hours a night, rolls out of bed and does two hundred push-ups, then takes a brisk shower and meets her at the hospital. After he walks his wife-to-be home, he heads straight to the courthouse.

Ron kisses Amy for what seems to Miles a moment too long, then nods to the guitar case dangling from Miles's right hand.

"Early morning rehearsal, Dr. Caffee?"

"I rent a little studio space in Chelsea. Playing helps me wind down."

"After ten hours under those fluorescent lights, I can barely make it home before I pass out," Amy says.

"Better get going, then," Miles says.

He stands at the curb, sticks his hand in the air as though hunting for a cab. Once Amy and Ron have turned a corner and are safely out of view, he heads for the subway.

He exits at the first stop in Brooklyn. The conditions are ideal: no fog or mist, the bridge in sharp relief against a bright moon.

Just like the photo.

He hops a fence and enters a small park on the water. The park is officially closed, but there's no one to stop him. The benches are empty after a chilly late autumn night; the homeless have sought out shelters, or maybe police came through and chased them away.

Always cautious, Miles hides himself in a small stand of bare trees and lays out his guitar case. He snaps the locks open, lifts the lid. Inside, hidden beneath the false surface of an archtop guitar and glistening from a recent polish, a Remington 700 bolt-action sniper rifle. The gun his father smuggled back from Vietnam, fitted with a contemporary, state-of-the-art adjustable scope.

Flat on his belly, balancing the rifle on a bipod, Miles is unable to angle the barrel high enough to take aim at the bridge. He will have to fire this shot standing. He does not mind: any challenge brings him closer to his reward.

At 4:30 a.m., there are next to no pedestrians. At 4:40, his opportunity arrives. A woman, alone, stops near the center of the bridge, leans her elbows against the railing, and stares out at a fixed spot in the distance. Like the woman in the photo, she is neither young nor old. There is a heaviness about her expression—a sagging under the eyes, a mottled complexion that suggests tears. Miles finds no longing in her gaze. She is past longing. A widow, maybe. Or a mother who outlived her child.

Miles watches her a moment longer, imagines she is reviewing her life, weighing the bad against the good, summoning the courage to jump. He will spare her this last bit of torture. He presses the butt of the rifle hard against his shoulder, rotates the scope, zeroes in.

Just one more breath, he thinks.

She grabs at her chest, then falls forward. Not quite the dramatic plunge Miles had been hoping for, with the road below, but graceful and painless nonetheless.

CHAPTER 3

THE MORNING AFTER RANDY'S visit I'm standing on a Brooklyn pier, watching boat cops and NYPD divers hoist a bloated female corpse ashore. Blond, middle-aged, turquoise rings and earrings. There's the kind of green tint to her skin that comes from soaking in New York waters.

"Single shot through the heart," Randy says.

"How'd you know where to look?" I ask.

"We've got dispatch flagging all suspicious death calls between midnight and sunrise. The early-bird jogger who phoned this in said the vic clutched at her chest and fell forward. He thought she'd had a heart attack."

I blow into my hands. It's late autumn with a touch of winter. The sun's been up a couple of hours, and the wind is harsh off the river. I look across at the skyline, scan the traffic on the bridge. The city didn't miss a beat while I was away.

Well, I think, *I didn't miss you, either.*

"You okay?" Randy asks.

"First day out of the asylum," I say. "It's like none of this is real."

Randy nods toward the vic.

"Doesn't get any more real for her," he says.

The boat cops lay the body out on a tarp, and we gather around. In addition to Randy, who still works the Lower East Side, the task force is made up of the best and brightest Homicide cops from each borough—dyed-in-the-wool murder police with clearance rates hovering in the mid- to high nineties. Kelly Byrd from the South Bronx—late thirties, pale going on pasty, wearing a pea coat that fits her like a burlap sack; Dennis Pfeifer from Staten Island—five foot nothing with pockmarked skin and a protruding gut; Pete Cohn from Queens—tall, dark, and handsome enough to play himself in the movie; and Patsy Bowles from here in Brooklyn—early fifties, short and plump, easy to mistake for a first-grade teacher. Patsy once went a decade without an open case. Collectively they look like they've slept about four hours in the last five years.

"You think she was shot from this side of the river?" Patsy asks.

Randy shrugs.

"Maybe the ME can tell us," he says.

"The killer could have been riding a tugboat, for all we know," Pete says.

"Someone check her for ID," Randy says.

Kelly slips on a pair of latex gloves, kneels beside the dead woman, searches her pockets.

"Nothing," she says.

"Probably had a purse," I say.

"If she did, it's sloshing around Long Island Sound by now," Dennis says.

The uniforms lift up the yellow tape at the end of the pier, and we watch a Crown Vic come veering toward us, then pull up short. It's Chief Branford, the kind of bureaucrat who was born wearing brass. He marches straight to the body. The best and the brightest all stare at their feet.

"This is him?" he says, to no one in particular.

"Looks like it," Randy says.

"That makes four," Branford says. "What's her connection to the other victims?"

"She was shot through the heart in the early morning hours," Dennis says.

Branford unleashes a long glare.

"I need more than that," he says.

"We haven't ID'd her yet," Randy says, "but these killings look random. Different boroughs, different ages, different races."

Branford presses one thumb against each temple, squeezes his eyes shut.

"We can't wait any longer," he says. "I'm calling in the media, putting the city on lockdown."

I step forward.

"That won't stop him," I say.

Branford looks me up and down, then takes Randy by the arm and pulls him aside. He's being dramatic, not discreet—he keeps talking loud enough for everyone to hear.

"You've got to be kidding me," he says.

"You told me to staff the task force how I saw fit."

"I thought she was AWOL?"

"On leave. Voluntary," Randy says.

"She's a liability."

"She broke the Bryzinski case."

"Bryzinski was a slasher who targeted ex-cons. I don't see the connection."

"The connection is we had nothing to go on then, either. She got inside his head. She knew what he was going to think before he thought it."

"Yeah, and the boy she shot is still on life support," Branford says. "On the city's dime."

"That kid fired on us," Randy says. "He caught me in the leg."

"Yeah, with a gun he found lying in a tenement hallway. An autistic kid who probably thought he was in a TV show."

I catch Dennis and Kelly eyeballing me, but I can't read their expressions.

"It was still self-defense all the way," Randy says.

"She's got to be invisible. It can't look like we promoted a white cop for gunning down a half-baked child in the 'hood."

It's like they're reliving my career for me—the high of slapping cuffs on Bryzinski, then the crushing low that came with shooting Jesse Smits two weeks shy of his thirteenth birthday.

Randy and the chief walk back over. Branford locks eyes with me.

"Any ideas, hotshot?" he says.

CHAPTER 4

HE'S SLEPT ONLY A few hours, has time to spare before his shift. He pays for his ticket in cash, heads down the museum's long, vaulted corridor to the room reserved for special exhibits. A placard outside the entrance reads: ALFRED JARRY'S DISTRESSED SOULS: A RETROSPECTIVE. Odd to call the exhibit a retrospective when Jarry is not yet dead, Miles thinks.

On a weekday afternoon, he is alone in the expansive gallery—just him and the security guard, a middle-aged man with a handlebar mustache who seems more interested in his phone than in Miles.

He sits on a bench at the center of the exhibit, surrounded by Jarry's photos of New York at night. Each nocturnal cityscape frames a solitary figure. In one, a homeless woman watches television through a department store window on Fifth Avenue, a passing taxi reflected in the glass pane, lights dim on the upper floors. In another, a sax player stands under the arch at Washington Square Park, backlit by street lamps, an empty hat on the ground in front of him, no audience in sight. Miles leans forward, hears notes echoing off the stone.

He rises, begins his tour. He is compulsive, goes out

of his way to view the photos in chronological order. It bothers him that the museum did not arrange the exhibit in this manner. In fact, he cannot find any order whatsoever to the arrangement. There are black-and-whites mixed with color shots, wallet-sized photos next to floor-to-ceiling images. Part of his work, Miles realizes, is to restore order.

Executioner and curator, he tells himself.

He imagines Amy is with him. Sometimes she holds his hand; sometimes she drifts away to look more closely at a particular photograph. He addresses his thoughts to her, introduces her one by one to the photos that inspired his early kills.

The first features an elderly and frail Chinese man using his full weight to draw down the metal security grid in front of his restaurant/discotheque. Miles traveled out to Flushing for that one, spent three nights canvassing before he found a close approximation.

Then came the doorman smoking a cigarette in front of a luxury building on Central Park West. He was easy to find.

Next, the gypsy cab driver stopped at a light in Bed-Stuy.

Finally, the woman on the bridge.

Amy would like Jarry's photos — Miles has no doubt. Jarry documented, bore witness. The people trapped in these photos, like the wounded who pass through the ER, are begging for release. Amy provides temporary release. Miles has found a way to bring her work to its natural conclusion.

This, he tells her, *is my true calling.*

The events and circumstances of his life, those sad childhood years on the compound, carved for him a singular purpose. As a surgeon, he possesses certain skills and is perhaps more gifted than most—but there are other surgeons. Should his vision blur or his nerve waver, who would step forward to take his place in this?

Amy is not convinced; his smile fails to reassure her. Miles watches as her uncertainty morphs into horror at what he's done. She steps back, holds up a hand.

Amy, wait, he says. *Please.*

He explains it all to her—slowly, painstakingly—as though everything depends on her understanding. She is his inspiration, he tells her. But that pain she makes disappear every time she draws the mask down will return, perhaps with greater force. Not the physical pain, but the deeper pain behind it. The pain steeped in fear and rage. The pain we're taught to conceal.

I'm fighting a war against pain, he tells her. *Rooting out those who suffer it most acutely.*

Little by little, she comes around. She nods, moves closer to him. She's struck by the beauty of Jarry's work—the beauty of *his* work. Her eyes well up.

Come now, Miles says. *As my muse, it's only right that you choose the next soul.*

He follows her from photo to photo, watches as she studies each image, measures each subject's need for release. She takes the responsibility seriously, will make a worthy partner. In time, she might come to think of him as more than a partner. In time, she might forget her precious little assistant district attorney.

Miles winks at the guard on his way out, but the man's eyes remain fixed on the phone in his palm.

CHAPTER 5

WE BREAK UP INTO pairs, spend the day tracking down local marksmen. Kelly and Dennis take the army post in Fort Hamilton; Pete and Patsy take Homeland Security. Randy and I head out to Rikers, check the correctional snipers' psych evals, interview the warden. We come away with nothing. The others come away with slightly less.

Later, the six of us sit around a fold-out metal table in the Lower East Side station house, brainstorming.

"It's gotta be somebody who knows the city," Patsy says. "I'm guessing someone who grew up here."

"Someone with a grudge," Pete says. "Someone who's taking vengeance on the city itself."

"So we're looking for a pissed-off native," Dennis says. "That narrows it down."

There's a prolonged quiet—a lot of throat-clearing and bodies shifting in their seats.

"What about the street cameras?" I ask.

"We've got a small army of uniforms poring over footage from every camera within a mile of every scene," Randy says. "So far, nothing."

It's going on 10:00 p.m. The group is starting to fade.

You can tell we're all hoping for that one great idea that will galvanize us, spur us on.

It doesn't come.

"We should break," Randy says. "Get some rest."

"What's Branford's plan for tonight?" Patsy asks.

"He's holding off on the curfew, but the governor's called in the National Guard. The city is flooding the streets with prowl cars."

"Great," Dennis says. "The Sniper's next target will be wearing a uniform."

Kelly gives Dennis a quick smack across the back of the head.

"Keep your phones on," Randy says.

The room empties down to just the two of us. Randy stands there, giving me the twice-over.

"You have a place to stay?" he asks.

"I lost my apartment when I checked myself in," I say. "I'll crash in the bunk room for now."

I can see he wants to offer me his fold-out, but he's wary of the hell he'd catch from his wife: Deb never liked him partnering with a woman.

"I know I'm throwing you into the fire," he says.

I wave him off.

"This is where I belong," I say.

"You sure?"

I can't tell if he's asking on his own, or if he's following Branford's instructions.

"I've only ever had one purpose," I say. "Besides, what trouble can I get into in a station house?"

"It's the pharmacy across the street I'm worried about."

"I can't score at a pharmacy," I say.

"It's a metaphor."

I smile, show him my middle finger.

* * *

The bunk room is as spare as spare gets—just four walls lined with double-decker beds. The space feels like a neglected public school classroom. Every so often baby roaches come pouring out of the radiator. Tonight, I've got the place to myself. Hardly anyone ever stays here of their own free will.

I dump my duffel bag on the floor, take a fitted sheet from a filing cabinet in the hall, and make up one of the bottom beds. I shut the light, lie on my back. Five minutes in, it's clear I won't be sleeping. I've gotten used to my roommate's mousey little snores, used to knowing exactly what will happen when I wake up in the morning. I feel a slight panic wondering what I'll eat for breakfast.

And then there's the adrenaline. I'm itching to hit the street. The competitive juices that made me a great cop and a lousy person are flowing again, and there's no way I'm strong enough to calm them.

It's got to be *me* who finds him.

Lying there in the dark, I already see the headline: **Child Killer Saves the City.** I'm already drafting the article about flawed heroes and second chances.

I tell myself I might as well do something useful. I've never been very good at sleeping anyway.

I get up, walk down the hall to the women's locker room, splash water on my face, swish around some Listerine. I fetch my camera from my duffel bag, then head downstairs to the sergeant's desk, where I check out one of the unmarked Cavaliers. Sergeant Teddy Romanski, ruddy-faced uncle to everyone in the squad, tells me I'd better be careful out there.

"Haven't wrecked one yet," I say.

He gives me a craggy scowl.

"That ain't what I meant," he says. "There's a vest in the trunk. You wear it, you hear me?"

"Teddy," I say, "those vests put ten pounds on a girl's figure."

He looks like he's going to lunge over the desk.

"I'm kidding," I say. "Only kidding."

But of course I don't wear the vest. Like everybody else in this city, I put my chances somewhere around one in eight million.

CHAPTER 6

I DRIVE OUT TO the first crime scene. I need to see it the way the killer saw it—at night, with the street lamps acting like stage lamps and the occasional pedestrian casting a long shadow.

Because, I tell myself, this has to be about place.

An elderly Chinese restaurateur, a thirty-something black doorman, a middle-aged female night stroller on the Brooklyn Bridge: there's no pattern, no connection between the dead. But not every aspect of the killings can be random—at least not for the killer. Even a disordered human mind makes connections.

So where is the logic? Take away people and you're left with place. Spend time at the scene and an impression will start to form. Stay with that impression, and you'll find your window into the killer's mind.

At 11:30 p.m. I pull up in front of the first victim's restaurant, on Northern Boulevard in Queens. I step out with my camera bag slung over my shoulder, looking like a tourist.

The restaurant is closed. The iron grid is covered with graffiti, most of it scrawled in Chinese. There's a sizable display of wreaths, teddy bears, and balloons on the sidewalk out front in memory of the victim, Mr. Zheng. Up and down the block, I see nothing but gaudy neon signage. Traffic remains steady on the boulevard. An ancient-looking man and his paramour huddle under a bus stop canopy. It's New York: even the elderly never sleep.

On the other side of the boulevard, there's an apartment complex: identical eight-story brick rectangles, one-time projects converted to livable homes for the middle class. CSI determined the bullet came from the roof of the building directly opposite the restaurant. I start across, catch a string of staccato honks from a cabbie who'd rather not use his brake.

I walk the complex grounds, taking in the lay of the land. There are four sets of fire escapes per building, two in the front and two in the rear. The killer wouldn't have to be very tall to reach one of the ladders. He'd be taking a risk passing by the tenants' living room windows, but at 3:00 a.m. the risk would be minimal. Besides, if the task force's working theory is correct—if he is ex-military looking to replicate his wartime experience stateside— then risk would make for part of the rush: stealth would be part of the skill set he was looking to revive.

Military or not, I think, *he's fighting his own war.*

It goes without saying that he's cast himself as the good guy. The question is: who has he cast in the role of villain?

My own stealth skills are lacking, so I walk back around to the front, stand in the entryway with my shield hanging from my coat pocket, and wait until a departing resident lets me in. The lobby is all marble and mirrors. The day's smells are starting to stagnate: ammonia, cabbage, an overly sweet tobacco.

I take the elevator to the eighth floor, then climb the

last flight to the roof. There's a sign in Chinese and another in English saying that roof access is prohibited, but I find the door unlocked. On the roof itself I find a long strand of balled-up police tape. There are lawn chairs scattered around, cigarette butts, empty bottles. There's even a small grill. I'm surprised by how much of the Manhattan skyline is visible—a clear vista from the spike of the Woolworth Building north to the blunt angles of the MetLife Building.

I screw a telescopic lens onto my Nikon, pull up one of the lawn chairs, sit watching the street below. An elderly Chinese man pushing a shopping cart full of plastic bottles stops in front of the pile of wreaths, bends over and begins to root through them, no doubt hoping someone memorialized Zheng with an object he might pawn. I capture him in a few hundred shutter shots, imagine my lens is the Sniper's scope. A woman leans her head out of a second-story window, screams at the man until he wanders off. I snap pictures of her, too.

By all accounts, Zheng was a beloved figure. He fed the homeless out of the restaurant's back door, employed local kids as waiters and busboys, catered neighborhood weddings and funerals on a generously sliding scale. According to the case file, detectives couldn't get through an interview without handing over the Kleenex.

But none of that matters, I remind myself. At least not to the investigation. The killer didn't know Zheng; for him, Zheng was just a prop. What I need to pay attention to here isn't the details, it's the larger impression. Why did the killer pick *this* scene? What did *he* see when he looked down at the street below?

An hour goes by, then another, before the impression crystallizes. I don't feel lonely so much as alone. The solitude is all the more cutting because I know there are eight million people hidden in the cityscape laid out before me.

I can't deny it: I want a benzo and a bourbon chaser. Or maybe codeine. Or Demerol. Anything to slow the world down, soften its edges.

But for the first time in a while I have a solid reason to stay clean.

The hunt is under way.

CHAPTER 7

THEIR SHIFT IS SLOW—maybe the slowest in Miles's ten years working the ER. News of the shootings has broken. Sure, there are still accidents that occur within the home, heart attacks, strokes. But unusually for this city, people are staying indoors. A little after 11:00 p.m., a teenage babysitter carries in a four-year-old boy who cracked his head open on a coffee table; at midnight, an addict comes in with a broken arm. That's it.

Miles has shut down five boroughs with four bullets.

"This lunatic's actually made the city safer," Amy says. "He's going to put me out of a job."

They're sitting in the break room, sipping coffee and waiting to be summoned via the hospital loud-speaker.

"Maybe NYPD should hire him," Miles says. "Find a way to keep people indoors after dark and you save the city a fortune."

Amy frowns.

"Don't say that. Someone's bound to take you seriously."

Miles bites his tongue, reminds himself to go slow: it's okay that she considers him a lunatic...for now.

"They're calling him the Night Sniper," Amy says. "Makes him sound like a comic book villain."

Miles looks at her with interest. "Who's calling him the Night Sniper?" he asks.

"The DA, the mayor's office, the cops. They've assigned six hotshot Homicide detectives to the case. The Night Sniper Task Force. Ron told me."

A situation Miles hadn't anticipated—Amy as his pipeline.

"The Night Sniper, huh?" he says.

It's catchy, but it reduces him to what he does and when he does it. For Miles, all that matters is the *why*.

"What else did Ron tell you?" he asks.

He spends the ride out to Queens studying the photo behind tonight's mission. He holds the image frozen in his mind like a slide on a stalled viewfinder. It's by far Jarry's most skillful shot—a male passenger glimpsed through the window of a moving subway car, colored light cutting diagonals across the composition. The man wears a baggy suit and trench coat, holds a paper bag in his lap. His face is a blur; his slumped posture suggests that he is alone, unaware anyone might be watching. Jarry snapped the photo from somewhere above as the train sped by. The timing had to be impeccable; no doubt Jarry's success was preceded by a slew of failed attempts. Miles won't have that luxury.

He exits at Thirtieth Avenue. Members of the National Guard stand with machine guns at either end of the elevated platform. They are young, well-groomed, self-important. Their camouflage uniforms look absurd here in the city. Miles remains the picture of calm as the tallest of them—a boy likely working his way through college, his pimples burning red against his almost translucent skin—asks to look inside the guitar case.

Miles pops it open.

"Just coming home from a gig," he says.

The boy stares down at the sunburst facade.

"Beautiful instrument," he says. "What's your genre?"

"Jazz, mostly."

The boy whistles with genuine admiration.

"I tried playing trumpet," he says, "but I can't keep time to save my life."

"You're young," Miles tells him. "Maybe you should try again."

He follows the elevated tracks for five blocks, then heads down a residential street and cuts into a narrow alley. The lights are off in the windows above. He selects a four-story building with a Dumpster parked under the fire escape, straps the guitar case across his back, and begins the climb. He imagines he is his father scaling a palm tree in the Mekong Delta.

His father: the distressed soul Miles failed to liberate, though he is making up for it now.

On the roof, he drops to his stomach and crawls to the ledge facing the street. His view of the tracks is not ideal: the angle is steeper, the distance less pronounced than in Jarry's photo.

But of course Miles can't be expected to replicate every detail. What matters is the essence.

CHAPTER 8

I GET BACK TO the station at a little after two in the morning. Randy and Pete are already there. Patsy, Dennis, and Kelly aren't far behind. We brew some coffee and sit in the conference room, all of us quiet, waiting.

It starts to look like the city might reach daybreak unscathed. Crime is down across the boroughs, and for the first week all year there hasn't been a single reported shooting. Even the gangs are inside. But it turns out that even if no one's there to hear it, the tree really did make a sound. The call comes in at 5:30: an MTA cleaning crew found the vic at a rail yard in Sunnyside, Queens. The train conductor had no idea he'd been chauffeuring around a corpse.

"The MTA's got a cleaning crew?" Dennis says.

Kelly gives him a smack.

We drive out to Sunnyside in two separate cars. The ME and his team are already there; the uniforms have unspooled a good mile of yellow tape. Branford's public announcement unleashed the media. TV crews and newspaper reporters are gathered around the periphery, chomping at the bit.

The DOA lies facedown on the floor of the train's center car. Bald crown, scuffed shoes, off-the-rack suit—a civil servant somewhere north of fifty. The blood outlining his torso is crusting over in the cool morning air. The ME puts the time of death around 3:30 a.m.

"Someone must have seen something," Randy says.

I point to a bullet hole in the opposite window.

"The shot came from outside," I say. "The vic probably had the car to himself. That time of the morning, with the city on high alert and people sticking indoors, a corpse could have coasted into the yard without anyone noticing."

Dennis takes a closer look at the bullet hole, smacks his lips together.

"Damn, this guy's one hell of a shot," he says. "He should give seminars at the academy."

"His first moving target," Patsy says.

"Maybe degree of difficulty is his form of escalation," I say.

The ME snaps a few pictures, nods for his lackeys to flip the body. Randy slips on a pair of latex gloves, crouches down, goes through the man's pockets.

"Well," he says, "someone saw this guy after he died. No wallet, no phone."

"If the shot came from outside, then it wasn't the killer who robbed him," Kelly says.

"Probably a bum riding for shelter," Randy says. "Finding him is our first priority."

"He won't have seen anything," I say. "Nothing more than that jogger on the bridge. A guy grabs at his chest and falls over. If it was a bum, he probably thought Christmas came early."

"Still," Randy says, "this hypothetical hobo might be able to tell us where it happened—between what and what stops. At least we'd know where to canvass. With all the cops and guardsmen around, it's possible someone saw something."

He's right—it's the next logical step—but my gut tells me no one saw a thing. Besides, witness testimony isn't how we catch this guy.

Branford shows up. He doesn't even look at the DOA, just walks straight to Randy and points in my direction.

"One of the chimps in that media circus out there spotted her," he says. "Now they're all asking questions. This is exactly what I said couldn't happen."

Something in what he says sparks an idea.

"That's how we draw him out," I say.

"What?" Branford says. "Why is she talking?"

"The media," I say. "We talk to him through the media. Say the right things, and he'll talk back."

Branford screws his face up into a portrait of skepticism.

"What kind of things?" he asks. "What is it you think he wants to hear?"

"It's more a question of what he doesn't want to hear," I say. "Right now, he's a God in his own mind. He perches up high and plucks people from the face of the earth. He's got the whole city scrambling. He's like sex—nobody goes more than eight seconds without thinking about him. That's exactly the kind of attention he craves."

"The same's true of any serial killer," Branford says. "Remind me how you're helping?"

"We knock him off his perch. Put out a profile that's so demeaning and humiliating, he won't be able to stop himself from contradicting us."

Branford turns his back to me like it isn't even worth discussing, but Randy looks past him, starts to nod.

"We trick him into dropping the script," he says. "This guy's planned every step. Make him improvise, and he becomes vulnerable."

Branford shifts his gaze from detective to detective, in search of a dissenter. No one looks back. After a while, he gives up, lets out a showy sigh.

"Does no one but me see the potential for this to blow up in our faces?" he asks. "Piss the guy off, and maybe he trades his rifle in for a machine gun. Maybe he schedules an afternoon shift."

"It's a risk," Kelly says. "But until he slips up, we've got nothing. No forensics. No witnesses. Every marksman in the tristate area accounted for."

Branford waits the obligatory beat before conceding.

"I want a department profiler on this," he says. "That way it'll at least look like we thought it through."

Randy starts to agree, but I cut him off.

"It should come from me," I say. "The disgraced cop. He'll take it as an insult, think we're cheapening his sacred mission."

Branford pivots, does his best to loom over me. I catch some hurt-feeling looks from my fellow detectives: I've overstepped.

"What part of *make yourself invisible* don't you understand?" Branford says.

I square my shoulders, grin up at him.

"Think of it this way," I tell him. "If this does blow up in our faces, you can lay it all on me."

CHAPTER 9

MILES SITS ALONE IN his wide Hell's Kitchen loft, sipping a power smoothie. Dark shades cover the windows; the thousand-plus square feet are lit by a single floor lamp. What furniture he has is a muted shade of gray: gray armchair, gray sofa, king-sized bed made up with a matching gray comforter. The bed he's barely slept in for weeks now, though his aim remains steady—as if some external force were reaching down to brace his hand.

He switches on the television in time for the morning news with Allie White. White is a striking young Harvard grad who somehow landed a news anchor gig after only a handful of years as a cub reporter. Miles has been tuning in ever since White inherited the broadcast from her aging predecessor, a man with leftist leanings whose words were half garbled by an excess of saliva. Watching White narrate his exploits gives Miles no small thrill.

At 6:15 a.m., the words *Breaking News* slide across the screen in blood-red italics. Miles leans forward, raises the volume. The camera closes in on White's face. She's wearing jade earrings and a tight blouse with a lace collar. Her blond hair is coiffed in a perfect wave.

"This just in," White says.

Miles wishes her writers had come up with a more original segue.

"The killer police are dubbing *The Night Sniper* has struck again."

As she reads from the prompter, the camera cuts to a train yard in Queens and pans over a wide expanse of empty subway cars before zeroing in on the crime scene. The immediate vicinity is crowded with bodies— a small sea of reporters all pressed up against one another behind the police tape.

Miles thinks: *Spread the word, Allie.*

White gives sketchy details of the crime. Police are uncertain as to where exactly the man was shot, how far he traveled before arriving at the yard. Going through the list of previous crimes, she lists similarities (a single shot through the heart) and differences (a moving target), then announces that *Wake Up, New York* has obtained an exclusive interview with a member of the Night Sniper Task Force—none other than Cheryl Mabern, the detective who shot young Jesse Smits in the Avenue D projects just six months ago.

Huh, a fellow killer, Miles thinks. *Or thwarted killer.*

He hopes that her notoriety will not distract the public, that her ignoble shooting of that boy will be in no way associated with his cause.

The camera frames a male beat reporter standing with Detective Mabern in front of a subway car, then zooms in on Mabern as the reporter asks if the task force has any leads to pursue. The detective, with shallow dimples and a slight cleft in her chin, is surprisingly attractive given her occupation. Not conventionally beautiful, like White, but subtly alluring—like Amy, only with harder edges.

"What we have on our side," Mabern says, "is history. History tells us everything we need to know about this guy."

"How so?" the reporter asks.

"If you stack up the profiles of every known serial killer going back to Jack the Ripper, you'll find only the smallest discrepancies in their biographies. They want you to believe they're unique—they want you to think they've been touched in some way that separates them from the rest of humanity—but the truth is they're all the same. They were picked on as kids. One or both of their parents were abusive. Their pets died violent deaths. They have no friends, have never been in a relationship that lasted more than a few weeks. They're usually white, usually male, just about always virgins, and anecdotal evidence suggests that most of them are impotent."

Miles digs his fingers into his thighs, feels his spine stiffen.

"So they've replaced sex with violence?" the reporter asks.

"That's part of their pathology," Mabern says.

"Aren't they also highly intelligent? Even brilliant?"

Miles locks eyes with Mabern through the television screen, willing her to give the right answer.

"That's pure urban legend," she says. "Most of them are actually feeble-minded. They were subpar students all through high school, and the few we know of that went to college flunked out. They're desperate to prove their worth, and that's why they stand no chance of long-term success: they're reaching way beyond their natural limits."

Miles is off the sofa now, crouched in front of the TV, ready to reach through it.

"You're describing a very sad character," the reporter says.

"He's not just sad," Cheryl continues, "he's broken. Society has no place for him. He's as close to human refuse as we get."

"Possibly," the reporter says. "But doesn't the skill involved in these killings suggest that you're dealing with a highly functional individual?"

Mabern gives a derisive sneer, then pretends to cover it up by coughing into her sleeve.

"You can train a chimpanzee to do one thing well," she says.

CHAPTER 10

MILES FORCES HIMSELF TO continue watching as White urges her audience to exercise caution, remain indoors after dark. When she announces the next commercial break, Miles switches off the TV, then replays the interview in his mind while striding back and forth across the apartment.

Feeble-minded. Impotent. Refuse. Chimpanzee.

"I'm a surgeon and you're a goddamned civil servant!" he shouts, then looks around as though he might catch his neighbors listening through the walls.

I only hope that Amy gets her news from another source, he can't help but think.

He continues to pace, finds even his own thoughts taking on Mabern's cadence.

She believes she's untouchable, he tells himself. *She thinks her badge grants her some kind of immunity.*

He will disabuse her of this notion. Her death will not be swift and merciful; he will not allow her a place among the Night Sniper's victims. She will come home to find him waiting with his scalpel. Maybe he will light candles, run a scalding bath, pour her a glass of bitter wine. He will make her last night on earth a very dark romantic comedy.

And then, all at once, his fury gives way to pity. Mabern, he realizes, was projecting, describing herself. Throughout the interview, it had seemed to Miles that she was trying to mask her hatred of the killer in order to appear professional, but in fact she'd been trying to disguise her own self-loathing.

She is stuck hating herself, Miles thinks, because the boy she shot did not die. She does not know what it is to liberate a distressed soul. To come so close only to fail: her psyche is damaged in ways she cannot possibly fathom. It is she who's broken.

But not beyond repair, Miles thinks.

He feels a compassion for Mabern unlike any he has experienced before.

Something about her reminds him of his victims: a vulnerability, a sadness.

He cannot fix her—he knows this—but he can put her on the path to self-healing. He can show her the way.

Her attempt to humiliate him was a secret cry for help—a cry aimed directly at him. He must respond, must reveal himself in order to save her. Not in a single flash: he must coax her to him in small, deliberate steps.

CHAPTER 11

I'M SITTING AT MY desk, eating pickled herring from Russ & Daughters and waiting for the phone to ring. It's been six hours since the interview. So far, nothing—not even a wrong number.

But I'm feeling good. I'm all the way back now, living and breathing the case, not thinking about Jesse Smits or the time I spent sequestered at the resort for wayward women. I wouldn't take a benzo if a bottle suddenly appeared on my desk, and no part of me wants that bourbon chaser. I'm the best version of me: alert and ready to work.

"You were making yourself a target, weren't you?"

It's Pete Cohn, the youngest of us, settling in at his desk with a cup of station-house coffee. We sit opposite each other in the conference room that serves as temporary task force headquarters.

I smile, feel what must be a sliver of herring stuck between my front teeth. I paw at it with my tongue, hide my mouth behind my hand. Pete has the strongest set of cheekbones in all the NYPD. He could have made ten times his current salary modeling sweaters and swimsuits for those flyers everyone chucks in the trash, but I don't think he knows it. I don't get a whiff of ego off Pete: he's all about the job.

"I mean in the interview," he continues, as though answering a question I'd asked. "You weren't just drawing the Sniper out—you were drawing him to you."

I finish clearing my teeth, put my smile back on display.

"I was starting an argument," I say. "Here's hoping our guy has a temper."

Pete leans forward, plants his elbows near the center of the desk.

"Is that how you caught Bryzinski?" he asks.

I want to believe he's showing interest in me rather than my career.

"Bryzinski was different," I say.

"Because he only killed men?"

"And because most of his kills were meant to throw us off track, hide his real target."

Pete takes a loud sip of coffee.

"I heard Randy say you were able to get inside Bryzinski's head, think along with him."

He says it like a question. I'm supposed to tell him how I did it. Now I know his interest is in Cheryl the cop. I try not to look dejected.

"The only way inside," I say, "is through the outside."

Somewhere behind me a throat clears.

"Sounds like one of those fortune cookies that ain't really a fortune," Dennis says.

He's standing over my right shoulder. I turn, see Kelly standing with him.

"Don't listen to Dennis," she says. "He thinks women cops are only good for busting johns."

Dennis starts to answer, but Patsy, now hovering over my other shoulder, cuts him off.

"Tell us about Bryzinski," she says. "Walk us through it."

They're on every side of me—like theater in the round. It's Patsy's stare that makes me understand what they're really asking. They want to know why I'm here. They want to know what makes me so special. How did a disgraced cop who locked herself up in a pseudo-asylum get called back for a career case? And where'd I get the nerve to do that interview without consulting them first?

"Listen," I say.

But I have nothing to follow it up. Instead, it's Randy, newly arrived to the circle, who speaks for me.

"You get inside the killer's mind by turning everything you know about the crime into a question," he says.

CHAPTER 12

AND WE KNEW PRECIOUS little," Randy says.

He gives them some background. Dead males were cropping up all over the five boroughs, stabbed with a crude instrument: possibly sharpened plastic, no longer than two inches, thin and wobbly, like the blade was taped to the handle. According to the ME, a simple kitchen knife would have made a more reliable weapon.

"That was the first hint of ritual," Randy says. "The first suggestion that there was something deliberate in his process, that these killings were personal for him. So the weapon itself became our first question."

"Why not swap out the toy blade for a real one?" Patsy asks.

Randy nods.

"And what did you come up with?" Pete asks.

"You mean what did Cheryl come up with?" Randy says. "She was the one who pieced it all together."

He gestures for me to take over.

"We cycled through a lot of possibilities," I say, "but

only one made sense: he was reliving some earlier, original crime."

I feel a team of detectives eyeing me, ready to pounce on the smallest mistake.

"He wasn't unsophisticated," I continue. "He knew how to cover his tracks. He didn't leave behind so much as a speck for forensics, and he threw us for loops by dumping the bodies in random places. And it wasn't a question of whether or not he could afford a better weapon: like the ME said, a kitchen knife would have been more effective. So these had to be trophy killings—the killer reliving some glory moment, playing it out in every possible detail."

Pete looks at me like he wants to be convinced. Dennis looks at me like he doesn't.

"So then what was the next question?" Patsy asks.

"Where?" I say. "There was hardly any blood surrounding the bodies, meaning he killed his victims somewhere else and then dumped them. But twelve murders into his spree, we still hadn't found an original scene. He had to have some kind of private killing ground. We were thinking a garage, someplace he could drive into with a living victim and drive out of with a corpse. So the next question was: *How?* How did he lure his victims to this place?"

I'm feeling it now. It's like the case has started up all over again. Maybe that's what Randy's hoping for. Maybe this is his attempt to get me back in the groove, because I can't imagine why else he'd want the story told. Or maybe he trusts me not to tell the whole story, to leave out the part where Bryzinski got the drop on him.

"We had good questions to work from," I say. "The problem was that each question had hundreds of possible answers. We needed a link, some concrete thread that wove all the questions together and made the right answers pop out.

"It was Bryzinski himself who gave it to us. We started to notice that a good number of his victims were ex-cons. All had been released from Rikers within the past month. There was a little something extra in the way Bryzinski killed them—slash marks and bruises to go along with the stab wounds, indications that the killer took his time, had some fun.

"Our first thought was a corrections officer," I say. "Someone who was doing on the outside what he couldn't do on the inside. But that didn't feel right to me. To snap like that...we were looking for someone who'd been abused. Not just abused, but systematically degraded, beat down. I tried to put myself in the killer's place, imagine what could be traumatic enough to keep him going. Only one scenario rang true: these killings represented the moment he fought back, reclaimed his life. We—"

Pete cuts me off.

"Bryzinski was a cabbie!" he says, half jumping out of his seat.

I smile.

"Yeah, but not even a gypsy company would hire a felon," I say. "It had to be someone entirely off the books."

"Are we closing in on your moment of triumph?" Dennis asks. "'Cause I gotta use the can."

This time it's Patsy who smacks him. Randy gives me a look that says it's okay to continue.

I'm about to tell them how Bryzinski found his jailbirds when my phone rings. We all signal at once for everyone to be quiet. I pick up.

"Task force," I say.

"You weren't very kind to me," a garbled voice says. I can't tell if he's using a voice distorter or just talking with his tongue pressed against the roof of his mouth.

I put a hand over the receiver, whisper: "Start the trace."

CHAPTER 13

HE STANDS IN TIMES Square during the lunch hour, stares up at the vertical triptych of neon screens. News of the Night Sniper scrolls across the bottom of an ad for a revival of *Cats:* City Hall has proposed a curfew; the NYPD is offering a six-figure reward for viable information. Miles tugs on the brim of his hat, pulls his scarf farther up the bridge of his nose, smiles to himself.

He takes the last unoccupied table in the narrow outdoor seating area, lifts the burner phone from his jacket pocket, and sets it in front of him. He is in no rush. More than ever, this is his city. The people swarming on every side might pretend otherwise, but they are thinking only of him. Why not bask a little?

A few hours at the library revealed that Detective Cheryl Mabern has made the news on more than one occasion. Heroine turned villain, she is now NYPD's blackest sheep. Miles feels prepared, back in control. With gloved hands, he dials the Seventh Precinct.

He is transferred twice: once by a gruff-sounding desk sergeant, once by a woman who answers "Detective

Squad" but otherwise does not identify herself. On the third try, Mabern picks up:

"Task force," she says.

Two short words and Miles recognizes the voice that's been playing in his head since early this morning. His pulse remains steady. He draws his scarf tight across his lips, assumes a deeper register.

"You weren't very kind to me," he says. "I mean in your interview this morning."

"You haven't been doing very kind things," Mabern says.

As though she were talking to a child! Miles holds the phone away for a beat, reminds himself that Mabern is lost. Her attempts to humiliate him are nothing more than a masked plea.

"On the contrary," he says, "I've been doling out the ultimate kindness."

Mabern laughs.

"Well, you know what they say? You have to be kind to yourself before you can be kind to others."

Miles takes a breath. He will not be rattled. He will draw her to him, give her what she believes she wants.

"That wouldn't suit either of us, Cheryl," he says. "You need me. I'm your chance at redemption."

"Funny, I never thought Jesus would come back as a serial killer."

Miles grins despite himself.

"I mean in this life," he says. "Capture me and the city forgets about that poor dim-witted child you shot in the projects. What's his name? Oh yes, Jesse Smits. Tell me, are you hoping he does or doesn't wake from his coma?"

Miles takes her momentary silence for victory.

"You're taunting me," Mabern says. "Trying to give back a little of what I gave you."

"Wrong again. I want to help you."

"So turn yourself in."

It's Miles's turn to chuckle.

"No," he says, "that wouldn't do. You have to work for it. You need to be good, not lucky."

"Then how are you going to help me?"

"I'll give you a hint."

"I've got a better idea," Mabern says. "How about you just don't kill anyone else?"

"But then you'd never find me."

"Don't be so sure."

There's another pause. Miles senses her changing tack.

"Where'd you learn to shoot like that?" Mabern asks.

"I'm a studious chimpanzee," Miles says. "And you're transparent."

"Transparent?"

"You want to keep me talking while your colleagues trace this call. Let me save you the effort: I'm in Times Square. I'm the guy on his cell phone."

He hangs up. All in all, he feels pleased with himself. Mabern knows now that she underestimated him. He is not that simpleton Bryzinski, acting out some trite revenge.

Miles stands, adjusts the angle of his hat. The wool scarf is wreaking havoc with his skin, but he will not remove it until the cameras are behind him.

He walks downtown at a brisk clip, enters Macy's from the north side, takes the elevator to the ninth floor. The men's room is crowded. He waits in a stall until he is certain the clientele has changed over several times, then exits, leaving behind his scarf and straw hat. He dumps the phone in a trash can on the first floor near the women's perfume section.

He starts back to Times Square, anxious to watch Detective Mabern at work.

CHAPTER 14

HE'S LEADING US BY the tail," Dennis says.

The trace confirmed the Sniper's location. Dennis, Patsy, and I are standing at the center of Times Square, hoping to find something that hasn't been trampled over a thousand times.

"He's probably watching us from the bar at the Marriott," Patsy says.

"Of course he's watching us," Dennis says.

I have a moment where I think everyone I see is him: the shirtless mime in silver body paint; the guy in the Raggedy Ann outfit who's handing out flyers for an adult-themed ice cream parlor; one of the countless hucksters drumming up business for theaters on and off Broadway—people who'd stand out anywhere but here.

We slip on elbow-high latex gloves, start rummaging through a row of garbage cans, our badges hanging from our pockets. No one in the horde of pedestrians seems to notice us. If we're lucky, we'll come up with a phone. If we're really lucky, we'll get a print off that phone.

Randy, Pete, and Kelly are rounding up surveillance

footage from local businesses and city cameras. There isn't much more we can do. We can't canvass for witnesses. What would we ask them? What would they have witnessed? A guy on his phone at midday in Times Square? Camouflage doesn't come any thicker. Still…

"There has to be a reason he led us *here*," I say. "Why not Grand Central, or…"

"You mean there has to be a reason he led *you* here," Dennis says. "We're just your merry band."

The smart move would be to ignore him, but I can't help myself:

"You don't seem that merry to me," I say.

Patsy grins.

"Maybe he plans to make his next kill here," she says.

"I doubt it," I say. "The only thing his victims have in common is that they were all alone when he shot them. Even at four in the morning, this place is crawling with tourists."

A middle-aged Hispanic woman dressed for office work stands a few feet away and stares at me. She sees me looking back but waits for Dennis and Patsy to take notice.

"Can I help you?" I ask.

She folds her arms across her chest, squares her shoulders.

"I'd rather have him out there than you," she says.

Dennis steps forward, looking like a watchdog who'd been dozing but is suddenly poised to attack.

"You had your moment," he says. "Now take your self-righteous smirk and move along."

She doesn't budge.

"I make it my business to speak for people who can't speak for themselves," she says.

"Yeah, you're doing God's work," Dennis says. "I'm sure you're anxious to tell your friends all about it, so don't let us keep you."

He's in her face now, veins popping on his neck. I try to pull him back. There's a small crowd gathering. Some of the onlookers might recognize me. Some just want to see what people are watching. A bike messenger in a skull cap and spiked leather gloves starts filming us on his cell phone. Dennis and Patsy spot the guy at the same time. Dennis heads straight for him. Patsy grabs the woman's arm—hard. The woman grimaces, struggles, can't break away.

"Did someone put you up to this?" Patsy asks.

"What are you talking about?"

"Did a man pay you to confront Detective Mabern?"

It's a good question. The Sniper knew we'd be here. He has every motive to humiliate me, and he craves the big stage.

"What man?" the woman says. "Let go of me."

I stand on a bench, scan the mass of people moving in every direction, hoping that somehow I'll be able to pick him out. Instead, my eyes are drawn upward to that gaudy trio of neon screens. There's a pubescent pop star I don't recognize drinking from a can of carbonated sugar water while he dances to a song we can't hear. And underneath, a news scroll: stock quotes, then weather, and then this, in flashing red letters:

ATTENTION! The city remains on high alert following four consecutive early morning attacks by the killer dubbed NIGHT SNIPER. Police have no leads. Citizens are urged to stay indoors…

He came here to soak it all in, to stand at the center of his own spectacle.

The woman is screaming now. Patsy reaches for her cuffs with her free hand. I lean forward, whisper in Patsy's ear:

"She's not involved."

Patsy whips her head around. I nod to the screen. She looks up.

"He wanted to watch his own movie," I say. "He wanted us to know he's a star."

Patsy releases the woman's arm, watches her scurry off, cursing over her shoulder. Onlookers fade into the larger crowd.

Dennis comes back.

"The kid's clean," he says.

"I thought he might be," I say.

CHAPTER 15

BACK AT THE STATION, we break into pairs and start combing over the surveillance footage. Randy pairs me with Pete. I let myself believe this is at Pete's request.

We sit side by side in front of a flat-screen monitor, looking for a man who stands in one place while talking into his phone. We've cut the footage down to the time of the Sniper's call: between 12:45 and 1:00 p.m.

Pete and I have been assigned to the outdoor seating area, a small island of red folding tables and chairs accented with outsize flower pots. I've always wondered why anyone would sit there, walled in by traffic on one side and bodies on the other, prey to the advertisements looming over you and the hustlers pushing up against you. It's like laying out a picnic blanket in the center of a battlefield.

The camera, perched on a streetlight, gives us a bird's-eye view, but the sky is overcast, the film grainy, and it's impossible to make people out beyond a ball-park description: thin or fat, tall or short, wearing bright or dull clothing. And even with the camera focused on a single area, there are so many people coming and going, cutting into and out of the frame, that it's hard to know where to look.

"I think that woman in the green jacket just picked that fat guy's pocket," he says.

"Is the fat guy on a cell phone?" I ask.

"No."

"Then we're not allowed to care."

We reach the end, hit rewind, start over.

"It's like *Where's Waldo?*" Pete says.

"Yeah, only we have no idea what Waldo looks like," I say.

We watch the same fifteen minutes of film a dozen or more times. With each pass I focus on a new cross-section. At the northern end of the area there's a man in a gold cape and white gloves performing what looks like made-up tai chi. People sit with their backs to him. Now and then a pedestrian stops to watch, but no one drops money in his bucket.

A little farther on, girls in bikinis work the tables, soliciting men to smear body paint on their bare stomachs. The mayor has sworn to drive them from the area. It's forty degrees out. I can only think how much the girls must hate restaurant work.

There are at least twice as many tourists with cameras as commuters with cell phones.

"So why is it," I ask Pete, "that I can never get away from the guy spilling his life story into a Samsung?"

Pete pushes back in his chair.

"Yeah," he says. "This is a bust."

"Let's give it one more pass," I say.

But our eyes are glazing over, our minds starting to drift. Pete turns chatty. He asks me again about Bryzinski.

"Why not just read the file?" I ask.

"I'm not much of a reader," Pete says. "So how'd you catch him?"

I keep my eyes on the monitor.

"We set up a sting," I say. "We tracked each of the cons Bryzinski killed back to Rikers. They'd all done recent stints. Rikers releases its prisoners at Queens Plaza. A white-and-blue bus pulls up by the pylons and spits them out."

"You figured Bryzinski was going right to the source?"

"Had to be," I say. "So we swapped out a busload of prisoners for a busload of undercovers."

"Clever," Pete says. "That your idea?"

I nod. I like that he thinks I'm clever. I start to lay it on thick.

"It was about this time last year," I say. "The bus rolls up at a little before sunrise—early enough so the cons don't mix with the workadays. I was parked in an unmarked car a block away. I remember there was frost on the windows. Each undercover had a tracking device in his belt buckle and a piece strapped to his ankle. We had helicopters on standby and about a thousand uniforms ready to swarm."

"All for one guy?" Pete says.

"All for one guy."

I let my voice trail off, wait for him to ask another question.

"So what happened?"

I tell him what I didn't know until afterward: that Bryzinski was there waiting for the bus, leaning against a lamppost and smoking a cigarette. He picked out his inmate, flashed the prison tat on his right forearm, played sympathetic ex-con—the type who turned his life around and wants to lend a hand:

How about a ride on the house? Anywhere you want to go.

What I don't tell Pete—what I can't tell him—is that Randy was one of the undercovers, and that Bryzinski picked him. Somehow Randy tipped his hand. Bryzinski saw right through the whole operation.

I'm about to take a shortcut to the end when Pete jolts forward in his seat, presses a finger against the monitor.

"How'd we miss him?"

"Miss who?" I ask.

He rewinds, keeps his finger glued to the spot he wants me to watch. All I see is a group of tourists in windbreakers huddled around what must be a map. But then they move on, and I see the guy Pete's talking about. He's seated at the last table, wearing a big straw hat and talking into a cell phone. He's on screen for just a flash before a fresh group of pedestrians blocks our view.

"Can we get a close-up?" I ask.

Pete rewinds, hits pause, zooms in. The image is fuzzy, but we can see the man's wearing a hat, gloves, and sunglasses. A scarf covers his face from the bridge of the nose down. We glimpse just enough skin to tell he's white.

"It's him," Pete says.

I nod. It has to be.

"Damn," I say. "I thought for sure Raggedy Ann was our guy."

Pete throws me a blank stare. I stand up, wave for Randy to join us.

CHAPTER 16

MILES, DECKED OUT IN surgical mask and gloves, leans over a twenty-two-year-old male cyclist who collided head-first with the scaffolding just outside the hospital's west wing. Knocked from his bike, he landed on the jagged end of a broken beer bottle.

The young man's wiry frame and taut muscle appear in stark contrast to his rotting teeth. A heroin addict, hooked in his early teens. The normal dose of anesthetic produced no effect—Amy had to adjust for tolerance.

Miles is distracted, cannot stop replaying his brief conversation with Mabern even as he removes shards of glass from the young man's upper back. Later, in the break room, he finds himself alone with Amy. She's been to a chic salon, had her shoulder-length hair sheared to just above her jawline. Ron, her assistant district attorney boyfriend, has been summoned—plus one—to dinner at Gracie Mansion. Amy bought a new dress to go with the new coif.

She turns her head first left, then right, inviting Miles to study her altered profile.

"You like it?" she asks.

He doesn't. The length is too uniform, the bangs

cut too straight across her forehead. From either side, it looks like she's wearing a helmet; from the front, she looks like a Dutch schoolboy. Everything about her seems suddenly juvenile to Miles.

"It's nice," he lies.

"That doesn't sound convincing."

"I'm tired."

In truth, he feels wide-awake. He is simply weary of talking, wishes he were alone to contemplate his next early morning excursion. He steers the conversation toward the only topic that interests him:

"Does Ron have any intel on the Night Sniper?"

"*Intel?*" Amy mocks. "Listen to you, Mr. Bond."

Listen to you! She's even taken on the cadence of a schoolgirl.

"I mean have there been any developments," Miles says.

Amy turns serious.

"Ron's worried," she says. "He didn't want me to come to work today. Our shift ends around the time this lunatic starts killing."

"But it sounds like the police are making progress," Miles says, fishing. "I hear they might even have a suspect."

"That's what they want you to believe, but Ron doesn't have a lick of faith in the task force. No one in the DA's office does."

"Why is that?" he asks, trying not to sound over-anxious.

"Apparently, one of the lead detectives is unstable. There's a rumor they pulled her from a nuthouse so she could work the case. Ron says he wishes the Sniper would make his next kill in Jersey, across state lines. Then they'd have to call in the FBI."

Nuthouse? Miles pictures Detective Mabern in a straitjacket, feels a glimmer of compassion. He thinks: *There is nothing quite like the bond between adversaries.*

Adversaries in circumstance, but allies in suffering.

This, he realizes, is the trouble with Amy: she has not suffered. So much of what he believed he saw in her was mere projection. Amy cannot understand the import of her work because she has never suffered herself, does not know what it is to need a reprieve, let alone permanent release. She's a technician. Nothing more. In a few years, she and Ron will move to Westchester, commence breeding.

"It's slow again tonight," Amy says.

Miles nods.

"I've got an idea," she continues. "Why don't you play something?"

"Play something?"

"On your guitar."

Miles masks his alarm with a smile.

"I'm a cut below hobbyist," he says. "I wouldn't want to torture you."

"Come on," Amy insists. "You're always carrying that thing around. I bet you're really good."

"Trust me, I'm not."

Amy doesn't seem to hear him.

"I can sing a little," she says. "I was in choir all through high school. Do you know any James Taylor?"

Her voice is rising with excitement. It's clear she won't let up.

"Ask me again," Miles says, "and I might have to kill you."

He'd meant to strike a playful tone, but Amy's smile is more than a little uneasy.

* * *

For once he does not have to travel far—just a twenty-minute walk to a pedestrian bridge on the West Side Highway. Of all Jarry's photos, this one might be Miles's favorite, though it is far from the most beautiful. The composition includes a truck and its driver, an otherwise bare strip of urban highway, street lamps bleeding streaks of light, silhouetted water towers in the distance. Each component is ugly in its own right, but something about the whole turns beautiful—in an eerie, industrialized way—when photographed in black and white.

This is the scene that will leave him most exposed, now when he is most fiercely hunted. He sits under a tree at the foot of the bridge, stopwatch in hand. The helicopters, he discovers, patrol at regular intervals; he will have just ten minutes to reach the center of the bridge, set up, identify his target, take his shot. The heightened possibility of being caught gives this kill the feel of a combat mission.

As he sits waiting for the next helicopter to pass, he finds himself addressing his thoughts to Cheryl. He explains to her, in tender detail, the relief he can bring.

"Is it true," he asks, "that you were hospitalized?"

He anticipates a reply, but now that he wants to hear it, her voice will not come.

"All in due time, Cheryl," he tells her.

He lets one more chopper go by, then sprints for the pedestrian bridge, guitar case in one hand, Cheryl's clue in the other.

CHAPTER 17

THIS TIME BRANFORD IS there ahead of us, standing with his arms crossed as though daring Randy to run him over.

"This can't be good," I say.

Branford is hovering on the driver's side before Randy can step out. As usual, he doesn't acknowledge me.

"You see that?" he says, pointing somewhere behind my back. I turn, look. On the opposite side of the yellow tape, maybe a few hundred yards away, a small militia of protesters sport homemade picket signs. It's me they're protesting:

Mabern's the Murderer...
May Burn in Hell...
Who's Policing the Police...
Night Sniper 5/ Mabern 1...
At Least the Night Sniper Ain't Racist...

"I told you from the start this was a piss-poor idea," Branford barks at Randy. "Then you go and put her in front of a camera."

"I put myself in front of a camera," I say.

Apparently my voice strikes a pitch Branford can't hear.

"She's a three-ring distraction," he says. "I want her sidelined. Now!"

"There's a problem, Chief," Randy says.

"What's that?"

"The interview worked. The Sniper reached out, asked for Cheryl by name. She's our only link to the killer."

"We've got him playing our game now," I say.

"Tell that to the dead trucker," Branford says. "Tell *him* this is a game."

"Okay, poor choice of words," Randy admits on my behalf. "But the Sniper's talking now. Cheryl clipped his ego. He wants us to know who he is. It's just a matter of time before he tips his hand too far."

"It isn't a matter of time," Branford says. "It's a matter of lives."

Branford the humanitarian. He must be practicing for his mayoral run.

Dennis and Kelly pull up, followed by Pete and Patsy. We form a small circle, with Branford at the center.

"We've got to examine the scene now," Randy says.

"Not her," Branford says, jerking a thumb at me. "Handcuff her if you have to."

"He said he'd give me a hint. He's left a clue for me," I tell Branford.

"Maybe he'll ask you to dinner next," Branford says. "If there's a clue, your colleagues can find it. This isn't an Easter egg hunt."

"Chances are he's here, watching," I say, nodding toward the crowd.

Branford squares his shoulders, steps to me.

"Believe it or not, I went to the academy just like everyone else," he says. "I've got cameras on the crowd."

I think: *Seems like the Sniper's ego isn't the only one I clipped.*

Randy turns to me.

"You'll have to sit this one out," he says.

I install myself dutifully in the back of the sedan, watch my task force teammates march to the scene. With helicopters circling low to the ground and a not-too-distant mob calling for my blood, there's no chance of a nap.

A long hour later, Randy returns alone, climbs into the passenger seat, back to the windshield.

"How did it play out?" I ask.

"He fired from an overpass," Randy says. "Through the heart, like always. The truck ping-ponged between the divider and a stone wall. The guy's torso is mangled pretty bad."

"Anyone else hurt?"

"There wasn't anyone else around."

He sees me wanting to ask.

"I'm guessing this is your clue," he says.

He hands over a creased postcard, its upper border stained with what I hope is mustard.

"Already been dusted," he says.

Still, I hold it by the corners, thumb and forefinger barely making contact. It's a black-and-white photo of a woman standing in front of a marquee. Top to bottom, the shot looks like a still from an old film noir. There's a heavy mist and a light fog. The woman wears a raincoat and holds up an umbrella. Her back is to the camera. She's svelte, with long blond hair. It's late at night, no one else on the street. The light from the nearest lamp-post looks like a Hollywood plant.

"Turn it over," Randy says.

Across the back, in big block letters:

FOR CHERYL.

"I guess he doesn't want to leave anything to chance," I say. "Where'd he place it?"

"In a garbage can, this side of the overpass."

"He saw us rooting through garbage cans at Times Square," I say. "Who found it?"

"Patsy. I asked her to keep it to herself for now."

"Good," I say. "If I'm going to be at all useful on this, Branford can't know. Not yet."

I open the car door, have one foot on the ground.

"Where are you going?" he asks.

I hold up the postcard, tap the copyright with a fingernail.

"Museum of the City of New York," I say.

CHAPTER 18

THE KID SELLING TICKETS looks confused when I show him my badge, like he's trying to remember if the museum has a discount for cops.

"I need to talk to the manager," I say. "Or director. Or whoever's in charge at a museum."

I wait while he fumbles with the phone, then tells a Ms. Hall that there's a detective here to see her.

"She'll be right out," he says.

I stand watching tourists pass through the lobby, catching snippets of German, French, a couple of languages I can't place. A few minutes later, Ms. Hall's stiletto heels cut through every other sound.

She smiles, extends an overly manicured hand.

"Detective…?"

"Mabern," I say.

If she watches the news, she doesn't let it show. She's young and thin, attractive in her custom-tailored pantsuit. She'd fit right in on Wall Street but seems out of place here.

I follow her to a windowless office—100 square feet she's done nothing to make her own.

"How can I help you?" she asks, gesturing for me to sit.

I take out the postcard, set it on her faux-mahogany desk. She squints like she's struggling to read the bottom line of an eye test.

"You recognize the picture?" I ask.

"Of course," she says. "It's one of Alfred Jarry's. He's the subject of one of this fall's special exhibits."

I snatch up the postcard before she can read the back.

"We found it at a crime scene this morning," I say. "We're pretty sure it was left there on purpose."

"Crime scene?" she asks. "What crime?"

"I can't tell you that."

"Then how is it you want me to help?"

I ask for every scrap of information she can pull on every museum employee. I ask for the receipt of every patron who's paid by credit card since the exhibit opened. I give her Randy's e-mail address. I tell her to take care of it personally.

It's clear I've ruined her day.

"Anything else?" she asks.

"Yes," I say. "I'd like to see that exhibit."

It's like a house of horrors past, present, and yet to come. They're all there: elderly restaurateur locking up shop in Chinatown; the doorman sneaking a cigarette in front of a swank facade; the woman on the bridge backlit by a bright moon; the subway passenger alone in his car; the truck driver alone on a highway.

The Sniper led us right to his source. Why?

He's presenting me with a puzzle, betting I'm too slow to piece it together. In order to solve the puzzle, I have to figure out the order: *his* order. How does he select the next victim?

He isn't working his way through the exhibit from left to right or front to back: victims one and two hang on opposite walls; victims three and four hang in a small side room. His approach isn't chronological: according to the museum placards, Jarry photographed the subway passenger a full year before he snapped the doorman's picture.

I walk the exhibit time and again, breaking the photos up into opposing categories. Figures in motion versus figures at rest. Black-and-white versus color. Male subjects versus female subjects. I consider types of architecture. Bridges, skyscrapers, brownstones, tenements. Nothing fits. No order falls into place.

I keep walking, keep looking. I start to feel dizzy. The people in the photos seem to be moving, or else the people are standing still and the buildings are moving. I sit on a bench at the center of the main room, shut my eyes. I see Jarry's photos overlaid with crime scene images. Every figure becomes a chalk outline.

I wipe sweat from my brow.

This isn't a game, I remind myself.

Branford was right about that much.

I hear voices, open my eyes. Three generations of Swedish women—grandmother, mother, and teenage daughter—stand in front of a floor-to-ceiling blowup of a junkie dozing on a bench in Union Square. Based on the few English words I glean, I guess the women are trying to hash out where their hotel is located in relation to this photo. The daughter points emphatically to a building in the background, her index finger nearly touching the glass. From across the room, a hoarse male voice snaps:

"Not so close, hon."

The security guard! Could it be that simple?

A man who stands alone with these photos for hours on end. A man who goes unnoticed save when he's scolding or giving directions. A man who could himself be the subject of one of Jarry's photos.

I spin toward him, make it obvious I'm staring. But his eyes are trained on the Swedish girl. And he's too short by far. Our estimate for the man in the hat was six feet; this guard is five seven at best.

I go back to brooding. Six victims so far, 120 photos in the exhibit. Jarry's photos on display for four months. One hundred twenty victims for 120 days. That means 114 lives might still be spared.

And then it hits me. That spark every investigator hopes for. The idea that feels true.

He's already told me who's next.

I stand, take the postcard from my pocket, hunt down the original. It's one of the smaller photos, no bigger than an eight-by-eleven-inch sheet of paper. Still, details I missed in the reproduction are clear. At the far left of the frame, just barely in focus, is the edge of a movie poster in a glass case. Across the street, on the opposite side of the woman, is the sliver of a facade I recognize as the ground floor of the Astrophil Hotel.

The woman is standing in front of the Marseillaise Theater.

And then it all falls into place. I know now what the Sniper wants me to do.

CHAPTER 19

AT THE STATION HOUSE, Randy takes my arm, leads me into the break room, and locks the door behind us. Before I can tell him about the museum he says:

"I need your gun and badge."

It's like the world's spun out of focus. I hear myself repeating:

"Gun and badge?"

"Branford's orders," Randy says. "He wanted to do it himself. I'm trying to spare you that much."

"Why?" I ask. "I don't understand."

"You haven't heard?"

I shake my head.

"There's a new witness," Randy tells me. "In the Jesse Smits shooting."

"That's impossible."

"A kid looking out his bedroom window."

"There wasn't anything more to witness. It happened the way I said."

"The kid claims Smits had his hands up. Claims he'd already dropped his gun."

Randy holds out an open palm as if to say: *Let's get*

this over with. I oblige. For a moment we just stand there.

"We'll fight this," he says. "We need you on this case."

I pretend I don't hear.

"Someone from the museum is going to be sending over receipts and personnel records," I say.

"Already has," Randy says. "I've sent them on to Hawes in Crime Analysis."

"Good," I say. "Hawes is good."

Randy looks eager to get me out of the room.

"There's more," I say. "That museum is his hunting ground. His kills are all taken from photographs."

"Photographs?"

"That postcard is part of a series."

I start to tell him about the Marseillaise Theater, about the Sniper's next kill, but then the door to the break room rattles, followed by a heavy and persistent knock. Dennis wants his coffee. Randy lets him in, then turns to me and whispers:

"I'm telling you, we'll fight this. I haven't forgotten. I know what I owe you."

The subtext is easy to read: *I'll make this right, but now it's time for you to go.* And part of me—the most childish part—thinks: *Fine, then. You figure it out on your own.*

CHAPTER 20

HE SHOULD BE ASLEEP, but the morning's events have left him jittery and full of questions. Why was Cheryl barred from the scene, sequestered in the back of an unmarked car? Are the protesters a curse or a blessing? Do they heighten Cheryl's need for salvation or simply draw attention away from his cause? Will the public see her liberation as an act of mercy or justice?

He gets up, switches on the television. He is not by nature a news junkie, but lately he cannot tear himself away.

It isn't long before the midday anchor turns his attention to the Night Sniper, or rather to Cheryl by way of the Night Sniper. Detective Mabern has been suspended. A new witness has come forward in the Jesse Smits shooting.

After a quick recap of the Smits case, a pundit with some vague affiliation to the NYPD speculates that this witness may be a plant—a convenient way of lifting Mabern from the task force without overtly bowing to public pressure.

Miles stands, starts to pace.

It's as if he is a mere sidebar, as if his kills are nothing more than a footnote to the ongoing coverage of Detective Cheryl Mabern's tumultuous career. She has become his rival in more ways than one.

But Miles cannot allow himself to be derailed by petty jealousy. Granting liberation to the person who would bring him low will be the Night Sniper's crowning achievement. In time, people will come to recognize his dedication and sacrifice. Miles will emerge on the right side of history. He will bring Cheryl with him.

The news cuts to a commercial. Miles begins to flip stations, stops when he notices an envelope shoved partway under his front door. No doubt a neighbor correcting one of the mail carrier's innumerable mistakes.

He shuts off the television, crosses to the entryway, pulls the envelope inside. Calligraphic writing on the front and back, *RSVP* across the seal. From Amy Winston and Ronald Affif. The card inside describes their impending marriage as a "blessed union."

Miles feels nothing but scorn. Their union is more banal than blessed—the joining together of two people as they march blindly down the path dictated by their narrow imaginations. A doctor and lawyer marriage— the white-class equivalent of cop and nurse.

That isn't love, Miles thinks. *It's people doing what they're told.*

Amy is the opposite of Jarry's distressed souls, the opposite of Miles's "victims." She is a pretty facade with no substance; there is nothing in her for the Sniper to liberate.

But Cheryl, on the other hand...

Cheryl, with her history of mental illness, is not only alone in the world, she is at odds with it. Now, more than ever, she must feel her solitude bearing down on her. Now, more than ever, she must long for release.

But how will he give it to her?

It occurs to him in a sudden and painful flash that Cheryl's suspension means she is no longer working the case. And if she is no longer working the case, then he cannot contact her at the precinct. What's more, she has no reason to talk to him, no reason to follow his lead.

Cheryl has ceased to pose any threat, but he will not abandon her. He will find alternate means.

CHAPTER 21

I HEAD NORTH ON Orchard, turn east on Stanton, duffel bag strapped to my back. I'm heading for a hotel near the river where I used to work busting johns.

This has been my beat for ten years now. I first saw these streets through a squad car window. Off-brand department stores, storefront churches, old stone churches, specialty boutiques (most have changed hands since I started), dive bars and night clubs and restaurants and cafés. Multiple generations sharing the same space. In short, a neighborhood.

I remember every arrest I've ever made. My third day in uniform, a woman pressed charges against her husband for "tickle-torturing" her. A week later, a gang of adolescent girls put on stiletto heels and stomped a budding cheerleader to within an inch of her life. Now I'm murder police. Detective Cheryl Mabern, Nebraska-blonde champion of the Lower East Side dead. Name any block between Houston and Canal and I'll tell you a story.

I cut over to Rivington, stroll past repurposed synagogues and community gardens. When I turn north again on Pitt, it becomes clear where I'm headed.

Probably I knew all along. The vacant lot where I shot
Jesse Smits.

It was a call we weren't slated to take. We'd been up in
Washington Heights, telling a seventy-year-old woman
who looked ninety that her grandson was shot dead in
a drive-by. She lived in one of those sprawling apartments it's impossible to find now. Sitting there on her
couch, which was still wrapped in plastic after a good
decade of use, I could feel the landlord willing her into
a nursing home so that he could break the place up into
three units, all renting at twice the original price.

She took the armchair across from us, spent a long
moment clearing phlegm from her throat.

"Was it quick?" she asked.

"I don't think he felt a thing," Randy lied.

Randy was always the one with the bedside manner.

The old woman looked at me.

"He was more than just a rap sheet," she said.

"I know," I said.

She nodded.

"As long as you know."

"Is there anyone who can stay with you?" I asked.

She got up, left the room. We saw ourselves out.

We were almost at the station house when a call came
over the radio: an undercover was taking fire on Ridge,
just south of Houston. We were two minutes out. Randy
stuck our siren on the hood. I punched the gas.

We found Detective Jason Juarez hunkered down
behind a station wagon with false mahogany side pan-
els, clamping a handkerchief over a bullet wound on his
right shoulder. The area was clear; the shooters must
have scattered when they heard us coming. There were

more sirens approaching—squad cars and an ambulance and what sounded like a fire truck. Lord knows why they always send a fire truck.

Randy and I holstered our guns, knelt on either side of Juarez. I knew Juarez by reputation—a tough son of a bitch with more commendations than I had years on the job. The salt-and-pepper buzz cut put him in his early fifties. He carried a lot of bulk that used to be muscle.

"They were kids," he said. "My son's age."

"We'll find them," I said.

He gave me a look like the world was a broken place either way.

"You're okay," Randy said. "What you've got there is a scratch."

"I see Percocet in your future," I said. "Maybe Demerol."

Randy stood, scanned the street. The sirens were closing in.

"I love that sound," he said.

A male figure cast in shadow leapt out from behind a row of garbage cans, fired a single shot, and ran. Randy stumbled, tripped over Juarez. There was blood pouring from his thigh. I started to kneel beside him, but he waved me off.

"Go," he shouted. "Run."

The shooter was a full block ahead of me. I jumped into the car, floored it. He saw me coming, cut a diagonal across Houston. A delivery truck swerved, the driver leaning on his horn. I hit the siren, turned with the shooter onto Avenue C, was on top of him when he dove through a hole in a chain-link fence and face-planted in a vacant lot. He came up limping, trailing blood. I was through the fence and after him at full speed, maybe six feet away when I raised my gun and screamed for him to stop. He spun, leveled his revolver. I fired.

Lights came on in the surrounding buildings. I started toward the shooter, gun trained on his body. He'd fallen face-first, arms spread. I kicked the gun from his hand, crouched, turned his head. A child, maybe twelve or thirteen. Still breathing.

I called dispatch, then collapsed in the weeds beside him.

And now here I am again, standing at the scene. Just as I did on that night, I take out my phone, start dialing. I stare up at the windows while I navigate an automated menu I know by heart. There are lights on, but no faces. I want someone to see me. I want my trial to happen right here.

I press three for the ICU. A cranky nurse with adenoiditis tells me there's been no change: Jesse Smits is still on life support.

CHAPTER 22

I GET A TOP-FLOOR room with no view. The bed is more cot than mattress; the sheets are spotted with cigarette burns. If I stretch my arms as far as they'll go, I can touch either wall with my fingertips.

I lie down, fully clothed, and sleep soundly for the first time since the clinic. I wake from a dream I can't remember beyond a vague sense that I've been hunted down and condemned. There's a moment before the room comes into focus and I understand all over again why I'm here.

That dream stuck pretty close to reality.

I sit up, rub my eyes, press a hand to my heart. I think maybe I'd cry if I hadn't trained myself not to. I'm as tired as if I hadn't slept. It occurs to me that I haven't eaten all day.

I think: *What will I do if I can't be a cop?*

But there's a more pressing question: Where do I go now? Back to the employment agency? Or maybe the clinic?

The shrinks told us that when we were alone and in a bad way we had to break the silence, get someone else's voice in our heads. But by the time you've reached a certain age, you have to wonder: if the only people I can reach out to are strangers, then what's the point?

Randy said he was here for me, but he isn't. He can't be. Not physically. Not in any other way.

I splash some murky water on my face, grab up my jacket, and step from the room. The smell in the hallway tells me I could make a week's worth of busts in one fell swoop.

I take the subway uptown at the tail end of rush hour, hair tucked under a knitted cap, sunglasses pushed far up the bridge of my nose. Not much of a disguise, but it should be enough to make the newshounds doubt it's really me.

Standing in the train, bodies pressing in on me from all sides, I catch myself wanting so many things at once. More things than I can hope to have. More things than I have a right to.

I want to snap bracelets on the Night Sniper. I want Jesse Smits to wake up and tell the truth. I want never to have shot Jesse Smits. I want to be partnered with Randy again — just the two of us, working cases. I want to live in a world that doesn't need Homicide cops. I want a nice one-bedroom in Brooklyn Heights and a cabin in the Catskills where I can romp through the woods with an Irish setter at my side. I want Pete to kiss me. I want to bring him home to my nice one-bedroom in Brooklyn Heights.

I exit the train at 103rd Street. I'm following a simple rule that kept me employed for more than a decade: Never score in your own neighborhood.

My dealer of choice tends bar at an easy-to-miss jazz club on 97th off Amsterdam. Andy, a Scottish guy with a thick brogue and a smile that says he passes judgment on no man, least of all himself. It doesn't hurt that he's easy on the eyes.

He has his back to the door when I walk in. I take a seat at the zinc, move my wallet from my pants pocket to my coat pocket. I'm the only patron. It's an in-between time: too late for happy hour, too early for live music.

He turns around, sees me, flashes that smile.

"I thought you'd broken up with me," he says.

"Is that gray in your goatee?" I ask.

"Oh, aye," he says. "Time has her fun with us all."

"Tell me about it."

"The usual, then?"

I nod.

"Wouldn't do to keep the stuff on the premises," he says. "I'll have to go fetch it. Anyone comes in, tell 'em we're giving self-service a try."

He leaves me with a pint of black and tan, on the house.

I think to myself: *I'm really going to do this*.

CHAPTER 23

HE TAKES THE SUBWAY to a downtown branch of the public library. Should his time on the computer leave a trace, at least that trace will remain forty blocks from his home.

He spends the six-stop ride rehearsing his next conversation with Cheryl, assuming there is a next conversation. It seems more likely that the bond between them will play out in action, not words. Nevertheless, he finds comfort in directing his thoughts toward her—more comfort still in imagining her quiet, sympathetic response.

"My father fought in Vietnam," he tells her. "He saw things that changed him. When my mother died, so did any hope of his changing back."

He imagines her seated next to him, her body jerking against his as the train approaches each station.

"How old were you?" she asks. "When your mother died?"

"Six or seven. It was cancer. I don't know what kind. My father wouldn't talk about it. He wouldn't talk about anything he considered past."

He feels Cheryl take his hand, then decides this is too much, too soon. Instead, she pats his arm, says:

"I'm so sorry."

He tells her things he hasn't shared with anyone else, things he has not allowed himself to dwell on for many years. He tells her about growing up on the compound in Idaho, about the long mountain hikes—marches, really—with his father. Fifty pounds of gear strapped to their backs, rifles at the ready. His father barking insults, striking him on the shoulders with a metal baton if his pace slowed.

"We were preparing for the Apocalypse," Miles says.

"There were times," he tells Cheryl, "I didn't think I'd make it back from those hikes. Times I thought for sure he'd leave my body in the woods."

He describes the relentless drills. Hours spent on his belly in the snow, well above the tree line, stripped of his coat and boots, waiting for an animal to emerge from a stand of Douglas fir while his father hovered nearby with a cattle prod. The long strings of sleep-deprived nights, his father chomping on pills to keep himself awake, shooting Miles with a water gun if his head started to nod. Dragging his son out at the first hint of dawn, forcing him to sight a target some 800 meters away.

"That's inhuman," Cheryl says. "I wish someone had been there to stop him. I wish someone had stood up for you."

But Miles senses the question she really wants to ask: Did your father live long enough to see you graduate from drills? Did he ever give you a human target?

He considers answering, then decides against it. He's told her enough. It is her turn to talk.

"I want to hear about you now, Cheryl," he says.

He realizes, too late, that he has said this out loud. The woman seated next to him—early fifties, plump, wearing three shades of nail polish and an obvious wig—leans back, gives him a quick once-over, then whips her head away to avoid eye contact. Miles knows he should be embarrassed, but he can't suppress a slight grin. He's always been a daydreamer. It was dreaming that got him through those long hours on his belly in the snow.

He sits alone at a bank of computers just beyond the children's section. It occurs to him that he is only three short blocks from task force headquarters.

Right under their noses, he thinks. *But then they wouldn't know me if I walked up and confessed.*

He types "Detective Cheryl Mabern, NYPD" into a search engine, hits return, is overwhelmed with a slew of recent news articles. He deletes "Detective" and "PD," tries again.

He is looking for some way to contact her outside of the precinct. It is less than unlikely, he knows, that her number will be listed in the White Pages or her e-mail address listed in some union database. But in the age of social media, no one is completely hidden.

Ultimately, it is easier than Miles could have anticipated: Cheryl Mabern has a LinkedIn account.

She must have opened it shortly after the Smits shooting, and, Miles guesses, just before she was institutionalized. The head shot she chose as avatar shows her hair chopped shorter than Amy's. Miles is glad she's let it grow out.

Her page is set up to attract security work. Under *Skills,* she's listed Crime Prevention, Surveillance Analysis, Field Training, Personal Protection, and Dignitary

Protection. Guilt over the shooting must have led her to seek a less volatile source of income—something, if not behind a desk, then at least off the street. Chances are she's forgotten by now that she ever opened the account.

Miles continues reading. Under *Experience,* Cheryl has chronicled a rapid rise through the department—from beat cop to Detective First Grade in just six years. After a short detail in Vice, she jumped straight to Homicide.

Cheryl's *Education:* a BA in criminal justice from John Jay, then a year of law at Fordham.

Miles thinks: *I wonder what kind of lawyer you would have made. I bet you're wondering right about now, too.*

He scrolls back to the top of the page, clicks on a blue icon marked *Contact info.* An e-mail address was the most he'd dared to hope for, but there is a phone number, followed by the word "cell" in parentheses.

CHAPTER 24

THERE'S NOTHING LONELIER THAN sitting at a bar even the bartender has deserted.

I take a long drag from my pint, look around the room. Maybe, I think, this is my personal purgatory, the holding cell meant to keep me until Jesse Smits recovers or doesn't, until the Sniper is caught or stops killing. If so, it could be worse. There's Louis Armstrong on the jukebox, and the bottles behind the bar look mostly full. I'd be okay here for a while.

So why do I feel so anxious?

And what's taking Andy so long?

I reach behind the bar, take up a bottle of whisky, top off my black and tan. One long swallow and I'm on the verge of floating away.

Here's what people don't know—the secret Randy's been good enough to keep. I've done some of my best cop work while drunk or high. I had a nice bourbon-buzz going the night we cornered child-killer Mike Mazza in a boiler room on Avenue C. I had a half-dozen oxycodone in me when we finally shackled Bryzinski.

The biggest secret of all: I was loaded on benzos when I shot Jesse Smits.

It's not a question of liquid or pharmaceutical courage. I was born with the kind of fearlessness that could go either way. Contract killers and serial killers have it. So do the most decorated soldiers and cops. Point a gun at me and my heart doesn't miss a beat. I'm not bragging: it's a gene you're either born with or you aren't. I have that straight from the shrinks.

So why drink? Why take pills?

To shut up the voice my mom and pop drilled into me because they knew that special gene might get me killed. The voice that says: but if I do X, then Y might happen, and behind Y lurks something much worse. It's the same voice that tells me to wait for backup, let SWAT take the door. If you don't hear enough of that voice, then your life expectancy plummets. Hear too much of it, and you end up paralyzed.

Right now, I'm in the mood to jump off the roof or kick down the door. I don't really care if I break my leg or take a bullet.

The band for the night shows up early, occupies the opposite end of the bar. Per Andy's instructions, I tell them to help themselves. The one with the sax-shaped case hops the zinc, searches out the most expensive bottle of Scotch. The rest of them whisper among themselves. Over Armstrong's scatting I catch the word "cop." Then I hear one of them say, "Still, she's not half bad."

At least I've got that going for me.

Andy returns. He's carrying a brown paper bag with twine handles, the kind you see at upscale department stores.

"Evening, gents," he says.

"We were hoping you wouldn't show," the sax player says.

"I can only give away so much of the boss's liquor."

The patter dies down, and Andy turns to me.

"Took you long enough," I say.

He hands over the bag.

"Go on," he says. "Have a look inside."

I realize this little show is for the benefit of the boozy quartet. Andy knows they've made me, and he doesn't want prying eyes speculating as to what that bag might hold.

I reach in, pull out what looks like a long box of gourmet chocolate. It's a good disguise. The box is even shrink-wrapped for effect. Holding it, my hand starts to quiver. I think: *It's been too long.*

"Only the best for my gal," Andy says.

How long has it been since someone called me his gal? Partly to play along and partly because the alcohol is kicking in, I lean across the bar, kiss him full on the lips.

Now the band is eyeing us hard.

"I've always wanted to do that," I say.

"Yeah," he says, "me too. How about we—"

"Hold on," I say.

I'm getting a text. The vibration in my pocket startles me. I stand, dig out my phone. Then I feel myself go white.

"What?" Andy says. "What is it?"

Just three words on the screen: Tonight in Marseille.

"I have to go," I say.

Andy looks confused, maybe hurt.

"But I thought—"

"I have to go shopping for a slicker," I tell him.

"A what now?"

"A raincoat."

I hand over a thick wad of cash, snatch up the bag, and run out the door. I hear the musicians laughing behind me.

CHAPTER

IT WILL BE HARD to pull this one off without leaving a trace. He needs access to a southern-facing window on a low floor of the Astrophil Hotel. The Astrophil Hotel, where Dr. Amy Winston and her baby district attorney will marry. The Astrophil, with its gaudy baroque flair reminding the world that America is just watered-down Europe.

His desire to liberate Cheryl has caused him to be hasty. Ideally, he would spend weeks, even months, planning this kind of kill. He sits now at a computer in yet another branch of the New York Public Library, searching for floor plans of the hotel, hoping to find a well-situated conference room that might be vacant in the early morning.

But then, even if he were to find such a room, he would need to know how often the security guards make their rounds. He would need to know where the security cameras are situated, and who is sitting at the bank of monitors, watching. Without time to prepare, he will have to risk collateral damage. A shootout at the Astrophil would make an unsightly sidebar to the Night Sniper's story.

Still, he does not feel anxious, but rather exhilarated, up to the challenge. He is smart and willing. His skill never wavers. He can allow himself to court danger. Not every time, but this time.

He finds his way in almost by accident, though he does not believe in accidents. In his search for blueprints and floor plans, he comes across a *New York Times* article about the recent conversion of a high percentage of Astrophil Hotel rooms to condominiums. The conversions are finished, the apartments sold, but the buyers do not move in for another month. The photo accompanying the article shows the exterior of the Astrophil at night, the majority of rooms pitch-dark.

It is simply a question of finding his way into one of these vacant apartments.

As luck would have it, this is his night off. At 7:00 p.m., he walks the southern block of the Astrophil, wearing accessories bought from a street vendor: large square glasses and a wide-brimmed cap that reads YES, I'M BALD.

He takes the same walk again at eight, this time in a BRING BACK LETTERMAN J jacket and a faux fur trapper's hat. At 10:00, in fedora and windbreaker, he joins the long line of film buffs waiting to see a revival of *Amélie* at the Marseillaise, though he does not buy a ticket.

He makes two more passes, at eleven and midnight, before settling on an empty fourth-floor condo.

CHAPTER 26

ANDY'S VICODIN CHOCOLATES HAVE me feeling warm and tingly and like I can float above whatever's out to do me harm. On the subway to Brooklyn, I sit straddling the twine-handled paper bag and my new purchase: a dark-gray raincoat with wrap-around belt, a close replica of the one in Jarry's picture.

It's 7:30 — rush hour for the industrious, the ones who stay late adjusting the columns of their spreadsheet or giving that drywall a final coat of paint. I look around, think: *These are the citizens I swore to protect.* And then that warmth I'm feeling spreads to all my fellow travelers, like Vicodin is some sort of Zen shortcut.

Before I checked into Lifeline, I stashed my stuff at Square Footage, a sprawling storage facility on Fourth Avenue, in the section of Park Slope we used to call Park Slump, though good luck affording an apartment here now. During peak hours, staff will ride you out to your unit on a golf cart, but now I have to walk.

My unit is at the far end of the far row. I punch in the code, open the bright orange roller door, pull it shut again behind me. I switch on the overhead light, stand staring at columns of cardboard boxes on one side, hastily stacked household items on the other.

I think: *Can all this crap really be mine?*

I've had the same furniture since college: dinged-up futon frame, mattress with duct-taped tears, the kind of floor lamps you assemble piece by piece, a flea market drafting table I use as a desk. No kitchen or dining room set, no armchair or loveseat. A bachelorette all the way.

I have a narrow aisle to maneuver in. I shuffle to the rear, start digging, pulling down boxes and stacking them beside me. The labels seem to refer to periods in my life instead of the junk inside.

Law Textbooks: a time when I saw myself trying cases, targeting not just criminals but crime rings, dismantling whole organizations one rung at a time. Cheryl Mabern, the crusader district attorney. But long afternoons in the library made me restless. No way I could be cooped up in an office or courtroom. Trophies And Medals: I bowled my first perfect game when I was thirteen. As a kid, I was into anything that got me dirty or sweaty or gave me calluses. In high school I tried to start a female wrestling team, but no one was interested except a heavily freckled redhead with bone disease who wanted to be the mascot.

Clippings, Etc.: A box crammed with dark-blue binders and a single photo album populated with relatives I mostly don't recognize. I remove the lid, pull out a binder marked Lower East Side: 1998, my rookie year. I open it, start flipping through. Street maps, subway tunnel blueprints, tenement floor plans, wedding announcements, obituaries, takeout menus—anything and everything having to do with the precinct I patrolled.

The last few laminated pages are dedicated to news

articles chronicling the strangest cases I caught that year. The identical twins who blamed each other for murdering their super. The bank thief who tunneled up into a safe only to have the tunnel collapse behind him.

I think: *You meant well, Cheryl. And you worked damn hard, right from the beginning.*

But what does it add up to if I'm no longer a cop?

I shuffle boxes around for a good half hour before I uncover the one I want. It's crammed with stuffed animals my parents gave me when they still thought they'd be raising a princess. The light-brown bear in the tutu and the pelican with ballerina slippers sewn to her feet have seen better days. At the bottom of the box I find what I came for: a tattered and oversized baby blanket. Wrapped inside are a revolver and a bulletproof vest.

Not that I know what I'll do with them. I have no plan—just rotating images stuck in my head. There's me laid out on the pavement, me standing over the Sniper's body. I can't say how I got there in either case.

Before I go, I take another dip into Andy's chocolates.

CHAPTER 27

THE HOTEL'S INTERIOR IS a study in contrasts. With angels painted on the ceiling and overwrought chandeliers, the place looks like the missing wing at Versailles, but its inner workings are worthy of *Travel + Leisure* magazine: hydraulic doors, surround-sound playing soft Chopin, a bank of flat-screens in the lobby silently broadcasting news from around the globe. Even the elevator, with its flashing control panel and wrought-iron door, is something new made to look old.

Miles exits on the fourth floor. He's replaced the guitar case with a Gucci valise on wheels, wears a Montecristi hat and Armani overcoat, an outfit designed to help him blend with the rich. Not that there's anyone to blend with: the floor is more than deserted—it's still under renovation. The hallway floor is covered in plastic tarp. Electric sanders and paintbrushes lie out in plain view. Miles is thankful no one works the red-eye shift.

By his calculation, the second apartment from the east end of the building should offer an ideal vantage point. He intends to force the lock but discovers that the door, freshly painted, is ajar.

He takes out a flashlight, steps inside. The apartment is little more than a shell, albeit an expansive shell: twelve-foot ceilings, a sprawling living/dining area, extra-wide archways. The walls are painted a tasteful shade of pale blue. The floors are oak.

But it's the sheer scale that makes the strongest impression. Miles shines his flashlight down a seemingly endless corridor. A small family could go for days without crossing paths. He is tempted to give himself the tour, see what kind of appliances the one percent favor these days, but it is nearing 4:00 a.m., and that is not why he's here.

He takes off his shoes, lifts up his suitcase, tiptoes to the living area's centermost window, and looks out. The theater and sidewalk are laid bare before him. The degree of difficulty will be low, even if the risk is higher than ever.

He kneels down, opens the suitcase, begins assembling his father's rifle. For the first time since his mission began, the Night Sniper feels his heart beating hard against his chest.

CHAPTER 28

I STOP FOR A caipirinha and a basket of fried plantains at a Brazilian place near the Marseillaise. The restaurant/bar is open all night, or at least I've never seen it closed. I've never seen it full, either. There must be something going on in a back room, but this isn't my beat, and the food and booze are priced right.

At 3:00 a.m. it's just me and the bartender. He's engrossed in a soccer match that's being played live somewhere in the world. I take a stool at the far end, away from the TV. He waits for a time-out to mix my drink.

Let's keep the edge going, I think, slipping another pill from the stash in my jeans pocket.

I scarf down six inches of fried plantain. Vicodin is good for that.

Call Randy, I tell myself. *Do it now.*

So why don't I reach for my phone?

Maybe I'm afraid if the cavalry shows up too early they'll spoil the show, because the Jarry-like image stuck in my head now—in black and white, for dramatic flair—features my corpse outlined in chalk. I see Randy leaning over me, Pete standing behind him. And there, in the not-too-distant background, are Patsy, Kelly, and Dennis, surrounding a cuffed Sniper.

They'll write songs about me. "The Ballad of Cheryl Mabern." Disgraced and misunderstood, she went out a hero.

It's a question of timing. I need the good guys to arrive after I've been shot, but before the Sniper has cleared the building.

But then if I want to die, why am I wearing my vest? It's like I'm hedging my bets. If he sticks to his routine, I live. But maybe he'll change it up, put one in my brain. Maybe the vest is faulty.

If I do live, I'll make the collar myself: a citizen's arrest.

Either way, I win.

The streets are deserted, the skyscrapers and lampposts lit for me alone. Jarry had it all wrong. What I feel now is the opposite of distress. There's no place I'd rather be.

Just a block to go. The Vicodin is taking over. The buildings and parked cars seem to be coming at me in slow motion, like 48th Street has been hoisted onto a malfunctioning passenger walk.

I lean against a mailbox, take out my phone. Just two rings before Randy picks up.

"I know where he is," I say.

As I start toward the theater, I imagine every squad car in New York switching direction at once.

CHAPTER 29

HE SPOTS HER WALKING up the block, moving in and out of shadow as she passes under the streetlights, wearing a raincoat nearly identical to the one in Jarry's photo. Her steps are quick but unsteady. Cheryl has been drinking. Miles feels a tinge of disappointment.

Now and again she glances up at the facing buildings. He wants to be seen, but not yet—not before the final moment. He will not take aim until she is in position.

There is no one following her, no eyes peering from parked cars, no helicopters lurking overhead. She has come alone—his first willing subject—evidence that the service he provides is a welcome one.

She reaches the theater, feigns interest in a film poster, her back to him, her body swaying. Miles cracks the window, rests the barrel of his father's rifle on the ledge. Cheryl turns, steps to the curb, stands directly beneath the streetlamp with her hands in her pockets, exactly like Jarry's subject.

Miles savors the moment a beat too long—Cheryl breaks the pose, bites at her bottom lip, furrows her brow. Miles is close enough to count the worry lines. He kneels down, unscrews the high-tech scope from his father's rifle. He will sight this shot on his own. The brief exchange between them will be simple, intimate.

He raises the rifle, presses the butt against his shoulder, then stops himself, brought up short by a faint tremor in his right hand. Once again, his pulse quickens. His palms turn damp.

He remembers his first kill: a corporate lawyer who'd quashed a lawsuit against big tobacco. He remembers lying motionless on his belly at the edge of a rock outcropping, watching the lake for hours before the lawyer arrived. He feels his father lying beside him, armed only with a pair of binoculars. He feels his legs trembling as his target wades out into the water, leans back to make his first cast.

"Now," his father said.

But Miles couldn't. He couldn't squeeze his finger, couldn't feel his arms or legs—not as though they were numb, but as though they were gone entirely. He braced himself for a hard blow, was surprised by his father's hand resting gently on the small of his back.

"Everybody dies," his father said. "All you'll be taking from him is time—time he'd spend poisoning man and earth for his own gain. A person like that has no qualms leaving the world worse off than he found it. So you just keep breathing, let your mind go blank, and pull that trigger."

Afterward: a ceremonial shot of whisky from his father's canteen. A rite of passage. The closest his father ever came to praising him.

Miles takes a breath, lets his mind go blank, sets the

rifle back in place. Cheryl is whistling to herself now. He can just make out the melody—anxious and broken. He wills her to look up. She obliges. Seeing him, her face goes calm.

She smiles, shuts her eyes.

CHAPTER 30

I RUN MY FINGERS over the vest but can't find the bullet, can't feel where I've been hit.

I think: *Taking the painkillers in advance, that was smart,* then laugh myself into a blackout. When I come to, I know it's the drugs and not the bullet holding me to the cement.

Time and again I fail to hold my eyes open, fail to raise my chest off the ground.

I see things: a helicopter with its blades on the bottom, a rainbow dripping blood, bodies falling from rooftops.

I see faces hovering over me, swelling and deflating, blurring around the edges. I see my mother, back from the grave, grimacing, not knowing how to soothe me. There and gone in a flash.

I see the girl I sat next to in homeroom freshman year. She still has the frizzy 1980s hair and the gum stuck in her braces, like she lived all this time without aging a day.

And then I see him. Smiling, leaning close, looking dapper in his old-style white hat with the black band. I try to reach for him, but my arms are molded into the concrete. His face changes shape like it's made of quicksilver. He raps his knuckles on my vest.

"Tsk, tsk," he says. "That's cheating, Cheryl."

I close my eyes, feel cold metal against my throat. I wait for the blade to break my skin, but when I open my eyes again it's Randy's face I see. His features are clear, distinct. He's holding me by the shoulders, lifting me partway off the ground.

"What did you do?" he says. "Damn it, Cheryl. What did you do?"

Little by little, I become aware of the chaos behind him: sirens blaring, bosses barking orders, uniforms running back and forth, not knowing what to do with themselves.

I hear a voice I think is Pete's say: "There's no blood. She isn't hit."

"Vest," I say. It comes out like a croak.

Randy drops his head in what I take for relief. I manage to reach up, grab his hand.

"It's all right," he says. "The paramedics will be here any second."

"No," I say. "No hospital. Get me out of here."

He knows right away what I mean: hand Branford my blood report and I'm done. Maybe he didn't need me to say it.

"I can't do that, Cheryl," he whispers. "Not this time."

But I'm not asking for my sake.

"You need me," I tell him. "I'm the one that got away."

When I wake up again, I'm lying on a cot in the cell we call the tomb. It's buried in the basement, across from the boiler room. We use it to hold suspects we want to scare—an hour down here and they understand just how easy it would be to get lost in the system.

Randy's in the cell with me, standing guard. He sees I'm awake, points to a tray on the floor. There's a pot of coffee, a dusty mug, a plate stacked with ancient-looking toast.

"Am I under arrest?" I ask.

"You should be," he says. "You might still be."

He pushes his back off the bars, steps toward me. It takes me an awkward moment to get myself out of a prone position.

"Coffee?" he asks.

Before I can answer, he pours me a cup, drops in a half-dozen sugar cubes, and stirs. I take a long swallow. Randy picks up a small trash can and sets it at my feet, as if to say: *Go ahead and heave, skel.*

The miracle is that I don't have to.

He gives me a beat to get my head right. I glance down, realize I'm wearing clothes I've never seen before: a St. John's hoodie, men's sweatpants, thermal socks. I look back up at Randy.

"Did you…?"

"I had to make sure you could breathe," he says. "And I couldn't let anyone find you down here wearing that vest."

I want the cot to snap in two and swallow me whole.

"So what was your brilliant plan?" he asks.

I stammer out an answer:

"I was setting a trap," I say.

"Really?" Randy says. "You might have clued me in earlier. Your stunt cost a man his life."

Now I'm all the way awake.

"What are you talking about?" I ask.

"We found the hotel's Chief of Security slumped on

the desk in front of his surveillance monitors. There was a small needle mark in his neck. Of course the cameras had been disabled."

I stare into my cup.

"It should have been me," I say.

I can't tell if I've said it loud enough for Randy to hear.

"The only question that matters now is, what do we do next?" Randy says.

I stand, start to pace. I'm more alert than I'd like to be.

"We set a better trap," I say.

"How?"

I think: *Time to come all the way clean, Cheryl.*

"I saw his face," I say. "He'll have to come for me."

CHAPTER

HE STANDS IN FRONT of the television wearing nothing but boxers and a T-shirt, toes gripping at the hardwood, fingernails digging into his thighs.

"Police are not releasing the name of the Night Sniper's first surviving victim," Allie White announces, staring into the camera with a look that seems to Miles more silly than sultry. "A spokesperson for the task force will only disclose that the woman is in stable condition. The Sniper, it seems, misfired for the first time."

Miles stops short of kicking in the screen.

"Do you hear that, Cheryl?" he yells. "Someone in the world thinks you're stable. You're hiding and telling lies."

He switches off the TV, drops onto the loveseat, lies on his side in a fetal position. He cannot say how many hours he's gone without sleep. Fatigue is catching up with him, violently and all at once. He shuts his eyes, sees himself kneeling over Cheryl, knife in hand, blade to her throat. He feels himself wavering, withdrawing.

His eyes snap back open.

"Pathetic," he barks. "Ridiculous."

He speaks the words aloud, but it is his father's voice he hears. A voice that hounds him, scolding and berating, refusing to let Miles sleep until he understands why his blade failed to break Cheryl Mabern's skin.

Instead of dreaming, Miles remembers.

The solid-oak sticks are barely padded. His father, seventy pounds heavier than the eleven-year-old Miles, holds nothing back. Miles blocks blow after blow until his forearms are a single, aching bruise. He falls to his knees, arms curled around his head, screams for his father to stop.

The sticks hit the ground. Miles looks up, but too late: the heel of his father's boot catches him square on the forehead. Miles comes to lying in the same open field, his father hovering above him, the lecture already under way:

"There's no saying uncle in war. You fight or you die. You understand?"

"But I…"

"There is no YOU. There's only the mission. And there is no failure, only death. You think a sniper is spared hand-to-hand combat? Say the enemy spots you, shells you out of your perch, surrounds you. You want to die alone, or take a few of them with you?"

From then on, the drills come nonstop. Early mornings spent in a meat locker, stabbing at a side of beef with a hunting knife, practicing thrusts and lunges, fingers locking around the handle, frozen. His father striking his bare calves with a willow branch whenever his technique faltered.

Afternoons in the baking sun, trying again and again to slip his father's chokehold, one leg shackled to a fifty-pound dumbbell.

Evenings blindfolded in the already pitch-black woods, listening for his father's footsteps.

All so that when the time came he wouldn't hesitate to see his mission through.

This morning he'd hesitated. He'd allowed a lifetime of training to be undone by whatever it was he felt for Detective Cheryl Mabern. And that after she'd already duped him, made him look like a fool.

Before Miles can continue, before his ultimate rendezvous with Cheryl, he will need to regain his confidence, prove to himself that he is worthy of his mission. His father, he is certain, would agree. Miles needs to prove that he can kill at close range.

It is Amy who, early the next morning, provides him with a plan. They are sitting in the break room, playing a hand of Rummy 500, waiting for their next call. Amy does the talking.

"Why the Astrophil?" she asks. "How many hotels do you think there are in New York? Why in the great wide world did the bastard have to go and pick the one I'm supposed to get married in?"

Miles takes a card off the deck, throws it onto the pile.

"I mean, I have to cancel now," she continues. "The place is tainted. It might as well be haunted. Ron says I'm being ridiculous. He says the fact that the woman lived is a good sign. Like God is looking down and blessing our nuptials. Now I ask you: who is being ridiculous?"

She throws down the queen of hearts, the card Miles has been waiting for. He picks it up, lays out three of a kind.

"Well?" Amy asks. "What do you think?"

He smiles to himself, the plan already forming.

"About what?" he asks.

Amy gives a rehearsed pout.

"Should we or shouldn't we get married in a place where that psychopath almost murdered a woman?"

Miles pauses for effect.

"I don't think it makes a bit of difference," he says. "I don't think it makes a bit of difference if you get married or don't. I don't think who the Sniper kills or doesn't has a thing to do with you."

Amy looks more startled than hurt.

"What are you saying?" she asks.

"I'm saying that you can't possibly love Ron because narcissists aren't capable of love. And he can't possibly love you for the same reason. I just hope that someday you'll both grow up and realize you aren't the center of anyone's universe but your own."

He could go on, but she's already running from the room, crushing tears with her palms. The stage is set for his apology.

I GLANCE AT THE skyline in the Cavalier's rearview mirror. We're surrounded by refineries, their smokestacks spewing black. We've timed it right, hit the late morning gap in traffic. Randy's going about twenty above the limit. He looks anxious, both hands on the wheel. We're on our way to meet Alfred Jarry.

"Remind me why I'm doing this," Randy says.

"Because I'm not fit to drive."

"You're also not a cop."

"I know," I say. "We're going to use that."

"Use it how?"

"You'll see."

He voices his objections all the way upstate, but he never turns the car around.

Jarry's driveway might be the longest part of the trip. It's a private paved road that keeps going and going through an autumnal forest with leaves turning every color. Randy hunches over the wheel, his jaw hanging partway open.

"Jarry owns all this?" he asks.

"His father was in steel," I say.

Randy shakes his head.

"What does this guy know about distressed souls?"

The road cuts through a meadow now. Randy takes his foot off the gas, points.

"Jarry has his own herd of deer," he says.

The asphalt gives way to a gravel parking area with a fountain in the middle. The fountain features little cherubic figures with their mouths open and no water coming out. Behind the fountain is a château-like mansion that looks to be closing in on disrepair—missing windows on the top floor, portico columns replaced with splintering wooden beams, stone chipping all around the facade.

"Looks like Jarry's about tapped out," Randy says.

Besides our Cavalier, the only car in sight is a two-door Civic from the late eighties.

"Can't be a lot of money in snapping pictures," I say. "The guy's ninety-four. That's enough years to stretch any inheritance thin."

I figure the Civic belongs to a nurse or butler, but it's Jarry himself who answers the door. He's smiling and spry, like he forgot to continue aging over the last twenty years.

"You're the officers who called," he says. "I'm sorry, I've already forgotten your names."

"Detective Hall," Randy says, extending his hand.

"And I'm Cheryl Mabern," I say. "I'm no longer a detective. I'm here on special assignment. That's what we wanted to talk to you about."

He leads us into a big open room furnished with what looks like a couch and an armchair—both are covered in white sheets like the room's about to be painted, but the sheets are covered in years' worth of dust.

Jarry takes the armchair. Behind him there's a

fireplace with a missing mantel and flakes of plaster where the ash should be. I imagine the chimney clogged with dead birds.

"Help yourselves," Jarry says, pointing to a pitcher of lemonade and a plate of crackers set out on a TV tray.

Randy fills two glasses.

"Now tell me," Jarry says.

I look him over. He's thin but not frail, his speech slow but still sharp. He's tall, with iron-rod posture like ancient yogis you see practicing in Columbus Park. His ring of hair is jet-black, and I wonder who he dyes it for.

Randy gives me a nod like this is my show. I lay out the major detail we've been keeping from the press: *his* photos as inspiration for the Sniper's spree. I'm half afraid he'll keel over with the news, but for a good while he doesn't react at all. Then:

"Those photos were part of my personal collection. They hung in this room."

He gestures to the walls, and I see the nail holes haven't been plastered over.

"I never meant for anyone to set eyes on them," he says. "But in case you haven't noticed, I'm old. When the people from the museum came calling last spring, my vanity got the better of me. I had nothing else to give them. I haven't picked up a camera—at least not professionally—in twenty years."

"Why not?" Randy asks. "If you don't mind my saying, you're a young ninety-four."

"Simple," Jarry said. "I lost my sight. Most of it, anyway. I can still make out shapes. Shadowy figures."

"I'm sorry to hear that," Randy says.

Jarry shuts his eyes as though to drive home the fact of his blindness. When he opens them again, he says:

"How exactly can I help?"

I don't pull any punches.

"We want to use you as bait," I say.

I expect him to show us the door, but instead he leans forward, smiles.

"That's a rare opportunity," he says. "Few people get to be of any use at the end."

CHAPTER

HE DOES NOT RING from the lobby for fear that Amy will refuse to let him in. He has a better chance, he thinks, if he appears directly at her door, brandishing the oversized bouquet of flowers he picked up at the corner deli. He waits, drifts in with a pack of adolescents returning home from school.

He has been to Amy's apartment once before, back when it was still just her apartment, when Ron was nothing but a blind date waiting to happen. She was new to the city, had invited staff from the ER over for a cocktail housewarming party. Miles brought a bottle of amaretto and, as a joke gift, a vintage model of the game Operation.

The evening would have been wholly forgettable had the alcohol not made short work of Amy's inhibitions. Early on, she called him "cute" in a tone he found ambiguous. Later, as guests sat cross-legged around his gift taking turns extracting fake shrapnel with tiny pliers, he felt her thigh pressing firmly against his.

Over the following weeks, he hesitated, failed time

and again to act. Before he knew it, Amy morphed into a doll programmed to say just one word: *Ron.*

He knocks, prepares to beg his way inside, is surprised when the door simply opens. He thinks: *You can take the girl out of the heartland…*

He has the impression that he is looking down on her, as though she were standing in a sunken living room, but then he realizes that he has caught her unaware: she has not had time to slip on her platform shoes. For an awkward beat, she stares at him, says nothing. Her face is flushed, her eyes red around the rims. Miles cannot tell if he woke her or interrupted a fit of crying.

"I wanted to apologize," he says, handing her the bouquet of flowers. "I haven't been sleeping, and I'm not myself. I didn't mean any of what I said."

She accepts the bouquet, but her expression remains sullen.

"I think you meant every word," she says. "It didn't exactly seem like something you were making up on the fly."

He hesitates, considering which way to play it, decides to go with what she most likely wants to hear:

"I was jealous," he says. "I am jealous."

"Jealous?"

He drops his head in mock shame.

"Can I come in?" he asks. "Can we talk?"

She looks down at the flowers in her hand, steps aside, and waves him in.

"Have a seat while I find a vase," she says. "Would you like some tea?"

"That would be lovely," Miles says.

The living room is just as he remembered it: a

characterless box. Her attempts to lend it character—sickly-looking plants, a West African tapestry she most likely bought on St. Marks Place—have only backfired.

The world will not miss her, Miles thinks. *It will merely adjust to her absence. And yet, not so long ago, you thought you were in love with her.*

No, he corrects himself. *I was in love with her work. That's an easy mistake.*

"I'm just waiting for the water to boil," Amy calls from the kitchen.

Miles has no desire to draw this out, no desire to watch her suffer. He bends forward, pulls his father's army-issue hunting knife from an ankle holster.

"Tell me," he says, approaching the kitchen, "when do you expect Ron home?"

"Not for at least a couple of hours," she says.

And then she turns, sees—even before she spots the blade—that it is not Miles standing there, but rather a pitiless shell in the guise of Miles, a manifestation of evil who will not spare her life no matter how hard she begs or bargains.

CHAPTER 34

HE EXPENDS WHAT FEELS like the last of his energy wrapping Amy up in a shower curtain and setting her in the tub. He is weary, would like to sleep, but he must be alert when Ron walks through the door.

He sits back down on the couch, switches on the television. His pulse quickens to see Cheryl's face once again taking up the screen. His bullet, it seems, did not slow her down in the least. She is standing in front of what looks like a low-rent château. An off-camera reporter holds a microphone in her face.

"It's true," she says, "that I'm no longer a member of the NYPD, but nothing in the terms of my suspension prohibits me from entering the private sector."

The anonymous male reporter counters with:

"But you say your work here is linked to your work on the Night Sniper Task Force. Won't the brass at One Police Plaza see that as a conflict?"

Cheryl flashes a condescending smile.

"I'm working security," she says. "I'm not investigating the Sniper: I'm protecting his most likely target. The NYPD should thank me."

"I don't understand," the reporter says. "The Sniper has never struck outside the city."

And he never will, Miles thinks. *You've gone from hot to very, very cold, Cheryl.*

She speaks slowly, deliberately:

"The man who lives here is, through no fault or intention of his own, the Sniper's inspiration. His name is Alfred Jarry. He's a world-renowned photographer, and we have reason to believe that the Sniper is choosing his victims based on a series of photos Mr. Jarry took in the late seventies and early eighties."

Miles is standing now, his blood pumping.

"These photos," Cheryl continues, "focus on solitary figures in the city at night. Our fear—my fear—is that once the Sniper has run out of photos, he will come for the photographer."

"Close the circle, so to speak?" the reporter says.

"Yes. Mr. Jarry is elderly, frail. He is himself a solitary figure. I don't plan to leave his side until the Sniper is brought to justice."

The reporter reminds his audience that they've heard it here first. Miles switches off the television, grins to himself.

Invitation accepted, Cheryl.

He runs a finger along the blade of his father's knife, willing Ron to come home early.

CHAPTER 35

WE'VE SET JARRY UP at his hotel of choice, assigned Kelly to stand guard. Dennis doesn't miss the opportunity.

"Here's your chance, Kelly," he says. "Widow Jarry will do quite well for herself."

Randy's manning headquarters back in the city, running interference with Branford. That leaves Pete, Patsy, Dennis, and me to cover ten thousand feet of crumbling château. There's no security system. There aren't even locks on the windows. And outside there's a perimeter of forest—an even 360 degrees of approach points to surveil.

And of course the operation is unsanctioned. No backup. No SWAT team hiding in the trees. Patsy, Dennis, Pete, Kelly, Randy: they've put their faith in me, gone rogue on my account. They're unlikely knights rallying around the disgraced princess in the dilapidated castle.

Or maybe they just want to catch a killer, save some lives. Either way, they're risking their careers.

We sit around a fold-out table in a sprawling kitchen that's been gutted but never renovated. We're studying a map of the mansion, a map we drew ourselves. Twelve large and mostly empty rooms on the first floor, fifteen slightly smaller rooms on the second floor. There's an endless unfinished basement, a loftlike attic that's been collecting cobwebs for untold decades.

"I know it's late to ask, but you sure this will work?" Dennis asks. "I mean, breaking in, killing at close range…the setup doesn't exactly fit his MO."

"Me and Jarry in one place?" I say. "The reward merits the risk."

Pete taps our blueprint.

"A lot of terrain," he says.

"Yeah," I say, "but lucky for us we aren't looking to keep him out."

"We still need to see him coming," Patsy says.

Dennis shivers.

"Jarry should charge the draft in this place rent," he says.

Patsy leans over the map, draws circles around four second-floor rooms: north, south, east, and west.

"Our lookout points," she says. "Between the four of us we can cover the full tree line. Whoever spots him jumps on the radio."

"So we sit at the windows, waiting for a sniper?" Dennis says.

"We'll have the lights off," Patsy says. "And the shades drawn."

I take the pencil, draw a fifth circle.

"Except for here," I say. "In a place this big, we need to know where he's heading. So we'll draw him to Jarry's bedroom. We'll leave the lights on and the TV turned up."

"He should buy it," Patsy says. "Everyone knows old people don't sleep."

I nod.

"Jarry's suite has double doors leading into each adjoining room. Once we've spotted him, that's where we'll set up. Two of us in the room to the east, two in the room to the west."

"We'll have to move like lightning," Pete says.

"Better make sure Dennis doesn't have far to run," Patsy says.

"Thanks," Dennis says. "I appreciate the consideration."

CHAPTER 36

TWO HOURS IN A cubicle at the midtown library yields the location of Jarry's home and a tour of the area via Google Earth. The mansion is secluded, surrounded by woods. The woods give way to national forest. Miles can leave his rental car on an access road, hike onto Jarry's property.

Under normal circumstances, he would have his choice of entry points and escape routes, but he cannot count on Cheryl playing fair: it is possible she will have a small army camped in the forest. The challenge excites him.

He'd hoped to find information about the interior of Jarry's home—a photo spread in *Architectural Digest,* or, better still, a blueprint in the registry of historical structures. But Jarry is not the type to open up, let others in. At least not the Jarry he imagines: a recluse who dislikes people yet feels compassion for them.

He has no doubt that Cheryl is using the old man. Jarry must be on his last mental legs if he's agreed to hire an NYPD outcast. Still, Miles cannot fault Cheryl: the game they're playing assumes the highest possible stakes.

He calls up a new search engine, types in "Alfred Jarry's Castle on the Hudson," then deletes every word but "Jarry" and "Castle." He skims the results, his mind spinning out questions and obstacles.

Questions: How will he arm himself? How will he circumvent the alarm system, if there is one? How will he find Jarry in a house that large? Will he find Cheryl, or let her find him?

Obstacles: Cheryl knows he's coming; he'd be a fool to believe she was alone.

Still, however many people Cheryl might have with her, there are only two targets Miles cares about. He can turn this to his advantage.

And then he finds it, buried on the fifth page of his search. Not what he was looking for, but the next best thing: Lage Coryell, the name of the architect who designed Jarry's house.

Miles begins a fresh search, learns that a graduate student in Ithaca manages a website dedicated to Coryell's work. An Overview tab claims that Coryell's designs are steeped in nostalgia: though he came to prominence just after World War II, he built in the Georgian style of the early nineteenth century. Apparently, he wanted to "restore a sense of grandeur to a traumatized world."

You mean to the rich, Miles thinks. *You would have been high on my father's list.*

The website's homepage is a photo of a Georgian-style mansion similar to Jarry's home. The windows of the mansion function as a menu. Miles moves the cursor from window to window until the word *BLUEPRINTS* appears on the screen. Miles all but leaps out of his seat.

He spends hours studying every line of the twenty-four archived prints, does not leave his seat until an automated voice announces that the library is closing. By the end, he's found the common feature that presents an opportunity. Coryell worked with a Cold War sensibility: every home he designed between 1947 and 1962, the year of his death, includes an underground concrete bunker linked to the main residence by fifty yards of tunnel.

Would Cheryl know this? Would the fading Jarry have thought to tell her?

Miles cannot be certain, but odds are against it, and every mission requires at least one leap of faith.

The trick will be finding the entrance to this bunker in a dense forest in the dead of night. Once again, Miles feels up to the challenge.

CHAPTER 37

WE'VE GOT A HALF hour till sunset. Pete and I are decorating Jarry's room for effect, making it up to look like his final resting place. We've loaded a TV tray with a dozen pill bottles and a six-pack of Ensure. We stacked magazines on the nightstand, set a chamber pot at the foot of the bed. We stuffed pillows under the comforter to make the shape of a body. The more the Sniper has to look at, the longer we have to take him unawares.

"I think we're done," Pete says.

"I think so," I say.

We stand there reviewing our work, neither of us heading for the door. I sense there's something Pete wants to say. After a long beat, he comes out with it:

"So Bryzinski picked up one of the undercovers?"

I'd been hoping for something else—something along the lines of a declaration.

"Yeah," I say. "He did."

"And then what happened?"

Of course I want to tell him: the story makes me look good. And this is a sleepover in a castle on a cold and windy night. We're supposed to tell ghost stories.

If only the undercover hadn't been Randy.

"And then we caught him," I say.

"That's it? No chase? No dramatic finish?"

I glance over at him. His grin says: "Come on, you know you want to."

Okay, I tell myself. *But you don't mention Randy by name.*

"Bryzinski made the undercover," I say.

"Made him how?"

Is Pete a gossip hound, or just eager to learn from other people's mistakes? Either way, I keep going.

"He asked questions the undercover couldn't answer, questions anyone who'd done time at Rikers would ace. What do they serve for lunch on Mondays? What do they call the special housing unit on the third tier? By this time Bryzinski knew we were getting close. He was playing it careful."

"Okay," Pete says. "But it's a cab, right? The undercover's sitting behind the driver, and he's strapped. Plus I'm guessing you've got a five-car tail and a battalion of squad cars at the ready. So why does it matter if the cop got made? There's nowhere for Bryzinski to go, and if he tries anything, then you know you've got the right guy."

"You'd think," I say.

"But...?"

We're sitting side by side on the bed now. Pete's looking at me. I'm looking out the window.

"Bryzinski had the car tricked out. Bulletproof glass dividing the front and back. Locks only he could open. And..."

I hesitate. I don't like remembering this last part. I don't like remembering Randy the way I found him—tied spread-eagle to a table, eyes red and swollen, skin turning colors, muttering a long stream of nonsense.

"And?" Pete pushes.

"And he had the back rigged like a gas chamber. He knocked our man out cold."

CHAPTER

IT TOOK BRYZINSKI FIVE blocks to lose four-fifths of our tail—everyone but me," I say. "He bolted a red light, ran over a pedestrian, then sped a hundred miles an hour the wrong way up a one-way street."

Pete's quiet now, maybe imagining himself in the back of Bryzinski's car.

"I followed them to Jackson Heights," I say. "Bryzinski turned so hard into an alleyway that I went skidding past him. The alley was lined with automatic garages. By the time I backed up, the car had vanished."

"So you call for reinforcements," Pete says. "Choppers, SWAT, the whole nine yards. Shut the block down."

"That's what Branford wanted," I say. "He was screaming at me over the radio. But cavalry would've got the undercover killed. If Bryzinski thought he'd gotten away, he'd take his time, enjoy himself. Especially with a cop. If he heard us bearing down, that cop'd be dead in seconds. I wanted to at least give him time to fight."

"How many houses are we talking about?" Pete asks.

"Seven or eight."

"So how'd you narrow it down? I'm guessing the mail hadn't been delivered at six in the morning."

"I saw the trash was out for pickup," I say. "A can for every garage. I figured Bryzinski might have tossed something I'd recognize. So I parked on a side street, took a blanket from the trunk, mussed up my hair, and played homeless.

"Third house in, I found dozens of empty packets of ramen noodles—like whoever lived there ate nothing else. That's con food. They make it in their cells to avoid the canteen slop. They get addicted to the stuff."

"Could've been a college kid," Pete says.

"I only had time for one guess. It seemed like a safe bet."

"And it was?"

"Yeah. I knew as soon as I went around to the front. The first-floor windows were blacked out with thick wool blankets. Whoever lived there didn't want anyone seeing inside. And they didn't want anyone showing up unannounced. There were about a dozen deadbolts on the door."

"So how'd you get in?"

"I took out my gun, wrapped the blanket around my head, and jumped through the window."

"Like an action figure."

"I didn't even think about it—there was no other way. When I looked up, I saw the undercover right there in front of me, tied to an operating table, drugged out of his mind. The entire place—floor, ceiling, walls—was wrapped in plastic. I was lucky. Bryzinski hadn't started cutting yet. The blade had come loose on his shank, and he was wrapping duct tape around the handle. He saw me, pulled out a real knife, and lunged for the table."

"And you shot him?" Pete says.

"I caught him in the throat. He bled out before the paramedics got there."

"The undercover have a name?" Pete asks.

"No," I say. "No name."

And then I bite my lip hard thinking how Randy has been held hostage all this time by what he thinks he owes me. Because I've put him through enough to chase anyone else away, and he was only in danger to begin with because he was following my plan. Just like Dennis, Pete, and Patsy are following my plan now.

"All right," Pete says. "I won't push."

I glance out the window.

"Almost dark," I say.

CHAPTER 39

THE ENTRANCE TO THE bunker is covered with a canvas tarp, its fabric tattered and stained from years of rain and snow. Miles holds his flashlight in his mouth, pulls the tarp back, watches the garter snakes scatter.

The round iron door looks like a rusted manhole cover. He takes a pair of bolt cutters from his backpack, removes the padlock, discovers a metal ship's ladder descending into a deep darkness. He starts down, pulls the door shut behind him.

The large, subterranean chamber is made of poured concrete and lined with enough bunk beds to sleep as many people as might reasonably live in the mansion. From the looks of it, no one has been down here in decades—maybe since the place was built. The mattresses are disintegrating. A shelving unit collapsed under the weight of canned goods, and now hundreds of tins of peaches and tuna fish cover the floor.

Miles shines his flashlight over the walls, finds the door-shaped crack that separates bunker and tunnel. He shoves aside one of the bed frames, lowers his shoulder, and pushes.

The tunnel is made of the same poured concrete. Miles feels a crunching under his feet, looks down, discovers a tapestry of long-dead beetles.

He is afraid the passageway from the tunnel into the house might be barred by something like a bank vault door, but instead there is only another rectangular crack in the wall. He switches off his flashlight, takes his revolver from his waistband, lowers his shoulder a second time.

There is no one waiting for him on the other side—just more darkness. Cheryl is unaware of the bunker's existence. Miles feels a slight pang of disappointment.

He switches his flashlight back on. The basement is cavernous, empty, deteriorating. Its cement floor is breaking apart. Its wooden beams are bowed and splintered. *The basement,* Miles thinks, *of someone who acquires nothing, has no past to hold on to.*

Gun drawn, he starts up the stairs to the main floor. Once again, he finds no one waiting on the other side—just a paler shade of darkness. He pockets his flashlight, gives his eyes a moment to adjust.

He is standing in a long corridor segmented by evenly spaced archways. The total silence is cut now and again by distant bursts of laughter—a television, the blue light he'd seen flashing in a second-story window. He takes off his tennis shoes, ties the laces together, dangles them over one shoulder. Heel-to-toe, he moves toward the sound.

He makes it to the second-floor landing without having encountered a soul.

Maybe, he thinks, *Cheryl really is alone with Jarry. Maybe she's come around, realized she wants what I can give her.*

He continues on, arrives at a bedroom door. He pauses, listening for voices that are not televised.

I won't leave his side until the sniper is brought to justice, Cheryl said.

Gun raised, Miles turns the knob.

Immediately, he senses something is wrong. Every object in the room points to a dying man, yet there is no smell of death. No whiff of sweat or urine, menthol or chicken broth. His eyes fall on the bed; he does not need to yank back the covers to know that there is no man lying underneath.

Slowly and silently, he backs from the room, shuts the door.

He stands in the hallway, listening, pushing down a swelling anger, running through possible scenarios. The most likely seems to be that he is alone in this house, that one or more lookouts were waiting for him to enter before they gave SWAT the signal.

But then they could not have seen him enter. The solution is simple: he will turn around, exit the way he came.

He takes a step, stops cold when he hears a faint cough coming from a nearby room. Worried his mind might be playing tricks, he waits until the cough is followed by the distinct sound of a man clearing his throat.

He inches forward, presses his ear to the door in question. Yes, there is someone on the other side. A heavy someone, shifting his or her weight on a rickety chair.

"Ready or not," Miles whispers.

CHAPTER 40

I'VE BEEN STANDING FOR hours, surveilling the western tree line through a gap in the blinds, trying hard not to blink. My eyes are dried out and my head's pounding. I'd be lying if I said I didn't crave one of Andy's chocolates.

My radio lets out a small explosion of static. I snatch it up, thinking the night has begun, anxious to know who's spotted him and where. But the next thing I hear is a gunshot. It comes muffled from some far end of the house, clear and loud through the radio.

And then I hear a long, guttural scream followed by a deep bellowing I know belongs to Dennis.

"Do I have your attention?" a voice says.

His voice.

"I'm listening," I say, hoping Pete and Patsy will know to stay quiet, make the Sniper think it's just me and Dennis in the house.

"Funny," the Sniper says, "the fat man I just shot looks nothing like Alfred Jarry. I thought we were going to have an intimate evening, Cheryl. You, me, and Jarry makes three. I keep wanting to trust you, and you keep betraying me. Were you really kicked off the force, or was this all a ruse from the start?"

A sound bite comes back to me from the academy: make the hostage human—give him a name.

"How bad is Dennis hurt?" I ask.

"A flesh wound," the Sniper says. "Lucky for him, he has a lot of flesh."

"Dennis also has a wife and kids," I say. "He isn't alone in the world. He isn't a distressed soul."

"He isn't dead, either," the Sniper says. "Not yet."

And then I hear Dennis, roaring up from the background:

"Don't think about me. You come and kill this—"

His voice breaks off with a groan.

"Hush now," the Sniper tells him. "You're being rude."

He's enjoying himself. Part of me thinks: *How did he get in the house unseen? Which one of us missed him?*

"So what will it take to keep Dennis alive?" I ask.

"You mean what do I want?"

"Yes."

"I want what you promised me," he says. "I want you. And I want Jarry."

"Jarry isn't here," I say.

"But you know where he is. The man let you occupy his house."

"Because he wants you to stop."

"And I want to hear that from him. I'd like a chance to explain myself. You have a habit of misrepresenting me. Take me to Jarry and your friend Dennis should recover nicely."

I can't think of any better way to stall, so I say:

"All right. Whatever you want."

"Good. Now, how many of you are here in the house?"

"There's just me and Dennis."

"Why on earth would I believe that?" he asks.

I think: *Sell it, Cheryl. Sell it hard.*

"There's something the press doesn't know," I say. "I was high when I shot that kid. Dennis is the only one who stood by me."

The air goes quiet while he makes up his mind. For a minute I'm afraid I've lost him.

"Keep your radio on," he says. "I'll be in touch shortly. If I hear you—or anyone else—moving in the house, I'll hurt Dennis a lot worse than he's hurt now."

"Understood," I say.

I hold myself stock-still, the radio shaking in my hand.

Think, think, think, I tell myself.

The door opens behind me. I spin, have my gun halfway raised before I see it's Pete. He holds up a hand. I lean against the wall, waiting for my breath to come back. Pete shuts the door, shuffles toward me in sock feet.

"Captain Stealth," I whisper. "You trying to get yourself killed?"

"You can't do it, Cheryl," he says.

"Do what?"

"Take him to Jarry. Or whatever else it is he wants you to do."

"I don't see what choice I have," I say. "He's got Dennis."

Even in the dark, I can make out Pete's hangdog expression.

"You won't be trading yourself for Dennis," he says. "That lunatic will just kill you both."

"Not if I play it right," I say.

Because there has to be a right way to play it.

A fresh burst of static has Pete and me grabbing up our radios.

"I'm ready for you, Cheryl," the Sniper says. "Meet me in the basement. Unarmed, of course. I've already taken a strong dislike to your colleague, so don't give me a reason to kill him."

"How do I know he's alive?" I ask.

"Don't you dare come down here, Cheryl," Dennis yells. "Don't you dare."

Then the line goes dead.

"Listen to Dennis," Pete says.

He takes out his cell phone.

"What are you doing?"

"Calling this in."

"No," I say. "You can't do that."

He looks down at the screen, steps to the window, checks again.

"I should have known," he says—more bitter than dejected.

"What?"

"He's jammed the signal."

I take Pete's arm, turn him toward me.

"Listen," I tell him, "I've got an idea about how to make this work."

"Do I get a say?"

"There isn't time. Give me a ten-minute start. Then you and Patsy find Dennis. After you drop him at urgent care, head straight for the hotel."

"To do what?"

"Get Jarry moved to another room."

"And?"

"Wait."

Before he can say anything more, I hand him my gun and bolt from the room.

CHAPTER 41

I STUMBLE OVER A loose floorboard, bang my shoulder on a cabinet I don't remember being there before. I can't imagine how Jarry, mostly blind, managed to live here alone.

The entrance to the basement is off the kitchen. I open the door, yell down the stairs. I want him to yell back. I want a sense of where he is in all that darkness.

"One foot in front of the other, Cheryl," he calls.

The words echo around the empty space, and I can't tell if he's standing in front of me or behind me, to my left or right.

I start down, holding tight to the railing. When I reach the bottom step, a beam like a spotlight hits me in the face. I throw up my hands, spin my head away.

"That's far enough for now," he says. "Turn around. Slow. Arms in the air."

He trusts his training, doesn't need to pat me down.

"Lose the phone," he says.

I tug it out of my back pocket, set it on the floor.

"Now come toward the light."

I take a step forward.

"Dennis," I say, raising my voice. "Are you all right?"

"He's resting comfortably."

"Where?"

The beam slides across the floor, reveals Dennis lying on his side, hogtied, a makeshift bandage wrapped around one shoulder.

"Did you...?"

"I gave him a sedative," he says. "I couldn't take another word. Now let's discuss whether he lives or dies."

The light is back on me, then at my feet, guiding me one step at a time toward the Sniper.

"All right," I say. "How do we keep him alive?"

"I told you: take me to Jarry."

We're just a few feet apart now, but I can't make out his face behind the beam.

"Let's go, then," I say. "He's in a hotel. We'll take your car."

He cuffs my hands behind my back, and we leave Dennis behind.

He's pushing me forward through a concrete tunnel littered with dead bugs. I know now how he slipped inside, got the drop on Dennis.

"Where does this lead to?" I ask over my shoulder.

"Why pose the question when you're about to see for yourself? Do you think chitchat will make us buddies?"

He isn't dumb. The next push comes hard.

We exit the tunnel, pass through a Cold War bunker that's bigger than any apartment I've ever lived in. Then it's up and into the forest. I catch my first glimpse of his face in the moonlight: early forties, olive complexion, angular features. That's as much as I get before he sees me looking, spins me away.

And then we're off through the woods with him on my heels, still pushing. I trip over a rock, scratch my face on a tree branch. By the time we make the access road where he's left his car, I'm bruised, bleeding, and winded.

It isn't like in the movies—he doesn't make me drive while he holds a gun to my ribs. Instead, he shoves me into the passenger seat, leaves my hands cuffed behind my back so that I have to lean uncomfortably forward. Maybe he thinks I'd hit the gas and aim for a tree. Maybe he's right. I remember what Jarry said: how many of us get to be useful at the end?

"So where's Jarry?" he asks.

"Take this road back out the way you came, then—"

"No, no, no," he says, clipping a GPS to the dashboard. "The name of the hotel. I won't have you driving me in circles."

I tell him. I only hope it takes us a while to catch up with the county road—long enough for Pete and Patsy to build a lead.

But then there's a break in my favor. He can't get a signal—not even a faint sputtering. He curses, beats on the steering wheel with open palms, slams back against the headrest. It's hard to believe this is steely-nerved Night Sniper. I take a long look this time. It can't be forty degrees out, but there's sweat streaming from his hairline. His skin is cadaver-pale.

He feels me looking, makes his first eye contact. His pupils are encircled by red. I wonder how long it's been since he slept. Whether I survive the night or not, he's breaking down, closing in on the end of his run.

I try my best to sound calming.

"It's all right," I say.

And then I soften my expression, look at him one more time, searching for something I can hold on to, some hint of kindness, some visible wound. Something to make me believe what I'm about to say.

"I want to help you. I was wrong before. I misjudged you. I see now that what you're doing comes from a place of love. Deep love."

His anger fades. For a moment I think he might cry. Beneath the exhaustion, he's a handsome man. High cheekbones, strong jawline. A rich crop of brown hair that's just starting to turn gray.

And the compassion comes easier than I'd thought. I've done enough interviews to know: there's a part of him—some buried part—that wants to be someone else.

"So you'll take me to Jarry?" he asks.

"I will," I say. "As long as you can find the county road from here."

He turns the key in the ignition, puts the car in drive.

There's something I've learned during my years on the job: a broken man will let himself hear what he's always wanted to hear.

CHAPTER 42

I KEEP TALKING AS he drives us through the blackness, the speedometer holding just under the limit. For now, my only agenda is to sound like a friend.

"Why do you think Jarry lives out here?" I ask.

"An accident of birth," he says. "Like most of what happens to us."

"What do you mean?"

"We think we make our own choice," he says, "but what we aren't born with, we're taught. And we don't choose what people teach us."

I want to ask—*What were you taught?*—but that would be too much, too soon.

"So Jarry saw people as lonely and isolated because he grew up out here?"

"I don't think he saw anything that wasn't there. I think his upbringing made him able to see."

"Until he went blind," I say.

There are eyes gathered on the side of the road, but I can't make out the animals they belong to. He sees them, too, slows without braking.

I decide to push.

"Can I call you something other than Night Sniper?"

He hesitates, seems flustered.

"You can call me Miles," he says.

The fact that he doesn't offer a last name tells me I have a ways to go—and not much time to get there. I jump all in:

"Let me kill Jarry," I say.

I can't tell if he's grinning or snarling. Either way, he doesn't look surprised.

"You mean you want to be partners?" he asks.

"More like an acolyte," I say.

"I don't know—"

"I've killed before," I tell him. "You don't have to worry about that."

He takes his right hand off the wheel. I think he might hit me, but instead he reaches into a pocket, pulls out the key to the cuffs, and sets it in my palm.

"Keep talking," he says. "Convince me."

I squirm in my seat, feeling for the keyhole. The cuffs drop off. I tell Miles he's doing God's work. I tell him I resisted before because I wasn't ready to believe, but now I am. Now only his mission matters. I set up at Jarry's not to capture him but to join him.

It's working. I feel myself winning him over. I put a hand on his knee. He blanches, looks a little lost, but he doesn't push me away.

Miles, I think, *really is a virgin.*

I've added a few small detours, but we're still getting too close, too fast. I can't gauge whether Pete's had enough time. I've got no choice: I have to stall.

"I think the turn's coming up," I say.

"You think?"

"I'm a city girl," I say. "I'm not used to wilderness and unlit roads. Everything looks the same out here."

"Does the road have a name?"

"It's in my phone."

I see his jaw muscles bulging.

"And you don't remember?" he asks.

I think: *Apologize, and he'll know you're playing him.*

"It's not like I expected to be giving you the tour," I say.

He's simmering, pushing down thoughts he doesn't want to have. He turns into a sharp bend without slowing down. For a moment, I'm thrown up against him. I think about grabbing the key from the ignition, but then I can't think of what I'd do past that.

"Here," I say, pointing. "Turn here."

He slams on the brake, but we've already gone too far.

"Are you sure?" he asks.

"I remember the road being off a blind turn," I say. "It's either this one or the next one."

Miles hesitates, then throws the car in reverse. It's clear he's having doubts about his acolyte. I reach over, stroke his cheek with the backs of my fingers.

"Trust me," I say.

CHAPTER 43

BY THE TIME THE hotel's in view, I've bought a good twenty minutes.

"That's it," I tell Miles. "There at the top of the hill."

He pulls off the road and onto a dirt shoulder. The hotel's a Victorian, as old and large as Jarry's mansion but in mint condition. The facade's been updated with cedar shingles painted forest-green. Towers topped with jet-black spires flank the east and west wings. The perfectly manicured lawn lit up by ornamental lamps planted along the walkway. A calligraphic sign reads: Hudson Manor. There's a line of cars parked where the curb should be.

"How do we do this?" I ask.

"There's a burner phone in the glove compartment," Miles says. "Call ahead. Tell whoever's with him that you've received a threat. Jarry needs to be waiting outside for you in five minutes. Alone."

His face has gone blank, his voice flat.

"If I say alone," I tell him, "then she'll know something's wrong."

"She?"

"His nurse."

For a beat I think he's going to call it off, tell me to drive on to some secluded place where he can have me dig my own shallow grave. I'm about to run my fingers through his hair when he says:

"Go ahead and call her. But put the phone on speaker."

I dial Kelly's cell, which is already a kind of code: if I were just checking in, I'd go through the hotel switchboard.

"Nurse Byrd," I say, "this is Detective Mabern. I'm sorry if I woke you."

I say it all in one breath, before Kelly can get a word out.

"What's wrong?" she asks.

"A threat," I say. "I need to move Jarry. Have him out front in five minutes."

I do my best to sound urgent, authoritative. I'm performing for two people at once.

"It takes me five minutes just to get Mr. Jarry out of bed," Kelly says.

"As fast as you can," I say.

I hang up, my mind racing, trying to guess what it is Kelly has planned.

"You heard her," I tell Miles. "What now?"

"The nurse will be outside with him," Miles says, "so you'll have to drive. I'll be in the back with my head down. You escort Jarry yourself. Don't let the nurse near the car."

He climbs into the backseat, and I slide behind the wheel. There's nothing to do now but watch and wait.

And for once I'm scared. Not for me, but for Pete, Patsy, Kelly. For Dennis, lying on a surgeon's table under the bright lights. For what will happen to Randy's career if we fail. I'm at the center of so many leaps of faith, and what happens next will decide whether or not they pay off.

The hotel doors swing open, and a wheelchair emerges with Kelly pushing. The figure in the chair sits hunched forward, wrapped in blankets and a scarf. He wears his knit cap down to his eyes.

"Here we go," I say.

"All right," Miles says. "Take the approach slow."

I switch on the lights, wait for Kelly to reach the end of the walkway before I begin creeping forward. I flash my brights. Kelly looks, sees it's me at the wheel, gives a slight nod. I hear the window behind me rolling down.

"Remember," Miles says. "Don't get too close."

I stop in the center of the empty road, just a few yards from Kelly and the fake Jarry I now recognize as Pete. Kelly steers the chair into a gap between the parked cars. Pete begins to rise. I jerk my thumb toward the back, start to open my door, but before I have a foot outside Miles is up and firing. Pete reels, falls from his chair. Kelly goes for her gun. The car is still moving so I pound the brakes. The jolt is enough to throw off the Sniper's aim. Kelly takes one in the leg, loses her footing, writhes in the grass.

Now Miles has his gun on me, the muzzle burning my temple. There's a sound like a car alarm echoing through my head. At first I don't hear him say:

"Drive, traitor."

I'm shifting gears when a final explosion turns me stone-deaf. I shut my eyes hard, open them again, suck in a breath. There's a beat before I realize the blood on the dashboard isn't mine.

I turn, see Randy running toward the car with his gun raised. Miles is slumped over, the top of his skull gone. When I turn back around, I see Patsy approaching from the front. They were hiding in the parked cars, waiting.

I jump out, yell:

"He's down. He's down."

I scan the lawn. Pete's stripped to a tank top and is crouching beside Kelly. I spot his vest lying on the ground where he fell.

CHAPTER 44

A WEEK LATER, RANDY picks me up in front of my motel. He gives me the news as we drive off: Jesse Smits is awake. He's corroborated my story.

"Corroborated how?" I ask.

"He kept saying, 'I lost, I lost,' over and over. It took a department shrink to tease it out of him. He thought the two of you were playing some post-apocalyptic video game. He wasn't running from you so much as leading you to that abandoned lot."

"Why?"

"Because it looked like a scene from the game. He was supposed to jump out from behind the rubble and shoot the cannibals."

Neither of us can think of a thing to add, so we leave it at that.

We're entering the tunnel now, headed for the Long Island Expressway.

"You're officially reinstated," Randy tells me. "Your job will be there when you're ready for it."

"Thank you," I say.

"For what?"

"Oh, I don't know," I say. "Saving my life. Safeguarding my secrets. Fighting to keep me on the force. Chauffeuring me around. Generally being there to protect me from myself."

"I wouldn't be here to protect you if Bryzinski—"

I cut him off.

"We're even now, Randy," I say. "You don't owe me anymore. If anything, you're ahead."

He brakes to let a station wagon enter our lane.

"I was never keeping score," he says.

And for a moment I'm ashamed all over again.

"What did you tell Branford?" I ask.

"About what?"

"Two cops shot, a few hundred miles from their jurisdiction. I'm sure he wanted answers."

Randy shrugs.

"I told him the Night Sniper was dead. I told him that was all he needed to know."

"What about Dennis and Kelly?" I ask.

"They should get commendations. But like you said, we were two hundred miles outside our jurisdiction, with no backup. No one wants to shine too bright a light."

"They're okay, though?" I ask.

"Yeah," he says. "Dennis is on desk duty for now, if you can picture that. Kelly's got another round of physical therapy before she's back on the street."

"They're damn good cops," I say.

"Heroes," Randy says.

"Yeah, well, they aren't alone," I say. "Tell me again how you happened to be there. I thought you were holding down the fort at the precinct."

He grins.

"I didn't want to miss the action," he says. "I was a mile from Jarry's mansion when Pete called."

I don't press him, but something tells me there's more to it. Some connection between us. Some kind of intuition that builds over years.

We're heading down the off-ramp into suburban Long Island. It's a clear, crisp morning—perfect weather for a fresh start.

"Dr. Miles Caffee," Randy says.

"A doctor?"

"A surgeon."

"Where'd a surgeon learn to shoot like that?" I ask.

"His father was a sniper in Vietnam," Randy tells me. "His mother died young. He grew up on a compound. Some kind of militia operation. They were going to take down the government, abolish taxes, build sky-high walls along the borders."

"So how did Miles end up in med school?"

"When he was sixteen, the feds started closing in on the compound. Instead of giving up, the militia members gassed themselves. Somehow Miles made it out. He wound up in foster care. He'd never set foot in a public school before, but he tested at genius level. Two years with a family in Boise, then straight to Harvard."

"It's sad," I say. "He had everything he needed to escape."

"Escape?"

"His childhood. The thing we never get past."

"Profound," Randy says.

"I'm quoting someone," I say. "Or at least para-phrasing."

He doesn't ask who.

"You heard about the DA who was stabbed to death alongside his wife-to-be?" he asks.

"Yeah," I say.

"The wife was an anesthesiologist. She worked on Caffee's team."

"Small world," I say.

"Yeah." Randy nods. "It sure is."

The houses are getting farther apart. There are clusters of gulls everywhere you look. Randy pulls up in front of Lifeline: A Haven for Women. We sit for a while, neither of us quite knowing what to say.

From the outside, it might be any other oversized home near the water. If anything, it's a bit worn. The gray shingles are breaking free in spots; the paint is chipping along the window frames. But maybe it's the defects that make me feel at home. I'm looking forward to six more weeks of beading and pottery, gourmet meals and group therapy.

"You're sure this is what you want?" Randy asks.

I lean across, kiss him on the cheek.

"I'm sure," I say. "It's time to finish what I started."

THE GOOD SISTER

SISTER

JAMES PATTERSON

with RACHEL HOWZELL HALL

CHAPTER 1

A PHONE ONLY RINGS at 12:38 a.m. on Monday morning for two reasons: a wrong number, or someone's dead.

So when my big sister Melissa's ringtone, Chaka Khan's "I'm Every Woman," blasted from my iPhone, my instincts told me this was no good.

It was late but the call hadn't pulled me from sleep. I was kneeling before my hallway closet, playing real-life Tetris with boxes of out-of-season stilettos, Mardi Gras masks, a pallet of parasols, and a heavy Hermès Birkin bag.

My sister's picture filled the phone's screen, a few feet away from me on the floor. The day I'd taken this shot, Melissa was sand-flecked, sun-kissed, and rum drunk, sandy-brown skin made golden by a Virgin Islands sun. She'd been so happy, the old Melissa I knew and loved.

Chaka Khan kept singing, and my heart tripped in my chest. I sat the shopping bag of gold-green-pink Mardi Gras beads in front of the shoeboxes, shoved the Birkin into a now-available rectangular slot, then slid the pallet of pink parasols over the bag. I closed the closet door, which immediately popped open, leaned against it, and grabbed the phone from the carpet.

"Hey, sister." I forced lightness into my voice, stretching out my long legs and wiggling my painted toenails. "What are you doing up?"

"Dani…" A sob escaped from Melissa's throat.

I closed my eyes, and pictured the beautiful sun-kissed woman who had danced the sexy merengue (*platonically,* she kept telling me) with a man who was not her husband. That night was just a year ago, but so much had changed since then. "Mel," I said. "What's wrong? What happened?"

Melissa kept crying—her sobs burst past my phone, against the mauve-painted living room walls, across the screen of my seventy-inch television, and into my carpet where tears that she'd cried yesterday, last month, and last year still soaked the padding.

"Mel, sweetie," I said. "Calm down, okay? Tell me what's—"

"I need you," she choked. "I need you to come over right now."

"Why?" I asked. "What's wrong?"

"I…I can't…Just come, okay? I can't say why, okay? I just need you here." Another sob, then a final, "You have to come over."

I tugged at the neck of my sweatshirt, then nodded even though she couldn't see me. "Okay. I'm on my way." My stomach cramped, making my toes flex. "Hey. Mel, listen. Are you listening?"

She hiccupped, and said, "Uh-huh."

"Good," I said. "Take a breath. Right now."

Melissa took a deep breath, hiccupped again, then slowly exhaled. Another deep breath. Another hiccup. Release. "I'm, I'm li-listening," she stammered.

With my eyes closed, I said, "Whatever's going on, trust me: it's gonna be okay. Okay?"

"Okay."

It's gonna be okay.

My first lie of the day.

CHAPTER 2

WHERE ARE YOU?" MELISSA sounded panicked again. No more deep breathing. No more relaxing. "Marina del Rey's not that far away." From my beachside condo to her house was just four miles.

"I don't want the cops pulling me over cuz I'm speeding." Butterflies the size of condors slammed against the lining of my stomach. "I'm almost there. Just turned on your block."

"Hurry up!"

"I'm hurrying," I snapped. "Calm the hell down."

Melissa lived on Don Lorenzo Drive, a magnolia-lined street in a fancy Baldwin Hills neighborhood that sat high above Los Angeles. The Talented Tenth lived here, in handsome Mediterraneans, sprawling California ranch-styles, and two-story colonials like Melissa's, with well-trimmed, well-watered lawns, drought be damned. They boasted MDs, PhDs, JDs, MSWs, E350s, and every letter–number combination that signified wealth and education. A Norman Rockwell Twenty-First Century Black Americana portrait south of the Santa Monica Freeway.

In this neighborhood, at this time of night, no one

stood on their lawns with joints and bottles of Hennessy. The only police cars around were those making late-night safety checks. The only clicking sounds came from sprinklers watering those well-tended lawns.

I parked my Escalade behind Melissa's late-model Lexus, then sat there, hands still tight around the steering wheel, listening to the engine tick…tick…tick.

A shadow at the house across the street lingered in the window, watching me indulge in these last moments of quiet. Probably a neighborhood watch captain, ready to alert the network about the strange Caddy with the tinted windows, doing something suspicious.

Cold night air tightened the pores of my face as I tromped up the walkway and to my sister's red front door. Small white clouds puffed from my mouth. Beginning to feel a lot like Christmas—but it was still October, and this cold spell was a special effects trick played on us by dwindling Santa Ana winds and global warming.

Those butterflies were still torpedoing my stomach as I slipped my key into the front door's lock. I stepped across the threshold and whispered, "Mel?"

Nothing appeared out of order—Jonah's Elmo roller-bag that he took to daycare sat over there on the foyer's tiled floor, and today's mail had been placed on the staircase's banister. The house smelled of burning jasmine candles, red wine, and…soiled diapers.

"Mel?" I said, louder. "Where are—?"

"Shh," she stage-whispered. "In here. In the living room."

Eyes focused on the white carpet, I tiptoed to the living room, where that candle-wine-poop smell was the strongest.

And there I found her, a tall, full-figured woman wearing a black and teal wrap dress with a plunging neckline and a tattered hem. With her hands clasped before her face, prayer-style, she was kneeling beside my brother-in-law Kirk Oakley. He was crumpled over, ass-up, facedown on the carpet.

A bottle of red wine sat on the dark walnut coffee table—a bottle of 2010 Burgundy I'd given Melissa as a push present three years ago. A wineglass had toppled, spilling its contents onto the white carpet.

"He pass out again?" I asked.

"Don't start," she hissed.

I rolled my eyes. "Fine. Is he *sick* again?"

"Stop being a—"

"He's a drunk."

"Can we not—?"

"What happened?" I asked.

She frantically shook her head, shrugged, shook her head again. "Don't know."

I narrowed my eyes. "What do you mean—?"

"Don't shout at me," she whispered.

I held out my arms. "I'm not shouting," I said, nearly shouting.

"He won't wake up, Dani. He was just lying here, I swear, and I tried to wake him and—"

"Breathe, Mel."

"Stop shouting at me," she shouted, eyes wild. "Don't you see that something's wrong?"

"I know—"

"Wake up, Kirk," she said, shaking his shoulder. "What's wrong with—?"

"Where's Jonah?"

That was the verbal slap that calmed her down, and forced her to focus and to breathe.

She took a breath. Held it. Slowly released it. "He's upstairs, asleep."

I pointed at my brother-in-law. "And you're sure *he's* not asleep?"

"He's dead," she whispered. "I think."

I saw no blood on the carpet. I saw no guts on the coffee table. Kirk looked as though he'd had too much to drink (again) and had simply passed out (again).

But then again, I wasn't a doctor, nor was I an EMT—I threw parties for a living.

From the stereo speakers, Jill Scott sang softly about being so gone.

So gone. Just like Kirk.

Melissa fixed the collar of Kirk's polo, then shook her head. "He won't wake up. I tried but he won't." She clutched her neck with trembling fingers. "I...don't know what to do." She brushed her knuckle against the stubble on Kirk's cheeks. "He's dead, huh?"

"Mel, I don't...Maybe...But..." Speechless. I wanted to rush over to my sister and hold her like we'd held each other that morning we broke Mom's favorite vase, like that summer afternoon we bent Dad's favorite 9-iron, like that day in college when I thought I might be pregnant. But I didn't dare move from my spot. Instead, I hugged myself, and asked, "What the hell happened?"

"I don't..." Eyes glistening with tears, Melissa shuddered as though ghost fingers had gripped her shoulders and shaken her. "I didn't want to call 911 yet cuz...I didn't call cuz it's my fault. I didn't call cuz...I did it. *I* killed him."

CHAPTER 3

SOMETHING COLD AND SHARP jabbed at my brain. "*You* killed him? *How?*"

The heater clicked on, the sudden *whoosh* making me jump.

Melissa pushed away from Kirk's body to stand. "I don't know. I mean, I *do* know but I didn't mean to. Dani, please believe me. Do you believe me? That I didn't mean to?"

I nodded. "Of course I do, but you can't say that anymore, okay?"

"Don't say what?"

"That it's your fault that he's dead."

"But—"

"No 'but,'" I said. "The cops will take that as the truth and arrest you. And you're not—"

A murderer? Even though she'd just confessed to me that she was?

My sister was a real-life do-gooder. As the executive director of KidsFirst, she advocated on behalf of orphaned and foster-care children of Los Angeles County. That's how she met Kirk, a social worker. A pretty wolf dressed in a do-gooder's cotton Dockers.

I finally took a step toward my sister. "Just tell me what *happened*."

"When I got home this afternoon, we got in a fight." She held out her hands to stop me from interrupting. "Not a physical fight."

I cocked an eyebrow. "This time."

She touched her forehead. "We fought about his cheating. We fought about—"

"*Her*. Again."

"Yeah."

A golden wedding band still hugged Kirk's stiff ring finger. It could have been a squirting flower or plastic dog poop since Kirk treated that band like a joke. A gag. A prop.

Melissa now twisted her own wedding ring. "And I told him that I was through dealing with his disrespect, and I told him that I deserved better. That *Jonah* deserved better. But Kirk…" She gulped and a tear tumbled down her cheek. "He said awful things to me. Awful, nasty things. Called me fat, and frigid, blind, stupid…" Her foot jerked and touched Kirk's hip.

Was that a kick or just a reflex?

"He's called you those things before," I said, arms folded, nerve twitching above my right eye. "I was there for a few of those—"

"I know." She dropped beside him again, and stuck her hand into the bulging left pocket of his cargo shorts. "But I *am* stupid. Every night I lay beside him, every time he came home, smelling like…I didn't do anything even though I wanted to burn him alive, even though I wanted to take an ice pick and drive it in his eye. But I didn't. I wouldn't because…"

"Jonah," I said.

My three-year-old nephew. Framed pictures of the

handsome little boy—*say "cheese," meet Santa, this is my mommy and daddy*—hung on every mink-colored wall, sat on every flat surface including the baby grand piano near the bay window.

Melissa shoved her hand into Kirk's right pocket. This time, she pulled out his cell phone. "He was texting her," she said, "even while he was fighting with me, he was texting her."

"Melissa, don't."

"What?"

"Don't erase anything. You shouldn't even be touching it."

She dropped the device as though it had bitten her.

"What were they texting about?" I asked.

She shrugged.

I glanced around the living room, still looking for any blood speckling on the yellow, purple, and green couch cushions. Any dried specks spattering the coffee-table book of Hawaiian volcanoes. Any drops on the crystal bowl Melissa had crafted at a glassblowing course last fall.

"I think I killed him," she whispered.

"I told you not to say—"

"I found these packs of Ecstasy in his closet," Melissa said. "And then I found some more in his jacket. And I found some of *her* shit in his closet, too. So this time, I had proof and I showed him my proof and he kept lying at first, saying that he'd taken the E from one of his clients, that the panties I found used to belong to me back when I was skinny. But I guess he realized how ridiculous he sounded and he finally manned up."

She looked up at me. "That son of a bitch *laughed* at me. Actually *guffawed* in my face. And then, he told me that he knew something that would destroy me, something that would upset my Wonderland. *Our* life together — he called it Wonderland."

My face numbed — I'd hardly taken a breath. "Destroy you? What did he mean by that?"

She shrugged, then said, "I couldn't take it anymore." She squeezed her hands, then pointed to the wineglass. "And I saw that he'd been drinking *my* wine from you, that I'd been saving, and so I took the E and dumped them into his glass when he left the room."

My eyes bugged. "Like…how much did you dump?"

Her lips quivered. "I lost count."

I gaped at her. "Oh, shit, Mel."

"I was mad," she shouted. "I wasn't thinking. The wineglass was just…*sitting* there, and the Ecstasy packs were in my hand, and…So after I did that, I grabbed Jonah and ran out the house before he could *destroy* me. I drove all the way to Orange County. Hours, just driving. Jonah was hungry so I stopped at McDonald's, bad mother again. But that's when I realized that this is *my* house. I bought it before I even met Kirk, and if anyone was moving, it was gonna be him.

"So, I drove back home to get rid of the glass before he finished it. It was quiet so I thought Kirk was gone. I put Jonah to bed first, then came back down here and saw that Kirk had already…He was slumped like this and he wouldn't move and that's when I called you."

I sighed, rubbed the bridge of my nose, then muttered, "Shit, Mel."

"Before I drove away," she said, "you know what I told him? I told him to drop dead." She bit her lower lip. "Drop dead: that's the first time he's ever done what I'd asked."

Kirk's phone buzzed from the carpet.

Melissa and I froze. "Who the hell is *that*?" I whispered.

The phone buzzed again.

"Should I check it?" she asked.

I nodded.

She dropped back to her knees and picked up the phone again. "Text messages." She swiped at the phone's screen. "It says, '*U RAT BASTARD WHERE DID U GO???*' And the second one says…" She took a rattling, deep breath, then: "It says, '*U DESERVE EVERYTHING THATS COMING TO U!!!*'" She looked at me with tearful eyes. "They're from Sophia."

CHAPTER 4

DON'T ERASE THOSE TEXTS," I blurted, then added, "We may need them."

"Okay." Melissa froze with the phone clenched in her hand. Her eyes glimmered with tears. They wouldn't fall—there was no time to cry.

The phone buzzed. Another text. *U FUCKING CAPULLO!!!*

I pointed to the phone. "Wipe off your fingerprints."

Melissa grabbed the hem of her dress and wiped the front and back of the phone. "Now what?"

I closed my eyes, tapped my right temple. *Think, think, think.* "Put his prints back on it."

"*What?*" She blinked at me, then gaped down at her dead husband. "How? Why?"

"The cops will wonder why there aren't any of his fingerprints on the phone. They'll know that you wiped the phone, and then they'll wonder why you wiped the phone, and then they'll start asking questions. Understand?"

Another text. *NO ME CHINGUES!!!*

Melissa grimaced as she lifted Kirk's dead right

hand and placed it around his phone. She turned the device this way and that against his fingers and palm. Then, she repeated this process with his left hand. Still holding the device with her dress, she slid the phone back into the pocket of his soiled cargo shorts. "Okay? How's that?"

I nodded. "Good, but—"

"Damn it." Melissa grabbed the tipped-over wine-glass from the coffee table. She got back on her feet, then scurried past me.

"We need to call now," I said, following her to the foyer. "Melissa—"

She knocked over the mail on the bannister as she raced into the foyer. She grabbed Jonah's Elmo roller-bag from the tiled floor.

I snatched up the mail, then snatched her wrist. "Mel, we need to call—"

Wild-eyed, Melissa yanked out of my grip. "I know, but I need to do something first." Perspiration had darkened the neckline of her dress, and now, the smell of sweat was mingling with the scent of candles and Kirk's last meal.

My sister darted into the family room with its stained cloth sofa and child-friendly rug thick with crushed crackers and spilled applesauce. From the plastic tubs of toys, she grabbed two Tonka trucks, then tossed them into the roller bag. From the pile of stuffed animals, she plucked out the fancy talking teddy bear I'd given Jonah on his first Christmas.

Melissa unzipped the bear's back, pulled out the bat-tery pack that made him talk, and shoved that pack deep into the tub of toys. She gathered all the leftover packets of Ecstasy, filled the wineglass with them, and slipped the glass into the bear's back, covered it with cotton batting, and zipped up the teddy. She lay the bear in the roller-bag, beside the trucks.

I squinted at her. "May I ask — ?"

Melissa ran back to the foyer and raced up the stairs, two at a time. She hurried down the hallway until she stopped at the closed door of Jonah's room. She took a breath, said, "Okay," more to herself than to me, then slowly turned the doorknob.

Golden stars and crescent moons from the space night lamp glowed and twirled on Jonah's walls and ceiling. So quiet and ordered in here.

Melissa tiptoed to Jonah's bureau and pulled out shirts, training undies, and pants. She grabbed his asthma inhaler and breathing chamber from her night-stand, then lay each piece atop the toys in the Elmo bag.

My nephew, now in a "big boys'" bed, slept with his butt in the air and arms to his side.

Just like his dad down in the living room.

We returned to the kitchen, where Melissa poured Cheerios from the box into sandwich baggies. She plucked tangerines from the ceramic bowl on the break-fast counter. The snacks went into the Elmo bag, too.

A whirlwind now, she swept back into the living room and over to the coffee table. Grabbed the wine bottle there, then spun back to the kitchen. She poured the leftover wine in that bottle down the sink, then ran the tap to rinse the basin. She wrapped one of Jonah's sweatshirts around the empty bottle, then placed it in the bottom of the Elmo bag. She whirled over to the sideboard in the dark dining room and grabbed a clean wineglass and a bottle of cheap California red, then swooped back into the living room. She poured a finger of wine into the glass, then knocked it over as though it had been the glass that had made the original spill.

The phone in Kirk's pocket buzzed again.

Melissa stood in the space between the living room and the kitchen. Slowly turning—wine bottle, toppled glass, wine stain, Elmo bag—her gaze finally landed on me. Her eyes narrowed and she cocked her head. "You understand what I just did?"

Breathless, I nodded. "Yeah."

"Stay here." She disappeared back up the stairs, and returned a minute later with a sleeping Jonah in her arms. He wore Elmo pajamas and clutched his favorite blanket in his tiny fist. She kissed the top of his head as a teardrop tumbled down her cheek and landed in his curls. "You'll take care of him tonight?" she asked.

"Yes." The lump in my throat was now the size of a comet and was just as cold. "What about Kirk's parents? Are you gonna call them?"

"Soon." Melissa kissed her son's head again, then offered him to me. "Here."

I was accustomed to carrying boxes of vodka and twenty-pound cartons of invitation stock, but not the heft of a sleeping three-year old boy.

Melissa patted her son's back, then turned her attention to the now-stuffed Elmo bag. She zipped it, stood it upright. "You'll have to take care of this, too. You can't forget about it. Do *not* let it out of your sight."

Her words made the weight in my arms even heavier.

She brushed my cheek with her knuckles. "You're a good sister."

I said nothing, just listened to my pulse banging in my ears, the soft snore coming from the sweetest boy in the world.

Melissa squared her shoulders, then gazed one last

time at the man she'd married just four years ago. "Guess I should call now."

"I love you, Mel," I whispered.

"I love you, too." She stepped over to the landline telephone on the kitchen wall, then lifted the receiver from the cradle.

The operator's voice cut through the kitchen's quiet. "911, what's your emergency?"

CHAPTER 5

WHAT'S YOUR EMERGENCY?

Melissa had lost her ability to talk to the 911 operator, so I'd plucked the phone from her shaky hands.

"There's a man collapsed on the living room floor, and we don't know if he's dead or alive." That's what I had reported, and now, ten minutes later, EMTs had rushed into Melissa's house to attend to her husband.

Someone had turned off the stereo—Jill Scott's smooth alto didn't fit the room's current mood.

A red-headed EMT with a treble-clef hand tattoo held the disc of a stethoscope to Kirk's back. He closed his eyes as he listened to…nothing.

The house was now filled with the noise of a crime scene. Camera clicks, police radio squawks, and the chatter of men and women wearing uniforms. The red-headed EMT closed his carrying case—the forty-two-year-old black male no longer needed saving. A second paramedic, a pudgy Asian guy with spiky hair, now attended Kirk Oakley's widow at the poolside patio table.

I stood in the kitchen with Jonah in my arms, and I

hadn't heard the paramedic pronounce Kirk dead. But I already knew.

Drowsy Jonah tugged at my raggedy ponytail with one hand and sucked the thumb of his other hand. "Dee-Dee, why the people here?" he asked me.

"They're just making sure your mommy's okay," I whispered.

"Daddy sick?" he asked.

"Don't worry, J-Boogie. It's gonna be okay." My face numbed from the lie I kept telling. *It's gonna be okay. It's gonna be okay.* The hell it was. But Jonah didn't need to know that, so I shifted him to my other hip, then kissed the top of his head.

"Where's the family?" A man's husky voice cut through the clicks and squawks of the cameras and radios.

"In the kitchen," a female voice said.

"Why the hell are they still in the house?" Husky Voice asked.

"Because it wasn't a crime scene at first," the woman explained.

Two men wearing bad suits entered the living room. The younger one looked in my direction. He had the clear blue eyes of a ventriloquist's dummy and a full mouth that reminded me of the candy wax lips I'd bought for a quarter back in third grade. His partner was an older black guy who could've earned millions as Danny Glover's body double.

The white guy tugged the sleeve of a passing female patrol officer, then whispered to her.

A moment later, the lady cop, Officer Robynn, held Jonah and I stood before Detective Gavin Elliott the Older and Detective Ian Anthony the Husky-Voiced.

"You're Danielle Lawrence, aren't you?" Detective Anthony asked.

I squinted at him. "Do I know you?"

"I'm disappointed," he said. "You don't recognize me?"

I flipped the pages of my mental "Back Down Memory Lane" photo album—shaggy-haired Brian, Kels the Lenny Kravitz clone, Magic Mike...

"We went to college together," Detective Anthony said. "Our second year, I lived two doors down from you."

Put a pair of Buddy Holly glasses on him, make those lips dry and flaky, un-straighten his teeth and... *Ah!* There he was!

I nodded. "Oh, yeah. You dated what's-her-face, the Raider's daughter."

"Everyone remembers that."

"You never let us forget. Neither did she." I frowned. "Wish I could say that I was happy to see you, but under the current circumstances..." I wrapped my arms around my shoulders, then slowly exhaled.

Ian thumbed back to the living room. "Who's the guy back there to you?"

"He's my brother-in-law, Kirk Oakley."

"This your house?" Detective Elliott the Older asked.

"No. My sister's."

"Not your brother-in-law's, too?" he asked.

"He lived here but he didn't own it," I said. "She does." I sounded petty but it was Monday at two-something in the morning, and Kirk was an asshole who had used and abused my sister. Just call me Petty LaBelle.

Ian pointed at Jonah, who was now playing with one of his toy trucks out on the terrace. "That your kid?"

"No. My sister's." I paused, then added, "And my brother-in-law's, too. The EMT—" I looked away as tears burned in my eyes. "Is Kirk...? Will he be okay?"

Ian's glassy eyes softened. "He's not. He's dead. I'm sorry. But don't worry. We'll catch the bastard who did this."

CHAPTER 6

WE NOW CONGREGATED IN Melissa's tiny home office behind the main house. The pre-fab module was a peaches-and-cream affair straight out of *Working Mother* magazine. My sister and I shared the love seat while Ian huddled on the ottoman and Detective Elliott sat behind the grand oak desk. Melissa's weeping had slowed into hiccups. Each time her breath caught, she tore at damp sheets of tissue in her hands. Pieces of that paper littered her knees and drifted to the carpet like snowflakes.

"For the hu-hundredth time," Melissa answered between hiccups. "I don't own a gu-gun. Why do you keep asking me about gu-guns?"

"*Because* someone shot him," Detective Elliott said.

"*What?*" Melissa screeched.

Ian glanced at his partner, then asked Melissa, "How did you *think* he died?"

"Like from a h-heart attack," Melissa said, tissue-ripping now set on high. "Or from a s-stroke."

"Only because we didn't see any blood," I said. "Are you *sure* he was shot?"

"Where?" Melissa asked. "On his body, I mean. Was

he shot? I can't think straight." She'd torn all the tissue paper and now clamped her ears with both hands.

Ian pointed to his belly. "Small caliber, shot in the abdomen, which is why you don't see a lot of blood. It's probably pooled on the inside. Bullet went in, probably ruptured major vessels, created internal bleeding. No one was here to get him to the ER, and that was that."

Melissa's trembling hand clutched her neck. "Oh, no. Oh, Kirk—"

Somewhere in the kitchen of the main house, a tray of silverware crashed to the floor.

We all—even the detectives—startled in our seats.

Tearing shit up—that's what Johnny Law was doing to my sister's house.

"What are they looking for?" Melissa asked, bug-eyed.

"Evidence," Detective Elliott said.

"There's evidence in my cutlery drawer?"

For the cops, evidence was *everywhere*. In the living room and kitchen, forensic technicians wearing khakis and blue nylon jackets had dropped plastic yellow tents with black numbers on floors and pieces of furniture. They swabbed strips of walls and carpet, and took pictures and pointed at invisible things. The wine stain had been marked with yellow tent 38, the wine bottle with yellow tent 25, and the wineglass with yellow tent 26. The numbers between marked those things that could only be seen with a microscope.

"…gonna have to do some testing," Detective Elliott was now saying. "Starting with you." He pointed at Melissa.

Melissa froze and her mouth hung open. "Why?"

"Because…" Ian used his pen to point at my sister's wine-stained palms and kneecaps.

Melissa gaped at her hands—she hadn't realized that she was now covered in Burgundy. "But it's not blood. It's from the wine in the carpet. I didn't shoot my husband."

Detective Elliott smirked. "We're supposed to just take your word for it?"

Ian shot his partner a glare, then said to Melissa, "It's all standard procedure, okay? We have to check everyone for blood and gunpowder residue because months from now, at trial, we don't want a defense attorney punching holes in our case because we'd neglected to run a few swabs over everyone's hands. That's reasonable, right?"

"But I *touched* him," Melissa explained. "When I saw him there, I thought he had passed out—"

"He passes out a lot," I added. "And she revives him a *lot*."

"I didn't know he'd been *shot*," Melissa continued, silencing me with a look. "I just saw him collapsed there."

"And so the tests won't be accurate," I said. "Blood or powder or whatever would've been transferred to her hands when she touched him."

"We'll deal with that once the test results return," Ian said. "Really, Mrs. Oakley. If you're innocent, you have nothing to—"

"Give me a break," I interrupted. "How stupid do we look? You think that *today* we can actually trust the cops to do the right thing? To look past the easy answer?"

"Are you insinuating that we're crooked cops?" Detective Elliott squinted at me, his thick black eyebrows wriggling on his forehead.

"Only if you're insinuating that she's a murderer," I

shot back. "And from where I'm sitting, it sounds like you are."

Detective Elliott glared at me. But I thrive under glares—the heat made me stronger. "Mrs. Oakley," he said to my sister, "you'll need to change out of your clothes."

With no more tissue to tear, Melissa now pulled at the tattered hem of her dress. "No. I don't think I want to do that."

"Mrs. Oakley, please," Ian said. "Work with us on this, all right? We need your cooperation and I know this is difficult but you have nothing to fear. I promise you. Trust us. Trust *me*." Then, he looked at me. *Please?*

Melissa slumped on the love seat as though her frame had separated from her muscles. She turned to me with worry in her eyes. "Dani?"

I took her hand and squeezed. "He's right. You have nothing to fear, because you didn't shoot him."

"Yeah." My sister took a deep breath that reunited her body again, then pushed off from the couch. She strode out of the tiny house and Detective Elliott shuffled behind her.

"Thank you, Mrs. Oakley," Ian called after her.

Melissa glanced back at me a final time.

I winked at her. *It's gonna be okay.* The truth this time—she *hadn't* shot Kirk.

A forensic tech was now scouring for clues out on the patio. "What's in the Elmo bag?"

My stomach lurched—I'd left Jonah's bag at the poolside table. The same bag that hid a poisoned wine glass and bottle, and blister packs of Ecstasy. A bag that could implicate my sister in the murder of her husband.

Shit.

CHAPTER 7

SOMETHING IMPORTANT HAD BEEN discovered in Melissa's cutlery drawer, and Ian Anthony moved past me on the patio and returned to the kitchen to check it out. Glass clinking, some rustling—sounded like they'd found empties in the trash can.

But something just as important had been discovered here at the poolside table, and now I needed to explain it away. Or else.

"It's just my nephew's bag," I told the man wearing the blue nylon jacket.

He was now squatting beside that bag, and his gloved hand rested on Elmo's face. "I'm gonna have to search it. You understand that, right?"

"Oh, yeah. Definitely." Ice crackled over my chest and scalp. *There's nothing to see here.* "Jonah's staying with me," I explained, "so he needed a change of clothes, some toys…Cheerios. I don't have Cheerios at home. No one over thirty eats Cheerios." *Move along, damn it.*

"I'm a Frosted Flakes man myself." He pulled the bag's zipper.

The backyard was becoming hotter and the dark sky seemed to be closing in on me like a coffin.

"His liver temp's at 87.8 degrees."

The man in the nylon jacket stopped un-zippering and turned to look through the living room bay window. There, a slight black man wearing wire-rimmed glasses and a jacket that said CORONER kneeled beside Kirk's stiff body, which had been flipped onto his back. Apparently the crime scene photographers had gotten everything they needed. He pulled a long thermometer from my brother-in-law's hip, then jotted a note onto his clipboard.

"Who's he?" I asked the man about to search Jonah's bag.

"Dr. Brooks," he said. "Deputy medical examiner from the coroner's office."

"Is he gonna move Kirk?" My brother-in-law's position looked unnatural, the hue of his skin a weird-mermaid blue.

"Not sure. It's a little hard since rigor's set in. And with that temp, seems your brother-in-law's been dead for about five hours. Now, let's see." He turned his attention back to the roller-bag.

Sandwich bags of Cheerios, five tangerines, two yellow Tonka trucks, a teddy bear, clothes, sweatshirt.

The man wearing the nylon jacket zipped Jonah's bag again and offered me its handle. "Thanks. Have a good night." Whistling, he trundled back into the kitchen.

Weak-kneed, I plopped into a deck chair. From my seat, I could see through the living room window—Dr. Brooks was still on his knees. A female forensics tech pointed to something on the carpet. Another tech held up the wine bottle that Melissa had planted on the coffee table. A man with a video-camera recorded something I couldn't see.

What had he found? What had we forgotten?

It was cold out here, and my breath clouded around my head. No crickets chirped—the noise from the cops and paramedics had scared every bug south of the Santa Monica freeway. Past treetops, I saw the Los Angeles skyline. The Staples Center glowed purple, and Klieg lights still roamed the dark skies. There had been a game hours ago—nothing compared to the one I was now playing, I was sure.

"You okay?"

I startled.

Ian was now standing at the patio table. He was quiet and watchful. He'd make the game harder.

I rested my chin on the Elmo bag. My eyes hurt from the lit-up blue of the swimming pool and from the jackhammer chiseling at the space between my eyebrows. "Just sitting here."

"You look worried." Ian dropped into the other deck chair. He could see that *I* could see into the living room.

"If not now, when? Kirk's dead. My sister's losing her mind. And a murderer's loose. It's all so…"

A white flash from a camera brightened the living room. The photographer who had taken the picture was kneeling to peer beneath the couch. He took another picture and a flash brightened the room again.

"It's all so *what*?" Ian asked.

"Surreal." My cell phone played from my sweatshirt pocket. R. Kelly's "Bump n' Grind." Talk about surreal. This time, it was my on-again, off-again boyfriend. Asher Davis was an ER doc, hence the late-late-*late* call.

The photographer reached beneath the couch and grabbed something. He held a small object up to the light.

And R. Kelly kept singing.

"Looks like he found a shell casing." Ian was also staring at that criminalist kneeling beside the couch.

"That's...*good,* right?"

He nodded. "Once we find the gun, it'll be wonderful. We'll match that casing to the bullet that's still lost somewhere inside your brother-in-law. Hopefully, that casing will have a fingerprint on it."

The medical examiner rifled through the pockets of Kirk's cargo shorts. Out came Kirk's cell phone as well as a pair of sunglasses and—

The man who'd found the shell casing now stood over Dr. Brooks and blocked my view.

"Do you need to answer your phone?" Ian asked.

My skin flushed as I dipped my hand into my pocket and clicked the Mute switch on my phone. "I'm good. He'll leave a message."

"So now it's your turn," Ian said.

I cocked an eyebrow at the man seated across from me. "For?"

Ian smiled and his now-perfect teeth glistened in the dark like a wolf's. "We need to test your hands."

CHAPTER 8

EXCUSE ME?" DETECTIVE IAN Anthony now had my full attention.

"We need to test your hands for blood and gunpowder residue."

That five o'clock shadow, that smug expression…I now clearly remembered both from our days together up in Santa Cruz, California. I wanted to smack it off.

Over at the house next door, the lights on the second floor flickered off. Mr. Jackson, a gnome of a man, was peeking out the window.

Ian whistled to the same forensic tech who had searched Jonah's Elmo bag.

The man returned, this time with a gray carrying case.

"This is Frank," Ian said as way of introduction.

Frank said, "Me, again."

"Mr. Frosted Flakes," I said.

"Like I explained to your sister," Ian said, "this is just part of an investigation. Oh—we'll also need a DNA sample."

I snorted. "Anything else? How about my blood type?"

Ian smiled at me. "Standard procedure. Nothing personal, Dani. Don't you want us to find the murderer and have a case strong enough to convict?"

I looked at him and the tech, then sighed. "It's not that—it's just that I really don't understand why any of this is necessary. This *is* my sister's house, my DNA's all over the place."

Frank sat his gray case on the table, opened it up. "Beyond my pay grade."

"Dani," Ian said, "I understand your concern—"

"And *Jonah's* gonna have all kinds of shit on him, too," I continued, "because Mel was holding him and then *I* held him and—"

Ian touched my knee. "Dani, breathe."

"I *am* breathing." Those clouds of cold air puffing quickly from my mouth and nose confirmed that I was. I pointed at Ian's hand on my knee. "I hugged Mel. After she found Kirk. Now, *you* have whatever the hell on you." My adrenaline was running high. "No one put us, like, in a holding pen to keep us from contaminating the scene and…and…"

Ian's smile was tight. "You're right—you wandered all over the crime scene because you didn't know that a crime had been committed. We'll know, okay? We're not a bunch of Barney Fifes. Let's get started, shall we?"

Frank chose a test kit from his case, then snapped on a pair of latex gloves. "This won't hurt a bit."

I rocked in my seat, still holding the Elmo bag tight against my chest. "You understand my concern, right? You understand why I'm a little stressed out? It's cuz we're innocent. We're not *those* people, okay? We've never had to deal with the police like this, and the swabs and the questions and the little yellow tents all over the place and…" Spent, I slumped in the deck chair.

"Dani?" That was my sister's voice.

"Out here!" I hopped up.

Melissa charged around the side of the house. She now wore black yoga pants and a gray UCLA sweatshirt.

I hurried over to hug her. "Are you okay?"

Her bloodshot eyes had nearly swollen shut from crying. "Shit, Dani." She pulled away from me and whispered, "They're about to arrest me."

CHAPTER 9

MRS. OAKLEY," DETECTIVE ELLIOTT was saying. He carried three paper bags in his thick hands. "You're making this far more difficult—"

"Because she didn't shoot him." I was chasing after the older black man as he and Melissa made their way past the side of the house to the front lawn.

The entire neighborhood had awakened from all the police activity and the glare of red, blue, and hot-white emergency lights. Clad in bathrobes and winter coats, every resident on Don Lorenzo Drive crowded the sidewalks. Every other person's fingers tapped on cell phone screens. Mrs. Gossett, a retired school teacher, was now being interviewed by a short, balding detective. She lived across the street and often kept Jonah for a few hours each month. *See something, say something* was her motto. The FedEx man tossed your package on the stoop a little too hard? A red Honda parked too long in front of your house? She'd tell you. The world needed more busybodies like Mrs. Gossett, I thought—except for days like today. Seeing her talk and point up and down the street, the detective's pen scribbling in his tiny notebook, made my pulse race. What had she seen? What was she reporting?

Detective Elliott led Melissa to a light-blue Crown Victoria parked behind my Escalade.

"Tell me where you're taking her," I demanded.

"Southwest station down on King Boulevard," he said. "You know, across from the Laundromat?" Amused, he raised his eyebrows and added, "I'm sure you know it."

"What the hell is *that* supposed to mean?" I whirled to face Ian. "Did you *hear* what he just said? He thinks I've been to jail, or I know people who've been to jail, that we're a bunch of hood rats. That's why I can't trust you guys to do the right thing."

Ian's mouth opened.

But I had already turned back to face Detective Elliott. "Is she being arrested?"

"We're just gonna talk," he said. "We'll talk about what happened tonight, about where she was, who could've done it. It's all good. Like you said, Miss Lawrence: your sister didn't shoot her husband. So there's nothing for her to fear from just talking to me down at the station, away from the noise and her nosy neighbors." He smiled, but it didn't reach his eyes.

Melissa took my hands and kissed the backs of each. "I'll call Kirk's parents when I get to the station. Take care of Jonah, okay? And don't forget to take his bag. He won't be able to sleep without his teddy."

"Don't worry," I told her. "I got him. I got *you*."

She squeezed my hands, then climbed into the back seat of the blue Ford.

A moment later, the sedan was cruising down Don Lorenzo Drive, then the car—and my sister—were gone.

That's when I let loose upon every remaining person

with a badge an assortment of colorful words that I'd learned at my Navy father's knees. For several moments, no one spoke. Frank the forensics tech broke the silence with, "Wow."

Ian grabbed my elbow and hustled me back to the patio.

The Elmo bag was where I'd left it—beside the table and unattended. I had to stop leaving that damn bag. I plopped back into the deck chair, then dropped my head between my knees.

Ian's shadow blocked the light. "You talk to Jesus with that mouth?"

I sat up and crossed my arms. "He's heard me say worse."

He chuckled and tilted his face to the sky. Finally, he pushed out a breath and looked at me. "You want my been-a-cop-for-twenty-three-years honest advice?"

I rolled my eyes. "Do I have a choice?"

"Whether your sister did it or not, doesn't matter. She needs a lawyer ASAP." He pulled out a pair of latex gloves from his jacket pocket. "I know, I know: she's innocent. Again: doesn't matter. You know *why* it doesn't matter? It's because the wife or the girlfriend or the boyfriend or the husband *always* does it. Because common wisdom says that no one else cares about you like that *except* for the person you're fucking or not fucking enough.

"And if your sister has any good sense and some money, she'll hire a good defense attorney who, if shit takes a wrong turn, can get her less time and a better deal. Who can get twelve strangers to see and accept that, I don't know, Kirk Oakley was a violent son of a bitch who pushed her around for the last damn time. Just don't be caught off guard, all right? Believe it or not, I accept that there are a few innocent people sitting on death row. I'm not the asshole cop you think I am. So that's my advice. Take it or leave it."

Ian tore open a pack of swabs. "Open your mouth. We can do this *here* or you can join your sister down on King Boulevard and we can do it there. In the meantime, your nephew would go to Child Protective Services and hang out with kids from *really* messed-up families. Lady's choice."

A vise tightened around my heart and lungs. *Jonah.* I had just promised Melissa that I'd take good care of him.

The cotton swab swirled against my cheek. Ian slipped the swab into a vial, then slipped the vial into his jacket pocket.

"You know what?" I said. "I agree with you." My tongue poked at my violated cheek.

"Oh?" Ian pulled the second deck chair closer to mine, then sat. "So you're saying that your sister—?"

"She didn't shoot him." I leaned back in the chair and stared up at the pale moon. "Kirk *was* a violent asshole. He was a player, too. And his current girlfriend is a stereotypical fiery Latina with quick fists and a mouth bluer than mine."

"Wonderful. Another good suspect. Tell me more."

I let my head roll to the side to look at him—the detective had his pen and pad ready. "What do you want to know?"

"Her name, for starters."

The truth was hidden behind twisted, thorny branches, daring me to reach in and grab it. Problem was: it didn't sit too far from the sort-of truth, which was just as tempting a choice. One led to freedom. The other...

"Sophia Acevedo." I felt light, now that I had uttered her name. "Sophia's probably stayed in your guest suites once or twice in her life. Right now, she's supposedly a social worker. Her main vocation, though—other than sleeping with married men—is an urban pharmacist. And Kirk Oakley was her best customer."

Ian cocked his head. "Kirk was cheating on Melissa with a drug dealer?"

"Uh-huh."

"So your sister really *did* have a reason to kill him."

I sucked my teeth, then said, "Occam's Razor, Detective Anthony."

"Right—the simpler, the better—and the simpler explanation is that your sister did it."

"If you knew my sister and knew Sophia," I said, "you'd also say that the ex-con with the temper did it."

Next door, Mr. Jackson had reclaimed his place at the second-story window. Since Kirk had moved in four years ago, the old man had certainly *heard* his share of arguments between my sister and her husband. But what had he heard *today*?

I smiled at Ian. "You want my been-a-woman-for-forty-three-years honest advice?"

Ian squinted at me. "Do *I* have a choice?"

I shrugged, then stared out at the pool.

Ian leaned forward until our knees touched. "Tell me."

"Find Sophia. Her DNA is gonna be all over Kirk. And *his* blood's gonna be all over *her*."

CHAPTER 10

OFFICER ROBYNN HANDED JONAH back to me and went to grab a coat from his closet. It was fifty-two degrees and damp, and the three-year old boy needed something warmer than the lady cop's embrace. Even as I held him close to my chest, we both shivered standing on the front lawn. The bright lights didn't offer a lick of heat, but they certainly made Don Lorenzo Drive look like the back lot at Universal Studios.

"Here you go, honey," Officer Robynn said, holding out Jonah's favorite Elmo coat.

I thanked the woman and helped Jonah into the jacket. "That better?" I covered his face with warm kisses.

Jonah whispered, "Uh-huh." He nuzzled my neck. He smelled so clean—like tangerines and laundry detergent. He was the only pure thing that had ever come out of Kirk Oakley.

Ian was staring at me from the front porch, and the heat from his gaze made me nervous. Despite my forced cheer with Jonah, the detective's intimidation tactic was getting to me. So much had happened in this house, and I wanted to get it off my chest. But no. I was many things, but a fool wasn't one of them.

On the lawn next door, the balding detective was interviewing Mr. Jackson. The old man had left his upstairs window, since the action had shifted to the streets. His arms were crossed, and he glared at the investigator before him. I caught just a snippet of what the old man had to say: "…treated that sweet girl like common gutter trash. If anybody was trash, he was."

And that was the truth.

On some evenings, Kirk would sit in his blacked-out 300M, blast his stereo and smoke who-knows-what, even though he lived in a house with a big backyard. He was the type who spoke too loudly on his cell phone, drank from brown paper bags on Sundays, let his gaze linger too long and too many times on neighborhood housewives. Despite his MSW, despite his wife's PhD, despite his two-story Colonial with the red door, Kirk Oakley didn't *belong* on Don Lorenzo Drive.

But Melissa loved him. Thought she could change him. Thought that a baby would transform this man-child into a full-fledged adult. She was wrong because here we were.

"Ready to go to my house?" I now asked my nephew.

Jonah nodded and yawned. "Dee-Dee, can we see Einsteins at your house?" Every time I babysat Jonah, we ate grilled cheese sandwiches in my bed and watched episodes of *Little Einsteins,* a cute show about smart kids doing smart things.

"It's kinda late for that, J-Boogie," I said. Rather, it was too early for that—the sun would be kissing the horizon in just two hours, the sky the color of popsicles.

"Can we go to the beach?" he asked.

"It's kinda late for that, too, sweetie pie. Maybe we'll—"

"Hey, Dani." Ian strode toward me, holding out his

business card. "For when you wanna give your forty-three-year-old advice again. Call me anytime. Really: Nothing's insignificant in a homicide investigation." He smiled down at sleepy Jonah and touched his head. "Hey, kiddo. You okay?"

"It's loud." Jonah turned his head away and stuck his thumb into his mouth.

Ian made a sad face. "Sorry about all this noise, okay? We're just trying to figure out some things."

Like who killed your daddy.

Ian pointed at the Elmo roller bag by my feet. "What's that?"

Numbness prickled across my cheeks. "Don't worry, Frank's already looked in it."

"And what did Frank find?"

I smirked. "Two nuclear bombs, six crack pipes, and a hammer with brains all over it. But since Kirk didn't die from any of that, Frank let me keep it."

Ian tossed me a lopsided grin and those dummy blue eyes of his almost looked human. "And if I look in it again?"

"Your face is gonna melt like the Nazi agent in *Raiders of the Lost Ark*." Ice rushed through my veins— I wanted to grab the bag and run down Don Lorenzo Drive.

"Dee-Dee," Jonah said, "I wanna go home now. It's too loud."

"I know, sweetie pie. We're going." To Ian, I said, "Can we...? I don't think he should see the coroner rolling out..." I nodded toward the house.

Ian turned back to see Dr. Brooks and his team pushing a gurney carrying Kirk's body to the front door. "Oh. Yeah. Crap. Quick question though: your sister have a security system?"

"Not that I know of. Why?"

"We could check to see when the doors were opened and closed." His eyes wandered to the house on the left of Melissa's and then to Mr. Jackson's on the right.

I squinted at him. "What are you thinking?"

He shrugged. "Maybe her neighbors have security cameras that face the street." He jotted in his notepad. "I'll ask them. Oh—last thing." He looked up at me. "What was the girlfriend's last name again?"

I told him and held my breath as he scribbled into his tiny notebook.

He nodded and grunted.

"Something wrong?" I asked.

"Nope. I'll call you later." He ambled back to the front porch.

Frank stood there with Dr. Brooks and the gurney. He held a baggie in his hand. And in that baggie— Kirk's cell phone.

CHAPTER 11

LIGHTS, CAMERA, ACTION!

Nothing said light and happy like the Aussie music group for kids, the Wiggles, now playing on my Caddy's stereo. Jonah, strapped into his backseat booster, clapped and sang along to their silly songs.

Down the hill I drove, the lightening horizon before me. The street-cleaning truck rumbled on the side of the dark road. On the sidewalk, a homeless man pushed a shopping cart filled with orange pylons and two small dogs. It was a little after three o'clock and people living in those Baldwin Hills Mediterraneans, sprawling California ranch-styles, and two-story colonials still slept.

"Dee-Dee, sing your part." Jonah's chipmunk cheeks were stuffed with Cheerios. Freckles speckled across the bridge of his nose, like Kirk's. "Sing, Dee-Dee!" he said again.

Sweet honey in the rock, it was too early for this. Too early for effin' Australians warbling about fruit salads and pirates and some damned octopus named Henry.

I caught my reflection in the rearview mirror—wind-tunnel hair and chapped lips. When was the last time I'd had something to drink? I needed something cold and liquid—preferably with dark rum and served in an icy glass. But I loved my nephew, so I sang. *"Welcome to our TV show!"*

My phone vibrated in the cup holder—I'd forgotten to turn the ringer back on and only now noticed that I had two missed calls and a long string of text messages. And the latest text message was not from the Hot Doctor.

STOP IGNORING ME PICK UP THE PHONE!!!

I dropped the phone back into the cup holder and hoped that Sophia Acevedo would grow bored or tired. And *alakazam,* just like that, she sent another text.

WHY THE COPS CALLING ME???

There was no punctuation mark Sophia Acevedo didn't like enough to triplicate. She spoke like that, too.

"Dee-Dee?" Jonah asked.

"Yes, sweetie pie?"

"Is daddy okay?" He met my eyes in the rearview mirror. They gleamed, those eyes. So close to crying. So close to falling asleep.

I opened my mouth to speak—the truth, a lie, I didn't know which had queued on my tongue. "Your daddy wouldn't want you to worry about him. He'd want you to get some rest and to be—"

My phone vibrated again, and took my lie away.

THIS DETECTIVE JUST TOLD ME!!!

What had Ian told her?

"Dee-Dee?" Jonah asked again.

"Yes, sweetie pie?"

"Where my mommy go?" He shoved a handful of Cheerios into his mouth.

"She had to go to a meeting but she'll see you later." Bile had already burned through my stomach and now it bubbled up my throat and into the back of my mouth.

"Why Mommy crying?" Jonah asked.

"She was just very tired today," I said. "You know how you cry sometimes when you're tired especially after a long day?" I glanced at him in the rearview mirror.

He nodded. "She gon' take a nap?"

"When she comes home, and I'm sure she wouldn't mind if you climbed in bed with her and helped her rest. She says you're the best nap-taker in the world."

Jonah pumped his legs in time with the music, then said, "Daddy makes Mommy cry. I cry, too. It's too loud."

"I know, sweetie. It won't be loud anymore, okay?" The truth, but oh, how I needed that drink.

My phone vibrated.

Sophia. Again.

IGNORE ME IF U WANT 2 BUT LET ME TELL U THIS!!!

WATCH YOUR BACK BITCH!!!

CHAPTER 12

NEVER ONE TO IGNORE advice, I watched my back.

That's why I stood at my living room window with frayed nerves and scratchy eyes that ping-ponged between the parking guard hut down on Marina City Drive and the smeared screen of my cell phone. Only a few rays of sunlight glimmered past thick fog hanging over Marina del Rey. Car lights burned through, then quickly blinked out, caught up in the Rapture.

It was almost seven o'clock. Monday had officially started.

Just a mile away from his home, Jonah had fallen asleep in the back seat of my Escalade. As I carried him from the truck to my bedroom, he hadn't awakened. He snored softly beneath the folds of my comforter, fifteen stories above the city.

I had not slept since Saturday night. Couldn't rest, not with Sophia Acevedo texting all morning. I re-read her last text message:

U CAN RUN BUT U CAN'T HIDE!!!

Six years ago, Sophia had seemed so...*normal*. She'd been a social worker, a product of the *barrio* who made it out. She was smart. Funny. Collegial. Melissa had hired her because of her ability to connect with struggling families. Back then, I'd swoop into the office, pick up my sister and her team, and treat them to my perks: happy hours and wine tastings, chef's tables and magic shows. Over tapas and flights of wine, we mourned the children swallowed up in the system and rejoiced after every Forever Family celebration.

But then, Melissa met Kirk Oakley. And then, *Sophia* met Kirk Oakley. Both women fell for him— but one bided her time until a weekend conference in San Diego. Only later was it discovered that Sophia had run up the organization's credit card on couples' spa treatments and bottles of pricey champagne. But her first mistake was answering Kirk's hotel room phone. The next week, Sophia didn't have a job, and Melissa discovered that she was pregnant with Kirk's baby.

Despite her affair with my sister's husband, Sophia still tried to maintain her friendship with me, inviting me to tequila tastings and Taco Tuesdays. I declined each invitation with a message—*Stop sleeping with my sister's husband!*

Now, here we were: me standing at the window, Sophia texting morning threats, my sister in not-custody at a police station.

Melissa still hadn't called, so I didn't know whether Detective Elliott truly planned to arrest her or if he had been blowing smoke like the bully he was.

My cell phone vibrated.

I KNOW WHERE U LIVE!!!

Down at the guardhouse, a cherry-red Mustang pulled to a stop.

Sophia drove a cherry-red Mustang. Before the affair, she drove a Chevy Malibu. But then fortune—and another woman's husband—had found her, and she found herself behind the wheel of a new red pony. Upward mobility in today's America.

At the guardhouse, the chubby security guard bent to talk to the driver. Randy turned away from the Mustang and grabbed a green parking pass from the kiosk. He handed the slip to the driver, then pointed to his left. The driver slowly turned left into the guest parking lot.

Shit.

My gaze skittered around my apartment—if I needed a weapon, what could I use? The ceremonial fireplace poker that had never met a flame? The silver frame with those sharp-edged corners? My eyes found that hallway closet, stuffed with boxes, Mardi Gras masks, and a heavy Birkin bag.

A bang from the hallway. Someone had slammed a door.

Voices echoed down the corridor. Male. Deep. The voices grew louder...louder. Came closer...closer.

"Which one?" one of the men asked.

Silence. Then: "This one."

A bang on the door. But not *my* door. "Hey, guys," the woman across the hall from me shouted. Laughter. Chatter. The door slammed shut.

Breathless, I trudged over to the intercom at the front door, and hit Gate. A squawk from the speaker, and then, "Mornin', Miss Lawrence." Randy's voice was as round and soft as he was. "How can I help you?"

"Hey, Randy. I'm expecting a friend today. Her name's Sophia and she drives a red Mustang. Could you call me as soon as she arrives? It's important—I'm surprising her with something."

"Sure, Miss Lawrence."

I spelled Sophia's name, thanked him, then hit the End button. Slightly relieved, I trudged back to the window.

Could I trust Randy to remember? What if he was on break when Sophia rolled up?

A light-blue Crown Victoria and a police cruiser stopped at the guardhouse. The driver of the Ford was a black man. Detective Elliott was a black man.

I leaned forward to get a better view but my forehead bumped against the windowpane. I closed my eyes and slowly exhaled. "What the hell am I doing?"

My parents—ovarian cancer for her, heart attack for him—had worked hard so that Melissa and I wouldn't have to be scared in our own homes. That meant extra jobs—more heads of hair to curl for her, more seasonal construction jobs for him after he'd left the Navy. That meant lots of frozen fish sticks and canned chili for dinner, all so that we could live in a View Park neighborhood that wasn't as fatal as the neighborhood we could truly afford.

Thirty-something years later, here I stood. Barely breathing, heart racing, terrified in my own home.

My phone vibrated again: *Just confirming mtg today at hotel to go over last details.* In two days, one of my best clients, the California Constitution Foundation, would be throwing its annual gala on Wednesday night—a gala I'd forgotten about until this text.

Something touched my hip.

I banged my forehead against the window again, then, spun around with a yelp.

Jonah, Elmo blanket in his hand, lay his head against my thigh. "Dee-Dee, I want some pancakes, please."

CHAPTER 13

PANCAKES, BACON, EGGS.

A normal breakfast for a normal American boy on an abnormal Monday morning.

Grease splatters and batter drips dotted the stove top, smoke from hot bacon curling at the ceiling—my galley kitchen hadn't hosted this much cooking since Election Night 2012.

Jonah, syrup on his chin, chipmunk cheeks filled with food, tore into his breakfast like LeBron James in Game 7 of the NBA Finals. He now poured syrup over his eggs just like Melissa did. I could only nurse coffee—I was a hollowed out, wrinkled mess that needed a shower and a week-long nap. I couldn't stand watch at the living room window all night and morning again. Some things—and some people—I wouldn't be able to control, no matter my willingness to deprive myself of sleep.

For the sixth time in an hour, I called my sister's phone number.

This is Melissa. I can't come to the phone—

I hit End Call—I'd already left five messages, imploring her to call me, to text me, *something*.

Over on the living room television, *Little Einsteins* played. On this episode, Rocket couldn't sleep and the little geniuses were teaching him how to count planets.

"Dee-Dee," Jonah said. "Watch this." He placed his bacon strip above his upper lip as a mustache. He held his last pancake to his face—he'd bitten out two holes for eyes.

I plucked the bacon from his fingers. "Gimme that." I pretended to eat the crispy strip.

"Hey," he said, "that's my bacon."

"Gimme a kiss and I'll give it back."

Jonah clambered onto my lap and planted a wet one on my cheek.

He snatched the bacon from my fingers and giggled. "Got it!"

I gave him a bear hug. "You did, and now it's time for you to get ready for school."

He *vroomed* back to my bedroom.

I crept back to the living room window—*no cars at the gate*—then fished Ian's business card from my sweatshirt pocket.

The detective answered on the first ring. "You remember anything?" His voice had that been-working-all-night rasp.

"No," I said. "Just looking for my sister. I've tried calling her, but she's— "

My pulse jumped. A red Mustang pulled up to the parking gate. Security guard Randy was not working the entry—Libby, a new hire, had taken his place.

"Melissa's still here," Ian was saying.

"As a free woman?"

The driver of the Mustang was black, male.

"Of course," Ian said. "I see that she took my

advice—Kopp is a damn good attorney. You guys don't play, do you?"

"This is life and death," I said. "Any other good advice you care to give?"

"Not at the moment," he said. "Lemme get your sister."

The phone rustled and a door opened and closed. Then, "Dani?" It was Melissa and she also had that raspy, up-all-night voice.

"Crap, Mel," I said. "I've been trying to call you. Are you—?"

"I'm fine. Kopp's on his way here to advise me on my formal statement." She sighed, then chuckled. "Maybe he can actually write it down for me since right now my handwriting looks like shitty Cyrillic."

"You're exhausted, sweetie," I said. "Need anything?"

"Maybe bring me lunch later? Don't know how much longer I'll be here."

"Well," I said, "they can't keep you—"

"Unless they charge me. I know this, Dani." She sighed again. "This is real life, and there are laws in real life, and ways to conduct yourself. Especially when someone you love has died."

My cheeks burned. "You heard about that?"

"Try not to curse out the people who are supposed to be helping us."

I squeezed the bridge of my nose. "I'm sorry."

"Give Jonah a kiss from me. Tell him...I don't know what to tell him."

"You wanna talk to him?" He was now brushing his teeth in the bathroom.

"No. I'll start crying if I do." She paused, then asked, "Are you watching *Little Einsteins*?"

I chuckled. "Busted. You call the Reverend and his wife?"

"I left a message but I didn't tell them that Kirk died."

"What about his sister?"

"Noreen's not answering, either. Hey. Gotta go. Here's Detective Anthony."

Just like that, Melissa was gone.

"I actually *do* have advice for you," Ian said once he came back on the phone.

I smiled. "Oh? You wanna tell me now or in person?"

"Is in person an option?"

I shrugged. "Sure. As long as I can come and go without restriction."

He laughed. "You're funny. Can you talk this morning? I haven't eaten breakfast yet. How about Café Laurent on Overland?"

I cocked my head. "Can you do that?"

"Have breakfast?" He laughed. "I'd take a bullet for bacon."

Outside, the fog was still breaking up, and pale sunshine was poking through the mist. No cars down at the guardhouse. Good.

I closed my eyes and slowly exhaled. My phone vibrated.

GET A GOOD NIGHT SLEEP??? Sophia had included three sleepy face emojis after the taunt.

I gritted my teeth—she *wanted* me to shoot her. I stomped to the kitchen and grabbed the hollow-handled utility knife from the bamboo block. Then I pawed through the catchall drawer. A pink canister of pepper spray rolled to the front. It had expired seven months ago.

As the ancient sages say, old capsicum is better than no capsicum at all.

CHAPTER 14

MRS. ROGERS, JONAH'S DAYCARE
teacher, had heard through the mommy grapevine that
Kirk Oakley had been found dead in his living room.
Wide-eyed, she whispered, "Is it true? Because they're
saying that he was…that he was…*murdered*."

I made a sad face, then nodded. "That's what we're
being told. Someone shot him."

She gasped, then slipped her wrinkled, thin hand
over her mouth. "Mr. Oakley was such a…" She swallowed her words and blushed. Her mouth moved as she
thought of positive ways to describe the slain man. But
even she knew the type of man Jonah's father was. So
she followed one of the golden rules of life: if you don't
have anything nice to say…

"Tell Melissa not to worry about Jonah." She
clutched her elbows. "What kind of monster…? I just
can't believe this type of thing could happen."

Of course, the owner of a pink and purple preschool
with gingerbread trim and fluorescent geraniums
couldn't believe people killed other people.

Jonah gave me one last kiss before zooming to his
cubby to stow the Tumi knapsack I'd let him borrow…

since his Elmo bag still hid drugs, a wine bottle, and a wineglass.

French bistro Café Laurent was located on a leafy corner in Culver City, a cute suburb of Los Angeles. Melissa and I sometimes stopped by after Jonah's Saturday morning swim classes at the rec center across the street. It was only two miles from Jonah's preschool but was far enough for a cherry-red Mustang to ram me from behind, then shoot into my car, *narcos*-style. My breath caught every time that silver pony emblem twinkled in my rearview mirror.

By the time I reached the café, I was a sweaty wreck with nerves tighter than piano wire—Ford had sold a lot of red Mustangs in Los Angeles County.

Café Laurent was tiny. An old couple stood at the glass deli counter, picking out cupcakes to take home. Ian sat at a table closest to the patio. He wore a blue suit with a crisp white shirt and red necktie, and his hair had been swept and gelled away from his face. His eyes were on his phone as his fingers tapped at the screen.

"Lemme guess," I said, approaching the table. "You're on level 438 of Candy Crush."

He stood up to pull out my chair, appraising my appearance with those blue eyes. "Close. Level 435. You look incredible."

"This old thing?" I wore a black and red floral Diane von Furstenberg wrap dress that cinched over there, and plunged down to there. My hair covered half of my face like the French lieutenant's woman. Not my usual Monday morning attire, but this wasn't a usual Monday morning.

I smiled as I took my seat. "And you, Detective Anthony, look very Young Republican. And before you ask, yes, I *have* accepted Jesus as my personal Savior, thank you very much." To the server, I gave the universal sign for coffee, then turned back to the cop. "Hey."

"Hey."

We grinned at each other like kids on a first date.

"For someone who's been up all night," he said, "you look like you're on your way to seduce some rich baron in Monte Carlo."

"Or a detective in Culver City." I thanked the server for the hot coffee she placed before me, then said to Ian, "Honestly? I feel like I'm on day three of the Hunger Games, and I'm two seconds from bursting into tears." I ordered lemon crepes, Ian a bacon and egg sandwich with extra bacon.

"So," I said, leaning forward. "What have you been doing since graduation?"

He had broken up with the Raider's daughter, returned to Los Angeles, enrolled in police academy, and married an accountant named Morgan. No kids. No pets. Divorced three years ago.

"You know..." he said casually, with the hint of a blush, "I had a *huge* crush on you back in school."

I cocked my head as my heart pounded in my chest. "You're just saying that cuz I'm wearing this dress. Don't hate me for saying this but...I didn't pay much attention to you back then."

Ian laughed, then nodded. "My teeth looked like I ate gravel and twigs, right?"

My shoe brushed against his calf. "Yeah. But worse."

"Well, I played plenty attention to *you*." His shoe moved against my heel. "Why aren't you married to some powerful attorney with a Subaru full of kids?"

"Cuz I hate Subarus." I shrugged. "I've come close a few times—but if you haven't noticed, I have a strong personality. Some men find it exhausting."

"I kinda like it." He dropped his eyes, then picked at a bit of bacon. "I shouldn't have brought this up. That I had, you know: *feelings* back in the day."

"You were young and foolish. It was the crazy nineties." I touched his hands, then squeezed. "You should've told me—we could've had a lot of fun."

"I missed the boat." He looked at me with hopeful eyes.

I sighed. "I'm not sure you want to hop on this ride at the moment." I rubbed the bridge of my nose and then my temples.

Accordion music blasted from the speakers. A group of moms and their toddlers now hogged the space in the center of the café. The coffeemaker whirred and hissed.

He reached to swipe my bangs from my face. "You okay?"

I looked at him with tired eyes. "Yes. No. I don't know, Ian. Suddenly, it's too much in here. Not sleeping and taking care of a three-year-old...my dress is losing control of my tear ducts and emotions." I shook my head and chuckled. "So I could use some advice now while I still have the capacity to listen."

"Trust me," he said, "this case is gonna take a while to solve. You can't burn out in the first few days. So, my advice is this: take a moment away and just...*be*."

I laughed. "Seriously? How? *When?*"

"How about right now?"

I blinked at him. "Okay...And go *be* where?"

"Anywhere but here." He cracked a smile. "You're no good to me or your sister if you can't think straight. Although my partner would say that your ragged state of mind is perfect because then, you'll slip up and admit that Melissa pulled the trigger."

I rolled my eyes. "And now, I'm gonna start crying."

"You wanna get out of here?" He reached in his jacket pocket for his wallet. "I live over in Fox Hills, so not far. We could go there, if you want. Walk around the park. You can cry. I can listen."

"And then you'll put me in touch with one of your counselors at some toll-free number?" I reached in my purse for my wallet, but Ian motioned me to stop. "You have more important things to do. Cases to solve. And me coming over to your place, when you're the detective on my sister's case?"

He smiled and shrugged. "We're old college friends. And really: who needs to know?"

I bit my lip. "Okay. Let's go and just...*be*."

CHAPTER 15

IAN LIVED IN A town house across the street from Fox Hills Park. At ten minutes to eleven o'clock, the only visitors were moms pushing strollers and old people moving tai-chi slow.

The detective kept a tidy home—clean hardwood floors, granite kitchen countertops with stainless steel appliances, and a dust-free entryway chandelier. The brown corduroy couch took up most of the living room, and pictures of his family (awful dental work, all of them) and Ian wearing his uniform took up most of the shelving. Vinyl record albums and CD cases crowded a glass-door cabinet, and the air smelled of spring rain.

I turned my back to Ian and wandered over to the patio doors off the living room, reaching discreetly into my bag where my phone rested. The view was of the park—at the basketball court, a buff personal trainer guided three women through squats and lunges. "You have your own fitness channel here, huh?"

"Yup." Ian came to stand behind me.

His body heat rolled over me, and his strong heartbeat pulsed against my shoulders.

I inched back until I bumped against him. Solid. Muscular. He was bigger than I thought.

He squeezed my shoulders. "Relaxed yet?"

"Almost. A little harder, please."

His phone rang and vibrated from his front pocket. We both jumped and laughed. Caught.

"Sorry." He glanced at the phone's screen. "I gotta get this—it's my partner. Be right back." He jogged up the stairs, but shouted, "Make yourself at home. There's OJ in the fridge."

I scanned the space around me—storage cabinet, faux mantel-top, armchair with cushions. Above me, the ceiling creaked from Ian's footsteps. If I was going to do this, I needed to do it now.

I darted to the armchair and nestled my purse between the armchair pillows, making sure that my hidden phone faced the couch. One last check and I casually wandered over to the bookcase.

Stephen King. Philip Roth. Doris Kearns Goodwin. Paul Beatty.

"Sorry 'bout that," Ian said, popping back downstairs.

"Do I need a rain check for my moment-away massage?" I asked, still studying the titles of his modest library. "Is work about to take you away from me?"

He stood behind me again. "Nope. You have me for another hour."

"Lucky me." My finger stroked the spine of a leather-bound edition of *Treasure Island*. I turned around to face him and smiled. "You read a little bit of everything, don't you?" I straightened his necktie, then let my hand rest on his chest before wandering up to his collar.

"All that liberal arts education in the woods." Ian kissed my wandering hand.

I cradled his face with my hand and brought him closer. "We shouldn't be doing this."

"Are you gonna say anything?"

I shook my head. "Are *you* gonna say anything?"

"Hell, no. This is just for us. For old times' sake."

Our noses grazed and I bit his lower lip and brought him closer. "I didn't tell you: I think you have really nice teeth now."

"Yeah?" he said. "I have other nice things, too."

I smiled. "Yeah?"

He nodded, whispered, "Yeah."

And then we kissed. His arms wrapped around me as we backed toward the couch.

I pulled off his tie.

He unwrapped my dress.

We fell onto the couch, across from the armchair where my phone nestled, recording it all.

CHAPTER 16

FOR AN EXPERIENCED DETECTIVE, Ian was surprisingly willing to throw discretion to the wind and walk me to my car.

We were leaned against his front door, our legs entwined, our hands on each other's hips. "You think that's wise?" I asked. "Someone could see us."

"And then?" His blue eyes were dewy and his expression relaxed.

"And then...I don't know," I said. "You're the detective. I just throw parties for a living."

He kissed me again and my belly fluttered. "And then, I'd say, 'Yeah, we just happened to see each other,' and you'd say, 'Yeah, I was just dropping my nephew at the preschool around the corner,' or something like that. Or you could stay, hang out until my shift ends."

My hand massaged his neck — I could feel his pulse banging against my palm. "Since this has been my first truly relaxing moment in days, believe me when I say that I want to tell you 'yes' — "

"But?"

"I have a meeting with a client, and you have work to do. A killer to catch, remember? The reason we're here."

He sighed, then gave me a quick kiss on the nose. "Yeah, I remember. Sorry."

I found a tube of lipstick in my purse, then faced the mirror hanging in the foyer. I looked relaxed, too—a weeklong getaway shoved into forty minutes. "You talk to Sophia yet?"

"So we're back to business. Yep. We've talked to her, and let me tell you: she guessed right off the bat that you gave me her name." He stood behind me, and kissed my neck.

"Did she deny even *knowing* Kirk?"

"No. She loves him. Wouldn't ever hurt him. Didn't see him yesterday. Didn't talk to him at all."

I squinted at his reflection in the mirror. "And you?"

"And *I* know that's she's lying. I know that she texted him all day, all night, and…" He turned me around to face him. "I know that the preliminary DNA tests on Kirk show that he had sex that day, and I'm betting that the DNA on his private parts won't be your sister's. Doesn't help that Sophia's text messages to Kirk confirm that they slept together on Sunday evening. And then argued viciously."

I raised a finger and said, "Aha!"

He cocked an eyebrow. "What's 'aha'?"

"I told you they slept together—she was there at the house that night." I squinted at him. "What were they texting about?"

He smiled, cocked his head.

I rolled my eyes. "Fine. Don't tell me. I could probably guess anyway."

"Did Kirk do drugs on the regular?"

I chuckled. "You name it, he smoked-popped-sniffed it. And then, he'd kick my sister's ass. I heard he slapped Sophia around a few times, too." I gave him a triumphant smile. "I've practically solved this thing for you, Ian. This one's free—next time, I want dinner at Mastro's and possibly something that twinkles around my neck."

"It's like that *already*?" He nuzzled my ear.

My hand found the place on his body that made him purr. "I lied: there's something else I'm gonna tell you, and it won't cost you a thing. Are you listening, Detective Anthony?"

He took my hand and placed it against his cheek. "I'm listening."

I reached down into my purse for the phone, deftly making sure only the home screen showed. "Sophia texted me all morning." I let him read Sophia's messages.

His eyebrows lifted. "There's a lot of rage coming off this phone." He looked at me. "And are you watching your back?"

I nodded. "Yeah, but I'm not her target—Melissa is." I pulled up screenshots of messages that Sophia had sent Melissa just two weeks before. From *U JUST MADE THE BIGGEST MISTAKE FIRING ME!!!* to *I COMING 2 UR HOUSE 2 SEE WHAT THE HELL U GONNA DO 2ME!!!* Then, there was *I'M GONNA BEAT THE LIVING SHIT OUT OF U!!!* and finally, three pictures of a naked Kirk sleeping in Sophia's bed.

Ian's lips pursed. "This is…"

"Troublesome? Scary? Jacked-up? To *imagine* your husband sleeping with another woman is horrible. But to see it in Kodacolor?" Tears burned in my eyes as I recalled Melissa spiraling on the day she'd received those pictures. She had kicked Kirk out of the house—and three days later, he had returned with his electric toothbrush in one hand and toxic libido in the other.

"What do you want me to do with this information?" Ian asked.

"You go where the evidence points you, correct?"

He nodded.

I slung my arm around his neck. "If I tell you a secret, will you tell me one in return? I know you enjoy reciprocity…"

He thought. "Okay. We found a pair of panties in the pocket of Kirk's cargo shorts."

I rolled my eyes. "Don't men do that? Steal ladies' undies?" A lock of his dark hair had slipped out of its gelled hold, and I pushed it back in place. "How do you know those panties weren't Mel's?"

"Because they're size two." He shrugged. "And your sister is *not* a size two."

I pulled away from him. "You couldn't help yourself, could you?"

"Sorry. That wasn't very nice of me. Forgive me." He pulled me back into his arms. "Okay. Your turn. Your secret."

I brushed that lock of hair away from his forehead. "My secret…" I stood on tiptoes and whispered in his ear. "In my purse, I'm carrying a Japanese kitchen knife and a can of expired pepper spray. And if Sophia Acevedo raises one finger in my or my nephew's direction, I'm gonna use one or both of those things to kill her. Then you'll only have one murderer to catch."

CHAPTER 17

FROM THE DETECTIVE'S HOUSE I went straight to the Southwest Division police department. I didn't want to push my luck with my newfound connection, but I had immediately accepted Ian's offer to get me in to see Melissa. That afternoon, I sat across from her in an interview room. The room's light-gray walls needed repainting, and the hard chair drove into my tailbone. Icicles formed along the edges of the scarred metal table, and ghostly stink waves made by dirty and angry men combined with the stinks of Pine-Sol and vomit.

I wanted to tell Melissa about Sophia, that our problem was nearly solved—but I couldn't risk bad acting. She didn't have much of a poker face. While the puffiness around Melissa's eyes had lessened, the whites were still filmy and bloodshot. Her sweatshirt hung like molting skin—being in not-custody for seven hours had caused sudden weight loss. She eyed my cleavage as I handed her a Double-Double—I'd stopped at In-N-Out Burger on the way over. "You have a meeting this afternoon?"

"California Constitution Foundation," I said. "Their

gala's on Wednesday night. I'm heading over there after this."

She peeled the white-and-red paper away from the burger. "I look like shit. Especially sitting across from you."

I winked at her. "You'll be back in fighting shape in no time."

She took two large bites from her burger. "Not if I keep eating these things."

I winced and forced myself to chuckle. *Maybe I should've brought her a salad.*

She wiped her mouth with a napkin. "How's my baby?"

I caught her up on Jonah: grilled cheese, *Little Einsteins,* bacon mustaches.

"He ask about me?" she whispered.

"He did," I said, nodding. "I told him that you were at a meeting."

"And Kirk?"

"I deflected."

"He cry?"

I shook my head. "No—but he got pretty excited when I made him breakfast. I told him we'd make grilled cheese for dinner tonight."

"Oh." She sank in her chair some, chewed slower. But then she brightened and sat back up. "Be firm about having to take a bath. I always have to beg him to take a bath."

I laughed. "Nope. He actually begged me—he likes my big tub and tonight, he wants me to put purple bubbles in it."

"Yeah, I put bubbles in the water," she said.

My smile faltered. "I think he's being nice to me because he knows I'm ignorant. Kind of how lions know that they can easily kill the trainer with a single swipe of a paw? Jonah's the lion and I'm the one about to be clobbered."

"Or, maybe being a mom comes easier for you. Everything else does." She picked at her burger. "I'm being a jerk—he's lucky to have you, Dani. Thank you for taking care of him."

We sat quiet for a moment with her staring at the table, with me holding my breath.

"When are they gonna let you go?" I asked.

She took a bite from her burger, then said, with a full mouth: "Soon. That's what they're telling me and Kopp. Once I complete my statement and then, do something else, I'm free—until I'm not anymore."

I twisted to look up at the camera. "Is this America? Is this how you treat victims? Mothers? *Americans?*" I twisted back around—Melissa had finished the burger and was now squirting ketchup on the French fries.

She pointed to the burger bag. "You didn't get anything?"

I flicked my wrist. "I gave it to Detective Elliott." The older detective had resisted letting my sister eat until I offered him one of the two In-N-Out burgers and fries in the bag. I twisted to peer at the camera again. "Since he's been working so hard to find the murderer."

She kicked me beneath the table.

"Ouch."

She hissed, "Stop."

I rubbed my kicked calf. "Relax. Geez."

Melissa shoved ketchup-drenched French fries into her mouth. "I need to start making arrangements for Kirk's funeral."

That snapped me back into the now. "Funeral? You're kidding, right?"

She stared blankly at me as she chewed. "He's my husband, Danielle. He's Jonah's daddy. What am I supposed to do? Let them bury him in a common grave?" Tears clouded her eyes. "I should make *her* pitch in—he lived with her half the time." She paused to bite a fry and compose herself, then asked, "How much do funerals cost?"

"One of those fancy affairs with pallbearers who dance like the Temptations? Or your regular home-going service with a family car, an organist, and color programs?"

Melissa traced a French fry through ketchup. "The color program one."

"Cremation or casket?"

"Can't believe I'm having this conversation." Melissa grabbed the large cup of soda and sipped through the straw. She grimaced. "Is this diet?"

My mouth popped open, then closed. "Yeah. Sorry. I automatically order diet Coke."

She said, "Ugh," then sat the cup back on the table.

I couldn't help but notice her dry lips and tear-stained cheeks. Ketchup and Thousand Island dressing smeared the wedding band and two-carat diamond engagement ring she'd "helped" him buy. The same woman who had graduated *magna cum laude* at Spelman College and had a PhD from UCLA. Recognized for her commitment by sororities and churches and families who she had kept together or helped to create.

Why hadn't she chosen a man like she'd chosen her schools, her career, and her fresh produce? Why—?

A sob burst from my chest, surprising me and startling Melissa.

"What's wrong?" She grabbed my wrist. "Why are you crying?"

I'd kept it together for so long, but my seams were giving. I took deep breaths to tamp down the hysterics. "You shouldn't be here. You shouldn't be in this situation." I hiccupped, then met her gaze. "I'm glad Kirk's dead. It's his fault that you're sitting in this wretched room. It's his fault that he's in somebody's steel drawer. Maybe if he would've controlled himself, maybe if he had respected you and——"

"Stop, Dani. No more." Melissa shook her head, then tossed me napkins to dry my face.

I blew my nose and wiped my face. "I'll shut up. And I'm sorry, okay? Last thing I want to do is make life harder for you." I plucked a French fry from the basket. "Hey, I have an idea."

Melissa let her head roll back to stare up at the ceiling. "Yeah?"

"What if, after the funeral, we take a trip back to Saint Thomas? This time, we'll stay as long as you want. Even better, you sell the house, I'll sell my condo. We can live like Caribbean queens. Drink all the rum we can stand. Read books, swim in clear water, eat jerked everything. Maybe open up a shave ice stand. Lead a simpler life. What do you think?"

She gazed at me, and a look passed between us, one that couldn't be caught on that video camera. Melissa smiled and there was light there, a glimpse of the sand-flecked woman who had danced the merengue all night with a stranger. "I'll think about it, okay?"

I held up the ketchup-dipped fry. "Here's to new beginnings."

She held one up, too, and touched mine. "To new beginnings."

But first, we needed a proper ending.

CHAPTER 18

NEW BEGINNINGS" MEANT MORE smiles, less humiliation. Respect. No drama except the kind you invited into your home via Netflix.

Kirk Oakley was dead. Someone had to pay for that. That someone should be the woman who drove a cherry-red Mustang. It seemed so obvious that Sophia Acevedo had killed Kirk—the lies, the violence, the panties, the texts—but as the afternoon progressed with no, "Hey, Dani, good news, we made an arrest" call from Ian, worry draped over me.

Why was Melissa still in not-custody?

If they hadn't arrested Sophia, who were they looking at now?

Were they looking at…*me*?

Shit.

Was it illegal to sleep with the detective working the case?

Had we been followed from the café to his town house?

Had Ian been arrested or demoted for sleeping with the sister of a possible murder suspect?

But I didn't have time to worry. I'd had a successful

meeting with my client and it was now five o'clock, when I needed to pick up Jonah.

Daycare was complete chaos. I could barely pick him out of the millions of children catapulting off the walls. How could the teachers stand it? The roar of wood blocks hitting each other. *The Wiggles* set on blast. This sea of small bodies with sticky hands made my ovaries shrink.

Jonah flew into my arms, then speed-walked to retrieve the Tumi knapsack he'd brought today. On the drive home, we chatted about his day—the construction paper jack-o'-lantern and ghost he'd made during art time, his tater tots and cut-up chicken lunch, the classmate who bit a boy who had tried to take her blanket. As I pulled into the underground parking lot, he asked, "Is Mommy in your house?"

"Not yet, sweetie. She's still at her meeting, but she'll be home tomorrow. Promise." My face warmed as I climbed out of the car.

"Grill cheese?"

I sensed before I saw the black Crown Victoria parked at the end of the garage. Only the orange parking lights were on. Shadows hunkered in the car's front seats.

Jonah slammed the car door shut.

The two men in the Crown Vic looked our way.

"Dee-Dee," my nephew shouted, "say 'echo, echo, echo.'"

I took his hand and smiled down at him. "Not now, sweetie. We should get moving." I glanced back at the black car. "The faster we walk, the faster we get to eat grilled cheese."

The air down here was still and heavy. Overhead, the fluorescent lights flickered—didn't I pay Home

Owner Association dues to prevent that from happening? I would write a strongly-worded letter after making dinner for my nephew. After this endless walk from my car to the elevator.

I heard the doors of the Ford thump.

Jonah dropped the knapsack. "Wait for me, Dee-Dee."

I glanced back at my nephew—and saw that the two men were climbing out of the car.

Jonah scooped up the knapsack, then dropped it again.

The two white men, both blond, wore sport coats and ties. They strode toward us, lock-step, like two Agent Smiths from *The Matrix*.

I grabbed the backpack and my nephew's hand. "Let's go, Jo-Jo." I thought of grabbing the knife and pepper spray from my bag; but assaulting police officers, if that's who they were, would not be the best move.

"Auntie," Jonah said, "Oww. You're holding my hand too tight."

My heart banged in my chest as we hurtled toward the elevator bank. My heels clicked against the concrete.

"Echo, echo, echo," Jonah shouted. "Say it, Dee-Dee."

"Excuse me, miss?" one of the men shouted.

The answer to my question—*who were they looking at*—had just been answered.

Jonah looked behind us—and what he saw worried him, made him walk quicker and closer to me.

"Wait, if you please," the other man called.

We'd been walking toward that green EXIT sign and the parked white Jaguar for days, it seemed.

Agent Smiths' heels clicked quicker against the concrete—they were walking faster.

I'd have that new beginning after all. One that included icy handcuffs, an orange jumpsuit, and Cup Noodles from the commissary.

Could Kopp represent both Melissa *and* me?

We finally reached the security door and I shoved my key into the lock.

A man's hand pulled open the door from behind me.

I let out a small cry.

Jonah hid his face in my dress.

"Sorry if we scared you."

The taller man was the one holding the door. "We need help, but first…" He smiled down at Jonah, then held out a pumpkin made from orange and black construction paper. "You drop this, little guy. Here."

Jonah peeked from behind my dress and plucked his project from the man's hands.

"Okay," the taller man said, "the parking lady point us to overnight parking but we don't know where overnight parking is." There was a lilt in the shorter man's voice. Norwegian?

I blinked at him, then barked, "Huh?"

The two men looked at each other, then looked at me. They smiled, then together, they said, "We're lost."

CHAPTER 19

THE NORWEGIANS WEREN'T THE only ones who couldn't find their way.

Unable to settle down, Jonah and I wandered from the kitchen to the bathroom to the bedroom, amped and anxious from our parking garage encounter. After dinner—grilled cheese sandwiches with hamburger patties—I gave my nephew a bubble bath. He climbed into bed and fell asleep ten minutes into *Little Einsteins*.

Glass of red wine in hand, I checked my phone for the fiftieth time. No calls.

Short hours later, the sun found the sky. Time to do it over again.

This time, Jonah wanted bacon and eggs. As we ate, we played Twenty Questions.

"Does it have fur?" I skimmed my fingertips across the boy's cheek.

Someone knocked on my door.

I glanced at my iPhone—only seven-twenty. I stepped over to the door and peeked out the peephole.

Copper spirally hair that always looked wet but was gelled hard. Eyebrows tweezed until they barely existed. Bright red lipstick and painted-on mole. Pink velour sweat suit and wedged Uggs. Sophia Acevedo.

"Is that Mommy?" Jonah asked.

I forced a big smile on my face. "No, sweetie. Just an old friend who…Come on."

With his plate of eggs and toast in one hand, I used the other to guide Jonah to my bedroom. "This won't take long," I promised him.

Back in the kitchen, I pressed Record on my phone and left it on the counter. In case Sophia got a little rowdy, I grabbed the cleaver from the knife block.

"Hey, Dani." Sophia Acevedo's skinny arms were crossed over her heavy bosom. Even though she didn't move, her cheap-smelling perfume wafted freely into my condo. "I know I shoulda called first but…" She tapped silver-polished fingernails across her arms. "But I figure with the circumstances, you'd understand."

"Your probation officer's still parking or did you make a break for it again?"

"Ha. May I come in?"

"Jonah is here, so don't bring your brand of nonsense into my home. Understand?"

She held up both hands. "I'm good—for real, I'd never hurt Kirk's baby."

I pulled the door wider and stepped aside as she entered.

"You didn't answer none of my texts." Her eyes flicked over my track pants and sweatshirt. "I thought we was homies."

"That was then. This is now," I said. "And you were threatening me."

She grimaced. "Threatening? You're joking, right?"

"All caps and exclamation points?" I said. "The 'get a good night's sleep' thing? 'Watch your back, bitch'?"

She shook her head. "I always keep the letters all-caps. It's just easier. Watch your back cuz someone hurt Kirk. I call everybody 'bitch,' you know this. And I hoped that you *did* get a good night's sleep cuz...I know I didn't." Her bright-red lips quivered, and her eyes shimmered with tears. "Do y'all need anything? Is the baby okay? He need anything? Kirk loved that boy."

I cocked my head and squinted at her. "This compassion act? It's just that, huh. An act."

She dabbed at her eyes with her knuckles. "I know me and your sister got beef, but I loved him, Dani. That's the God's honest truth. So whatever y'all need—"

"Why did you do it?" I asked.

"I sure as hell didn't do it. I woulda married that man if he had asked." Her gaze dropped to the weapon in my hand. "C'mon, Dani. That knife really necessary?"

"It's a cleaver. What do you *want,* Sophia? Why are you *here?*"

"I came cuz I wanted to be a comfort—I didn't want to, you know, mourn all by myself." She raised her chin. "But I guess you don't want that from me. And anyway, the detectives cleared me as a suspect."

Something inside of me exploded and I coughed. *"Excuse me?"*

"I got an alibi." She reached into her Vuitton clutch.

I flexed my fingers around the handle of the cleaver.

"Since you wanna go there, let's go there." She pulled out a thin square of paper in the air. "This right here? It's an ATM receipt. It says I got out money at 9:03 in *Hollywood* when Kirk was killed. Hol-lee-wood. Not in Baldwin Hills." She roamed my living room, stopping to peer out the window. "There's video. I'm on camera getting money out."

I shook my head.

Her nostrils flared. "See? That's your problem. You ignore the truth even when it's right there in y'all's face, even when it's on camera. I was sleeping with Kirk all over that house, and in her bed. And what *she* do? Look the other way.

"And he chose *me*." Sophia's braggadocio flagged and her hand clasped her neck. "I don't know what I'm gonna do without him. Oh, Dani…" She looked at me with wet eyes.

What did she want from me? A hug? A "that's okay, sweetie"?

"I wish I could take it back," she said, shaking her head. "We had an argument the last time we was together. I told him…" She sniffled, shook her head again. "I didn't think, when I told him 'good-bye' that I'd never see him alive again."

I tapped my foot, glanced at the imaginary watch on my wrist. "I'm not gonna stand here and tell you that it's gon' be okay. You should probably go now."

"Fine. You wanna know who killed Kirk even before he dropped dead on Sunday?" Her eyes gleamed with cold fury, and she pointed at me with a rigid finger. "Your sister. She didn't deserve Kirk, and she was jealous of us and killed him. And because of that? Best believe that I'm gonna do everything in my power to destroy her."

Someone knocked on my door.

Sophia smiled, and said, "Starting right now."

CHAPTER 20

ARE YOU GOING TO let us in?" Reverend Leland Oakley stood at my door, fedora in one hand, and the elbow of his wife—Kirk's mother—Virginia in the other.

Virginia Oakley wore her fall coat, taupe with fox fur collar and cuffs. Her eyes were as swollen as the pearls around her neck, and her café au lait complexion was splotched red. A thin woman, she looked skeletal in that big coat.

With a close-lipped smile, I opened the door wider, and allowed the couple to pass inside.

"Oh, Sophia, honey." Virginia took the mistress's face into her hands, then kissed her cheeks. "Thank you for sending us Dani's address—I had it somewhere, but with everything going on, I just couldn't put my hands on it."

Reverend Oakley held out his arms for a hug. "Come here, girl."

He was a big man, and smelled of pipe tobacco and lavender.

"I'm so sorry," I said—and I was.

He tugged at the brim of his fedora. "We were leading a marriage retreat up in Vancouver when Melissa called and told us the news."

Virginia came to kiss my cheek. "I still can't believe it. I keep telling Leland, 'they made a mistake, it can't be true, not my baby.' Not my Kirk."

With a sad smile, Sophia rubbed the woman's back. "If you need *anything,* please let me know. Kirk was like a big brother to me."

I cocked an eyebrow and said, "Sophia was just on her way out."

Reverend Oakley's expression mirrored mine—he knew the devil on sight.

After Sophia left my condo, I turned to them. "I wish I'd known you were stopping by. I would've had breakfast—"

"We didn't come to eat." Reverend Oakley placed his hat on the breakfast counter. "We came to retrieve Jonah."

My gut clenched. "Huh?"

Virginia touched my wrist. "Thank you for watching over him, but we're here now. His bedroom is ready."

"At *his* house?"

"No," she said. "At *ours.*"

I pinched the skin at my throat. "That's really unnecessary. He's fine—"

"Relax." The minister held up his hand. "We're only following instructions that Melissa and Kirk left in case of severe emergencies. Didn't she call you and let you know?"

I shook my head, and pinched my throat harder. "I'm not sure what you mean."

Virginia pulled from her purse a thick sheath of paper, then handed it to me.

If my wife does not survive me, or is unable to care for my children, and it is necessary to appoint a guardian,

I appoint Melvin and Dolores Lawrence guardians of my children. If for any reason Melvin and Dolores Lawrence do not act as guardians, I appoint Leland and Virginia Oakley as guardians of my minor children.

In the event *his* parents couldn't care for Jonah, Kirk's sister Noreen would be next. My name came after everyone else had died. I was stunned and numb—my name was so far from Jonah's.

"And even though Melissa's alive," Reverend Oakley was saying, "she *is* incapacitated. She admitted as much when we talked to her yesterday."

Yesterday? I'd *seen* Melissa yesterday, and she never mentioned that the Oakleys were taking Jonah. What the *hell?*

"Pop-pop!" Jonah raced into the living room and threw himself into his grandfather's arms. "Nana!" He reached more delicately for his grandmother.

The trio hugged, kissed, and nuzzled, and soon, lipstick covered Jonah's face.

Leland squeezed his grandson's shoulder. "Wanna come stay with us?"

Jonah shouted, "Yeah!"

My heart broke—he'd chosen them over me. Like Melissa had chosen Noreen over me. But then, way out in Yorba Linda, nearly forty miles away from Los Angeles, the Oakleys had three dogs, a deluxe jungle gym, a swimming pool, and all the grilled cheese sandwiches Jonah could eat.

Hell, I'd choose to live with them, too.

"I'll help you get your things together, Jo-Jo," Virginia said.

Jonah led his grandmother to my bedroom.

"You tell him about his father yet?" Reverend Oakley asked.

I shook my head and sank to the couch. Speechless—my broken heart had also broken my mouth.

The minister sat next to me and took my hand. "Believe me, Danielle, this is hard on all of us."

Jonah ran back into the living room and headed to the kitchen to grab his Elmo bag.

I jumped up from the couch. "Oh, you can't take that bag, J-Boogie."

"I want my bag," the boy said. "I'm going to Nana's house."

"It's broken, remember? That's why I let you use—"

"I want my *teddy*." He lay the bag on the ground and searched for the zipper.

"How about we leave Elmo," Virginia said, handing her husband the borrowed Tumi bag, "and we take the teddy bear?"

I shook my head. "The teddy bear's broken, too. The battery pack..."

"I want my teddy." Tears shimmered in Jonah's eyes. "Pop-pop, I want my teddy."

Shit. No. He couldn't have—

"Give the boy his teddy, Danielle," the minister said with a stern smile. "I don't think he cares if it's broken. He's been through enough, don't you think?"

I sighed, then, unzipped the bag with thick fingers.

As soon as I lifted the top, Jonah snatched the bear from the bag. "Thank you, Dee-Dee."

After writing down the Oakleys' address again, and being assured that I could visit Jonah anytime I liked, I escorted Kirk's parents and Jonah to their BMW. As they pulled away, Jonah waved at me from his car seat.

I waved good-bye, too—to him and to the teddy bear filled with Ecstasy.

CHAPTER 21

LOST.

For the first time since Sunday, I didn't know what to do.

The worst had happened—my nephew had been taken from me and critical evidence linking my sister to Kirk's demise was also gone. I'd failed Melissa twice.

I drove around Los Angeles for hours, trying to figure out my next steps. My wandering led to a cupcake shop, as wandering sometimes does. It was close to five o'clock when that "next step" popped in mind.

Today, the park across the street from Ian's town house had gained visitors and now bustled with activity. Grade-school kids carried soccer balls and water bottles to wide grassy fields. Figures in yoga pants and basketball shorts jogged around the dirt track.

The door finally opened. Ian gawked at me and then, at my outfit.

I wore a tight, vintage *Star Wars* T-shirt and snug Levi's worn only on special occasions. Like this one. "Thought you'd want a proper dessert." I opened the box's top.

Four perfect cupcakes—two salted caramels, two strawberries—waited to be devoured.

He flushed and leaned against the door, literally swooning. "You're kidding me."

"What?"

His gaze met mine. One of his eyebrows cocked. "The cupcakes, the shirt, the jeans."

"Coincidental."

He lifted an eyebrow.

"Okay. Engineered. Want me to leave?"

"I didn't say *that*."

"I've had an awful day, and now, I need your advice again."

"I heard about Jonah." He stepped aside. "Come in."

I carried the cupcakes into the kitchen. The stovetop was splattered with red pasta sauce. In the living room, *Family Feud* played on the television. On the couch, documents spilled from an expandable file folder—in one of them, I glimpsed a photo of Kirk dead on the living room floor. A large, three-ring binder sat on the coffee table next to a bottle of Corona.

I left the box on the kitchen counter, then headed back toward the front door. "I don't want you to think…Part of me, of course, wants to get in good with you. The other part of me finds you terribly interesting. The cupcakes—these are out-and-out manipulation."

"I love your honesty, but there's nothing I can do. Jonah's guardianship is above my pay grade." Ian shoved papers from the couch cushion into the folder, then ambled into the kitchen. "Let's see now…" He opened the cupcakes box. "Oh, wow. Salted caramel and strawberry. My absolute favorites." He cut a caramel in half and offered a piece to me.

I dragged my finger through the frosting. "Before Kirk's parents came to get Jonah, I got a special visitor today."

He blinked. "Umm…"

I plopped onto the couch. "Not *that* kind of special visitor," I reached for his Corona and took a swig. "Sophia Acevedo."

"What?" He sat next to me, took the beer, and drank. "Why didn't you call me?"

"I knew she wouldn't do anything crazy with Jonah there. I thought of not answering but I got sick of hiding. I just wanted to get it over with. Looking back, it was probably a stupid thing to do but then I haven't had a clear thought since Sunday."

"So, you're here. What about her? Is *she* still alive?"

I laughed. "I didn't stab her, nor did I pepper-spray her even though she threatened my sister again." I grabbed my phone from my purse, then played the recording of Sophia vowing to hurt Melissa.

He bit into his cupcake, then smiled. "I love the taste of manipulation in the evening."

"Tastes like victory." I dabbed at frosting and crumbs left on the corners of his lips.

"Sophia's crazy," he said, "but do you think she's actually *dangerous*?"

"Hell, yeah, she is." I fished out a battered envelope from my purse. It was stuffed with pictures of Mel's damaged black Chrysler, repair quotes and invoices, and police reports. The pictures showed that the car's headlamps had been smashed; the windshield wipers had been pulled off; and "BITCH!!!" had been scratched into the car's hood and driver's side door.

"This all happened in August. Mel took out a restraining order against her last month." I handed him a copy of the temporary restraining order that forbade Sophia to come within 500 yards of the Oakleys. "Of course, Sophia ignored the order."

"Of course," he said.

"But this is why her alibi is bullshit," I said. "She admitted that she and Kirk argued the last time they were together."

"But there's ATM video…"

"She could've easily taken La Brea that night." La Brea Boulevard ran for nearly fifteen miles from near the airport, passing Baldwin Hills and ending in Hollywood. "It was a Sunday," I continued, "so there wasn't a lot of traffic. She still had time to kill Kirk, then withdraw money. She practically says that she shot him. And now she's gonna hurt my sister. You have to do something. Did you take her DNA?"

"We did."

"That's her on Kirk."

"Probably."

"What about Mel's neighbors? Did any of them have security cameras?"

"Nope. Old people don't bother with that shit."

"Sophia says you guys cleared her as a suspect."

Ian squinted at me. "You believe a woman you told me lies as much as she breathes? Relax, Dani."

"I can't." My eyes burned—I wanted to cry. I took the Corona from Ian's hand, took a few hard swallows, then handed the bottle back to him. I shoved the rest of the cupcake into my mouth. "I don't mean to be a Debbie Downer, spoiling your night of spaghetti and beer. I've disturbed your peace, and I'm sorry. I'm just scared, okay?"

"You bought me dessert." He rubbed his finger against the neck of the Corona bottle.

I winked at him through my tears. "And I bought you cupcakes, too."

He traced that cold finger along my ear. "I'll keep looking into Sophia, okay?"

"Okay. Thank you."

"We done talking business?"

"Yes. So, first, there's this..." I climbed onto his lap and planted tiny kisses on his face and neck until he shivered beneath me.

He chuckled. "Is this you or is this manipulation?"

"It's whatever you want it to be."

His hands slipped beneath that tight *Star Wars* T-shirt. "You were so worth the wait," he whispered in my ear.

No hidden phone recording this time. This time, I was just...*being*.

CHAPTER 22

FOG HAD ALREADY HIDDEN the sun, and was now rolling off the Pacific Ocean. Something like it washed over me and made it hard to breathe. It was Ian. He was like sunlight winking through the trees. A dime glinting in the sand. A surprise.

I *liked* sunlight and found money.

My heart had lost its map and directive playing this game with him. Our late-afternoon tryst had ended on the couch, naked, stuffing our faces with cupcakes, drinking Corona, and watching *Family Feud*. It had been a perfect hour.

Until I remembered: Jonah was gone. And so was the teddy bear.

My condo had become a coffin with his absence. I'd paid too much money to live in a coffin, and I didn't like the idea of Jonah discovering drugs in his toy.

But what could I do?

After pacing and thinking, drinking wine and thinking some more, I came up with a great excuse to drive way the hell to Yorba Linda—Jonah's inhaler and breathing chamber were still in the Elmo bag.

After a nearly two-hour drive, I stood on the porch

of the Oakleys' European Rustic home of many gables, thanking goodness for allergy-induced asthma.

"He needs it," I said, "especially being around all the dogs."

Now, it was Virginia Oakley's turn to gape.

Virginia led me through the great room with her purple satin robe trailing out behind her. "I'm so glad you remembered before he started wheezing. Sorry you had to drive way out here, though. Jonah's fast asleep, but can I get you something to eat? Folks have been dropping off food since we got back into town."

"Yes, please." My stomach growled to prove the point.

We moved through the formal dining room where a large framed photograph of Kirk wearing his graduate school cap and cowl sat in the middle of the table. Vases of flowers and candles surrounded the portrait.

In the family room, the hardwood floor was littered with Legos and the breakfast table near the kitchen was covered with filled Tupperware and Corningware—and Jonah's beloved teddy bear.

"Jonah's moved right in, hasn't he?" I nodded to the toys.

"He's such a sweet boy." Virginia grabbed a paper plate from the counter. "He reminds me so much of Kirk, especially with those freckles. I slipped and called him by his daddy's name a few times."

I smiled as bile burned the back of my throat. "How are you holding up?"

She scooped, dipped, and plucked from platters, bundled foil, and containers. "I'm keeping busy. Noreen should be here tomorrow—she's in shock, too. Really: It's such a surprise. Who would do something like this, and to such a *good* man? I'm thinking it was one of those kids he was helping. Some folks you just need to leave alone."

She set a plate filled with fried chicken, macaroni and cheese, red beans and rice, collard greens, and sweet potato pie in front of me.

I wouldn't have to eat for a week.

The doorbell rang.

Virginia glanced at her wristwatch and gasped. "That's right—the head deaconess is dropping off more food. Will you excuse me for a moment?" She hurried to the front door.

I grabbed the teddy bear. My hands shook as I pulled apart the Velcro flaps. I winced from the noise, then shoved my hand into the teddy bear's back.

Fabric. Stitching. Cotton batting and...*nothing*.

The wine glass and the blister packs were gone.

CHAPTER 23

I SANK INTO MY chair, near tears. Where was the glass? Who took the E? Had I actually *seen* Melissa place both into the bear back on Sunday night? Was this the *right* teddy bear?

"Did you want to kiss Jonah good night before you left?" Virginia placed the deaconess's dishes of bread pudding and peach cobbler on the breakfast table.

I forced myself to stand from my chair and trudge down the hallway to Jonah's bedroom. Dodgers pennants and posters of cartoon baseball players mixed with pictures of Kirk and Melissa, and Virginia and Leland Oakley. The boy had fallen asleep with his butt in the air again. I kissed his head and whispered, "I love you."

"He'll be fine," Virginia assured me as we left the room. "We need him here—he's helping us more than we're helping…" Her breath caught and she clutched her neck. "You'll help us plan something really special for Kirk, won't you?"

A lump formed in my throat, and all I could say was, "Yes."

Reverend Oakley stood in the doorway to his home

office with his hands shoved into the pockets of his corduroy slacks. He'd aged since I'd seen him hours ago—his whiskers looked whiter, his back more hunched. "You heading out, Danielle?"

I nodded. "Thank you for dinner. If Jonah needs anything else, just let me know. I'll bring it—I don't mind the drive."

"I'll walk her out, Ginny," the minister said. "You go rest up."

After one more hug and kiss from Virginia, Reverend Oakley led me into his office. The room smelled pleasant, that pipe tobacco aroma and lavender. Pictures of young Kirk and Noreen sat on the desk alongside a Bible open to Ezekiel and a glass mug of tea.

"How's Melissa doing?" Reverend Oakley asked. "We didn't get to talk for long."

"She's exhausted and confused." I plopped into the armchair across from his large walnut desk. "She hasn't had time to mourn or to really process any of this. They keep asking her but she has no clue who killed Kirk."

Reverend Oakley held his chin in his hand as he peered at me. "*She* didn't shoot him, now, did she?"

Anger flared in my gut. "Melissa would never hurt Kirk, even though he—" I clamped my lips together.

"Even though he...*what,* Danielle?"

The greasy chicken bubbled in my stomach. "I should probably get back." I bent over to grab my purse from the floor, then looked back at Kirk's dad.

Melissa's wineglass now sat near the Bible.

He held the blister packs of Ecstasy. "Is *this* why you drove all the way out here?"

I said nothing. Just stared at my sister's secret now in her father-in-law's hand.

"Was the rest of your sentence, 'Even though Kirk was an alcoholic, a chronic drug user, and womanizer'?"

I whispered, "Yes."

"I found all of this when I was trying to fix Jonah's teddy bear."

I swallowed but no spit came.

"Is this evidence?"

I didn't answer.

"The police need to know it exists," he said. "It's only right that I tell them what I found." He reached for the telephone that sat on the corner of his desk.

I blurted, "Wait."

"Why?" His hand rested on the phone receiver. "You don't want me to tell them that you hid evidence in my grandson's toy?" He chuckled, then waved his hand. "Danielle, I know who my son was. I know what he was up to when he married Melissa, and I know about his relationship with that awful Sophia woman, and what he did with Melissa's money. I know Kirk was no angel. But he didn't deserve to be killed." His voice broke, but he held my gaze.

"I don't know if he was killed by a scorned lover, a drug dealer, hell, a damn cartel. And that tears me up. But whoever did it, he's gone. So, let's make a deal: you don't tell the police anything that will posthumously implicate my son in a crime, and I don't tell the police about…" He waggled the packets of Ecstasy. "I like you, Dani. And I love Melissa and I think she deserved better. But Kirk was my son, understand? And I have a reputation, here and across the country."

He sat back in his seat. "How would it look to my parishioners if they found out my son got drunk all the time, got high all the time, and was about to rip off his wife and run away with his girlfriend?"

I squared my shoulders, then said, "It would be the truth."

"Yes, but do you want the *entire* truth to come out?" He furrowed his brows. "Kirk told me a lot during one of our more...*sober* discussions. Your sister's not all meekness and light. She's done some things with my son. And from what I hear, you aren't a paragon of virtue, neither."

My cheeks burned, and I dropped my head.

"Hear me, and hear me good," Reverend Oakley said in a measured tone. "You take my son down, and you *all* go down. And when you think you're at your lowest, I'll make sure that neither you nor your sister get even five minutes with Jonah ever again."

CHAPTER 24

REVEREND LELAND OAKLEY WOULD prefer that his son's murderer walked free so that *he* wouldn't look bad. And here I thought that the minister was a good man. But as the reverend pointed out— what and who was "good" in this mess?

His threat was effective, and his words stayed with me as I made my two-hour drive back to Marina del Rey. By the time I took my place at the living room window, anxiety had burned through the soul food I'd eaten at the Oakleys' table.

My phone vibrated and played "I'm Every Woman" from my back pocket. *Melissa!*

"Hey," I shouted.

"Free at last, free at last," she said. "For the moment, at least."

"So, Jonah—"

"I know, and I should've told you."

I plopped into the armchair. "About the Oakleys taking him? Or about being a guardian after the Oakleys' French poodle?"

"Stop it."

"First, you *didn't* even tell me you had a will. And then, you put Noreen, a legitimate wino, in charge of Jonah—"

"She wasn't always a wino."

"I'm your *sister*. I'm the one who—"

"Stop whining, Danielle, and get over here. And bring the Elmo bag."

I chuckled without humor. "Oh, yeah. About the bag. Oh, yeah. About the bear, too." I told her about my conversation with Reverend Oakley. "What are we gonna do?"

She said nothing for several seconds, then, "Why didn't you tell Jonah, 'No, you can't have the stupid bear'? Never mind. Come over and bring the bag."

I grabbed the Elmo roller bag from the kitchen, and headed to grab my purse from the bedroom. But my steps slowed as I neared the hallway closet. A moment later, I was kneeling in that closet, pushing aside the Mardi Gras masks, the shoe boxes, and parasols to find my Hermès Birkin bag.

It had been a gift from an old friend who'd thought he'd finally found a way to turn my "no" into a "yes." The Birkin was a rare and precious thing crafted from deep-red ostrich leather. At $10,000, it would carry whatever the hell I deemed necessary.

Two bags in hand, I took the elevator down to the garage. The air was heavy, and those fluorescent lights were still blinking. No lost Norwegians followed me this time, but a black Dodge Challenger had blocked in my Escalade.

I stopped mid-step as the ground rolled beneath me.

The driver's side door opened. A husky white dude wearing a gray T-shirt and clean jeans climbed from behind the steering wheel. He had a salt and pepper buzz cut and the scratchy ease of an undercover cop. He said, "Hey."

Sparks shot from my chest, down my left arm and to my fingertips. I said, "Umm..."

"Wait a minute," a woman shouted from behind me.

The voice belonged to an Asian chick with two long, shellacked ponytails. She scampered past me, and said, "I'm Leah," to the white guy.

He said, "Airport?"

She said, "Uh-huh," then whispered, "Sorry," to me before sliding into the Charger's backseat.

The driver shrugged. "My bad. Have a good night." He dipped back behind the steering wheel. The tires squelched against the concrete as the car rolled out of the garage.

I stood there, shaking.

Was this now my life? Being terrified and breathless all day?

Was "losing my freakin' mind" my new normal?

If so, then...

Crap.

I COULDN'T LOSE MY mind. I needed to ignore the constriction in my chest, ignore all that pressure building up. Because surrendering to the crazy would mean the end of life as I knew it. No condo. No parties. No freedom.

The good guys had left Melissa's house in a state similar to homes battered by tornadoes. A fine, black dust covered nearly every flat surface, and it seemed like the house had paled, its soul stolen by the forensic tech's flash photography.

Melissa looked like a survivor in the wreckage, wearing a funky UCLA sweatshirt. "Please don't hate me," she said. "I'm sorry. I just want what's best for Jonah."

My face flushed—how could I argue with that?

She now pushed her hair back from her face, then said, "Wanna help me clean up?"

I shook my head. "That's okay."

She laughed. "Don't blame you."

"Why don't you go take a shower? I'll get started on...this." My eyes skittered over the scattered envelopes on the floor, the coffee table books also on the floor, and the magazines scattered throughout. "Couch cushions are a great place to start. Incredibly do-able."

I grabbed the first pillow: brocaded, yellow, and now with a man's heel in its center. I tossed it back on the couch. "See? The living room's already looking better." I stayed busy placing cords of firewood back into the leather holder. I fixed pictures, and arranged clay jars from Mazatlán, Belize, and New Mexico just so. The spot on the carpet where Kirk had lain dying was stained and smelled like soiled diapers—I'd let Melissa handle that.

But she was now squeezing the bridge of her nose. "Kirk and I, we should've never been together. I should've listened to you. I should've listened to that tiny voice in my head. I didn't, and now I'm gonna be arrested for killing him. Either way, I'm losing Jonah."

I stared at the pillow in my hand: brocaded, green, footprint. "You didn't shoot him."

Melissa snatched magazines from the floor. "Tell that to Detective Elliott. He's just waiting for DNA evidence to come back in, and then…"

"He's trying to scare you into a confession." I tossed the pillow on the couch, then took my phone from my pocket. "And he's working with old information. If he tore his eyes away from you for just one second, he'd solve the case."

Melissa stepped toward me. "You sound more confident than usual."

I told her about Sophia Acevedo's early-morning visit, then played the recorded conversation. "Detective Anthony listened to this, too. Seriously, every time Sophia sends either a crazy text message or makes a house call, she's one step closer to a cell in San Quentin. And throw in her lipstick, sunglasses, and panties they found on Kirk…It all points *away* from you and it points away from *us*. *She's* gonna throw him under the bus in order to save herself. We can't control what she says."

"And the Oakleys?"

"They'll turn their anger on where it belongs—with Sophia. You just have to amp up your grieving widow act a little more. Say only good things about the asshole you married."

She nodded. "I can do that."

I grabbed another pillow from the carpet—quilted, purple, too busy-looking for the sofa. "Does this one go on the armchair?"

Melissa didn't answer. Her face had twisted more than the curtains hanging over the windows.

My lungs pinched in my chest. "What's wrong, Mel?"

She took a deep breath, then slowly exhaled. "I need to tell you something."

CHAPTER 26

PARTIES WEREN'T MEANT TO last, *Dani.*

My skin prickled across my chin and cheeks. "I don't think I can handle anything else." I forced myself to chuckle even as I crumbled inside.

Melissa covered her mouth with a trembling hand.

I offered the fakest smile in the history of fake smiles. "I'm joking. What's up?"

Her eyebrows crumpled. "Before you came over on Sunday night…" She twisted the cuff of her sweatshirt. "I planted all of that…everything on him."

The clock on the mantel ticked, and kept time with my pounding heart.

"Planted all of *what?* On *who?*"

"It's easier if I just show you." She headed toward the staircase. "I should've told you sooner but I couldn't really talk with Detective Elliott hanging around."

I barely felt my feet as I followed Melissa down a hallway that looked too slick and too bright to be real. My phone vibrated in my hand—Ian's number brightened the screen.

"Hey," I said, forcing light into my voice. "You just finished dreaming about me?"

"Umhmm." He sounded loose and lazy, just like I'd left him hours ago. "Where are you?"

"At my sister's. Helping her upright the chiffarobe y'all knocked over when you were looking for the bloody candlestick holder."

He chuckled. "Call me later?"

"Certainly," I said, and ended the call.

Melissa was gawking at me. "Who was that?"

"I, too, didn't have time to tell *you* something. Ian— Detective Anthony—and I were at Santa Cruz together. We lived in the same dorm during our second year. Small world, huh?"

"Are you…? You and him…?"

"This is a very good thing." I paused, then added, "It's best that you don't ask any questions." I reached out to close her mouth. "What did you want to show me?"

The master bedroom was in disarray, just like the rest of the house. The down comforter that cost a fortune lay on the ground and had been trampled. The pillows were stripped from their cases. Drawers were bleeding clothes. That fine black dust dirtied every surface. The wedding picture of Kirk and Melissa that had lived on the nightstand had fallen to the carpet. There was another footprint on the glass but the glass hadn't cracked. Of course it hadn't.

I pointed at the bed. "You're getting rid of that as soon as possible."

She nodded. "Trust me: I'd rather sleep on shark teeth than sleep on that thing again."

I rolled my eyes. She'd said that before. Piranha teeth that time. And she'd stayed.

We entered the walk-in closet. Classic Talbots in no particular order hung on Melissa's side. Kirk's side was color-coded, with most of the space dedicated to his collection of baseball caps and athletic shoes. There were also two small bureaus in the closet.

"Remember when I told you that I'd found packs of Ecstasy and some of Sophia's things in here?" Melissa pulled open the bottom drawer of the bureau on Kirk's side, then removed a box from beneath a pile of jeans.

Among the collection: panties, body oil, pictures of naked women.

She plucked two pairs of panties—blue lace and pink satin. She lay both pair on the carpet. The blue lace panties were twice as big as the pink satin. "Two different sizes," she said. Next, she pulled a B-cup bra from the pile, then found a bra with cups bigger than my head.

My face was now completely numb because I *saw*. "These—"

"Belong to two different women, at *least*. Not just from Sophia."

I groaned and sank to the carpet. I hid my face in my knees. "Oh, Mel…"

"I was angry, Dani. I wasn't thinking. I just started grabbing things."

I looked at her with tired eyes. "You should've warned me."

Her face darkened. "*When*? And don't take that tone with me."

"Here I am, trying to pin this shit on *Sophia,* and now, you're telling me that Lorraine from Kentucky could be the rightful owner of those panties in his pocket? You're telling me this but you're concerned about my *tone*?" I ran my hands over my face. "Anything else you didn't have a chance to tell me?"

Melissa swallowed, then nodded. "About Jonah's bag…"

CHAPTER 27

I SIGHED. "WHAT ABOUT Jonah's bag?"

"It's easier if—"

"You just show me, yeah," I interrupted, shaking my head.

Melissa led me back to the kitchen, glinting with scattered cutlery and displaced dishes. The Elmo bag sat on the breakfast counter. Melissa placed Jonah's extra clothes near the sink, remembering to keep the wine bottle wrapped in the sweatshirt. She tossed the last bag of Cheerios into the snack bowl, then sat his Tonka trucks on the windowsill.

"I told you," I whispered, "the teddy bear—"

"There's something else. Look." She pointed inside the bag.

There was a zipper in the gray lining—a zipper I hadn't noticed until she tugged at it. The lining separated, and brushed gold metal caught the kitchen's light.

I whispered, "I'm scared to guess what that is."

She pulled out her mini iPad.

I cocked an eyebrow. "Again: scared to guess."

She offered me the device. "Go to my search history."

The iPad's wallpaper was a picture of Kirk and Jonah sitting behind home plate back in August at Dodgers Stadium. Peace fingers and big smiles, Dodger caps turned backward.

I tapped the browser icon, then selected History from the menu.

- POISONING—4 days ago
- DIVORCE—4 days ago
- ECSTASY OVERDOSE—4 days ago
- MANSLAUGHTER VS MURDER—a week ago
- COUNTRIES NO EXTRADITION—a week ago

Drums pounded in my head. "So it wasn't spur of the moment, you dumping…?"

"Ecstasy in the wine? Kind of. But killing him in general?" She took the device from my hands. "I'd been thinking about it for a while. Only because I knew that he'd never go, and that I'd never let him go. I knew he was planning shit with Sophia and that they were close…"

Cold dread crackled over me, and I placed my forehead against the granite countertop. "This isn't good, Mel."

She laughed. "No shit. So now, the cops can't find this." She pointed to the iPad. "I didn't shoot Kirk, but if they saw this history, they wouldn't believe me. It's obvious that I wanted him dead. And I knew they would turn the house upside down trying to prove that. That's why I hid it in Jonah's bag." She swiped at the iPad's screen.

"Stop." I grabbed her hand. "What are you about to do?"

"Clear the search history."

"No." I tightened my grip. "You can't. Nothing's ever truly erased in search histories. You'll only look guiltier if you clear it."

Melissa's eyes bugged. "It can't just *stay* there. What am I gonna do?"

"We'll figure out the internet stuff. They'd need a warrant anyway to look at IP addresses and all that. But this—" I pointed at the iPad. "We have to get rid of this, like, right *now*."

The kitchen was silent until the refrigerator's ice-maker rumbled.

Finally, Melissa said, "*You* know, and *I* know that they're watching me. I can't get rid of it."

"Yeah." My stomach cramped from the icicles now growing there. I lay my forehead against the cool countertop again, then sighed. "Fine. I'll handle it, then."

CHAPTER 28

I'LL HANDLE IT.

As though I knew about dumping murder-plotting iPads and laced wine bottles. Hell, I'd never smoked a joint, had never taken Ecstasy, and sometimes blessed my food before I ate, but now, here I was, an effin' heroine in a Quentin Tarantino movie. Handling it.

With a brick in my belly, I sped away from Melissa's house and down the hill.

Crenshaw Boulevard and Leimert Park were a hot mess. The new subway construction had brought endless concrete barriers and posted traffic signs that prohibited turning, speeding, and just about everything else. Heavy steel plates covered open trenches—sometimes. Drivers now avoided this stretch of street, where big trucks ferrying metal crap dropped metal crap that banged up your car, shattered your windshield, and punctured a tire or two.

The houses surrounding the park had been built in the 1930s and 1940s. Spanish-styles, many boasted ceramic-tiled roofs and neat front yards. Security bars hung on the windows of every third house—windows now aglow with lamp and television light.

Even with ongoing construction, Leimert Park still acted as a cultural center. It had a black bookstore, a performing arts theater, and community center—as well as homeless, the mentally ill, African drum circles, and vendors hawking sticks of incense, bootleg DVDs, and cheap T-shirts.

I rolled past it all, then made a U-turn at the beginning of a residential street to drive past it all again. No one cared—I didn't stand out here. Just another black girl rolling in her black Caddy in South LA.

My phone rang, and for the second time that night, Ian was calling me. "Hey," he said. "I have a crazy idea. How about you, me, late-night pizza, such and such?"

"Such and such?" I said. "Sounds intriguing. A little naughty, even. When?"

"Tonight. That is, if you're not tired of me yet."

I smiled. "I can't tonight. Mel's finally home and she doesn't want to be alone, especially since the Oakleys have Jonah and you guys have yet to arrest Sophia."

At the red light, a Camaro pulled beside me. The woman driving was smoking a cigarillo and singing along to Drake, now blasting from her stereo.

"Sounds like you're driving," Ian said.

Oops. "Yep. Just down the hill." Phillips Barbecue sat to my left. A long line snaked from the order window to the parking lot. "Getting ribs for Melissa."

Ian clucked his tongue. "I'm jealous—that sounds better than pizza."

"Will the offer for such and such still be good for tomorrow? I'm getting home late from the gala and I'll need to wind down. You could help with that."

"Protect and serve," he said. "And I enjoy serving you."

Yes: I *was* losing my effin' mind. No: I *couldn't* help myself.

I slowly rolled through the dark streets around Leimert Park, passing barbershops, hair salons, car repair garages. At the beauty school, I found an empty diagonal parking slot between a Dodge truck and a Toyota Corolla. There was an open sewer grate below the curb. No streetlights burned except for one halfway down the block. Moths the size of pterodactyls banged against the orange bulb.

I slid the Cadillac into the empty space, then turned off the car. Even though I was parked, I gripped the steering wheel tight enough to crack it in half.

And then, I listened.

To my pounding heartbeat...to the pounding at the drum circle...to trickling water...

A living sewer that ran to the Pacific Ocean?

I reached for the bag I'd hidden behind my seat and placed it on my lap. As I glanced in the rearview and side mirrors, I ran my fingers along the Birkin's supple leather. Trembling, I peeked inside the bag. What I saw there made me dizzy.

CHAPTER 29

Previous Sunday

IT WAS A LITTLE past nine o'clock and I sat in my Escalade one house down from my sister's stately Colonial. Every twenty minutes, dog walkers tromped past my truck, pausing only to let their pups pee and poop on someone's grass. Melissa's tearful words from our telephone call still played in my mind. Her words were now a familiar song.

"We had a fight. A big one."

"Kirk and Sophia, they're sleeping together again."

"I'm leaving him, for good this time."

Earlier that afternoon, I'd fed private investigator Dominic Carducci a porterhouse steak, creamed spinach, and lobster mac and cheese. In return, he'd fed me more proof that Kirk was, indeed, planning to rip off my sister. And that Sophia was planning to rip off Kirk.

All of that proof had lived in an expandable file folder that sat on my passenger seat.

Photographs of Kirk and Sophia checking in at beachside hotels up and down the California coast. Kirk and Sophia standing in line at banks around the city and in Las Vegas. Mug shots, criminal arrest records, copies of Facebook posts. Those things that Dominic couldn't do without a warrant, I did with my sister's unspoken permission—from snooping around her house and putting a tracker on Kirk's car, to downloading cellphone records.

Sophia Acevedo's red Mustang was parked in the driveway.

I was recording the scene with my cell phone as Kirk and Sophia stormed from the red front door and stomped over to the Mustang. Their voices carried in the quiet.

"You tired of me now?" Kirk demanded.

"I'm real tired of you now," Sophia said. "And you know what? I wish you'd drop dead, bitch, that's how much I'm tired of you."

He grabbed her arm, pulled her close to him, shoved his tongue down her throat.

She pushed him away, slapped his face, then opened her car door.

"Love you, Soph," he said, chuckling.

"Fuck you, Kirk," she spat. "I'm gon' get you back. Trust."

My recording joined an album filled with other recordings of Sophia kissing Kirk, Sophia kissing other men, Kirk buying Sophia jewelry, and Sophia pawning that jewelry.

I'd started this file four years ago.

And now I stood on the dark streets of Leimert Park. Forty degrees out here, and frost-covered car windows and blades of grass. The drum circle had quieted. No more laughter, no more pontificating. The smells of weed and cigarette smoke were getting closer. Those shadows in the park were trudging toward me. Water rushed through the sewer. The Birkin bag gained a ton every second it remained in my possession. I threw one last glance around to see that my only company was a giant possum now waddling across the street and disappearing beneath an RV. I squatted in front of the sewer, then dropped the Birkin down it. I took a deep breath, then swiped my eyes with the back of my wrists. But that reclaimed breath caught in my throat.

Crap, crap, crap.

A gray Crown Victoria was parked across the street from the RV. I couldn't see if someone was sitting behind the steering wheel. It wasn't there before…*was it?*

Crap.

The Elmo bag was still inside the Escalade.

At the end of the block, a black and white patrol car crossed the intersection.

My eyes fixed back on the Crown Victoria.

A ticket was stuck beneath the windshield wipers. Fallen leaves gathered at the wheels. The driver's side back tire looked flat. The car had been parked for a while.

I think.

Crap.

Not knowing for sure, and seeing that patrol car roaming the streets…

I couldn't get rid of the iPad right there, right then.

I needed another sewer.

Los Angeles had plenty of those.

CHAPTER 30

I COULDN'T SLEEP—EVERY time I came close, I startled awake, sweaty, breathless, and near tears. I dreamed of handbags and possums, Kirk lunging at me with bloody claws, falling into dark, wet holes, drowning in water that stank of urine. Not a good thing, insomnia and nightmares, since today would be a long day.

The sun had barely kissed the horizon when my iPhone started vibrating with last-minute e-mails from the foundation. Two glatt kosher meals. Another three comped tickets. Seat changes at the CEO's table.

I arrived at my office an hour earlier than normal. My eyes were on my phone as I hurried down the corridor—and right into Detectives Gavin Elliott and Ian Anthony.

The older man had chosen to wear his undertaker's suit, and the triangular shape of an iron glistened in places. "Funny seeing you here," he said to me.

I offered him a wry grin. "Especially since this is my office."

Ian wore his hair Agent Smith–style. He had also dressed for mourning in a midnight-blue suit, dark-gray shirt, and tie. He pointed at my handbag, my carry-all, a cardboard carafe of coffee, and the cell phone. "You look like a Sherpa. Can I take something?"

"Keys. In here." I cocked my right hip.

Ian blushed, then dipped his fingers into my pocket.

After he'd opened the door, I led them through the offices of Morley, Greenwood, and Lawrence, An Entertainment Company. Only three people were in— Mark stood at the copier, Diana stuffed envelopes for tonight's seating, and Stephanie tapped at the laptop on her desk. I waved at the trio, but kept moving down the hall until I reached my office with its bright sunlight, mustard-yellow pillows, and distressed wood furniture.

I dropped the coffee and my purse on the glass conference table. "Hope this won't take too long. I have an event tonight."

Ian said, "We'll make it quick."

Elliott pointed at the carafe. "Is that…public?"

"Would you like a cup, Detective?"

"Only if you're offering," Elliott said.

I forced my curled lip into a smile. "Sure." My hands shook, I hoped not noticeably, as I filled two MGL mugs and placed both, along with packets of cream and sugar, before my guests. I sat across from them and said, "So how can I help you gentlemen?"

"We never got your fingerprints Sunday night," Ian began.

I lifted my eyebrows. "I thought Frosted Flakes took them—he took everything else."

The older detective produced a kit from his briefcase. Five minutes later, he had my prints captured on a piece of white cardboard.

"Anything else?" I asked, wiping my fingers with a wet towelette. "A kidney? A filling from my back tooth? A fallopian tube?"

Both men laughed, so I joined uneasily.

Ian fished out his steno pad. "Still upset with your sister?"

I cocked my head. "About?"

"About Jonah being with the Oakleys."

My heart thudded as I stared at him. I'd told him that while naked.

"Guess it's a blow to the ego," Detective Elliott said.

My gaze lingered on Ian a moment more, then slipped over to his partner. "It hurt some, but Jonah's well-being is more important than my ego."

"Has it always been that way?" Ian asked. "Melissa gets in trouble, you run to rescue her, and she winds up helping someone else win the game?"

What?

"She did that when she met Kirk, right?"

I shifted in my seat. "Not sure what you mean, Detective Anthony."

"She chose him over you all the time, that's what I mean. Even when she told you time and again that she wouldn't. She chose to stay with him, despite the hell he gave her."

Elliott leaned forward to refill his cup. "That's gotta hurt."

I rested my chin in my hand. "Is there a point to this?"

"You need to start being honest with us," Ian said.

"I *have* been honest."

Ian's face darkened—he didn't believe me. "Then, tell me now. Did you and Kirk Oakley have an affair?"

CHAPTER 31

THE OFFICE FELL INTO silence—even the copier out in the shared space had quieted.

My pulse raced and for a second, I thought I would die from a heart attack.

"We asked Melissa the same question," Detective Elliott said as he stirred his coffee. "She had a very interesting response. Broke my heart, but then there are worse things in life. Like, you know, murder."

Once feeling had returned to my face, I said, "I hated Kirk more than I hate sin."

"You didn't answer the question," Ian said.

"I love my sister. I love my nephew. I only want the best for them."

Elliott turned to Ian. "I don't think she's gonna answer your question."

I cocked an eyebrow. "I didn't have an *affair* with Kirk. How's that?"

My phone vibrated on the coffee table with text messages. It was Lucas, the events manager at the Beverly Wilshire Hotel.

"Where were you at nine o'clock on Sunday?" Ian asked.

I squinted as I recalled that night. "Stuck on the 10 freeway after having an incredible dinner with a good friend."

"A lady friend?" Elliott asked.

I offered him a sly smile. "No."

"What's his name?" Ian asked.

"Dominic Carducci."

"Sounds familiar," Elliott said.

"Where'd you have dinner?" Ian asked.

"Mastro's in Beverly Hills."

"Fancy," Elliott said.

"Their rib-eye is the best. So is Dom."

"Then what did you do?"

"Then I drove home."

Elliott said, "That took, what, ten minutes?"

Both Ian and I laughed. I said, "I live in Marina del Rey, Detective Elliott."

"And? So?"

"The 405?" Ian and I said together.

The older man waved his hand. "Okay, so that took about…?"

"A little over an hour. I pulled into the garage around ten-fifteen. Put my leftovers in the fridge, took a shower—"

"Alone?" Elliott asked. "Or with this Dom guy?"

Ian studied his steno pad.

I said, "Alone. Then I watched TV."

Ian cleared his throat, then asked, "What did you watch? Netflix? HBO?"

I shook my head. "Just regular TV." No downloads. No streaming. No time-stamps.

"When was the next time you left the house?" Elliott asked.

"Close to midnight or a little after," I said. "Mel

called, asking me to come over. She didn't say what had happened. Just that she needed me."

"And you went in blind like that?" Elliott asked.

I nodded. "Of course I did. She's my sister."

The cell phone vibrated and shimmied across the conference table.

"Should you get that?" Elliott asked, pointing at the device.

I nodded. "I should—the hotel's calling me about tonight."

Ian stood from the couch, then waggled the print card. "Thanks for cooperating."

I walked them back down the hallway to the frosted door. *What had Melissa told them?*

Elliott thanked me again for the coffee, then exited.

Ian squeezed my arm and whispered, "It's okay."

This visit had told me that nothing would be okay ever again.

CHAPTER 32

I WAS NUMB FROM the knowledge that my life had changed.

But I didn't have time to cry.

The California Constitution Foundation had paid my firm big bucks to throw a great party. Mr. and Mrs. Goldstein needed their glatt kosher meals. The fussy music executive required an extra seat for his tireless assistant. The guy who worked the teleprompter needed another extension cord. And I looked like the last, beaten-up bag of dog food on the grocery store shelf.

At two o'clock, the traffic on the 405 freeway flowed. I called Melissa as I drove—*what had she told Detective Elliott about me?*—but she wouldn't answer. I reached my condo in under twenty minutes to change into the perfect dress, another Diane von Furstenberg, this one red, white, and blue. I'd only been home for ten minutes, and had barely changed when the doorbell rang.

Ian and Detective Elliott stood at my door with their satchels and shit-eating grins.

My mind went *ka-BOOM,* and I blurted, "Are you fucking kidding me right now?"

Ian's gaze paused at my boobs then stopped at my hips. "Great dress."

"I'm about to get out of here—I'm working."

"We need to talk to you again," Ian said, not budging.

"Can this wait? I need to get to the hotel by five—which means I need to leave *here* in ten minutes."

Elliott leaned forward. "The longer we stand here, then…"

I groaned and opened the door wide.

Elliott whistled as he wandered to the living room window. The light over the turquoise ocean was aflame with oranges and reds. A prelude to one of our epic sunsets. "That the Pacific over there?"

"Since the second day of creation," I said with my arms folded.

Ian settled on the love seat. "Sorry for coming over right now. Couldn't be helped."

"You live a pretty fancy life, don't you?" Elliott asked, settling in the armchair. "Glamorous job. Condo on the water." He ran his hand over the chair's nubby fabric. A perfect slice of sunlight fell across his cheap Oxford.

I could feel his loathing ooze toward me. I said, "I work fourteen-hour days. About twenty percent of my clients stiff me. Brides are crazy people. And I have a bad back from carrying boxes of Jordan almonds across a wet grassy golf course back in 2007. Yup, it's all glamour."

Elliott leaned forward, elbows on his knees. "Probably wondering why we're here."

I shook my head. "I thought it was a social call."

He chuckled. "We have some good news and some bad news."

"A few test results came back," Ian said. "So first, the good news: the DNA from the underwear and finger-prints taken from the lipstick and sunglasses came back today. None of those results match Melissa."

I glanced at my watch: three twenty. "That's terrific news."

"We thought you'd like to hear that." Then, the older cop pulled from his satchel a plastic evidence bag. He tossed it on the coffee table. "Recognize these?"

CHAPTER 33

MY SPINE RIPPLED AS though someone was pulling apart the vertebrae, *click-click-click.*

Gray. Silk. Boy shorts. Fancy panties for a fancy lady living a fancy life.

I owned about a dozen pair of these boy shorts in different colors—including gray.

"Are these yours?" Ian asked, an edge to his voice. "The DNA tests say that they are."

"If you haven't guessed, Miss Lawrence," Detective Elliott said, "this is the bad news."

How…? But…My…?

"For the second time," Ian said, "I'll ask this question again: Did you have an affair with Kirk Oakley?" His blue eyes had hardened into cold, blue stones again.

Four years ago, when he and Melissa had just started dating, Kirk and I bumped into each other at the Raven in San Francisco. Packed dance floors. Music videos playing on the walls. Disco ball throwing shards of light. Color exploded in time to Biggie Smalls and Kanye West. Friendly, Kirk and I bought each other drinks. Danced. Drank. Drunk. Touched. Pulse racing. Lightheaded. Slipped into the bathroom. Ten minutes. Done.

"It was before Mel and Kirk eloped," I said, my voice weak. "Kirk and I had sex in a bathroom at a club up in the Bay Area. We were both drunk. There was nothing intimate about it. I didn't give him my underwear that night. Knowing Kirk, he stole these when they came to visit once. Our...ten minutes together four years ago meant absolutely nothing to me. It was no *affair* and afterward, I'd hoped that..."

Melissa would've canceled their wedding?

Kirk would've found another mark?

"Hoped that what?" Ian asked.

I clasped my neck and shook my head. "I'm innocent." The words wriggled and poked in my throat like burrs.

Kirk and Melissa eloped to Las Vegas after dating for five weeks. They returned to Los Angeles two weeks later. Didn't take long for her to get pregnant and for him to start sneaking out to lunch with a family court attorney named Anne, and then, drinks with Riley, and of course, everything with Sophia. He'd smirk at me, dare me to speak out so that he could tell Melissa about our fling.

I had swallowed my anger, causing waves of nausea to wash over me. He made me sick. *I* made me sick.

Detective Elliott stood from the couch. "You're gonna have to miss tonight's party."

"What?" It came out as a shriek. "Why?" The natural light that I loved so much was now blinding me.

Ian also stood. "We need to have this conversation down at the station."

"I didn't kill Kirk," I blurted. "But I know who did."

Ian and his partner smirked at me, then smirked at each other.

"I figured it out with the PI," I said, barely breathing.

"That's who Dominic Carducci is. You know him—he was a hotshot in the Robbery-Homicide Division. I had him investigating this case long before you two even knew who Kirk Oakley was. Which is why Reverend Oakley told me to keep quiet about what I found."

"That's a little convenient," Elliott said.

Tears burned in my eyes. "I promise: I'll come down to the station after my event tonight. I'll bring Dom and we'll give you everything you need."

Elliott glared at me. "We're supposed to trust a woman who slept with her sister's husband?"

"He was barely her boyfriend then, and yes, you *have* to trust me."

The older man laughed, then shook his head.

I raised my chin. "I'll give you my passport. I have no intention of running except to the Beverly Wilshire Hotel."

Detective Elliott canted his head. "And then to the Caribbean to open a shaved ice stand?"

So he *had* been listening to my conversation with Melissa. "I'm not going anywhere. I'll give you everything tonight. I promise."

CHAPTER 34

WHAT THE HELL WAS I gonna do?

Wanting to cry, I paced the carpet with my eyes closed—the living room was now too hot and too bright, and the lingering scent of Detective Elliott's cologne made me want to puke. Dying was a possibility. I could just open one of the many windows and jump.

Or...

The expandable file folder containing dirt on Kirk and Sophia sat hidden on a shelf in my closet. But Reverend Oakley had been clear—if I talked, Jonah would disappear from our lives forever.

Someone knocked on the door.

I looked through the peephole to see Ian standing there and squinting as though his eyes hurt. I gritted my teeth and threw open the door. "I'm on my way out."

He rushed past me without waiting to be invited. "You're not going anywhere."

"You've been a tremendous *asshole* to me lately, and I don't—"

He grabbed my hand. "I followed you."

I paused and tugged my hand out of his. "What? When?"

"Last night." He dropped his postman's bag onto the coffee table. "Good thing I was nearby, too." He pulled a large plastic bag from his satchel, then placed it on the table. "Because you dropped something."

That Leimert Park sewer.

My eyes had burned with tears as I shoved the Birkin through the sewer grate. *Plop!* The bag was $10,000 down the literal drain, with gunpowder, gun oil, little drops of blood, and Kirk's DNA all over its inside. But now, it was back in my condo.

"That sewer?" he said. "It only drops a few feet to the catch basin. It was a little disgusting, but with some help from a friend at the water department…"

Buzzing filled my head, and my knees nearly buckled. *Trapped*.

The walls of my apartment closed around me and everything—the couch, the television—had a weird looking-glass sheen to it. There, but…*yesterday*. One thought kept me from blacking out, and I took a deep breath first before sharing it. "Off the record?"

"Of course." But Ian's posture had stiffened. His smile was cold and shark-like.

I squared my shoulders, then said, "I killed him."

CHAPTER 35

THEY SAY CONFESSION IS good for the soul, so I told Ian everything. About my suspicions around Kirk and then hiring a private investigator. About watching Kirk and Sophia argue in the driveway Sunday night.

After Sophia had raced down the block, after Kirk had stumbled back into the house, I'd climbed out of the Escalade. Birkin bag slung over my wrist, I marched to the front door and used my key to enter.

Maxwell was playing on the living room stereo. Kirk was singing off-key.

I dipped my hand into the bag.

Cold. Hard. Deadly. The .22 had been Dominic's idea. "Just in case," he'd told me. I'd resisted asking, "In case of what?" because the reasons for anyone carrying guns tended to be the same.

I stepped into the living room breezeway.

Wineglasses sat on the coffee table. Kirk was sprawled out on the couch, attention on his phone, fingers tapping at the screen.

"Congratulations," I said. "You are now the alpha and the omega of abusive assholes."

"*Thafuck?*" He fumbled his phone, then sat up to face me. "Who do you think you are, coming in my house?"

I strolled into the living room. "I was sitting in my car, watching you and your girlfriend fighting. A different episode this time—usually, you're making out. I know this because I've seen it happen all around Los Angeles County, Palm Springs, Las Vegas...." I let that sink in. "And then, I've watched *her* make out with some dude named Frankie Herrera in many of those same places. I have pictures and recordings of everything. And records. And statements. Some of it is prosecutable. You're going to jail."

"Says who?" Kirk was sweating. His eyes were glassy, and his pupils were the size of quarters. High as hell.

"Says the private investigator I hired back in January as one of my New Year's resolutions." I shrugged, smiled. "So. Guess what? You and Melissa are done."

He clasped his hands behind his head, then sat back on the couch. "Or what?"

I glared at him but didn't speak.

"Thought so. How about *this?* I tell Mel everything."

Cold sweat prickled beneath my arms. "And then what? Nothing changes. You're still trying to take away her house and her money, and Sophia's still planning to pull a switcheroo on *you* with her real boyfriend."

Kirk blinked at me, then whooped. "You think Mel would appreciate knowing that her little sister—"

"That was four years ago—"

"But who's counting?" He grabbed the wine bottle from the coffee table.

"You and Melissa weren't married," I said.

He chugged from the bottle, then wiped his lips on

his wrist. "Think she'd believe that?" He clenched his teeth, then rubbed his face again. "Especially since I got proof confirming that I tapped. That. *Ass*." His smile didn't last long before his teeth started grinding again.

"I'm not bullshitting, Kirk." I reached into my purse, then brought out the gun and pointed it at him. "See? This is me, not bullshitting."

He froze and put his hands in the air. Sweat rings had darkened the underarms of his polo shirt. But then, he laughed and his hands dropped. "You hard now, girlie? Where you buy that gun? Nordstrom? Saks?" He winked at me. "You sexy as *hell* when you mad."

"Leave this house," I said, my voice as cold and hard as the pistol in my hand. "Leave my sister. Never come back. If you do, I swear I'll kill your sorry ass."

"C'mon, Dani." He was still smiling as he stepped around the coffee table. "You ain't shootin' nobody. Gimme a hug, girl. C'mon."

My finger sat on the trigger. "Leave this house, leave my sister and—"

He growled, then lunged for me.

I flinched.

A *pop*.

Kirk grimaced, gripped his belly, then sank to his knees. His left arm shot out as he tried to slow his descent, knocking over one of the wineglasses and sending precious Burgundy to the carpet.

I'd frozen with my hand outstretched.

Kirk muttered, "You...bitch."

His words forced me to move, and I stepped back... back...back...until my butt banged against something solid—the front door. That's when I realized I was shaking.

I gaped at the gun in my hand—I had shot him, I'd

actually shot him. *Wow. Shit.* I shoved the weapon back into the handbag. My mind cleared enough to decide not to leave through the front door. Instead, I rushed to the kitchen, glancing one last time into the living room.

Kirk was still on his knees with his forehead on the carpet. "Shot…me…Shot…"

I slipped out the kitchen door.

Don Lorenzo Drive was empty, and you could almost hear Maxwell's singing from the stereo. Cold drizzle drifted from slow-moving clouds and kissed my face. Heart racing, I hustled to my truck, then dipped behind the steering wheel. My eyes fixed on Melissa's red door until the drizzle broke my view into millions of beads of water.

Would that red door open? Would Kirk come stumbling out?

No lights blinked on at a neighbor's house. No one opened their doors, looked out to the street with cocked heads and squinty expressions.

No one had heard me shoot Kirk.

CHAPTER

IAN'S BLUE EYES FOCUSED on something beyond me—he flushed pink, then darkened to fire-engine red.

I took a shaky breath, then released it. "You gonna say something?"

He reached into his jacket pocket and produced a pair of handcuffs. He dangled them before me and smiled. "This is the easiest case I've ever solved. Thank you, Miss Lawrence."

"Just like that I'm *Miss* Lawrence again?" My voice broke asking that question. "I thought we had something."

"C'mon, Miss Lawrence." He smirked. "You were really falling for me?"

"You weren't falling for me?"

He paused, and his smile died some. "I do what I have to for justice."

"So you faked it," I said bitterly.

His smile transformed into a smirk. "Well, not *all* of it. Some things you can't fake, know what I mean?"

"I *do* know what you mean." I grabbed my cell phone from the breakfast bar. "For instance..." I swiped through the photo album until I found it. I pressed Play and immediately, banter between Ian and me from Monday morning filled the room.

"Relaxed yet?"

"Almost. A little harder, please."

I held up my hand. "Wait. It's about to get *really* good."

In the recording, Ian's breathing had quickened as I whispered his name. He had chuckled, then gasped, then moaned "Dani," over and over again, louder and louder each time.

That Ian was then. The Ian standing here now hated me—his glare was made of arsenic-tinged razor blades and hydrogen bombs.

I held out the phone so that he could see us going at it.

He didn't want to but he looked down.

There he was, naked, my leg around his neck, moving against me on the couch in his living room, his parents and young academy cadet Anthony looking on from the mantel.

"So good, baby. So good."

I fanned my face. "Don't know, Ian, but that sounds genuine to me. Certainly *felt* genuine."

"Dani—"

"Oh, I'm 'Dani' again?"

His nostrils flared. "You did this…with me…on purpose?"

I shrugged. "I do what I must."

He ran his fingers through his hair and tried to smile. "C'mon, babe. You can't—"

"I *can,* especially since you've broken my heart. So, you're caught. If I go public with this"—I waggled my phone—"you'll have zero credibility. And your career?" I watched his mind race. "Oh, and yes, I thought to send a copy to Dominic. Just in case anything should happen. Scorned women are bitches—thought you knew."

His eyes were bright. "So, what's next?"

I glanced at my watch, then out the window—the sun now sat low over the Pacific Ocean. "Well, I have a party to throw. Before I go, how about one for the road?"

I pulled a bottle of Burgundy from the wine rack near the breakfast bar, then grabbed two glasses from the cubby. "Don't worry, Ian," I said as I poured. "I'm not leaving for good, and I'm not leaving you alone to figure things out. Here you go."

He took the glass I offered, and stared into its darkness.

"After the party," I said. "I'm gonna take a quick trip. To Narnia, Wonderland, Oz…You know, somewhere safe."

"To do what?"

I pointed at the plastic bag filled with the dress, the gun, and the designer bag. "To drop that off."

Ian finally looked at me. Beads of sweat had popped above his top lip. "And then?"

"And *then,* you're gonna take all that Dom and I found on Sophia Acevedo, and you'll arrest *her* for the murder of Kirk Oakley. Then, we win. Sound good?"

He didn't speak.

I poked him. "Cheer up, dude. You'll do great. You're a natural liar. Hey—do you like shave ice?"

He paused, then nodded. "Why?"

"Cuz I'm opening a stand soon in Saint Thomas. I'll need someone to chip ice."

His hands were shaking—the wine sloshed against the glass.

I smiled and held up my glass. "To new beginnings."

ABOUT THE AUTHORS

James Patterson has written more bestsellers and created more enduring fictional characters than any other novelist writing today. He lives in Florida with his family.

Robert Rotstein is an attorney with over thirty-five years' experience in the entertainment industry and is the author of three legal thrillers, featuring lawyer Parker Stern. He lives in Los Angeles.

Christopher Charles is author of the crime novel *The Exiled*. He has lived in Normandy, Paris, and Brooklyn, and currently resides in Denver with his wife, the author Nina Shope.

Rachel Howzell Hall is the author of six novels, including *A Quiet Storm* and *Trail of Echoes*. She serves on the Board of Directors for the Mystery Writers of America and currently lives in Los Angeles with her husband and daughter.

JAMES
PATTERSON
RECOMMENDS

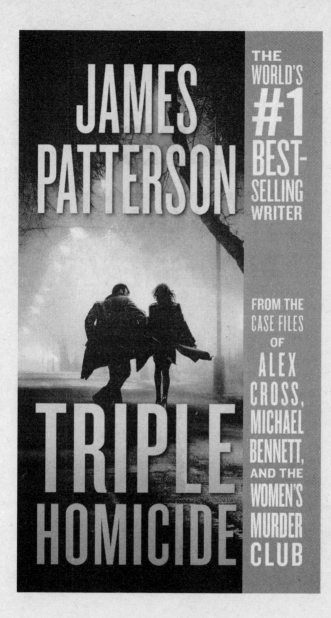

JAMES
PATTERSON

TRIPLE
HOMICIDE

TRIPLE HOMICIDE

I couldn't resist the opportunity to bring together my greatest detectives in three shocking thrillers. Alex Cross receives an anonymous call with a threat to set off deadly bombs in Washington, DC, and has to discover whether it's a cruel hoax or the real deal. But will he find the truth too late? Then in possibly my most twisted Women's Murder Club mystery yet, Detective Lindsay Boxer investigates a dead lover and a wounded millionaire who was left for dead. Finally, I make things personal for Michael Bennett as someone attacks the Thanksgiving Day Parade directly in front of him and his family. Can he solve the mystery of the "holiday terror"?

JAMES PATTERSON

"No one gets this big without amazing natural storytelling talent—which is what James Patterson has, in spades."
—LEE CHILD

3 NEW ELECTRIFYING THRILLERS

THE MOORES ARE MISSING

THE MOORES ARE MISSING

I've brought you three electrifying thrillers all in one book with this one. First, the Moore family just up and vanishes one day and no one knows why. Where have they gone? And why? Then in "The Housewife," Maggie Denning jumps to investigate the murder of the woman next door, but she never imagined her own husband would be a suspect. And in "Absolute Zero," Special Forces vet Cody Thurston is framed for the murder of his friends and is on the run, but that won't stop him from completing one last mission: revenge. I'm telling you, you won't want to miss reading these shocking stories.

JAMES
PATTERSON

THE HOUSE
NEXT DOOR

THE
WORLD'S
#1
BEST-
SELLING
WRITER

BIG
THRILLS.
SUSPENSE
THAT
KILLS.

THE HOUSE NEXT DOOR

The most terrifying danger is the one that lurks in plain sight; the one that is always there, but you don't notice it until it's too late. Here are three bone-chilling stories about exactly that.

In "The House Next Door," Laura Sherman is thrilled to have a new neighbor take an interest in her, but what happens when things go too far and things aren't really as they seem? In "The Killer's Wife," when six girls have gone missing, Detective McGrath will do anything to find them, even if that means getting too close with the suspect's wife. And finally, "We. Are. Not. Alone." proves that we aren't the only life in the universe, but what we didn't know is that they've been watching us…

JAMES PATTERSON

THE 13-MINUTE MURDER

The perfect
murder takes
only a few
minutes.

THE 13-MINUTE MURDER

I've really turned up the speed with three time-racing thrillers in one book! In "Dead Man Running," psychiatrist Randall Beck is working against a ticking clock: he has an inoperable brain tumor. He'll have to use his remaining time to save as many lives as he can. Then in "113 Minutes," Molly Rourke's son has been murdered and she's determined to expose his murderer even as the clock ticks down. Never underestimate a mother's love. And finally, in "The 13-Minute Murder," Michael Ryan is offered a rich payout to assassinate a target, but it ends in a horrifying spectacle. When his wife goes missing, the world's fastest hit man sets out for one last score: revenge. Every minute counts.

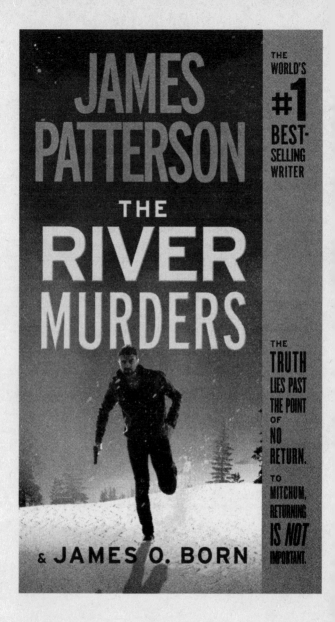

JAMES
PATTERSON

THE
RIVER
MURDERS

& JAMES O. BORN

THE RIVER MURDERS

Mitchum is a relentless man and I've really cranked up the tension with three stories just about him. In "Hidden," after being rejected by the Navy SEALs, he becomes his small town's unofficial private eye. But he never could've imagined that investigating a missing teenage cousin would lead to a government conspiracy. Then in "Malicious," when Mitchum's brother is charged with murder, he'll have to break every rule to expose the truth—even if it destroys the people he loves. And finally, in "Malevolent," Mitchum has never been more desperate, as one by one, his loved ones have become victims. Now there's only one way to stop the mastermind: going on the most dangerous hunt of his life.